The Brothers Mecarnin Series

The Last Victim in Hichester

Book One

Sarah Flanagan

ISBN: 978-1-63522-019-3

Printed in the United States of America
10 9 8 7 6 5 4 3 2 1

Rivershore Books
8982 Van Buren St. NE • Minneapolis, MN 55434
763-670-8677 • info@rivershorebooks.com

Prologue

The flame that licked across the field gave a fiendish glare to the usually friendly light that covered the countryside. A few shadowy figures lingered here and there across the darkened field as they scanned the hundreds of bodies that lay across the course, dry ground. They walked slow with their shoulders hunched forward. This was no time to do otherwise.

One particular figure was taller than the rest, walking slowly and occasionally lifting his hazel eyes to scan the field for sight of his comrades. He could see several of his friends helping wounded people to their feet while others knelt beside the bodies of fallen comrades in prayer.

He looked about again as he ran his bloody, sweaty hand through his wavy brown hair. He was in mid stroke when he spied something that made his blood run cold. Charging across the field, leaping over bodies and avoiding the small licks of flame that still ate at the dead grass, he hurried to a particular body.

Falling to his knees, he grabbed up the limp pale hand that lay on the ground and rubbed it. The head of the person barely turned, but in the dim light of evening, the long black hair and the bright green eyes of the girl looked glassy and empty.

"Come on," the young man whispered gently, "I'll get Elys . . . she'll fix you right up."

The girl slowly shook her head but cringed as a pain ran through her body. "No, Hirrun . . . there is no point now."

"Don't say that!" Hirrun snapped angrily, not angry at the girl but angry at the realization that she was right. "You'll be fine!"

A soft smile appeared on the girl's face and she gripped Hirrun's hand. "Promise me something . . ."

Hirrun nodded weakly, tears appearing in his eyes. "Anything . . ."

The girl gripped his hand tighter as if trying to make him understand how painful it was. "Promise me that you take my daughter . . . She is just a baby . . . she won't understand. Take her . . . to Gerhenia . . . place her in Chris's hands . . . I don't trust anyone else."

Hirrun was about to nod again and protest further, but the girl's shaky breathing stopped. Her bright green eyes stared at him from faraway . . . and there was silence. Biting his lower lip angrily, Hirrun reached over with one soiled hand and gently drew her eyelids closed.

Letting go of her hand as if it was on fire, Hirrun stood up and looked to the sky. "Take her soul, Lord . . . Take it . . . please! It was a beautiful soul!"

He felt his shoulders begin to shake and his legs felt like putty. He was prepared to fall to the ground in a fit of agony, but a pair of gentle arms wrapped about his shoulders and he buried his face in Elys's long, strawberry-blonde hair.

"Why?" he whimpered, allowing the girl to hold him close. "Why did He have to take someone . . . so perfect?"

Elys slowly shook her head as she stroked Hirrun's dark hair. "I do not know . . . but like she taught us: we cannot dwell on the past . . . but look to the future. I have a feeling that what will come from her death will be just what this world needs."

Chapter 1

There are all types of legends and myths that I heard in my life, but none of them could match the one that would change my life and the lives of my brothers. There was a legend that we had heard but always thought was make-believe. Needless to say, we found out what fools we were and how wrong that assumption had been.

Bentley Hichester was an educated daredevil, determined to excel in his work as a scientist but also to prove to everyone around him that he had no limits . . . that he was invincible.

Bentley was a man of great integrity and curiosity but also of great arrogance. He had heard legends and myths of creatures in the world that were considered by some to be immortal. Believing that he had control over the people of the world, Bentley located the last five remaining of these peculiar creatures, naming them: changelings.

Through serious research and tests, he discovered that they were in fact mortals, but truly different from every other human. Seeing this as a chance to prove his superiority over other people of the world, Bentley decided that he needed to "breed" a new race of these creatures.

Three of his "specimens" died from stress and other unknown causes, leaving him with the last two remaining changelings in the world. Bentley knew he was running out of time, but his arrogance fought on until he discovered that "breeding" new changelings wasn't as simple as he thought. Nine out of every ten of the offspring were not changelings but normal human beings. His self-confidence, arrogance, and self-pride overcame his judgment and, in his attempt to solve the issue, he failed to notice that his work had been infiltrated.

Another scientist, just as wizardly smart and arrogant as Bentley, had been hunting down the last of the creatures for his own experiments. He was known as Nohte Respure, and his plan was not to find the origin of changeling reproduction, but to change their genetics to suit his cause.

One thing that many people did know about these changelings was that they were believed to be "angels" in beast form. They had loving, caring hearts that always sought to do the right thing. Nohte, however, was a step ahead of Bentley and had discovered a way to change this special trait of the changelings through torture. He just needed the physical specimens.

One of the changelings, a young girl by the name of Gianna, had an indescribable love for goodness. This frightened Bentley so much that he refused to work with her. There was something about the girl changeling that made him feel strangely uncomfortable.

Sending one of his most trusted scientists to infiltrate Bentley's secret facility, Nohte managed to kidnap two of Bentley's few changeling specimens. This passed directly under Bentley's nose and soon proved his downfall, for Nohte wasn't done with Bentley.

After conducting his own procedures on the kidnapped changelings, Nohte returned the creatures to Bentley's facility without him knowing. Of course,

Bentley didn't notice that several of his "specimens" were beginning to show rebellious and almost aggressive traits. He didn't discover the truth . . . until it was too late: Nohte had created the first Underbeasts. What was worse, by placing the tortured and now aggressive changelings in Bentley's facility, Bentley was framed for enabling such an evil to appear.

Bentley's now-famous facility of breeding changelings was now greatly marred. He was seen as a traitor, a liar, and much worse, for he had seemingly created the underbeasts: a race of changelings that had been shaped and chiseled into an evil and wicked race of beasts through the evildoings of Nohte.

Bentley's pride though was too strong. Feeling that he was in no way to blame for his loss in publicity and trust in the political leaders, he took out his fury on the changelings. Not three years prior, he had been trying his hardest to discover the genetics of these creatures, not for their own good but for the publicity that he would gain from doing so. Now, he was trying his hardest to destroy them.

Bentley's only son and heir, young Walter Hichester, was an excellent child, feeling drawn to the changelings because of their goodness and uniqueness. He helped the creatures escape his father and made it seem like they were destroyed. However, the political leaders ordered Bentley to lock up the underbeasts or kill them. Walter's involvement in aiding the changelings went unnoticed by Bentley until he heard rumors that the changelings were making a rapid recovery on a remote island off the coast of Scardihn Caan.

3

The now-crazed scientist did the last thing anyone expected: he released two of the underbeasts and sent them off to find out the source of the changelings' recovery. The result was stunning: Young Walter Hichester had created a safe haven for the creatures in the Western part of South Scardihn Caan. There they had prospered, though there was something else that the underbeasts discovered: the changelings were beginning to show more signs of human traits and personalities, almost to the point where they were nearly identical to humans. This caused great distress in Bentley, especially since the changelings were now considered "angels in human form."

Bentley sent his underbeasts back to infiltrate the safe haven to find out how these beasts were somehow beginning to show similarities to humans. The answer. . . was Walter. After leaving home to study at a university, Walter had swapped places with a young, intelligent farm boy who couldn't pay for his own education. While Walter allowed the farm boy to take his place at the university, Walter escaped to South Scardihn Caan and there married one of the changelings, causing a change in the changeling's features and traits, though the trait of natural goodness stayed. There were also a handful of human friends of Walter's who also joined the cause.

Bentley still couldn't admit that he himself was the cause of all this trouble, yet he decided that it was for the good that he had. His mind, now twisted into a tangle of lies and deceit, caused him to go on a wild crusade to destroy every last changeling; to do this, he bred an army of underbeasts.

While Bentley may have been arrogant, he was a coward. He sent his army of underbeasts to Scardihn Caan with the mission of leaving no changeling alive. No one knows which side won, or which one retreated, but there was never any sign of changelings or underbeasts again. After the disappearance of his own army and the changelings, he received horrible news that his son had been fighting alongside the changelings . . . and three months later, on Walter's nineteenth birthday, Bentley was presented with the body of his son. Walter had been found on the battlefield in South Scardihn Caan . . . killed by his father's underbeasts.

Bentley shut himself out from the world. He never tried any other attempts associated with science. He wasted away his life on grief and mourning, yet he still couldn't blame himself for the deeds he had done that had eventually led to the death of his son. Five years after receiving news of his son's death, Bentley died of hypothermia.

Little did he know that, through all of his faults and evils on an innocent race, good had woven a plan through it all. Though his son had died before Walter had even become a man, Walter had brought forth a son: Bentley Hichester II.

Walter's goodness and compassion for the changelings brought out goodness from the dark, yet there was still the punishment that Bentley had brought upon his son and all his children to come. Bentley's acts would one day prove to be for the good of the future, yet there was still the price for Bentley's injustice toward the changelings. And from that time forward, one of Bentley's male heirs from each generation would suffer a troublesome punishment: never being able to age.

Though Bentley Hichester II was cursed with this uncomfortable punishment, he was the foundation of the good that would come from it all, and he would be the one to open the chance for future souls to right the wrongs that Bentley Hichester first brought when he thought he could change the world.

That is basically how the legend goes, and from what the three of us learnt, almost every word of it is true. No one could ever match a more complicated, action-filled, decisive adventure as this . . . that is, until someone knocked the daylight into us.

Chapter 2

Shadows passed back and forth in front of the door as the two figures hurried from the bedroom to the kitchen and back again. A pair of eyes watched them through the small crack in the door that stood ajar just slightly.

"What did you see?" a little voice whispered.

The figure at the door slowly closed it and began to fumble about in the dark, searching for a light source. The glare of a torch flickered on, and the boy started as the light struck his eyes. Quickly moving the light away from his eyes, he pointed the light at his brother's chest, so as not to blind him.

"I couldn't see momma . . . I think I saw pa," the one with the torch whispered.

The younger boy rubbed his pudgy little fist across his nose, smearing his cheek with a handful of tears and mucus. He then ran the same hand through his unruly brown hair, causing his older brother to give him a disgusted look.

"Stop doing that," the older brother remarked. "It's gross, Deke."

The two brothers were not exactly what people would call "similar." The oldest had spiky black hair and a stern brow and natural sarcasm. His left eye was a light green, while his right was a dark gray. His face was slightly pointed, firm, and had an early maturity somewhere in the way he held himself, despite the fact that he was only five.

The younger of the two, Deke, had wild brown hair that was cut slightly shorter than his brother's but never stayed in one place. His eyes were a bright liquid blue, and his features had no rhyme or reason to them. He still had the roundness in his face, but his figure was slender and small compared to his brother, who was only a year older.

"They've been in there a long time, Neil ... What do you think is happening?" Deke whispered, sniffling as he did so.

Neil cocked his head to the side and raised one of his dark eyebrows. "How am I to know? I was a baby when you had the flu."

Deke rubbed his hand through his hair again, causing it to look unrulier than it already was. "It's gotten really quiet out there."

At once Neil reached back over and opened the door again. He didn't poke his head out this time but just peered out with one eye, for the crack was too small for his whole face to look out. The shadows had stopped passing back and forth into view. There was now a dreadful silence, which caused his stomach to churn.

"I can't see anything," he hissed back at his brother. "I wish pa would hurry up."

Suddenly the door began to creak open and light flooded the dimly lit room. Standing in the doorway was a tall man with sandy hair and bright blue eyes ... though they weren't very bright anymore. A serious look was on his handsome young face.

"You can come out," he whispered.

The two boys leapt to their feet and quietly followed their father to their parents' bedroom. Their father stopped in the doorway of the bedroom and slowly turned to the side so the boys could peer inside. Lying on the bed was their mother. Her face was deathly pale, and sweat was drenching her brown hair and the top of her shirt. There was no color in her mouth, and her skin had a strange pasty look to it as if she was covered in wax.

Deke took an impulsive step forward, but his father placed a hand on his shoulder. "You have to stay out, Deke."

Neil and Deke glanced back up at their father at the same time, then slowly back at their mother. "But . . ." Neil stammered. "What . . . happened?"

Being only five, Neil didn't know much when it came to sicknesses, but from what he had been told, the flu was not something to fear that greatly. Something about the way his father's shoulders sagged to the side and the look on his mother's face told him that there was something he was missing.

At the sound of Neil's voice, their mother slowly turned her head to look at them. "It's all right, Frank . . . we don't want to scare them," she replied in a voice that sounded like it was coming from the other side of a tube.

The two boys slowly slipped past their father and then picked up speed once they were clear. Both reached the bed at the same time but were careful as to not place too much weight on the bed as they skidded to a stop.

"Are you all right, momma?"

"Why doesn't pa want us in here?"

Their mother smiled and patted each of them on the cheek. "There is nothing to worry about . . . I'm just very tired. Your father doesn't want me to wear myself out."

Neil quickly took his mother's hand and tried desperately to force a smile onto his worried face. Her hand felt strangely hot . . . not a normal hot but

9

in such a way that he almost couldn't hold it. Deke meanwhile had another thought that struck his mind.

"Momma . . . What about Gene?"

Their mother's face at once relaxed as if she was pleased that their thoughts were no longer on her. "He's over on the floor bed."

Deke turned fully around, and his eyes fell on the mattress in the corner of the room. Careful as to not walk too loudly, he crept over to the mattress and peered at the face that was barely visible beneath the blanket. Gene was almost three years younger than Deke, with platinum blond hair and the same blue eyes as Deke. Now, his eyes were closed, and his hair was drenched in sweat. His face, though, didn't hold the pasty look nor the unusual paleness that was showing in their mother. He just looked exhausted and was squirming back and forth as if he couldn't get comfortable.

Deke slowly turned to look back at his mother when he noticed a figure standing on the other side of his mother's bed. The figure was small—half his father's size. It was the nurse . . . but not what Deke had expected. She wore a trim gray dress with white lace at the collar and sleeves. Her graying brown hair was piled high on the top of her head and, though the woman looked to be in her late forties, her eyes and smile showed cheerful childishness.

Deke became exceedingly aware that the woman was looking directly at him nonstop. Her deep eyes were staring directly into his in such a way that Deke felt himself begin to become fidgety. She was summing him up to see if he was also sick.

"Is he . . . better?" Deke inquired in a soft voice.

Both of his parents and the nurse smiled at the obvious worry on the boy's face. The nurse was the first to reply, "Yes, child. Your brother is a strong patient. He just needs rest and silence for a few days."

Deke slowly sank to his knees beside the mattress and pressed his brother's hand . . . it was cold. He reached over and moved the blanket aside just a little to get a better look at Gene's face. Though his eyes were closed, and he looked as if he was in pain . . . there was something about that face that had somehow changed over the past several hours. It wasn't the exhaustion that was evident but the sudden strength that shined through that young face . . . a strength as if he knew of something Deke didn't, as if he had climbed the mountain Deke hadn't encountered yet.

All at once, the front doorbell began to ring, and Frank Mecarnin quickly left the room to check who it was. No one was paying heed to the voices that were muffled down the hallway . . . that is, until the door closed with unusual boldness.

All the heads in the bedroom moved slightly toward the bedroom door, waiting to hear if the slamming door would be followed by another sound. Everyone waited to hear if the person had left or if Frank had gone out to speak with him. Suddenly, Frank reappeared in the doorway and directly behind him was a tall, rigid figure.

His face was long, and his eyes were like small pinpoints, though too close to his long nose. He wasn't as tall as Frank but was gangly and thin, wearing an overcoat that didn't help in making him look less sickly.

11

"I'm glad to see that you and the baby are improved, Morgan," the man remarked in a thick Gerhenian accent as he stepped past Frank into the bedroom.

The mother didn't frown or smile at the man but just looked at him as if he was a piece of wood painted brown. "That is the first time that you have come to pay your respects, Alec."

Alec clapped a hand to his chest as if insulted. "I'm surprised, Morgan. I am only concerned about your welfare."

Neither Morgan nor Frank Mecarnin replied to that remark but pretended that he hadn't spoken. Alec sensed their dejection and annoyance toward him, so he turned toward Neil. Taking a step toward the boy, he placed a hand on his shoulder and patted it.

"The lad has grown," he remarked. "He looks a lot like his father."

Neil at once realized that he didn't like the man. His overcoat had a fowl stench that he didn't recognize and the way the man walked, it looked like he had a board nailed to his forehead.

"What is the point of your being here, Alec?" Frank demanded from the doorway. "You didn't just come here to compliment my son on his growth."

Alec turned, and an amused look came into his face. He shook a finger at Frank and grinned mischievously. "You should know better by now, Frank, that there is only one reason why I am here."

As soon as those words were out of his mouth, Frank and Morgan's faces began to show signs of red fury. Alec pretended to not notice and reached into his coat pocket, drawing out a rather thick blue envelope with large white letters on the front.

"You refused about three and a half years ago, so I'm here to point out that the sooner you agree, the better," he remarked, waving the envelope in Frank's face.

Frank grabbed Alec's wrist with one hand and with his eyes, he stared down at Alec with deep ferocity. "Matilda, would you be so kind as to take the boys into the other room?"

The nurse quickly rounded the bed and caught Neil and Deke by the hand. Pulling them after her, she hurried past Frank and down the hallway. She guided the two boys into the bedroom they had left not long ago and closed the door behind her.

As she did this, Deke caught a faint glimpse of what appeared to be an expanding shadow. As soon as the door was closed behind her, Matilda drew the two boys close to her and pressed her hand against their ears to block out any noise.

Everything sounded muffled to the two boys except the beating of their own hearts. Once or twice, Neil thought he could feel Deke's heart through his hand but then he thought that he was just trying to get his mind off the fact that his own heart was beating furiously.

After what seemed like decades to the boys, Matilda slowly released them and turned to the door. She gently touched the door handle with her hand, and then turned to look the two boys deep in the eyes.

"I want you boys to go out the back door and stay there until I come get you," she whispered. "All right?"

The two slowly nodded and Matilda opened the door. Stepping out, the boys felt as if there was a great weight on the air. Matilda turned them toward the end of the hallway opposite the bedroom and gave them a nudge. "I'll be right there."

The two boys started down the hallway, but about halfway down, Deke stopped and looked over his shoulder. Matilda had just disappeared into the bedroom that his mother was in. Neil didn't notice his brother had stopped until he had almost reached the door. As he turned with his hand on the handle, he saw that Deke had turned to follow Matilda to the bedroom.

"Deke," Neil called, "come on!"

Deke ignored him and looked into the bedroom. There was something going on, and he wanted to know what it was. Even though he was barely four, he was smart enough to know that the looks his parents had shown Alec were not welcoming ones. The sight he saw was one that Deke would never forget.

Matilda was holding a white sheet from the bed and using it to block Deke's view of whatever was on the bed. He could make out the rough shape of his mother on the bed, but he barely got a glimpse of her face before Matilda blocked his view. Her face had looked calm . . . as if all the pain of the sickness was gone . . . yet there was no color in her face still and her closed eyes had looked heavy and sunken in.

The next thing he realized was one that puzzled and frightened him. As Matilda blocked his view, he became increasingly aware that his father and the man Alec were nowhere to be seen, and the sheet lying on the floor next to the bed was stained bright crimson red.

Deke had poor eyesight unless it was very close, but the sight was enough for him to cry out in horror and shock. Matilda spun on her heel, startled to see Deke in the doorway.

"Go to the back door, Deke," she yelled in a strong voice.

Frightened at her sudden boldness and strength, Deke didn't linger, though his natural instinct jumped in first. Rushing across the room, he shook Gene awake but discovered that the boy was already awake, just cowering under the sheets.

Deke pulled him to his feet and the two rushed for the door as Matilda continued to cry at them to move. She was gathering things up from the floor and about the room such as sheets and pillows. As Deke hurried Gene through the doorway, he saw out of the corner of his eye that Matilda was piling the linens and pillows in a corner of the room and fumbling with something small in her hands.

Before Deke could see what she was doing, his foot brushed against something on the ground. Looking down, he realized that it was the blue envelope that Alec had been holding. Deke glanced at Matilda to see that she was about to turn back around. Quickly he snatched up the envelope, stuffed it down his shirt, and hurried after Gene.

As he reached the back door, he found Neil waiting with Gene. He tumbled down the brick steps onto the grass and turned to see Matilda close behind, running at top speed when suddenly they heard a ringing sound.

Matilda stuffed her hand into a large pocket in her skirt and drew out what looked like a small radio to the boys. She put it close to her mouth and, while panting, spoke, "What is it, Father?"

"Do you need help? I just got a report that you went to the Mecarnin's," a voice remarked through the radio.

Matilda looked down at the three boys before her and let out a deep breath before speaking, "Let's just say . . . the plan didn't work. Prepare a place for some guests . . . I'll be at the Church within thirty minutes. And you had better call the fire wagon."

She said this just as the house enveloped in a cloud of smoke and the boys could hear the sound of   kindling   crackling.

Chapter 3

Sunlight was streaming in through the small window. Gene was watching the light as if it was the most fascinating thing in the world. His turquoise blue eyes stared up at the light, and then they would glance about the room at the bodies nearby that rose and fell as they breathed deeply.

Suddenly, he heard a voice nearby whisper and he turned to see Deke looking up at him from where he lay beside him. Deke's light brown hair was tousled and matted to his head in strange places from sleep. His bright blue eyes almost looked blurry as he squinted up at Gene, for he wasn't wearing his glasses.

"Any sign of him?" he whispered.

Gene slowly shook his head, his straight blond hair waving as he did so. "I've been up since five thinking about him . . ."

Deke slowly nodded and laid his head back on the pillow. "Have you counted the days recently?"

"No . . . have you?"

Deke nodded again and looked up at the bare ceiling. "Tomorrow it will be exactly 1,826 days since we've seen them. Chances are that we probably won't see them for another 366 days."

Gene slowly turned his eyes back up to the light and drew his knees close to his chest. Almost five years ago, he and his two brothers had been brought to the home for the homeless of Saint Matthew's Church. There, they had met Father Fischer, one of the greatest men they knew. He wrote them constantly, giving them support and encouragement, but they hadn't seen a single sight of him, or the nurse Matilda, since the three had been left in the care of the sacristan: Mr. Stafford.

Gene glanced around the room and sighed to himself. Of all the twenty people who slept here regularly, he only knew eight. Most of them were older men, while two out of those eight were probably in their early twenties. They were decent fellows, always ready with a joke or laugh. Most of the time, Gene and Deke passed their days listening to the men talk and laugh while Neil went out to play with some boys outside. About three times a week, the two younger boys would join Neil, but rarely did the older boys let the two join their games.

Letting out a deep breath, Deke pulled himself to a sitting position and rumpled his hair with his hand. "I wonder if Father is any different . . . I hope not, because then we won't recognize him!"

As Deke sat up, he felt a pinching pain in his back and began to rub it with his hand. Almost immediately it disappeared. That was a normal feeling, especially when he first woke up. It happened to Gene and Neil as well, though Neil was the only one of the boys to openly complain about it. It wasn't as bad for Gene and Deke, but surprisingly less for Gene.

Deke scratched his head and yawned but barely finished before he saw the large bruise on Gene's forehead that wasn't there before. "Hey, Gene . . . what happened?"

Gene didn't make eye contact with Deke but merely shrugged. "Jeff didn't want me to play with him and Neil last night."

A quick memory flashed through Deke's mind. Gene was the one that most of the older boys picked on because when they began to beat Gene up, he wouldn't squeal or even make a noise. He would simply look them passively in the eye and let them beat him to a bruise. It was something about Gene that Deke could never understand.

The two boys were suddenly jolted from their calmness by the entrance of one of the homeless adults: Sef. He was a tall, gangly young man of about twenty with sandy blond hair and deep, sad, brown eyes. Now, his eyes were no longer sad. Instead, they were on fire.

"Wonderful news," he hollered. "Wake up, everyone! Have you heard the news?!"

Everyone at once began to leap out of their bed, thinking that possibly it was another attack. However, when they saw who was shouting it, they slowed down. Sef continued to run back and forth between the closely cramped cots, waving a newspaper over his head in triumph.

He had repeated his cry at least four times before a large, serious man known as Reid stopped Sef by grabbing him by the collar. Gene and Deke stared in surprise as Sef dangled, his feet at least a foot from the ground.

"Tell us the news before I drop you. It had better be good news if you decided to wake up the whole house at six a.m.," Reid remarked grumpily in Gerhenian.

Sef waved the newspaper in front of Reid's face. "Can't you see?"

Reid glanced at the newspaper, and then back at Sef. "I cannot read. Tell me," he remarked in Gerhenian.

Gene saw that Reid was about to lose his patience with Sef. None of the men liked waking up this early, and Sef didn't know enough about Reid to know that he was in danger of getting a boxing. The real problem was that Sef didn't understand a word of Gerhenian and Reid didn't understand a word of Catasbanian, like most of the men in the room. Leaping from his bed, he hurried through the maze of cots and pulled up in front of Reid.

"I'll read it to you . . . But can you put Sef down?" he asked in his clumsy Gerhenian.

Reid had to look way down at Gene, then way back up at Sef, who was hanging level with his head. "You know how to read, half-pint?"

Gene nodded. Reid looked back at Sef, then down at Gene before setting Sef down, none too gently. Before Sef had time to move again, Reid had snatched the newspaper from him and handed it to Gene.

Gene slowly took the large newspaper but realized that the front page was crumpled in half due to Sef's clumsy grip on it. Slowly he opened it, careful as to not rip the page. When he did, he realized that it was in Gerhenian. He should have known! Being full blooded Scardihn Caan, Gene and his brothers had been taught their lessons in Catasbanian, not in Gerhenian, though Gene had learnt some words by listening to the Gerhenian homeless.

Squinting at the page in the dim light, he began to read the words aloud in Catasbanian. Everyone grunted in confusion except Deke and Neil (who had been forced awake by Sef) who stared at Gene from across the room with growing eyes.

"What did you say, half-pint?" Reid asked in Gerhenian.

Realizing his mistake, Gene apologized in Gerhenian and read the bold headlines aloud in Gerhenian, then in Catasbanian again: THE WAR IS OVER.

There was a long silence in the room as everyone digested what Gene had just read, and then a whoop roared out so loudly that Gene had to clamp his hands and the newspaper over his ears, so he didn't go deaf. Deke and Neil began to bounce on their beds since they didn't want to get crumpled by the cheering adults.

Gene felt strong hands grab him by the shoulders and lift him off the ground. He opened his eyes and ears just as Reid lifted him to his shoulders as he pumped his fist shouting the news in his deep Gerhenian voice.

Gene managed to catch sight of Deke over everyone's heads and he saw Deke seemingly freeze and look over his shoulder. Gene knew that what was over Deke's shoulder was the wooden wall of the house and on that wall were hundreds of tick marks: marking the days since they had last seen Father Fischer.

Deke then looked back at Gene and both knew what the other was thinking: Father Fischer was waiting   for   the   war   to   end.

Chapter 4

When the boys broke free of the cheering inside the building, they had little plans of having breakfast. Neil had hurried his two younger brothers through dressing because he wished to find out what the reaction was outside.

The three boys had to pass through the sacristy to get to the front door of the Church and therefore had to quiet their voices so as to not startle anyone within the sacristy, especially the small sacristan who was easily startled by every noise. He was the kind of man who jumped whenever the bells began to ring before Mass started.

Finally, the boys managed to reach the front door, but that was when they discovered that they couldn't open the door all the way. The streets were jam-packed with people of all ages, spreading onto the lawns and steps of all the buildings, including the Church steps.

"How are we going to get out?" Deke inquired, glancing nervously out the window as though he wasn't sure if he would last long in that racket.

He felt his arm almost get jerked out of its socket as Neil caught hold of it and bolted back through the sacristy. Gene was close behind and remembered to close the sacristy door so that the sacristan wouldn't hear them open and close the back door. The back door wasn't nearly as crowded as the front, but Neil was only able to push it open enough to let the three of them squeeze out.

The noise difference was obvious. Their ears had begun to ring inside the Church because of the silence, but now they were exploding with cheers, chants, and screams from the street. People were leaping up and down, waving their hands as if trying to get everyone's attention.

Neil began pushing through the crowd in an attempt to reach the street. Gene and Deke grabbed each other's hands and helped each other through while keeping Neil in sight. It felt like endless winding turns around big people that never seemed to end. If anything, the people only got larger and denser as they continued to push through.

"Neil, we can't go any further," Gene called. "We'll get lost!"

"I can see the street!" Neil called back. "We're almost there."

Gene was clutching Deke's hand, trying not to lose him but also trying to stay as close to Neil as he possibly could, but Neil had disappeared under the legs of a tall person. Gene was about to help Deke after Neil, but a few bodies began to slam into the two.

Gene almost let go of Deke's hand but managed to grab his sleeve before he lost him. Another person rammed into his head, causing Gene to feel dizzy, and then he felt Deke suddenly go down onto the ground. Gene quickly composed himself and looked down at Deke, hoping that he hadn't been crushed.

Deke was kneeling on the only bare part of cobblestones that wasn't taken up by feet. In his hands he clutched a small object that seemed to have no definite form. Gene melted to his knees beside Deke, for he recognized the object as Deke's glasses.

"I'm sorry, Deke," Gene whispered.

Gene knew that the glasses were important to Deke. They had been a gift that Father Fischer had sent Deke for his eighth birthday, since Deke had been diagnosed with nearsightedness. It had enabled Deke to excel better in school, but also it had been the only thing they had to remember Father Fischer by other than memories.

The glasses were completely bent in half, one of the lenses was gone, and the other was cracked badly . . . there was no way to fix them. Deke closed his hands over the glasses and held them to his chest. Slowly, he rose to his feet but didn't take his eyes off the ground.

"I'm going back into the Church," he murmured almost in a whisper.

He pulled his sleeve out of Gene's grip and headed back the way they had come. The going was much easier that direction because no one was pushing that way. Gene watched him go until he couldn't see his brother behind all the other bodies. Turning around, the boy began to push through the crowd in search of Neil.

Meanwhile, Deke had made it to the back door of the Church and was pushing into the building. He pressed his back against the door as he closed it as if trying to hold off the sounds outside. It was quieter in the Church, and cooler. This part of Gerhenia could get rather warm in the summer.

Deke waited until he caught his breath before he started toward the sacristy. He quietly pushed the door open and stepped in, leaving the door open behind him. There was no sign of the sacristan, so Deke headed through, toward the entrance to the homeless building.

He had barely set his hand on the handle when he heard a voice behind him: "Deke?"

Turning around, he expected to see the sacristan or one of his brothers. However, the man that stood before him was not what Deke remembered. He was rather tall with wild pepper-colored hair that stood up on end, dark brown eyes, and a scar on his chin from an accident in his childhood. He wore black dress pants, clean black shoes, and a white shirt underneath a black jacket but the only thing that made him different was the white collar around his neck.

The man's eyes lit up as Deke turned around, and a smile creased the man's face. "You haven't changed."

Deke's blue eyes began to grow and didn't stop until he heard the sound of his brother's feet tramping quickly toward the sacristy. "Deke, we heard that . . ."

The two boys pulled to a sharp stop in the doorway. Obviously, they had heard about the visitor, so they weren't as startled as Deke. The three boys stared at the man while the visitor looked from boy to boy, smiling to himself.

"I promised I would come back," Father Fischer remarked, looking directly at Deke as he said this, "and now the time has come . . ."

The brothers looked at each other from across the room in confusion. Neil was rubbing his black hair with his hand and Deke was still trying to get over his shock, so Gene asked the long-awaited question.

"Time for what, Father?"

* * * * * * * * * *

26

"Matilda and I have managed to find several people who are interested in adopting a child," Father Fischer explained, leaning his elbows on the table.

The three boys and Father Fischer were sitting at the desk in the sacristy. The sacristan had returned from the streets, given his greetings to Father Fischer, then declared that he had to go clean the altar so he left them to their chatting.

Neil opened his mouth, about to point out that there were three of them, but Father Fischer could see the remark already coming. "We also knew that you three shouldn't be separated, so we called on several old friends and asked if they knew of anyone who would be willing to adopt more than two kids."

Deke and Neil glanced at each other and since Gene was sitting between them, he thought they were looking at him for a reaction. "You didn't find anyone?"

Father Fischer grinned brightly. "If I hadn't found anyone, I wouldn't have come to raise your spirits then to just drop them."

The three boys at once sat straighter and placed their folded hands on the table as if ready to listen to anything now. Deke, however, kept one of his hands in his lap; the hand that held his destroyed glasses.

"One of my oldest and dearest friends; he is a special person . . . He told me about a friend of his who lived alone and was always looking for company. I went to call on the gentleman . . . and he seems to be the perfect man for you three," Father Fischer explained.

"What is he like?" Deke inquired in a low voice, as if the question would be hurtful.

Father Fischer smiled. "I honestly can only say from the hour talk I had with him, he seemed to be a very decent gentleman."

The boys didn't seem satisfied by this reply and looked at each other in distress. Who knows what the man really was like! Father Fischer could sense their doubt and at once spoke the remark that he knew he should have said at the first moment:

"He agreed to let you boys come and stay with him for a few weeks. Just to see how you like him, the house, and the people nearby. At the end of those few weeks, if either you boys or Mr. Wetherby feels that it wouldn't work, I'll keep looking and bring you to stay with Matilda and her family."

Gene slowly pulled his hands off the table and clutched his knees. He didn't want to seem too confident or his brothers would have him make the choice. Neil rubbed his hands through his hair, trying to not make eye contact with either Father or his brothers. Deke watched his brothers' reactions and knew that the only other person to decide was him.

He thought of the long days in the building across the street ... the sleepless nights, the lonely meals. This might be the chance to have an actual childhood. He felt the sharp object of his glasses in his hand and gripped it tightly. He drew in a deep breath and let it out.

Looking down at his lap, he took a last look at the glasses, and then let them fall out of his hand onto the carpet under the table where no one would see them for a long time. He then placed both hands on the table, folded them together and nodded seriously.

"We'll do it."

Chapter 5

Gene looked out the window again, squashing his nose against the window pane. He couldn't help but watch the rows upon rows of trees pass by. Neil had curled up on the far end of the car bench and had managed to fall asleep about an hour ago. Deke had opened an encyclopedia and was earnestly looking for some information on where they were going.

Matilda and Father Fischer had refused to tell them exactly where their destination was, for they wanted it to be a "surprise." None of the boys believed this. Neil later told his brothers that he thought they were hiding something from them, while Deke mainly just thought that possibly they didn't want an important location to get into the wrong hands. This only brought on more suspicion from his two brothers.

They had, however, told the three that they were going to a place known as Break Neck Creek. This proved to be very helpful, but not to Deke, who had been trying his hardest to prove to his brothers that everything would be all right. However, it was helpful to Gene and Neil, for that gave them another reason to suspect that where they were going was not for the faint of heart. Neil, of course, hadn't thought that maybe Deke had a faint heart. He probably should have thought of that.

"Found anything yet, Deke?" Gene inquired.

Deke shook his head, though with Gene still looking out the window, the latter didn't see his brother respond with movement, so he repeated the question.

"Anything, Deke?"

"No," Deke replied in a slightly impatient voice. "Just let me know when you come into sight of a creek. We should be there soon."

"If we're nearly there, why are there only rocks?" Gene inquired.

Deke snapped his head up from where it had been bowing over the book and crowded to the window. Sure enough, the trees had disappeared and the whole place was rocky, gray, and the sky looked as if ready to rain.

"Neil," Deke hissed, leaning over to rouse his brother. "Neil, wake up!"

Neil groggily groaned and sat up. "It had better be important!"

"We're here," Gene whispered. "The car is slowing down."

Sure enough, Father Fischer's automobile was slowly pulling to a stop. Neil sat up straight and pushed to look out the window over his brothers' heads. As the car slowed, the foggy atmosphere began to show dark shapes that the kids at once guessed were buildings.

Father Fischer opened the door, and the cold air outside the car surrounded the three boys as they slowly climbed out. Their shoes at once felt damp, for they were standing on brown, dying grass that was soaked from a recent rainfall. The air seemed exceedingly light, but the moisture in the air was so great that they could feel the dampness on their faces.

"Where are we?" Deke shivered. "It was never this cold before . . . at least where we come from."

Father Fischer smiled. "We've headed further north. It's cold here a great deal. Very rarely does it warm enough for the attire you boys are wearing."

Automatically, all three of them looked down at the clothes they were wearing. Sure enough, they all wore knee-length shorts, short-sleeve shirts, ankle-high socks, and sneakers. They were in no way prepared for this weather.

"I'm glad that we arrived early then," Matilda pointed out as she climbed out of the car. "That gives us enough time to suit them up before they freeze into permanent ice cubes."

As she stepped out, she reached into the back bench and pulled out three leather jackets. Handing these to the boys, she helped them pull them on before they followed her advice in becoming ice cubes.

She was just helping them button the coats, for their fingers were too cold, when car wheels sounded behind them. They all turned to see the glare of car lights appearing through the fog toward them at a decent pace. The lights continued to grow as they got closer but stopped just directly behind Father Fischer's car.

Matilda stood up, having finished buttoning the boys, when a loud voice broke through the fog from the direction of the car: "Fischer? Father Fischer?"

Out of the mist appeared four gloomy figures; all four seemed to grow massive as they drew nearer, but as soon as they broke free of the glare of the car lights, the boys realized that two were adults and the other two were kids about their age: a boy and a girl.

"Schneider," Father Fischer called in a similarly loud voice. "Didn't think you ever came home this early in the school year!"

The tallest of the adults came forward and the boys saw that he was a giant of a man with wavy, thick brown hair that was brushed up out of his laughing hazel eyes. He was incredibly good looking even though he looked to be in his late thirties. He wore a dark black coat that came down to his hips and pants that suited the weather.

"Well, Whip is starting his fourth year. I felt that all his checks needed a little more of an update. Bill was getting onto me about that last semester," the man replied in a definite Gerhenian accent.

The second adult came into view, and she turned out to be a lovely petite woman with long blonde hair and big, round hazel eyes. She also wore a dark brown coat and her light hair against the coat seemed to suit the almost wintery feel of the place.

The kids were the next to approach, and at once Gene felt excitement, for the youngest was a boy his age. His brown, curly hair was piled on his head but long on the top and cut short around his ears and the back. His eyes were brown like his mother's but more of moderate size like his father's.

The girl was obviously at least a year older than the boy but looked to be tall for her age. She was slender, graceful, and had a sort of regal character about herself but also toughness underneath. Her hair was light like her mother's and came down to her shoulders. Her eyes were a deep hazel and slanted, not oval or round like her parents'.

"Who do you have with you this year, Father?" the woman inquired in a soft Catasbanian accent.

Father Fischer turned and began introducing the three boys, placing a hand on their shoulder as he introduced them. "This is Neil—he is ten—and Deke—he's nine—and then Gene, who is almost six. This is Mr. Schneider, his wife, and his children, Seraphina and Whip."

Mr. and Mrs. Schneider smiled at the three boys as they were introduced. Whip grinned brightly and waved at the three boys. Gene was the only one who returned it, for Neil and Deke were still trying to take in everything around them. Seraphina, though, seemed vastly interested in Neil, who was also looking at her in surprise.

"Well, since you are also here for status and health checks, could you possibly take the boys along with you?" Father Fischer inquired. "I still have other things to see to."

Mr. Schneider grinned brightly. "No need to ask, Father; we would be glad to! I can drop them off at their bay, too, if you would like."

Father Fischer had begun to help Matilda back into the car when he stopped to acknowledge the offer. "If you could, Colton, that would be swell. Their bay is 7.19. Their pick up should be here in another hour."

"That is perfect timing," Mrs. Schneider remarked, stepping over to the three boys and smiling at them. "Our bay leaves in an hour, too."

"We'll take care of them Father," Colton called.

Father Fischer closed the door behind Matilda, then turned to the three boys. All three of them were staring up at him in shock. The way things were looking, they weren't going to be in his care anymore . . . their life was an open book now.

Father Fischer could read the dejection and worry in their faces. He gently knelt down despite the fact that the dead grass was wet. He put a hand on Neil and Gene's shoulders; he couldn't on Deke's, since he was squashed between the two for warmth.

"Take care of yourselves," he remarked, waiting to look into each of their eyes before continuing. "Help each other out . . . but the most important: don't be afraid."

The three boys slowly nodded as Father Fischer let go of their shoulders. He touched each of their faces with his hand, patting them on the cheek before rising to his feet. He rounded the car and began to climb into the driver's seat.

"Wait," Deke cried, rushing to the window where Matilda was sitting. "I need to know . . . did you know who we were when Mom . . . died?"

Matilda looked deep into Deke's eyes and smiled sadly. "I cannot say I did. I was a nobody then . . . at least no one of importance. If I hadn't found you, I wouldn't be on the crusade to finding the answers, finding your father, and making sure you lead the life your mother would have wanted you to."

Nodding, Deke stepped away from the car back into the shelter between his two brothers. Matilda slowly raised the window but watched them through the foggy window as the car slowly roared backwards and away, back the way it had come.

Mrs. Schneider quickly stepped over to the three boys and put her arms around their shoulders. "You three are freezing! We should get inside."

She turned them toward the buildings and began walking. Whip and Seraphina hurried to keep up with their parents.

Chapter 6

"So, this is the first time you've come here?" Whip inquired, hurrying up the stairs to catch up to the three brothers. He had inherited his mother's clear Catasbanian accent while Seraphina had the clear, crisp Gerhenian of their father.

Gene nodded. "That's right ... what about you?"

Whip grinned. "I actually live near here. We were only on a vacation during summer break. Dad wanted to come back early this year because my diagnostic tests aren't up to date. You have to update them every three years."

"What are the diagnostic tests?" Deke inquired, while he climbed the stairs behind Whip and Gene.

Whip and Gene turned around to acknowledge the question, but Seraphina beat Whip to replying, "It's a series of tests that look for health, athleticism, intelligence, and other important facts."

"You boys are lucky because you get to also do the whole signing in thing. I always thought that was fun," Whip remarked.

Just then, the kids reached the porch of the building, and that was when the fog didn't seem to blind them any longer. The three boys looked up at a small building that was obviously an old log cabin. The door was painted a bright red but was chipping in several places. The windows were covered by dark green curtains and each corner seemed to be infested by cobwebs. It truly looked deserted.

Mr. Schneider stepped forward and pulled the door open. It creaked loudly, though neither of the adults, Seraphina, or Whip found this strange. In fact, it seemed familiar to them. As Mr. Schneider held the door open, Mrs. Schneider, Seraphina, and Whip hurried into the cabin. The three brothers went in at a slower pace, for they didn't know what would be on the other side of the doorway.

As they entered, the three boys at once felt their frozen limbs thaw out. The interior of the cabin looked the complete opposite of the outside. It was clean and polished, with not a cobweb in sight. There were handmade carpets on the wooden floors, and a soft glow from candles and a fireplace filled the room.

There was a long desk directly opposite the door and a long bench on the far side of the desk. To the right of the door was a large fireplace that was roaring with warmth, and several benches were positioned in front of the fire. On the left of the small square room was a huge bookcase, piled high with papers but not a single book.

"Anyone home?" Mr. Schneider called in his deep voice.

Neil almost thought that the call would echo, but instead it was met by the sound of bare feet padding on the wood floor. The three boys became aware of a staircase behind the desk and three small figures that were now descending the stairs.

"What do you know, Schneider," one of the figures remarked in a masculine voice. "Has Mrs. Schneider finally taught you how to be early?"

Mr. Schneider grinned and ran his hand through his brown hair. "I think it might be working, Brother Ken."

The three figures stepped off the stairs into the light and turned out to be three little monks. They were barely taller than Mrs. Schneider and half the size of Mr. Schneider, who was over six feet tall. They wore long brown robes that fell to their ankles, with hoods that rested on the backs of their heads.

Their hair was thickly laid on the top of their heads, and though they didn't have the bald spot as custom for some monks, they wore large, hand-carved, wooden rosaries around their waists. The first to walk over was a small skinny man with a long face and beady little brown eyes. The next was a slightly taller, medium-built man with strawberry-blond hair and bright brown eyes. He looked to be younger than both other monks. The third and last was taller than the first two but slightly on the round side. His face was bright and smiling and almost reminded Neil of a barn owl. His hair was brown and straight, not curly or gray.

The first two monks shook Mr. and Mrs. Schneider's hands before sitting down at the desk. The third shook the parents' hands, and then he went to shake each of the kids', giving them a bright grin as he did so. He then joined his brothers at the desk and pulled out a pen and large brown book that was tied shut by a piece of thread.

"What is new for Seraphina?" the small skinny monk inquired. "Just updates?"

Mrs. Schneider shook her head. "Seraphina is all up to date. Whip is the one who needs a new update."

"What about these three lads?" the oldest monk inquired. "I assume they're here to sign in?"

The three brothers nodded slowly, not sure what was happening. The round, bright monk smiled at the three boys and motioned them over to him.

Gene, being the first to realize that this wasn't a trial, stepped over to the monk with his brothers close behind.

"Don't be nervous," the monk whispered. "Brother Ken and Brother Weiss might seem stern, but they are really dear hearted men. I'm Brother Lawrence, by the way."

Gene smiled brightly at the monk. "I'm Gene . . . these are my brothers Neil and Deke."

Brother Lawrence smiled at the three and then turned to his book. "I just need some random information to put in here," he explained as he opened to almost the last page. "Let's start with the oldest."

Neil stepped forward and Brother Lawrence gave him a reassuring smile. "Were you given a specific bay number?"

The boy stared at the monk for a long time. He knew the number, but he had been too busy wondering about the weather to remember the bay number that Father Fischer had mentioned. Deke, at once seeing that his older brother was in a crisis, wanted to give the number, but his shyness suddenly kicked in and quickly he ducked his head.

"What was that?" Brother Lawrence inquired, looking around Neil at Deke. He was sure he had heard the younger boy speak. "Did you say something?"

There it was again; the boy's mouth moved, and a faint voice replied, but it was barely audible. Gene had been watching the nervous, confused looks passing between the monk and his two older brothers. Standing between Neil and Deke, he had

41

been able to hear what Deke had said, so he stepped slightly forward and answered the waiting monk.

"He said it was bay 7.19."

Brother Lawrence blinked, looked at Neil, then blinked again. Neither Neil nor Gene could tell whether the monk was confused, surprised, or impressed, for he merely stared at the three brothers in stunned silence.

"7.19, you say?" the monk asked again, louder this time.

The Schneider family had been signing paperwork with the other two monks, but at the sound of Brother Lawrence's confused voice, all of them, including the monks, looked in his direction.

"What's wrong, Lawrence?" Brother Weiss inquired, leaning over Brother Ken so as to see the situation better.

"7.19," Brother Lawrence replied, not taking his eyes off the three brothers.

Brother Weiss suddenly jolted and sat back in his seat, but now his eyes weren't calm and serious but wide and with a look of either surprise or horror. He slowly turned his head and looked directly at Mrs. Schneider.

"Don't you realize . . ." he started, but Mrs. Schneider interrupted him before he could go further.

"Yes, Brother, I know," she remarked, turning to look at the three brothers with a look that puzzled them . . . a look that almost seemed to hold all the answers. "That bay hasn't been used since HUDGE broke up."

Chapter 7

"Didn't you find their behavior kind of strange?" Whip whispered to Gene and Deke.

Gene nodded but Deke merely hugged his arms to himself in the attempt to keep warm. After the strange exchange between the parents, the three brothers, Whip, and Seraphina had been given small tabs of paper to pin on their coats, though Whip and Seraphina had advised them to wait.

They were now heading across the sandy, damp road that separated the small line of cabins, to another cabin opposite the one they had just left. The kids were huddling together to keep warm with Seraphina and Whip on the outside since they had warmer coats, though they still felt the cold, for their coats were meant for autumn weather and this was the weather of mid-winter.

"Incredibly," Deke replied, his teeth chattering between his words. "Has that ever happened before?"

Seraphina and Whip shook their heads as they rubbed their arms. "Everything has become rather strange since we arrived here," Whip replied. "First they act strange, then the weather drops to almost zero!"

"It was already cold when we arrived," Neil pointed out. "What's so strange about that?"

"I suppose just nerves," Whip remarked.

The kids had just caught up to their parents on the porch of the next cabin. They stomped their feet loudly on the steps and hurried into the door as Mr. Schneider held it open. As they hurried inside, they were welcomed by the familiar feel of a warm hearth.

The room was perfectly silent like the others, but it was furnished quite differently.

The walls were lined with pictures and portraits that looked older than the present. Instead of colored pictures, they were black and white. One half of the room was loaded with huge bookcases, but instead of shelves there were dozens and dozens of small drawers lining them with a particular number on each. Almost all the bookcases were painted a rustic green, but there was a single lone bookcase that was dark blue with white designs painted elaborately on each drawer.

The left half of the room looked like a hospital room, for there was a high bed against the wall with pure white sheets, a small table on wheels, and several cabinets on the walls that were labeled with names that the three brothers couldn't even pronounce.

"Sister," Mr. Schneider called loudly as he closed the front door behind him.

Somewhere in the back room, something crashed and from the sound of it, it was probably glass. A tall woman buzzed through the door and stopped short when she saw the new arrivals. She wore a long brown dress just like the monks' that came to her ankles, but instead of being barefoot, she wore a huge pair of bog boots. Her bright red hair was pulled back and most of it hidden beneath a brown veil that was tied snugly behind her ears.

"So, Sister Maria wasn't imagining things when she said she saw you pull up!" the nun remarked in a bright, feminine voice. "Here for a health update?"

At the very mention of those words, the three brothers froze. In being raised in a building for the homeless, they never had "health checks" and they had no clue what it could possibly be like. While Whip merely lingered, Seraphina rushed forward and threw her arms around the nun.

"Hello, Sister Anne!"

Neil, Deke, and Gene snapped their heads at the sudden energetic sound of Seraphina's voice. For the past hour, she had barely spoken and when she did, it was in such a soft voice that they could barely hear her.

The nun smiled brightly down at the girl and patted her on the cheek. "It's good to see you again, Seraph. I see you've been hanging out with your mother recently."

Mr. Schneider raised an eyebrow at the nun and crossed his arms. "What is that supposed to mean?"

Sister Anne grinned mischievously. "As a kid, you were never the sentimental or emotional kind. While your wife would have hugged someone to greet them, you found that a little too friendly."

"Just get on with the health checkups, Sister," Mr. Schneider groaned.

The nun at once busied herself, rushing back and forth between shelves, drawing open a specific drawer as if she had all million of them memorized. Every time she opened one, she removed a small vial or other object of some kind and laid them on the table. After a moment of work, she sat down on the roll chair and turned to the children.

"Who's first?"

When all four of the boys hesitated, Seraphina stepped up boldly and held out her left hand. Sister Anne pressed her two fingers on Seraphina's wrist and watched a stopwatch for about a minute. She then scribbled something down on a piece of paper nearby. Pulling out one of the vials, she dripped three drops of a blue liquid on Seraphina's hand and rubbed it in.

By now, the boys had slowly inched forward and were watching the whole procedure with extreme interest. The blue liquid absorbed quickly into Seraphina's fair skin and before long, all they could see was a pale blue marking on her hand. Sister Lillian turned Seraphina's hand back over to reveal that Seraphina's veins in her underarm were now much more noticeable and a deep purple.

While Neil and Gene's eyes grew wide, Deke's squinted smaller in the attempt to see what was making the purple smear on Seraphina's wrist (at least that was what it looked like to him). Sister Anne then resorted to pressing Seraphina's veins. As she did so, the veins returned to their natural color and size. Before long, her veins were barely visible.

"Did any of that hurt?" Sister Anne inquired as she bowed over her notepad.

Seraphina shook her head. "It only felt cold."

The nun nodded in seeming satisfaction before scribbling something on her notepad. She then began to do the boring, basic health checks. She checked Seraphina's ears, mouth, nose, and eyes. She then tested Seraphina's sight, smell, taste, and hearing abilities. After that, she let Seraphina go and turned to the boys.

"Next?"

Whip, Deke, and Neil still hesitated. Whip had done this before but that was five years ago, and he still wasn't sure what to make of it all. Deke was still puzzled about the whole thing since it all seemed so vague to him, while Neil was suspicious that this might all be some sort of prank.

In that case, Gene stepped up to the table, receiving a grin from Sister Anne. After checking his pulse, the nun drew out the vial and dripped three drops of the blue liquid on the back of his hand and rubbed it in. As it began to absorb into his skin, Gene looked the nun right in the eye.

"What does that liquid do?"

Sister Anne smiled. "You know, you're the first boy to ever ask me that. The girls are always the inquisitive ones. It's a testing substance. You see, the materials in the liquid will turn a particular color if something is wrong in your bloodstream. If you have blood poisoning, it will turn yellow. If you have an infection somewhere in your body, it will be red. If there is nothing wrong with your blood or your blood stream, it will just be purple. The liquid also causes the veins in your wrist to expand for a short period until I put pressure on them, which enables me to get a better look at the color of your veins."

Gene's eyes grew wide at the strange miracle that the almost clear blue liquid could create. Deke meanwhile had been listening with such rapt attention that he hadn't noticed that he was standing right on top of the two, absorbing every word as fast as the liquid was absorbing into Gene's skin.

Sister Anne grasped Gene's hand gently and slowly turned it over. After hearing what the liquid could detect, Gene had become rather nervous about seeing what color his veins were. It wasn't until he saw the overly expanded purple veins that he fully relaxed and let out the air that he had been keeping in his body for the past few seconds.

Gently, Sister Anne pressed each vein until they all receded back to their normal form. She then drew out her checklist. "Did you feel any pain?"

Gene shook his head. "No ma'am . . . could I do it again?"

The three adults let out cheerful laughs at the boy's enthusiasm, but the nun gave him a gentle look. "Sorry, Gene but the swelling chemical in the formula is just enough to inflate your veins. Too much of it may cause something more critical to inflate . . . possibly permanently. That is why you can only have a health check every five years."

Reluctantly, Gene allowed the nun to test his eyes, ears, nose, and mouth. He then stepped back to allow Neil up to the table. Neil's check was just like Gene's and Seraphina's, and sister Anne was pleased at his sight especially since his different colored eyes had her concerned.

Whip's check went well, though his sense of smell was rather poor. It wasn't until he was halfway through his sight test that Sister Anne realized that Whip had a slight stuffy nose from a recent cold, which had caused his sense of smell to deteriorate for the time being.

Deke had been watching the whole check with suspicious interest. Through Whip's check, Neil and Gene had tried their hardest to convince him that there was nothing wrong with the check and it was for their own good. When Sister Anne turned to Deke, he at once felt the impulse to hesitate but then an almost firm, determined look crossed the nun's face and Deke quickly stepped up to the table.

Sister Anne had mixed up the order of Whip and Neil's checks merely for the sake of keeping the kids attentive and not boring them to death. First, she checked Deke's senses and confirmed that he needed a new prescription of glasses soon. She then rubbed the liquid onto his hand and gave it a few seconds to absorb.

The notepad she had been using was overflowing with the notes from the other checks, so she reached down to grab a new notepad. When she did this, Deke suddenly felt a desire to sit down. He moved slowly away from the table and sat down on the clean bed, sinking onto it as if he hadn't sat in weeks.

He glanced over at the others. Gene and Whip were chattering together near the warm fire, laughing merrily while Seraphina and Neil were listening to the talk of the parents with interest. Sister Anne was still hunting for a notepad in a lower drawer . . . and no one was looking at him.

Deke's head began to swim before him . . . he could feel something strange happening in his hand. Slowly he looked down, but everything looked blurred . . . more than usual. He slowly turned his wrist over just slightly and barely got a glimpse of his inflated veins before a voice broke the horrible ringing sound in his ears.

"Deke," Neil called, "what's wrong with you?"

Deke slowly wavered his eyes up to meet his brother's and that was when everyone present in the room started. Deke was slumped on the bed as if he was ready to topple over. All the blood had left his face and looked waxen and thin. His eyes were bloodshot and falling shut.

Sister Anne looked up from the drawer and at once rushed to her patient. Grasping Deke by the shoulders, she eased him down back onto the bed and then snatched up his hand. Slowly she turned it over, but one look told her that there was nothing wrong.

"Back up, please," she said in a shaky voice. "Give him some air."

"He's delirious," Seraphina whispered.

It was true. He was tossing his head back and forth wildly. Sweat was pouring down his face as if he had stuck his whole head into the hearth. Moans and whimpers were filling the room, causing the children to back up in fright. Who knew what he would do . . . who knew if he would cry out. Truth be told, they didn't want to break their eardrums if he did.

Suddenly, his words began to make sense. "No . . . Neil, no . . . Gene needs you . . . Don't . . . no . . ."

Deke meanwhile was experiencing a strange "vision" that was flashing before his eyes. He could see things of the past . . . past faces . . . past pains. The bloodstained sheet, the blue envelope on the floor and Gene shivering on the floor bed . . . he saw the faces of Sister Anne, the Schneider family, Neil and Gene hanging over him. Their voices seemed to come from the other end of an iron pipe and half of their words were muffled by a strange wall that seemed to separate them.

The things that began to flash before him now were ones that were strange . . . foreign and unknown to him . . . ones that he hadn't experienced before . . . or yet while some were from things he had seen before. The first he saw was Neil and Gene, about two years earlier when Neil was trying to teach Gene how to hold a football correctly. He saw faces of people, young and old, who were unfamiliar to him yet seemed to have significance to him. He saw water lapping around him . . . clear blue skies through a watery view . . . and then everything changed. He saw faces that seemed strangely familiar . . . yet strangely different as if there was something altered about them . . . something about the faces that seemed aged. He saw a young figure in front of him, facing away from him.

On the other side of the figure, Deke saw a sight that made his blood boil. The ground seemed red, though he knew that it wasn't just the flames that lingered about the dead grass, nor was the clay red ground beneath the millions of bodies that littered the ground . . . the ground was stained with blood. Suddenly, a strange shape appeared at the other side of the plain of dead. He felt himself tense for some reason, and the figure in front of him suddenly started forward as if in pursuit of the shape.

Deke felt himself call out to the person, who stopped and turned to face him. The young man's face was streaked with blood and his straight blond hair crusted with dried blood and dirt . . . it was Gene! Though it was as if . . . he was aged somewhat.

"You would do the same for those you love," Gene said in a voice that was foreign to Deke . . . a voice that was cracking with pain and sorrow . . . a voice that Deke had never heard out of Gene.

This altered Gene turned away from Deke and hurried off into the darkness, leaving Deke standing in stunned horror. Deke felt himself suddenly start to follow where Gene had gone . . . and that was when he heard a sharp sound pass by his head.

He turned, just in time to see a long arrow pass by him . . . missing him by an inch just because of his move. He followed the movement of the arrow as it soared through the air and struck the body of a human who stood nearby. Deke felt his face grow increasingly hot, then cold, then stale . . . the person was tall, slender, and his black hair was plastered to his head by sweat and blood: Neil!

Deke and Neil's eyes met just for a second before Neil's eyes closed and he slowly sank to his knees. Deke felt his chest rise into his throat and a blood-curdling scream broke from his body with such fury that he felt his head splitting . . . Then he felt strong hands rocking him back and forth and he felt his eyes snapping open . . . it was a dream.

His eyes opened, and he saw the familiar, unaltered faces of Neil and Gene over him, shaking him violently. Sister Anne was trying desperately to stop the two boys from messing with Deke, but when they saw his eyes open, they all stopped.

"You were crying out our names," Gene explained. "What happened?"

Deke felt his eyes sting as tears rose up in them, then he felt a sudden relief settle in his chest, but a strange puzzlement struck his mind. "I . . . I saw the future."

Chapter 8

Gene slowly slipped on his coat, making sure to not take his eyes off of Deke. Deke's recovery after his strange encounter with the past, present, and possible future was so rapid that everyone was slightly on edge, ready to catch him should he topple over.

Deke had refused to detain them any longer, so Sister Anne had filled out the forms for their health updates, handed them over to Mrs. Schneider, and they had headed out of the cabin.

"How much time do we have?" Whip whispered to his sister.

Seraphina glanced down at her wristwatch, and trying to decipher the numbers in the dim light of the foggy outside, she answered, "We got here at about eight and the bays begin to leave at nine. We have about fifteen minutes."

"That's more than enough time to get our supplies and find our bays," Mr. Schneider called from ahead.

Whip shivered as a cold hand seemed to run down his spine. "I hope the shipment of new capes has arrived. Sister Anne promised that they would be pretty great."

Gene and Neil glanced at each other over Deke's head, and it was evident to each that the other was thinking the same thing. It was Neil who voiced the question passing between the two of them: "What is the deal with all these health checks, signings, and stuff?"

"Precautions," Whip replied. "You see ... Hichester District is the most unknown, secretive, and best-protected place in the whole world. There is only one way into Hichester, and that is the bays. It just so happened that the bays are connected to this old town, so the monks and nuns cared for it. Since then, they have protected the use of the bays by all these signings and precautions. The health checks are for the safety of the inhabitants. Since the mayor has added the health checks, no diseases or unusually dangerous sicknesses have been brought to Hichester."

Neil looked over at Gene to see if his brother understood any of that, but Gene had already formed another question in his small mind: "What in the world is Hichester District?"

The whole group stopped short in their tracks. Both the parents, Seraphina, and Whip turned to stare at the three brothers, who were looking at them expectantly.

"You honestly don't know?" Seraphina inquired in her soft girlish voice.

The three boys slowly shook their heads in unison. Seraphina and Whip looked at each other in shock and seeming horror while Mrs. Schneider smiled kindly at the three boys.

"Let's just say that Hichester District is pretty much paradise on earth."

* * * * * * * * * *

Whip pulled the wrap over his head, causing his already unruly hair to go flopping about and over his eyes. He reached up with one hand and brushed his hair to the side so that he could see.

"Are you sure you'll be all right without us?" he inquired as he shifted the wrap on his shoulders so that he could reach the pockets.

They had just emerged from the supply cabin, where they had been supplied with water canteens (one each), medium-sized bog boots to protect their feet from the dampness, and wraps. The wraps were Whip's favorite part of the day, for the shipment of newly designed wraps had just arrived.

Simply cut, the wraps were square pieces of cloth with a slit in the center where the head could slide in. There was a collar on each that you could turn up and it would cover your ears. There were rows of pockets on the inside of the wraps, all different sizes and shapes. The wraps were somewhat waterproof, though they had no head protection, so the boys were given flat caps of the same material while Seraphina received a knitted hat that came lower over her ears.

Neil hesitated in answering, for he wasn't sure if he was confident enough to go on alone with his brothers, but Deke and Gene nodded for him. "Thanks Whip," Deke remarked in a soft, low tone. "We'll be quite all right."

Whip nodded as he pulled his hat lower over his head to protect his ears. Gene watched him a moment before looking down slightly so as to not meet Whip's gaze. "Will we see you again?"

A grin creased Whip's face and his brown eyes danced with humor. "Oh, I'm sure we will. Hichester is a small town; you eventually know every living being there within the first week."

"Great, just great," Neil muttered to himself, not loud enough for anyone other than Deke to hear, who gave him a firm look of disgust.

Mrs. Schneider finished fishing through the bag that Mr. Schneider had been carrying and now drew out the tags that the kids had received from Brother Lawrence. Bending down, she carefully clipped the tags onto the chest of each child where they could be clearly seen.

As she was pinning on Deke's, she looked up into his eyes and for a moment, Deke almost thought that he could see her face plainly. She placed a gentle hand on his shoulder and gave him a bright smile.

"Stay strong, Deke. Those things you saw were possibilities of the future, though there is a way to alter them for the better," she whispered in a low tone so only Deke could hear. "Remember . . . there will always be something there for you, so be there for others."

Deke slowly nodded his head, causing his brown hair to flop about his forehead. Mrs. Schneider smiled at the boy before rising to her feet and turning to her own children. "We had better go now. Say your goodbyes."

Whip turned around to realize that Deke and Gene were right in front of him. Giving them a mischievous grin, he crossed his arms in front of him and, grasping one of their hands with each of his, he gave them strong, vigorous shakes.

"See you in a few days," he remarked cheerfully. "Don't get lost!"

Neil raised an eyebrow in mock humor. "How could we possibly get lost in a small town?"

Whip seemed to be warming to Neil's sarcasm and had a quick reply ready. "Oh you'll see."

Chapter 9

Neil was still pacing . . . up and down, back and forth. He seemed to have a rhythm for the way he was pacing. Deke began to wonder if he was trying to draw an imaginary picture with it. He glanced over at Gene . . . he was the complete opposite of Neil. Sitting there, wrapped up in his cloak, Gene was merely watching the huge wall before them that obviously had an important part to play in the arrival of the bay.

They were seated on a bench in a wide alleyway between two of the cabins. There was a wall that connected to the backs of the cabins, joining them together, in a way. Mr. Schneider had told them to wait there until the bay arrived and he said that it would arrive in the next twenty minutes.

"He could have had the decency to tell us from which direction the bay was coming!" Neil remarked crossly.

Deke turned his attention from Gene to Neil, still not sure which side he should agree on. "Maybe we should just give it a few more minutes," he suggested hopefully.

Neil didn't stop his pacing but turned to glare his brother. "So you're siding with Gene now? Don't you think that's kind of irregular?"

"I prefer to look at it as uncontaminated predisposition," Deke replied in a low tone. "Besides, there are no sides when it comes to you two."

"If Gene is not choosing to make another side opposite me, then what is he doing?" Neil demanded, turning back to his pacing.

Deke looked over at his younger brother, hoping the two could dissolve the tension and impatience without placing him in the center. Gene, however, was watching the wall intently, resting his chin on his arm. "Haven't either of you noticed that the wall is moving?"

Neil let out a sharp laugh, though he didn't stop to take even a glance at the wall. "Seriously, Gene; don't try to convince us that there is anything special about that solid piece of plywood."

When neither of his brothers replied, Neil turned to realize that they hadn't even heard his remark. They were staring with wide eyes at the wall . . . that was indeed sliding to the side, behind one of the cabins!

As the wall slid to the side, the three brothers saw only a dense thickness of fog that didn't want to enter the alleyway but stayed where it was. Gene was preparing to rise to his feet when a soft, melodious sound split the chilly silence . . . the sound of a flute. A gentle, long note rang out, then was followed by a soft trill on a higher note before a few more notes followed in a scale fashion.

Deke slipped his hand into Gene's, and at the feeling of his younger brother gripping it back, Deke felt a sense of security and relief. Gene drew Deke to his feet, without taking his eyes off of the fog.

"Where are you going?" Neil hissed in a whisper as if the fog would retreat if it was frightened.

Gene pretended to not hear Neil's question but rather cocked his head to the side as if listening. "The flute . . . it's getting louder."

"What is that supposed to mean?" Neil demanded in a louder tone.

Gene grasped Deke's hand tightly and reached out with his free hand to grab Neil's. "It means we're going in," he whispered.

Neil desperately tried to pull back, but there was a strange strength in his little brother that he couldn't fight. Also, that strange look in Gene's eyes told him that this was not a time for second guessing.

Gene's eyes were fixed on the wall of fog, trying to decipher any shapes that might appear. Gene was the first to enter the fog, for Deke was gripping his arm from behind while Neil was trying to keep a distance between himself and the fog for as long as possible.

As his bare face touched the moisture of the fog, he felt suddenly at peace . . . warm and content as if all the answers were right there . . . all the goodness of the world seemed to be in the very air he breathed. That was another thing, for the air no longer smelt like damp earth or dead grass . . . but a soft, fragrant smell as if something good was cooking over a smoky fire or a field of flowers was near.

Gene turned slightly to look Deke directly in the eyes. There was almost a wall between the two of them now, for Deke was trying to not enter the fog. However, as Gene's turquoise eyes met Deke's dark blue ones, Deke could tell there was something special beyond the wall of fog . . . something that made Gene's face seemingly glow with happiness.

Deke slowly allowed Gene to pull him into the fog, and as he did, he felt Neil brush his shoulder as Gene pulled both brothers all the way into the fog. As Neil and Deke absorbed the fullness of the air, Gene released their hands and took several steps forward to see if the blinding fog was thinner ahead.

61

"No matter what this countryside is like," Deke whispered, "Mrs. Schneider wasn't kidding when she said this was like paradise on earth."

"And I'll say this," Gene remarked, "the monks were right in giving us these bog boots . . . I've found water."

Deke and Neil's eyes snapped open (they had closed them so that they could pay attention to the smell of the air). They could barely see the dark silhouette of Gene ahead. They watched as Gene took several more steps forward . . . becoming barely visible to them now.

"Guys," Gene remarked in a surprised tone, "I think you need to see this."

Grasping Neil's arm, Deke slowly followed his brother to where Gene was standing. The fog seemed uncommonly thick as they ventured further into it . . . then all of a sudden it lifted. Deke's first reaction was to look behind him, for there was a perfectly flat wall of fog behind him . . . yet he stood in a semi misty environment.

Turning around, Deke looked to where his brothers were staring, and he felt his heart leap in his chest. They were standing ankle deep on the bank of a river. The water of the river was barely moving, as if it was still water but it was too clear to be stagnate. There was a soft golden glow to the lighting on the river for a soft glow from the sun shone through the branches of the trees that lined the opposite side of the river. The side of the river they were standing on stretched out perfectly straight for about eighty feet before both ends curved sharply away from the cabins.

The only thing that stood out on the glass like river was the dark silhouette of a figure who seemed to be standing on the water itself. It wasn't until the figure was upon them that they realized that it was a human standing on a flat barge. The barge was about ten feet long and barely two feet wide. The person stood in the center of the barge, holding a long pole in one hand and holding the other out to them.

The brothers couldn't see the stranger's face, for he was completely garbed in a golden outfit that had the same rustic, soft hue as the water. He wore a long-sleeve shirt that was loose and relaxed, not tight and snug. His shirt was tucked loosely into a pair of similarly colored pants. The pant legs were tucked into knee high boots that had no sharp, rough edges. A long narrow cloth, made of similar material to the rest of his outfit, was wrapped many times around his shoulders, under his arms, across his chest, and around his neck and head, concealing all of his upper body. The ends of the cloth were wrapped loosely around his face like a hood, concealing all skin except around his eyes and part of his forehead. On his hands were slender, snug gloves with the fingertips cut off, so only his fingers showed.

If any one of the three brothers had imagined a bargeman to meet them on this remote river, they would have expected a simply dressed human. This man was dressed simply in a relaxed sense, but the elaborate golden embroidery along his boots, pants, sleeves, and across his chest showed that there was obviously a significant or important meaning to this bargeman.

Without a word, the man reached over with one hand, almost touching the boys. Gene slowly took it and realized that it didn't feel like a hand ... it felt like flowing water! The bargeman lifted him out of the water with his one hand as if Gene weighed nothing. He placed the young boy in front of him, and Gene impulsively knelt down so as to not fall off the narrow barge.

Deke and Neil were similarly brought aboard and placed behind the bargeman since there was more room behind than in front. Grasping his rod with both hands, the bargeman submerged it deep into the river and pushed on it. The barge smoothly surged forward.

The water made absolutely no noise as the flat barge with its slightly upturned front glided down the still river. There was no sound that split the air except for the soft hum of a passing dragonfly, the bargeman inserting his pole into the water, and the sound of the wind brushing against the river side rushes.

Gene leant over so he could see around the bargeman's legs at his two brothers. Neil and Deke leaned over as well and gave him a confused, quizzical look. Gene glanced up at the bargeman, who seemed to concentrate entirely on his rowing.

Gene turned around and moved his legs around so that they wouldn't fall asleep on him. He glanced over the edge of the flat barge at the water that slowly glided past him. He extended a hand to touch the water when a voice suddenly cracked behind him, causing him to spin around.

"Don't touch the water!"

The boy stared up at the bargeman, for it was obvious that he was the speaker. His voice had been soft and kind, yet firm, with a slight crack to it as if overly cautious or as if he carried a heavy sorrow on his shoulders.

"Wha . . ." he stammered, "what's wrong with it?"

The bargeman didn't answer right away but instead he laid his pole on the barge and knelt down where he stood. He grasped a rope that was tied around the middle of the barge with both hands and seemed to be finding a comfortable place to hold it.

"This river is known for its toxic fumes. Some of the water from this river runs from the Smothering Marshes, farther north. The Smothering Marshes flow around a rare plant known as *lenthon,* which gives off a fume into the water that can knock a man unconscious for hours," the bargeman replied.

He straightened himself up, then his arms suddenly tensed, and he yanked at the rope. The barge suddenly seemed to curve on the sides as if it transformed into a canoe. At least, that was what it looked like, but what really happened was that the wood of the barge was so flexible that a sharp, strong pull on a certain part would make it curve.

The three boys jolted and grasped the sides of the barge at the movement, but the bargeman didn't seem to notice. He grasped his pole but remained on his knees. While kneeling, he grasped the pole in the center so that equal length of pole was sticking out over the water.

It wasn't until they turned around that they saw that the water was now moving them along at a faster pace. Gene slowly glanced back at his brothers. Neil was merely shrugging, not sure of what was going on, but Deke's eyes were wide open. His ears had caught

the sound of strong raging water . . . And he knew
why the bargeman had just suddenly knelt down.

Chapter 10

Neil, Deke, and Gene were all clenching their teeth so hard that their heads began to throb. The bargeman seemed completely relaxed, as if it was every day that he was speeding his barge toward a waterfall at top speed.

"Are you sure we shouldn't try paddling back upstream?" Neil asked, over the roar of the approaching waterfall.

The bargeman didn't meet Neil's eyes but kept his own fixed on the edge of the waterfall. "Unless you want to reach a dead end and then have to turn around and come back this way."

Neil and Deke leant over to stare at Gene. Their younger brother was busily racking his head for a way out of this, but nothing was coming. The roar of the fall was so strong now that Gene couldn't even hear his own breathing, which happened to be in gasps.

Gene was just about to make up the most random excuse when the bargeman did the last thing either of the brothers expected. Standing up hastily, he grasped his pole in one hand and spun around, so that he was facing the back of the barge.

He gave Neil and Deke one glance before leaping into the air. All three boys closed their eyes and clapped their hands over their ears as if trying to block out the sounds of the bargeman striking the water . . . but that sound never came. Instead, they felt like they had just been lifted off the water slightly.

Neil was the first to open his eyes and when he looked around, he realized that the bargeman was no longer in front of them and the barge was now tipping backwards as if there wasn't enough weight on the front. If Neil was Deke, he would have realized what had happened just by seeing the unbalanced weight of the barge. However, luckily for Neil, Deke was sitting right in front of him and before Neil could make some frightening assumption, Deke had pointed out that the bargeman was standing behind Neil at the back end of the barge.

The bargeman had landed on his feet, with his back facing the boys. He was holding his pole in both hands and barely glancing over his shoulder at the fall. The water was now raging around them and there was no way they could have stopped their descent now. The front of the barge was literally centimeters from the edge, when everything seemed to happen.

The bargeman began to toss his weight back and forth, rocking the barge as if preparing to overturn them all. Just when the barge was tipping it's furthest, he cried out to the boys in a voice that caused them all to jump.

"Lean to the left!"

The boys at once obeyed. for the barge was tipping fully to the right, but it wasn't until they were all leaning to the left that they realized that they were leaning directly toward a huge cliff of solid stones, about five feet from them!

For a moment, they were on the brink of completely tipping over and possibly hitting the side of the river, but the bargeman had everything situated. He shot his pole forward, holding onto the very end of it, and jabbed it onto a small stone that stuck out from the smooth stone of the cliff.

None of the boys had noticed anything peculiar about that rock, for they had been too preoccupied worrying about the falls. If they had noticed, they would have seen that the rock seemed on the brink of falling out and it had a reddish hue to it, not the rough gray-and-black color of the rest of the cliff.

The bargeman pressed all of his weight into the pole, and that was the first time the boys noticed the stone, for it suddenly clicked forward like a light switch does when you flick it on. The water directly in front of them seemed to slow down, though the bargeman continued to lean to the left so that the barge wasn't perfectly flat but almost completely leaning to the left.

If the light had been any worse, it would have looked like they had begun to fly off the falls, but with the almost dim light around them, they could plainly see that it wasn't a miracle, but a huge log had suddenly appeared from over the edge of the waterfall and leveled out perfectly with the falls.

The log was cut completely in half and carved out in the center to take the form of a slide, though it curved sharply to the left, directly into the cliff past the falls. As the log seemed to levitate and connect itself to the edge of the falls, water began to flow down the log branch as well as down the falls. Before the brothers could think, the bargeman had steered the barge directly at the log!

They all grasped the edge of the boat in the hopes that the log wouldn't suddenly fall apart when they flowed through it. The water flowing along the "log channel" was much faster, and as they spun around the sharp corner water sprayed up into their eyes. But that water wasn't enough to hide their view from where they were headed.

From their view on the main river, it had seemed that the log curved directly into the flat side of the cliff, but what they couldn't see from that viewpoint was that there was indeed a cliff opening that was just large enough for them to speed through without the bargeman getting his head knocked off.

Everything became extremely dark, especially as a stone rolled across the entrance of the cave as if it was perfectly naturally for rocks to move themselves. The thing the boys did know was that they were obviously in a cave, for it was cool and they could hear the trickling of water falling from the roof . . . and also that they were going much slower.

"Uh . . . can anyone see anything?" Neil muttered from out of the darkness.

"Just hang on there, little sir," the bargeman remarked from behind. "You'll soon be able to see."

The boys listened silently as if waiting to hear the strike of a match . . . but instead they could hear the bargeman either moving around or messing with his clothes. Then it sounded like he had set his pole down on the barge . . . And then that noise broke the silence . . . the whistle of the flute. It was the exact same sound that they had heard when they first entered the fog bound. It was a haunting sound that sent a chill up their spine.

The whistle echoed off of the walls of the cave and came back to their ears as if he had repeated the song. There was a long, dead silence, the kind where you are just listening for the next echo . . . but there was nothing. Everything seemed to have stopped,

71

even the gentle plinks of the water dripping from the roof of the cave . . . it was all deathly silent.

That was when it happened . . . A crack of light split the pitch darkness, striking the people on the barge directly in the face. Slowly, that crack of light began to grow upwards, not from side to side like when a door is opened, but like when a garage door is raised.

There was a soft trickling sound that had begun to grow with the light, and finally it sounded like a small creek was flowing nearby. As the light continued to grow, the boys realized that there was a huge rock that had blocked the exit and it was now rolling upwards out of the way. On the other side of the rock was a small waterfall that covered about a half of the entrance.

Without a word, the bargeman submerged his pole into the water and pushed them gently forward. Surprisingly, the water flowing from the small falls didn't seem to make the job any more difficult. As they neared the entrance, the rock completely lifted out of sight, leaving a small circle-shaped opening, just large enough for them to squeeze out.

The bargeman removed his staff from the water and holding it in both hands, he held it out in front of him, then suddenly drove it into the water with all the strength in his body. The barge flew forward and leapt over the side of the waterfall. As soon as they felt the jolt, the boys had covered their eyes and grasped the side of the barge, fearing that they would start to go fast again . . . However, they weren't moving.

Neil, being the one furthest in the back besides the bargeman, felt the man touch his shoulder from behind. He turned around before opening his eyes. The bargeman wasn't looking at him, but ahead, with a strange look in his eyes.

"Welcome to Hichester District," he whispered.

The three boys slowly opened their eyes and at once felt all their air escape their bodies in deep gasps. Small, bright-green, rolling hills covered all sight before them. Winding through them were different branches of the river and forests of trees, sprinkled with reds, oranges, and yellows as fall was progressing.

Far ahead, through several hills and trees, the boys caught sight of a semi-flat area with houses lined with ivy and rose bushes. Yet, everything about the small town seemed more like a countryside village than a town.

It truly looked like they were looking down on a paradise.

Chapter 11

Gene gently touched the water below him with the tips of his fingers. After leaving the cave, the bargeman had informed them that the water in the river was no longer polluted, due to drainage in the cave that freshens the water before it reaches the district. The water pricked his fingers with a sharp stab of coldness, yet it felt too welcoming for him to notice the cold.

Deke was squinting in vain at everything that passed them. All he could see were the blurs of color that slowly passed them. Finally, having found that it was useless, he gave up and merely watched the sky above them.

Neil glanced back at the bargeman. The man looked like he could carry on the rowing for hours, yet there was something about the bargeman that Neil couldn't place. He knew that the man wouldn't carry on a full conversation while rowing, for Neil had tried it before.

"Could I paddle?" he inquired.

The bargeman looked down at him a moment before a kind smile lit up his eyes. Nodding his robed head, the bargeman slowly knelt down behind Neil. He placed the long pole in Neil's hands and slowly wrapped the boy's fingers around the staff.

All at once, Neil felt like a sudden peace . . . strength had seeped into his body through his hands. It was like the bargeman had just handed him a new strength in the staff. Patting him on the shoulder, the bargeman sat down while Neil slowly climbed to his feet.

His first impulse as he stood up was to stick the pole into the water to prevent his falling. His brothers quickly shot him horrified looks as the barge rocked greatly for a short moment. Neil slowly pushed his weight off the barge and bracing himself by spreading his feet apart, he slowly removed the pole and pushed off, allowing the barge to move forward.

"Can I ask you something, sir?" Deke inquired, looking back at the bargeman to let the man know that he was talking to him.

The bargeman's eyes smiled kindly, though they couldn't see if he was actually smiling. "My name is Lyle. What is your question?"

Deke slowly reached back and rubbed his neck nervously. The bargeman seemed like a nice man, but the questions the brothers had asked since they had joined him had been practical and not personal. Deke honestly didn't know how this stranger would react to what Deke was going to ask. In that case, he decided to start with a simpler question.

"Are you the only bargeman here? I mean . . . aren't there other people who run the barges?" he inquired.

"Most certainly, young sir," the bargeman replied. "I am just one of about twenty other bargemen. We are all assigned five different barges that run at different hours of the day. For about a week every few months, all twenty of us are constantly running barges like today. After I drop you off, I have two more barges to run before five."

Deke glanced at Gene, for he felt a strange silence coming from the front of the barge. Gene slowly turned his head just slightly so one of his eyes could look back at Deke. Deke couldn't clearly see Gene's features, but he knew that Gene was giving him a passive look that meant only one thing: Gene knew what Deke wanted to ask.

Sighing deeply, Deke cleared his throat twice before he could get the next question out. "Is that . . . Is that all you do? Run barges?"

There was a long silence that was slicing Deke's confidence in half. The boy slowly looked behind him to see the bargeman watching him calmly. Lyle glanced down at the water and slowly ran his fingers through the clear water.

"Pretty much. You might think that it isn't the most fascinating job in the world, but there is nothing else I would rather do."

Neil leaned over to give Deke a confused look over Lyle's head. "Why do you say that?"

A soft chuckle broke the confused silence, causing all three boys to look at Lyle in shock. His shoulders were slightly racking as he laughed softly, shaking his head as he did so.

"I say that because . . . if it hadn't been for Crispin, I wouldn't have a place in the world," Lyle explained in a soft tone.

Suddenly, he removed his hand from the water and reached up with one hand to his left shoulder. Grasping the wrap that was wound around his neck, he pushed it away from his shoulder and pulling his collar down almost to the shoulder.

The boys were watching in silent confusion when suddenly they saw something that made their blood run cold. As Lyle pulled his collar back, they realized that once he reached his shoulder . . . his arm just

76

stopped! It was scarred and slightly pink as if his arm had been removed in a harsh way.

"What happened to you?" Neil gasped in shock, forgetting to paddle.

"The same thing that happened to them," Lyle replied simply, nodding his head toward where they were heading.

The boys turned to realize that there were four barges approaching them, going the opposite direction. The barges were empty of passengers except for the bargemen who occupied the space. Just like Lyle, these bargemen were dressed in the same attire, but they had rolled their sleeves up past their elbows and their pant legs past their knees. They had also unwound their wraps and left them on the barges next to them.

Neil almost wanted to hurry to the other end of the barge and cover Gene's eyes, but his little brother seemed to be taking the sight rather well. All four bargemen had different facial features and bodily builds, but the one thing they had in common was that they were all about twenty years old, and they had no arms!

Starting from their shoulders all the way to their hands, there was no arm, at least not the normal kind with skin and bones. Instead, their arms were made of water! It was the same for their legs. The most shocking part though was their faces. Their eyes were normal, surrounded by skin . . . but their cheeks and foreheads were water . . . on the left side of their necks was a section of skin missing that was occupied by water . . . it was as if these people had been mortally maimed but then healed with water prosthetics.

Their hair was normal, but instead of being cut normal and of the normal color, their hair was straight, long, and unruly but had a sort of naturally flowing tameness to it . . . and all their hair was blue . . . like water.

Slowly the other four bargemen paddled past with strong strokes and were soon lost to sight around the bend.

"But . . ." Neil gasped, "how . . . how did that happen?"

Lyle slowly shifted his weight from on knee to the other, meanwhile removing the glove on his right hand. As he removed it, the kids realized with shock that it was also made of water!

"People," he muttered in a voice that had pain but surprisingly, no sign of anger. "I suppose you heard of the persecution of 'disfigured' people at the beginning of the war several years ago?"

Neil and Deke's eyes suddenly met. They hadn't told Gene about their knowledge of the matter, for they didn't want to frighten him, but now there was no hiding it. Slowly, the two brothers nodded.

"Every one of these bargemen, including myself, are some of the 'disfigured' people who were persecuted. While hundreds of us were killed . . . a few of us were saved . . . but just barely," Lyle remarked as he pulled his glove back on. "Crispin . . . and the HUDGE members were the ones who saved us. They found us in the piles of dead bodies and were able to replace our missing bodies with water."

All at once, the three brothers let out a rush of questions:

"What is HUDGE?"

"How did they use water?"

"Why didn't they save all of you?"

Lyle held up his hands and laughed kindly. "Woah! One at a time! First off, not all of us were still alive. They were only able to save the ones who still had some life left in them . . . Barely one percent of us were even breathing."

For a moment he paused as if remembering that terrible time . . . he was probably just a teenager when it happened. Taking in a deep breath, he continued, "HUDGE is a group also known as the Humanity of Uniting Distinctive Gifted Elementals. There were only eight of them . . . Wonderful people. Very few of them are still alive today . . . due to . . . a catastrophe. Anyway, Crispin's wife was one of the eight members of HUDGE and they were known as the 'saviors' in the Golden Age. They were kids, just like you . . . and they had the heart to save a bunch of disfigured and maimed humans . . . Ah, we're here."

Devastated that they wouldn't hear the rest of the story, the brothers turned around to see that they were nearing the end of the river. It became rather narrow at the very end, just the right size for the barge to slip in perfectly . . . if Lyle had been driving . . . but it was Neil, so he scraped the side of the barge on the ground just slightly.

As it pulled to a stop, the bargeman rose to his feet and took his staff from Neil. He then spread out his legs wider so that they were almost falling over the sides of the barge. That was when Gene realized that Lyle's feet were longer, yet rather graceful and seemed to suit his tall, agile, and graceful features. With his feet being rather long, about half of his foot was on the ground, holding the boat in place so that it didn't rock.

One by one, the boys slowly climbed off of the barge, grasping their cloaks and hats onto their bodies, for a sudden breeze caught up around them.

"Go straight down the road until you reach the second fork. Then you take the *Chick Pea Drive* for about a quarter mile, and your destination will be on the right. You can't miss it. There is an old white mailbox out front," Lyle explained, nodding his head toward the small, narrow brick road that was about twenty feet away from the barge.

The boys turned to see where he was nodding, and right away they were able to see the road.

"What exactly is our . . ." Deke began, but when he turned back around . . . Lyle was gone.

Chapter 12

"I don't care what you think, Deke," Neil remarked, "but I find all of this unnerving and rather suspicious."

Deke shrugged his thin shoulders and pulled his cap further down over his eyes as if trying to hide the fact that he was squinting desperately to see the world around him. "Father Fischer would not have sent us here if there was anything to be suspicious about. It may be unnerving, but I suppose everything has a strange side to it. I know humans do."

"That's just it; other than the monks and nuns at Break Neck, we haven't met a single human being. And I wouldn't exactly count the bargemen as pure humans. They're more like a cross between human and water spirit," he added, for Deke had opened his mouth to point out that the bargemen were humans.

"I don't know . . . I think I like it here," Deke remarked.

Neil rolled his eyes. Inside, he was writhing with excitement and curiosity, but he didn't want his brothers to think he was a "weakling." The brick road, more like a path, looked like it had been there for centuries, for vines and grass grew in the cracks and on the edges, which were rounded by erosion. There were a few bricks missing here and there, but other than that, it was in rather good shape.

The houses weren't as close together nor as many as you would see in a neighborhood. There was about one to two blocks distance between each house and between many of them were bushes, trees, and hand-carved wooden fences that gave it a countryside, relaxed, and peaceful sort of look.

Glancing over his shoulder, Neil saw that Gene was purposely walking slower and giving each house a good long summing up before moving on to the next one.

"What in the world are you doing?" he demanded.

Gene turned around and grinned at his brother. "I'm trying to guess what kind of people live in these houses."

"Who said they wouldn't all be Gerhenian?" Deke pointed out.

"And who said that they were even humans. These houses may be habited by ghosts for all we know," Neil added.

Gene raised on eye in a pathetic and almost amused look. "Then what would you call *them*?"

The boy pointed ahead of them and the two older boys turned around to see that two new boys were walking their way. They were barely fifty feet away, but the brothers could easily tell that they were identical.

Their faces were perfectly oval shaped with an olive color, almost a dark suntanned color. Their slightly slanted eyes were dark brown with epicanthus. Their noses were small, slender, and slightly upturned, and their small faces, firm lips, and jet-black hair that was cut short in the back and long in the front gave evident proof that they were Uthanian. They looked to be between Gene and Deke's ages. They wore matching white shirts with starched collars and long black pants.

Before any of the brothers could say anything to each other, the two boys had quickened their pace and had approached the three brothers. They both grinned and a glint of mischief and energy flashed in their eyes.

"Welcome to Hichester District!" the one on the left remarked in a quick voice, his "s" sounds being rather prominent, almost like he whistled short and fast whenever there was an "s" in his words.

The other one stuck out a hand toward Deke with a bright grin. "I'm Reed. Thith ith my twin brother Roy."

Right away, the three brothers realized that the only way they could tell these two identical brothers apart was how they talked. While Roy was fast with obvious "s" sounds, Reed spoke slower and with a firm lisp.

Gene reached out before Deke could and shook Reed's hand. "I'm Gene. This is Deke and Neil. We're brothers too."

Roy and Reed both grinned (identical grins) and took turns shaking the brothers' hands. "How long have you been here?" Roy inquired.

"About fifteen minutes," Deke replied. "We just had to walk from the end of the river."

Roy and Reed both glanced over their shoulders and they gave each other a knowing look. "You muth be heading to 202 Chick Pea Drive," Reed remarked. "We heard that Mithter Wetherby wath having thome kidth thtay with him for a while. We didn't know they would be boyth."

Neil's eyebrows had been going up and down the whole time, but now they went down. "How did you know we're new to Hichester? And how did you even know where we were going?"

Roy grinned. "Small town, word gets around rather fast. Besides, you get to know everyone here within the first week. Also, we're Chris Wetherby's neighbors, so we hear about what is happening during his day from our dad. Dad and Mr. Wetherby are pretty tight."

Deke had been squinting at the two brothers for a long time. There was something familiar about the brothers, but he couldn't place it. It wasn't the Uthanian features nor the skin tones, but the wild hair, the laughing eyes, and the mischievous smile . . . he had seen them before on another person, but he couldn't place it.

"Excuse me for asking," he remarked in a soft voice, "but . . . what is your last name?"

Roy and Reed both raised an eyebrow in confusion. They didn't know why the boy had just asked that, but there was nothing about the brothers that they could suspect as being suspicious.

"Fischer," Roy replied. "Why?"

All three brothers almost jumped out of their skin at the mention of the name. While Deke and Neil looked at each other in puzzlement, Gene gave the twins a curious look. "Do you by any chance know a certain Father Fischer?"

The twins let out bellowing laughs and shook their heads as they did so, obviously shocked that the boy had asked. "Father Fithcher ith our dad's couthin," Reed explained. "Uncle Fithcher and our dad are couthinth. They're Adieu and Ahoy Fithcher."

The already-surprised expression on Deke's face slowly changed, to that of confusion. It was as if those names were strangely familiar. He had never heard Father Fischer's first name before, yet there was something about it and the name of his brother that seemed to stick in Deke's mind. Sure, the names were unusual and rather strange . . . yet there was still that thing about them that was itching the back of Deke's head.

Roy glanced down at his wrist watch and nearly jumped out of his skin. "Gosh! We've got to get going. We still have to stop by the Salerno's for pa's book! Ma is going to have a fit, Reed! I hope she doesn't keep us home from the Homecoming Party tomorrow night!"

Reed stuck the knuckle of his pointer finger in his mouth and began to gnaw on it nervously. "Pa thaid that if we pathed curfew again, we would get it!"

"We got to go," Roy explained, grabbing ahold of his brother's collar and preparing his legs to move. "Nice meeting you guys! See ya around!"

With that, the twins were gone as quickly as they had appeared. The three brothers watched them go as long as they could before the two skidded around the corner of the road and disappeared.

"'Probably all Gerhenian,' huh?" Gene remarked, grinning cheekily at his brothers.

Neil gave him a crooked smile while glaring at him with his eyes, showing that he wasn't going to carry on a debate on the subject. "Okay, maybe I was wrong about that . . . but I would like to know if we'll reach our 'destination' before this century ends."

"Keep your shoes on, Neil," Deke remarked from where he had wandered off about twenty feet ahead of them. "I've found it."

Chapter 13

"You're sure you heard the directions, right?" Neil inquired, leaning his head to one side, then the other, sizing up the large gate that stood before them.

Deke rolled his eyes and rubbed his forehead. "Trust me. The bargeman said to take Chick Pea drive for a quarter mile and the destination will be on our right. Father Fischer also told me before he left us at Break Neck that the address is 202 Chick Pea Drive."

Neil took a quick look at the iron letters that were hammered into the brick wall beside the gate. Concluding that either fate was against them or something strange was happening, he decided to test his brother's intelligence. "But you're nearsighted. How can you tell for sure that this is 202 Chick Pea drive? It could easily be 108 Swamp Road."

"Sorry, bro," Deke remarked, giving his brother an annoyed scowl, "but 108 Swamp Road just so happened to be the blue-roofed house about eighty meters back that way. The one with the hydrangeas in the front yard. Now, even though I'm nearsighted, those letters are large enough for a blind bat to read!"

Neil glanced down at his little brother to see that Gene was grinning beneath the hand that he had used to cover his mouth. Neil looked back at Deke and realized that there was no way out of this one. Both his brothers knew that this was the place, no matter how much Neil doubted that it was. Deciding that there was nothing to do but try it, Neil grasped the huge iron handle of the gate and pushed.

Now, this gate was in fact not very large at all and was probably a decent size, but to the three brothers, everything seemed big. It was probably their fears and worries that made everything look . . . larger. As Neil pressed his weight into the handle, what he didn't know was that while he and Deke had been debating, Gene had gone and undone the latch that unlocked the small door that was part of the gate so that the whole gate didn't need to open.

Neil had expected the gate to weigh a great deal, so he pushed extra weight into it, only to go flying through the normal-sized door part of the gate. He grasped the handle of the door in the attempt to not fall on the gravel but almost slammed into Deke, who had hurried after him. Both brothers caught hold of the other, trying to steady themselves and each other so that neither of them had to taste gravel.

"Watch it, dude," Deke remarked in a teasing tone. "You nearly gave me a true blue headbutt."

"Well, don't look behind you because you will get one," Gene whispered from the gate.

The two older brothers glanced at the boy first, before slowly turning to see what sort of building awaited their entry. The first thing that their eyes fell on was the wooden door with metal brackets. A small stained-glass window shaped like a crescent moon on its side rested above the curved top of the door.

On either side of the door were two glass windows with lace curtains closed on the inside. The house wasn't square, round, or rectangularly shaped like most of the houses they had passed so far. This one seemed to be all points. It was, or so it seemed to be, at least three- to four-stories high with two small towers making up the fourth floor. Windows of various sizes and shapes were sprinkled about the house in an organized and understandable manner.

Having been raised in a square brick building behind a Church, the brothers had never encountered a house like this nor of this size, so to them it seemed like they were looking upon a castle in the middle of a neighborhood.

"Now what do we do?" Deke whispered.

Gene had already slipped ahead of the two and had reached the front door. Neil had watched him go and now gave Deke a mischievous look. "Knock naturally."

Feeling that Neil needed a little lesson on sarcasm, Gene reached up to the large metal door knocker that hung just within his reach. Neil's eyes at once grew wide, causing the green and gray in his eyes to brighten. "You're not actually going to do it, are you?"

"You suggested it," Gene replied, glancing over his shoulder just slightly.

"Yeah, but . . ." Neil remarked as Deke slowly joined his brother on the front stoop, "that was just a joke . . ."

Gene lifted the knocker, which was surprisingly light, and rapped the wooden door twice. "Come on, Neil, it's not like the door will be answered by a gingerbread man."

Suddenly feeling foolish and cowardly, Neil hurried to join the younger two in front of the door, so, should someone answer it, he wouldn't look like a distant passerby. There was a momentary silence, full of worried glances, deep breathing, and counting their blessings before they met their fate.

During that course of what seemed like hours (it was only three minutes), Neil had wrung his hands so much that they were sweating, Deke had mussed his hair completely over his eyes, and Gene had located the large metal handle that was on the wrong side of the door.

Gene watched the handle as if his eyes were drawn to it like a magnet. Slowly it began to turn, then it stopped . . . posing in the air. The door slowly opened, creaking in protest, and the three boys found themselves looking up at a tall, slender man. He wore a long, brown, suit jacket over a matching brown vest and white, starch, collar shirt. His face was slightly long with a high forehead, slightly pointed chin, and long nose. His lips were slightly full and held a strange comedy behind the professional seriousness.

His brown hair was sleeked back away from his eyes, and his brown eyes looked way down at the three brothers. His hands that looked to be almost larger than his face clapped behind his back as he bowed low. Gene, being the one in front, had to duck so that the man's head didn't crack him on the skull.

As the man lifted himself back into the erect position, a simple smile appeared on his face. "Welcome, young sirs. I am Macaroon at your service."

Gene blinked twice and barely heard Neil lean over to Deke and whisper: "That's close enough to a gingerbread man."

Macaroon spun on his heel, stepping to the side, and waved his long arm toward the inside of the house. "Please come in. Master Wetherby is awaiting your arrival."

The three boys slowly stepped into the house, and all at once, their feet seemed to sink into the carpet. It was so thick and soft that they could barely see the bottoms of their shoes. They were standing in a large circular room with two doorways on either side and a large staircase opposite the front door.

A large chandelier hung from the ceiling, made of hand-carved wood with bright red wax candles resting in the holders. The walls had a relaxed cream color to them and dark frame pictures and portraits hung in an orderly fashion from the walls.

As they stepped inside, Macaroon closed the front door behind them and made his way briskly and smoothly to the right-hand door. The boys slowly followed him, marveling about how their shoes were making no noise on the carpet.

They entered the hallway to realize that it was similarly situated with pictures on the walls in between the doors (three doors on either side) and a tall, stained-glass window at the end of the hallway.

Macaroon led them to the end of the hallway and stopped in front of the right-hand door. This door was obviously different from the others, for it was of a darker wood and with iron brackets like the front door but with a larger handle. The man rapped loudly on the door with his knuckles three times.

A muffled voice from inside spoke an almost inaudible admittance to which Macaroon reacted immediately. Pushing the door open, and giving the boys a gentle nudge, Macaroon announced their arrival: "The young gentlemen have arrived, Mr. Wetherby."

"Thank you, Macaroon," the same voice replied but clearer now.

The boys barely noticed this exchange, for they were looking around at the walls in surprise. Every inch of the wall was covered in shelves and cabinets, all full of papers . . . no books. A huge desk stood at one corner with a red, straight-back leather chair. Seated in the chair was a man who looked to be in his mid-fifties to early sixties.

He was a rather large man, both tall and strongly built. He was what Gene had always imagined Santa Claus would look like. His hair was pure white and bushy, sitting on the top of his head. His moustache and beard were just as pure white and came just about to his chest. His eyebrows were thick and full of expression. His eyes were small but full of energy and excitement, with wrinkles around them as if he always smiled.

His slightly deep voice cracked in a tone that Gene at once recognized as Falfinian: "You made it safely!"

Macaroon slowly closed the door behind him as he quickly left to leave the boys alone with his employer. Mr. Wetherby rose to his feet and walked over to the boys. He towered over the small lads, so he squatted down in front of them until he was relatively level with them.

"I trust your journey was all right?" he inquired with a kind smile.

Deke at once felt all his fears vanish and a smile lit up his boyish face. "Yes, sir! It wasn't exactly the journey we anticipated."

Mr. Wetherby let out a bright chuckle that erupted from his belly. "It is that. I assume you met

93

those crazy twins next door? I heard them hollering not long ago."

Gene nodded his head vigorously. "It's amazing about the people we have met. I mean . . . we met the Schneider family and they're nothing like what we are used to . . . neither are the Fischer twins."

"Ah, so you've met the Schneiders?" Wetherby remarked in a bright, curious tone. "So you've got about a half dose, huh?"

"Half dose sir?" Neil inquired, not fully sure that what they had seen of this place wasn't one to fear . . . too much.

Wetherby nodded. "It's a long story. One that would suit for another time. Anyway, you three had better settle in before dinner. Philippa will have a fit if I keep you three too long. I think she is the most excited of us all that you're here."

Almost as soon as he said this, there was a loud pounding at the door. Not three smooth raps but multiple raps with no sense of organization. "Mr. Wetherby? Macaroon says that the lads have arrived! Are you there, Mr. Wetherby?"

The large man rose to his feet and crossed the room to open the door. A young girl who looked to be about seventeen almost stumbled into the room, having been leaning on it with her full weight. Her hair was short and a dark green color that seemed to suit her but was what greatly attracted the boys' attention. It was cropped in a feathery and snug way so that it lay close to her face, framing her pointy figure. Everything about her was points and edges; her nose, chin, eyes, and even her ears were pointy! Her eyes were a bright green that matched her hair, but there seemed to be an unusual glimmer in her eyes.

She wore a green-and-blue dress that framed her petite, slender figure and the long sleeves exposed her small, delicate hands. Over the dress she wore a white apron that was slightly smudged with handprints and water marks. Her face was full of energy and surprise with a bright smile all ready and charged up.

"Sorry to interrupt, Mr. Wetherby," the girl apologized.

The man smiled kindly at the girl and waved a hand toward the brothers. "Phillipa, would you be so kind as to show the boys to their rooms and help them get settled in? I have strict orders from Gertrude that dinner will be an hour early today."

Phillipa saluted clumsily and clicked her shoes together in vain (due to the fact that they were leather). "Yes sir! Leave it to me."

The girl leapt out of the room to make space for the boys to exit. As soon as they were clear, Mr. Wetherby gave them a kind farewell and closed his door. Once it was closed, the boys relaxed. They had been around grownups all day and had been acting proper and professional, but around someone like Phillipa, they felt at ease.

"Come with me," Phillipa chirped. "I'm so glad you've finally arrived! Father Fischer has told us that you hold promise!"

Chapter 14

Despite the fact that Neil had almost dampened their enthusiasm and curiosity, the quick tour that Phillipa gave them of the house was enough to raise their spirits. She showed them the library which also served as Mr. Wetherby's study. His office was mostly his business office. The library was a huge open room carpeted in red, setting off a welcoming soft light that reflected off the papers that lined every inch of the shelves.

Taking them to the second floor, Phillipa pointed out the kitchen, dining room, Mr. Wetherby's room, and also the back balcony connected to the sun room that looked out back into the trees that grew behind the house. She then took them to the third floor where their rooms were located. There were three spare rooms besides the ones that had been prepared for the boys.

"I hope you don't mind, but we thought you might like your own rooms," Phillipa was saying. "Mr. Wetherby suggested that space might be to your liking after the homeless house. Of course, Macaroon doesn't know anything about preparing rooms, so I had to do it. If there is something that isn't to your liking, just let me know. I'm not used to preparing rooms these days."

Gene at once pounced at her pause in chatting to speak up, "That's all right Phillipa . . . may I ask you something, though?"

"Absolutely," the girl replied as she fumbled through her apron pocket for the bedroom keys.

"How did Macaroon get his name?"

Phillipa's huge brown eyes met Gene's and a flicker of amusement flashed in them. "That is probably the most straightforward question I have gotten asked in the past week. As it turns out, Macaroon was an orphan when Mr. Wetherby's father found him. Mr. Wetherby and Macaroon grew up like brothers and Macaroon was seen as such a 'cookie' that Mr. Wetherby gave him that name. It's not really his name, but it suits him."

"So, Macaroon isn't a butler?" Neil inquired. "I mean, since he and Mr. Wetherby grew up together."

Phillipa raised her eyebrow in confused interest. "Macaroon is as much a butler as I am a maid, but to us, it feels like we're part of Mr. Wetherby's family. He has taken all of us in and we live here as if we were his children or brothers and sisters."

Gene and Deke glared at Neil, who merely shrugged, despite the fact that he might have hurt Phillipa's feelings. The girl, however, didn't seem to pay any heed to the source of the question and drew out three keys which she handed to the boys.

"These are to your rooms. If you need anything, I'll be around. Oh, since Gertrude will be having dinner an hour early, you should come downstairs by four or she'll have a fit."

The girl spun on her heel and began to skip back the way they had come as if she had nothing better to do. Deke glanced down at the key in his palm, then back at the girl. "Thank you, Phillipa."

The girl waved her hand without looking back and hollered a reply, "YOU'RE WELCOME!"

Slipping the blue ribbon that was tied to the key onto his finger, Neil began to swing the key around even though one key on its own wouldn't make any noise when jostled. "Well, you're right so far, Deke. This place isn't too bad."

Sighing, Gene took his key from Deke and headed toward the bedroom that Phillipa had pointed out as his. Gene and Deke's rooms were across the hallway from each other, while Neil's was the next door down beside Deke's.

Gene quickly unlocked his door and slipped inside, closing the door softly behind him. Neil did the same but gave Deke a competitive look as if saying: "You were right . . . so far." With that, Neil slipped into his room, leaving Deke alone in the hallway.

"There's nothing to lose, right?" Deke asked himself as he fumbled with his key. "Just step right in and close the door behind you. It's not like there will be an anaconda waiting in there for you."

He finally managed to insert the key and turn it. The door silently swung open to reveal a darkened room. Stepping in blindly, Deke fished around in the dark for a light and switched it on. The sudden brightness blinded him, so he covered his eyes with his arm and closed the door as he stepped inside. Rubbing his eyes with his pointer finger and thumb, he looked up to get a better look at the room he was in. All at once, his mouth dropped open.

Despite the fact that he had rather poor eyesight, Deke could clearly make out almost everything in the room. It was the size of a master bedroom and the walls were made of strong, ancient-looking, dark brown boards. In the far-left corner was a large queen-sized bed with blue-and-gray sheets. Next to the bed was a small, gray, painted wooden nightstand with a lamp on top.

At the end of the bed was a large wooden chest that looked pretty ancient but in relatively clean shape. On the direct left corner of the room was a large wardrobe, painted in a dark blue color that seemed to match the dark brown walls. In the far-right corner of the room was a massive desk (dark blue colored) with a black, leather chair with wheels enabling the chair to spin around. The desk was supplied with paper, binders, folders, and all other necessities.

Directly to the right of the door was a large beanbag next to a small shelf of books. Between the beanbag and the desk was a door built into the wall that was almost impossible to see. Deke slowly crossed the room and opened that door, finding it the most curious part of the room. It took him a moment to realize that the door opened out, not in. Once he got it open, he poked his head inside, only to collide with several hangers. It was obviously a built-in closet.

After dropping his knapsack onto the floor next to the bed, he plopped down on the bed and began to remove his boots and wrap. Laying them on the bed next to him, he straightened out his shirt and shorts, considering the room around him. His eyes fell on a large window that was opposite the door. A half-circle seat was attached to the large window, making a window seat.

Walking over, Deke ran his fingers over the soft fabric of the seat. Looking up, he realized that he could see the tops of the trees that grew in a cluster behind the house. He was just about to sit down in the chair when he noticed that something was reflecting the sunlight toward his window. Squinting his eyes almost completely shut, he realized that it wasn't a tree that was just visible over the tops of the trees but the top of a building . . . but what building was that tall?

Suddenly, he heard the sound of a fist rapping on the door and Gene's voice came through though it, sounding like his mouth was pressed against the keyhole: "Hey, Deke . . . you in there? Phillipa says that she wants to show us something if you've gotten settled in."

Opening the door, Deke poked his head out and gave his younger brother an inquisitive look. "You know, from the way you spoke just now, anyone would have thought you have lived here for years."

A smile spread across Gene's young face. "I finished getting unpacked, so I went to explore. Macaroon showed me the shed out back and I even got to meet Gertrude. Oh, just to let you know, she prefers being called Cook. Macaroon says that she had a dog that she named Gertrude and when the dog died, Gertrude refused to have people call her by her original name in her presence."

Chapter 15

There he was, doing it again! Neil wouldn't stop looking Gene directly in the eye and then nodding toward Mr. Wetherby. As soon as Deke or Mr. Wetherby looked up, Neil would look back down at his plate as if he didn't want them to know he was trying to communicate with Gene about something.

Gene decided to not make eye contact with Neil to see how his brother would react to that. Gene didn't know it, but Neil then began trying to get Deke's attention. Deke, not realizing what his brother was trying to say, nor having the thought to ignore him, spoke up: "Mr. Wetherby, I saw the top of a building out my window over the trees . . . do you know what it is?"

Neil's eyebrows swerved in complete confusion. He glanced over at Gene, who was biting his lower lip to prevent himself from choking on his meal. "That's what you get for trying to silently communicate with Deke," Gene was thinking to himself. Little did he know that Neil was thinking the same thing, only directed at himself.

Mr. Wetherby finished chewing his bite of green beans before he replied to Deke's question. "Yes, indeed. That is the tower of SOHE, built by the HUDGE members."

Neil didn't even need to look at Gene to know that his little brother's head at once snapped up with rapt attention. "What exactly is HUDGE? We've heard it before . . . but we still don't know what it is."

Mr. Wetherby took up his napkin and wiped his mouth with it. He looked down the table at Macaroon, Gertrude, and Phillipa, who were all purposely trying not to make eye contact. All three of them knew what HUDGE was, but none of them wanted to be the one to speak of it.

Sighing deeply, realizing that he was the center of attention at present, Mr. Wetherby set his napkin down and looked directly at the boys. "HUDGE . . . *was* a group of extremely talented young people who had the dream to save the world. They dreamt of the day when war was dead and peace was alive. They stood up for humanity, for human rights, and for the goodness that was given to every human being . . . but squandered by many."

"So, they were a group of spies?" Neil inquired, brushing a handful of hair away from his eyes. "Is that why they have that strange name?"

The old man smiled kindly and shook his head. "They weren't really spies. What they really were was a group of people who . . . understood that goodness cannot work on its own. They were ordinary humans like you . . . but they did all the things that no one else wanted to do, just for the sake of protecting others. They worked as spies, smugglers, politicians, soldiers . . . but they were really warriors: warriors of faith."

"And the name HUDGE is an abbreviation," Phillipa pointed out before she realized that she had spoken.

Smacking a hand over her mouth, the girl realized that now everyone's attention was on her, which was the last thing she wanted. Phillipa was a very kind and friendly girl, but she couldn't stand being the center of attention, especially at dinner.

Mr. Wetherby could see the girl's dilemma, so he explained for her, "The abbreviation HUDGE stands for the Humanity of Uniting Distinctly Gifted Elementals. I'm sure Lyle told you that much. The name pretty much described them . . . in every aspect. Their goal was to unite all people under one banner . . . one faith."

There was a long silence during which the brothers looked from Mr. Wetherby to the other grownups to realize that all four were bowing their heads and not even eating . . . something was wrong. Deke, being the one closest to Phillipa, reached over and tapped her on the arm.

"What happened to them?" he whispered.

Phillipa slowly raised her head to reveal that she had been crying. Taking in a deep breath and choking down tears, Phillipa slowly choked out a reply, "At the prime of their lives . . . one of their dearest friends . . . was killed. After that, things started falling apart. One by one the members began to die and the hope that they had kindled up . . . was dying with them."

Gene and Deke's eyes met across the table and the glimmer in each other's eyes was enough to tell them that they both were thinking the same thing.

"Um . . . the bargeman told us that one of the members of HUDGE . . . saved them by giving them prosthetic limbs made of water . . . is he or she . . . still alive?" Gene inquired, fishing around with his food while he spoke as if trying to not be heard.

All eyes at once turned to Mr. Wetherby, who had been watching Gene with a calm look of passiveness on his face. Gene, realizing that no one was staring a hole through his head, glanced up to realize that a small smile had appeared on Mr. Wetherby's face.

"Yes, Gene, he is still alive. There are three of the eight still alive. Though the son-in-law of two of the members, Finn . . . I wouldn't really say he is alive," Mr. Wetherby replied.

The three brothers slowly looked at each other. "What do you mean?" Neil inquired.

"Finn has acted rather strange ever since . . ." Phillipa started but she had to stop for a second, "ever since the members died. He has kept to himself . . . almost drawn himself into another world. It will be a miracle if anyone ever gets the guts out of him again. He used to be such a spirited, kind man."

Mr. Wetherby suddenly let out a deep grunt and cleared his throat rather loudly while setting down his fork. "Before we all lose the spirit to eat, maybe we should change the subject. I suppose you boys have realized that the summer is coming to an end?"

Slowly the three boys nodded. They knew that any conversation beginning like that would lead to the talk on school. Their education back at the Church was decent, but due to the fact that they had been considered "homeless" at that time, few people even spoke to them. Deke had fared better than both of his brothers, though Gene had done well in different languages than Deke. Neil always seemed to be more interested in the physical things of life rather than the brain.

"We have thought about that . . . Somewhat," Deke replied in an unsure voice that spoke volumes of nervousness.

Mr. Wetherby smiled kindly at the boy, noticing that all three had suddenly stopped eating and were now fingering their plates with anxiety. "I think you'll like the school here. I'm afraid that since Hichester

105

District is so small, there is only need for one school. All the children in Hichester District go to this school and seem to like it a great deal. There is a welcoming party in a few days for all the students who are coming back or newly entering the school."

When the boys didn't reply, Mr. Wetherby sensed that he needed to build up their ego again. Looking across the table, the old man caught Macaroon's eye.

"Macaroon. Don't forget that I have a business venture tomorrow. When the boys are fully settled, would you be so kind as to take them to the Wagner Department Store for school supplies? I would have Phillipa go, but they also need a good supply of 'northern Gerhenian' attire, if you get my drift."

Macaroon smiled a crooked smile. "Consider it done, Mr. Wetherby."

* * * * * * * * * * *

"Gene ... Gene? Are you in there? Gene Mecarnin," Neil hissed through the keyhole, raising his voice by every word. "Gene, is the door open?"

"It's open," a voice inside the room replied calmly.

Letting out a huff, Neil pushed the bedroom door open. "Golly. You took your time replying! What world were you in any ... What are you doing?"

Gene looked just slightly over his shoulder at Neil from where he sat on the window seat of his room. Gene and Neil's rooms were similarly furnished to Deke's, though of a different color. While Deke's was a dark blue theme against the brown walls, Gene's was dark green/brown and Neil's was dark silver/brown.

"I'm counting the nettles on the trees outside my window," Gene remarked with a slight hint of sarcasm in his voice. "Why do you ask?"

Neil closed the door behind him as if trying to hold off anyone hearing him. "You know what I'm talking about, Gene," he remarked in a low voice. "You've been acting really strange for the past twelve hours, thirty-three minutes, and twenty-two seconds . . . Twenty-four right now, actually. You're lucky that I'm the one who decided to confront you about it rather than Deke . . . twenty-eight seconds."

Gene smiled and glanced back out the window. "You've kept an exact count? When did your watch learn to do that? Also, why wouldn't I want it to be Deke?"

"Stop trying to change the subject, Gene! Deke wouldn't have been so . . . nice about it. Now, are you going to tell me why you're acting so strange, or do I have to go get Deke? He's already uptight about finding out before we leave soon with Macaroon," Neil remarked in an impatient voice.

"You're not being so nice about it yourself," Gene remarked calmly, despite the fact that Neil was glaring at him. "I've just been thinking about how . . . there's got to be some reason for all of this."

Neil's dark eyebrows slowly raised in confusion. "What does that . . ."

Gene turned to give his brother a look that told Neil to not interrupt. "All this . . . security. We first went through health checks and had to be signed in before we could take a secret barge through highly secured caves to a place that probably no one knows about. Also . . . there seems to be something else . . . something about everyone that we've met. It's as if they know something I don't."

There was a momentary silence as Neil considered this observation. He hadn't really noticed it himself, but now that Gene mentioned it, he began to see that it made sense that something would cause his brother to be wary.

"Well, if you are done with your brooding, Macaroon is ready to leave. He says he wants to get there before the 'rush' starts . . . I assume he means the lunch hour," he remarked, shaking off the thoughts in his mind.

Gene spun around, planting his feet firmly on the floor. "I'll be right down."

"Great," Neil remarked as he opened the bedroom door. "On your way down, why don't you grab Deke?"

About three minutes later, Neil was standing on the front stoop with Macaroon, waiting for Deke and Gene to hurry up and join them. Neil was tapping his foot impatiently, arms crossed over his chest.

"If they don't come out soon . . ." Neil started to say, but Macaroon lay a large hand on his shoulder.

"Give them time. If we're a little late, we'll just have to deal with rush hour," Macaroon remarked in a calm tone that sounded like he was talking through his nose.

Almost as soon as he finished the last three words, a strange sound erupted from the open doorway and the two missing brothers blew through the door. Deke was clutching his jacket under his arm, while trying to stop his quick descent by grabbing the frame of the door with Gene right

108

behind him and colliding into his back, causing Deke to cringe.

Gene flew against the opposite side of the door, but his feet reached the door before his hands and his legs went flying from under him, letting out a loud thud as he crashed onto the front stoop.

"Very embarrassing, guys," Neil remarked, giving them a dark look. "Way to go."

Gene looked up at his brother with no apparent expression on his young face. He grabbed a hold of the stray shoe he had been pulling on when he had collided with Deke on the stairs and drew one of his knees close to his chest to help himself climb to his feet. "What are brothers for?"

Neil turned back to give the boy a look that confused Gene. While Neil's eyebrows went down almost vertical, his lips curled into a disgusted look. Gene was three years younger than Neil, but that look told him that something was awry.

Chapter 16

Gene brushed his long bangs out of his eyes and stared up at the bright-red sign that hung above the door. "How long has this place been here? It looks ancient!"

Macaroon paused in the doorway of the shop, holding the door open for Neil and Deke. "It's actually not that ancient, but Mr. Wagner built this shop shortly after his wife died. He made it 'old fashioned' to match the style back in the 60s."

Gene continued to stare at the unique old wood painted a friendly chestnut color and the drapes in the windows that were each a different pattern. He wasn't watching where he was going when he stepped into the shop as he collided with a girl about his size.

She was slightly taller with straight, light-brown hair that came to her shoulders, with feathery bangs framing her forehead and the side of her face. Her eyes were a silvery blue and there was something about them that almost had a flicker.

The most surprising thing to Gene was her outfit. Growing up the way he did, the only other kids he hung out with were the kids at school, and they were always in uniform. This girl, meanwhile, was dressed in dark gray slacks, a long-sleeve, bright pink shirt with a dark gray, short-sleeve shirt over it. She had a jacket tied around her waist and was holding a pink baseball cap in her hand.

"I'm sorry," Gene apologized as soon as he had figured out who he had bumped into.

The girl shrugged. "No big deal. I'm glad you weren't bigger, or I would have been trampled."

"Destiny?" a small voice called from around a table near the door. "What's going on?"

Gene and the girl leaned over to see another girl, slightly younger than Gene, who was sitting at the table by herself. Right away Gene knew that the girl was blind, for her eyes were an unusual pale blue, too pale to even look blue. Her hair was dark brown, almost black, and straight like Destiny's but much longer. She didn't have the bangs, either, but there were several strands of hair falling about her face. She was dressed similarly to Destiny but with blue colors rather than pink.

"Oh, I ran into someone. It's all right, Silver," Destiny replied.

Silver had just nodded to show her understanding when another girl, completely different from the first two, leapt over to Gene and took his small hand in her long, slender one. "You must be Gene! I've heard so much about you! I'm Emma, by the way, and I see you've met my sisters Destiny and Silver. Welcome to Hichester!"

Gene stared up at the girl, not sure whether to reply or allow his surprise to play out. The girl was almost a foot taller than him with light brown hair, slightly lighter than Destiny's, but it fell about her shoulders in perfect ringlets, and she wore a dark-green slouch hat on her head, which brought out the dark green in her eyes. Gene realized that obviously this family remembered their children by their favorite colors, for the only color Gene saw on Emma besides gray was green, while it was the same for Destiny and Silver, but pink and blue for them.

"Yes . . . that's right. I'm afraid I met your sisters . . . though I wouldn't call it meeting but more like

111

ramming into them," Gene remarked, trying to remember everything Emma had just ranted out. "Wait . . . how did you know who I was and who told you about me?"

Emma smiled brightly and almost bounced where she stood, still clutching Gene's hand. "Roy and Reed Fischer came in earlier for school supplies and they told us all about you and your brothers. Then Whip and Seraphina Schneider followed and told us about your meeting in Break Neck."

Gene's eyes at once lit up. "You know Whip and Seraphina?"

Destiny rolled her eyes and turned away to go back to what she was doing while Emma nodded her head vigorously. "Of course I do! Seraphina and I are in the same class! Also, they live three houses down from ours."

"Emma!"

Emma spun around. She didn't give Gene time to see who had called her, for she grabbed his hand and pulled him over to the far counter of the store. "Oh, you've got to meet my brother!"

As Emma pulled Gene to a stop, the boy rammed into Deke's shoulder, hitting his chin. At first, he couldn't see where Neil was but then saw him out of the corner of his eye near the candy jar shelves. Gene turned back around to see that he was looking up at a boy who was stocky in build with brown hair slicked over his eyes, covering his view from what Gene could see, and he wore clothes as if he was part of a secret agency.

"Did I hear that you're Gene? The Mecarnin boy?" this new boy inquired in a husky voice.

Gene slowly nodded. "That's right . . ."

112

"Huh," the other boy remarked, making an uncomfortable sound with his nose and scratching his shoulder. "Not much of you. The Schneider pipsqueaks overdid it in their descriptions."

Deke stared at this obviously tough boy. He wasn't sure why Gene was merely meeting the boy's glare with a calm, passive look on his face. Emma quickly stepped over and placed a hand on Gene's shoulder as support. "Hey, Barret, go easy there."

The boy turned toward Emma and lowered his eyebrows, though it looked like his hair curved upwards. "Stay out of this, Wagner. I don't want your sisters causing a riot because I 'hurt their feelings' just by talking to this kid."

Gene glanced slightly over at Destiny to see that the girl had suddenly tensed. Her eyebrows were down and her blue eyes shining a defiant and firm glow. Gene slowly looked back at Barret without changing his almost-bored expression.

"Hey, Barret, what's going on here?"

All eyes turned to the back of the store where the voice had come from. Standing there was a boy that didn't look like he was exactly "even." His legs were unusually long, giving him a great height, even taller than Emma. His bright-orange hair was wildly curly and piled on the top of his head. He had a pair of huge wide-rimmed glasses resting firmly on his nose, reflecting the gray in his eyes. He carried an armful of books under one arm, and with the other he was brushing a handful of curls out of his eyes.

"Nothing that concerns you, Oliver," Barret replied, giving the tall, gangly boy a dark look.

The whole commotion had gained the attention of Neil, who had stepped over to Deke, who was

113

standing behind Gene. He looked from Oliver to Barret, wondering which of the two boys would win the ground in the store.

However, Oliver didn't say another word, but merely looked Barret directly in the eye. For a while, Neil thought they were having a staring contest, but then he saw Barret almost shiver. The stocky boy turned long enough to give Gene an ugly smirk before heading toward the door.

"See you later, losers," he called over his shoulder before slamming the door.

Macaroon had been standing at the side of the door and when Barret slammed it, he jumped. "Thanks for stepping in, Master Wagner. It was starting to get ugly, but you know: I don't like breaking up fights that usually end with me being on the bottom."

The tall boy smiled a small smile but didn't say anything. He stepped over to Emma and nodded toward the three brothers. "I'm Oliver."

He held out his large hand and Gene readily shook it. However, as he let Oliver's hand go, Gene felt a strange almost loss. There was something about that quiet tall boy that was almost hidden behind his spectacles.

"Thanks for . . . saving my self-confidence," the boy remarked, grinning.

Oliver smiled back but then tilted his head forward to look Gene directly in the eye. "It didn't look like you needed help. In another few moments you would have stared a hole through Barret's head." Without another word, Oliver glanced down at the floor as if trying not to be noticed.

Emma leaned over to Gene and whispered in his ear, "My brother doesn't talk much. He's better with his brains than his voice."

Gene nodded in understanding. "It's still a pleasure to meet you, Oliver. Actually, it kinda reminds me of my brother Deke. He's kinda quiet too but not a lot. He likes inventing things."

"Oh, tosh," Deke remarked, desperate to not be the center of attention. "Did I hear right? Your family owns this store?"

Emma smiled brightly. "That's right . . . but they don't run it. Since my mum died . . . My dad has refused to come here. I think it reminds him too much of mum. Uncle runs it, though . . . actually, he's not our uncle, but we call him that. He should be in the back of the store."

With that, Emma bolted off around the counter to the back door that led to the back of the store. As she left, Gene was able to get a better look at his surroundings. The shop reminded him of the small sweet shops that can be found in antique malls, but this was slightly different. It had a little of everything, from books and paper to meat and flour.

Gene caught sight of Deke and Neil who had snuck over to the far side of the store to the bin full of school supplies. Gene slowly joined them, and as he peered in, he realized that the bin was almost empty with about eight binders left. Each was a completely different color.

"Don't be surprised," Destiny remarked. "The bin was full yesterday, but everyone has been stocking up before school starts."

"Hey, Gene," Deke called from where he had stuck his upper body into the barrel, "would you like a green, blue, or red one?"

"I'll do green," Gene replied. "I know you will want blue."

Gene hadn't really been paying attention to his brother, for his eye had fallen on a small wooden box that was on a shelf next to the candy jars. For some reason, the fancy designs and lovely, hand-painted wood seemed to catch his eye more than the colorful school supplies.

Stepping across the room, Gene reached up to touch the box just as a voice near his elbow caused him to jump. "That belonged to my dad's childhood friend. His name was Colton."

Gene looked slightly down to see Silver sitting near him. She wasn't looking at him, but her ear was turned toward him. "How did you know I was going to touch it?" he inquired.

Silver smiled. "That is something I learned from my mom. Bring it over here and I'll explain."

Gene slowly took the small box in his hand; it was barely bigger than both of his hands put together. He placed it on the table between himself and Silver as he took the seat opposite her. Silver reached out with her pale hands and touched the box. She opened it expertly as if she wasn't blind. As the lid fell back, Gene looked into the box to realize that it was coated in black velvet with a small bundle that fit snuggly in the bottom. The bundle was wrapped perfectly in black silk with a silver ribbon looped around it several times and tied in a knot at the top.

"I don't think I quite understand," Gene pointed out as Silver reached into the box.

Silver chuckled a soft laugh that sounded far off but gentle like a breeze. "This diary belonged to Colton's father: Res. I guess you could say that Res's story was . . . a fairy tale."

"What happened to him?"

Silver stopped for a moment to run her fingers over the bundle in the box, then removed her fingers as if it was too painful to think of. "For the longest time they had thought that he would . . . just stop or do something rash. Surprisingly he didn't; he actually found comfort in the arts. He is actually still alive . . . he lives on the other side of town."

Gene closed the box with a soft click but furrowed his brow. "You said 'they' . . . who are 'they'?"

"The HUDGE members," Silver explained. "The eight members. My grandparents were two of the members. Whip and Seraphina's grandfather's brother and sister-in-law were also members."

The boy's eyes at once expanded beyond their normal size. He grasped the arms of his chair in an attempt to keep himself from jumping up. He glanced around to see if anyone was watching. Deke was still halfway in the barrel, with Oliver trying to help him out. Neil was leaning on the counter, staring into space, while Destiny and Macaroon were talking about the color of pencils.

Leaning across the table, Gene spoke in a soft voice, "You mean the members of HUDGE live here? Here in Hichester?"

Silver smiled kindly, though Gene could barely see it, for her mouth was almost deathly pale, but a realistic, not sickly, pale. "They all live here . . . at least the ones that are still alive."

117

Gene looked over his shoulder to check before he whispered again, "Who are the other members?"

"Ahoy and Adieu, Fischer's fathers . . . they're dead; my grandparents . . . who are also dead; Sky Muller's mother . . . she's still alive; Mr. Nielson's father is still alive; and Mr. Schneider's uncle and aunt . . . his uncle isn't alive, though . . . Mr. Schneider's father is Res . . . Res Richardson Schneider."

Gene didn't have a moment to absorb that information, for Emma reappeared from the back of the store, leading a man by the hand. The man looked to be in his mid-forties with wild orange hair like Oliver, ocean-blue eyes, and a large chin but a look full of understanding.

"Gene," Emma called, hurrying over to the two, "this is Uncle Nielson. His real name is Mr. Hummer Nielson."

Chapter 17

"I still don't know if we should open it, Gene," Deke whispered, eyeing the box suspiciously. "If this was made by someone who is still alive, don't you think we should consult him first?"

"You mean Mr. Res Schneider?" Gene inquired. "I asked Silver where he lives. However, I doubt we'll have time to go visit before the Welcoming Party tomorrow evening."

Neil glanced up from the book he was reading. What he was really trying to do was to not make his brothers think he was curious, for he wasn't. Deke supposedly noticed his brother's lack of concentration, for that was the next thing Deke brought to the light.

"You haven't turned a page in thirty minutes," the boy pointed out, before quickly reverting back to his other brother. "I still don't know . . . don't you think it's invading privacy?"

A smile appeared on Gene's young face, twisting his face into a smirk. "If Res Schneider was trying to avoid invading privacy, why would he place the chest in the only supply store in the middle of town? Besides, if Mr. Nielson thought it all right to let us have it, don't you think that we have a right to look?"

The two boys were interrupted from their lively debate when Neil slammed his book shut and tossed it onto his bed. "If you two don't mind, I would like the privacy of my room back."

Deke, being the slower of the two brothers to react to Neil's sudden outburst, merely stared at his brother in confusion. Gene, sensing the strain that had suddenly appeared in the air, grabbed the box and his brother's hand before jumping to his feet.

"Absolutely, Neil. Sorry," he quickly apologized as he pulled Deke toward the door.

Deke stumbled out the door and even before he caught his balance, Gene handed him the box so that he could turn around and close the door quickly. Gene then pressed his back against the door as if trying to hold in everything in the room.

"That was close," he whispered.

"What was that all about anyway?" Deke whispered.

Gene took the box back from Deke and began to head down the hallway. "Honestly, I don't know . . . but I think we've upset Neil in some way."

"So . . ." Deke started, glancing from Neil's door to Gene, "it wouldn't be a good idea to bring my latest experiment to the party tomorrow? I don't even have a place to put it."

Gene pursed his lips together in concentration. "Probably not."

Shrugging, Deke headed toward his own door. He was just closing the door behind him when Gene realized what Deke had said. "Wait . . . what experiment?"

However, Deke's door was already closed, and he didn't hear the question . . . or so Gene thought.

* * * * * * * * * *

As the three boys neared the corner in the road which turned toward the town square, Gene hesitated. Neil continued to walk, trying not to pay attention to his brother's strange behavior, but Deke noticed and at once stopped in his tracks.

"What is it?"

Gene glanced over at Neil, who had stopped some twenty paces ahead and was giving him an impatient look. Gene didn't feel like making Neil upset again, but what was going through his mind at present was fighting against that urge.

Seemingly reading Gene's mind, Deke walked back over to his brother, shifting his knapsack further onto his shoulder. "Come on, Gene; Neil may be trying to dampen our enthusiasm, but he won't succeed . . . at least not tonight."

Gene looked slightly up at his brother. There was a look on Deke's face, one mixed with worry, fear, and pleading. Right away the boy could see that his brother didn't understand. Deke thought that it was just some brotherly concern that Gene held toward Neil's unusually stern behavior lately.

Shaking his head, Gene looked down at the cobblestones below his feet. "It's not like that, Deke; there is something here that I cannot place . . ."

Deke cocked his head to the side, taking in what he had heard. However, he was never able to inquire further, for at that moment a bright voice broke the silence that separated Gene from his brothers.

"Gene and Deke Mecarnin!"

Deke spun around on his heel, almost slipping on the wet stones (it had rained the night before), but Gene grabbed his elbow to help steady him. Standing at the corner where Neil had been was no one else but Whip Schneider!

Gene flew past Deke, almost knocking the boy down, and catapulted into Whip, who was prepared for Gene's assault. As they parted, the two looked into each other's eyes and both held different expressions. Gene's turquoise eyes were brimming with tears that were fighting to break the surface. His lip was trembling and he was almost gasping for breath as if he had run a mile.

"Oh, Whip," he muttered, half sobbing half whispering.

Whip's dark eyes softened, and he smiled at the boy who was exactly his size. Patting Gene on the shoulder, he gripped the boy's hand firmly and squeezed it hard. "I know, Gene . . . I felt it once, too."

Deke watched this exchange from a few feet off, not close enough to hear the words that passed between them, but close enough to see that they were indeed talking. As he finally approached, Gene hurriedly wiped his face with his sleeve and sniffled loudly.

"Hey, Whip . . . what is going on?" Deke inquired, trying to talk in a low voice even though Gene was standing right there.

Whip grinned up at him with a glimmer of mischief in his eyes. "I'll explain later, but I think you need to meet some people."

True to Mr. Wetherby and Macaroon's word, the town square was indeed lit up even though it was relatively dark outside. Christmas lights hung from sign posts and window ledges all around the square with papier-Mache lanterns hung on long blue ribbons from the lamp posts. About ten long tables were set up at all different parts of the square, with checkered tablecloths and piles of food and beverages.

The square looked even brighter, for almost every part was filled with kids of various ages. The boys couldn't exactly see kids their age, for they were so small that the older kids and teenagers were towering over them. Music was pouring from a large radio set at the far side of the square.

Whip grabbed both Deke and Gene by the hand and began to pull them through the bustling crowd of people. Finally, Whip stopped.

"Here is the gang," Whip remarked in a louder voice, since the music was almost deafening.

Deke was the first to regain his balance and control. He brushed his hair out of his eyes and found himself face-to-face with several familiar—and one unfamiliar—faces. The faces he did recognize were Seraphina Schneider, Roy and Reed Fischer, and Oliver Wagner. The unfamiliar face was that of a girl about Deke's age. Her bright-red, curly hair was piled on her head and it was a miracle her head was still on, for all of her hair could have possibly weighed eighty pounds even though it barely came to her waist. Her eyes were a deep green and freckles were sprinkled across her face. She wasn't exactly pretty, but there was a look about her that held great curiosity.

"Oh," Whip remarked, realizing that he had forgotten introductions, "This is Denise Nielson . . . Uncle Nielson's daughter. And, of course, you know Oliver, Roy, and Reed."

The two brothers smiled brightly at Denise, for she looked a lot like her father, at least when it came to hair. Seraphina, of course, scurried across the stones to snatch the two boys up in a hug. As she released them, she backed off to give them air but looked down at the ground as if trying to not get anyone's attention.

"It's nice to see you too, Seraphina," Deke remarked.

"So," Denise started, tossing her red curls out of her face in vain, "you think they'll work as part of the clan?"

The two brothers glanced at Whip, not sure what they had missed or what they were supposed to know. Whip, meanwhile, was just grinning brightly. "I think so, Denise. They'll help fill in the gaps."

"Wait, pull the horse back," Deke remarked, not realizing he had used the phrase wrong. "What are you talking about? What clan?"

Roy and Reed both started talking at the same time and the surprisingly thing was, even though it was difficult to sometimes understand them by themselves, together they sounded like one person. "We have a tight-knit group. Mostly it consists of the two of us, Denise, Whip, Seraphina, Oliver, and sometimes Emma. We hang out together whenever we're at school or at SOHE. Would you be interested?"

"What is SOHE?" Gene inquired, taking a step closer to Deke for moral support.

At once all eyes were on him, and Gene felt his neck turn red.

"You aren't part of SOHE . . . are you?" Denise inquired with almost a look of satisfaction.

The two slowly shook their heads, not sure if that was good or bad. As soon as they did this, though, everyone else present shrugged their shoulders and sighed. "Well, that wouldn't work, then," Roy remarked.

125

"Couldn't they thtill be a part? Even if they aren't in thohe?" Reed demanded, tripping over his own words.

Gene, Deke, and Whip all looked at Oliver. The boy had been watching the whole scenario silently from his place leaning against a light post. He was clutching a book to his chest as if he couldn't live without holding a book. He was watching them through his large, round glasses, a faraway look in his eyes.

"What do you say, Oliver?" Whip inquired, and as if guessing that the first question was too much, asked one that Oliver could answer simply: "Should we just let them join?"

The red-haired boy seemed pleased that Whip had given him a question that didn't require a vocal reply, so he nodded. As soon as his head began to nod up and down, the twins, Whip, and Seraphina all began to cheer, but Seraphina kept hers very minor and almost unnoticeable.

"Welcome to the team, guys," Whip cried, grabbing hold of Deke's shoulders since he was closest to him.

Deke grinned back but felt strangely jostled by the energy that Whip had put into that grasp.

"Hey, guys!" Emma's voice called as the tall girl appeared. "I think Mayor Rupert is going to make his speech. We had better get a closer place."

Chapter 18

Emma quickly pulled everyone who was smaller than her from behind taller people until they were right on the edge of the crowd of kids. Everyone was now turned to face the small platform that stood at the far-right side of the square where the radio had been set up.

Mayor Rupert was already on the platform, hands held behind his back, waiting for silence before he would speak. He was a large man, strongly built both in height and in strength. He was the kind of man whom you wouldn't want to mess with and seemed to suit the figure of a police chief rather than a mayor.

"Welcome, everyone, to the eighteenth Welcoming Party for Hichester District," he called out in a voice that sounded like a pounding drum.

A cheer rose out from the back of the crowd and grew until it was blaring in everyone's ears. When the noise had finally settled, Mayor Rupert continued: "I know that I am interrupting your last large party before school begins next week, so I won't take up too much more of your time. However, I would like you all to join me in singing *The Flower of Gerhenia.*"

At once everyone in the crowd hushed into soft tones, for even though barely fifty percent of those present were Gerhenian, everyone knew the importance of the national anthem of any country.

"Now," Mayor Rupert added just before he stepped off the platform, "I know you're all thinking about how terrible my singing voice is. You have no need to worry on that, because I am going to hand the job over to Rodge Schneider."

Gene and Deke exchanged looks of surprise as a ripple of cheers and claps rose up from many of the sections of the crowd, mostly the older kids. Deke, being the closest to Whip, tapped the boy on the shoulder. "I didn't know you had a brother!"

A smile creased onto Whip's face. "I promise you, after Rodge there aren't any other surprises from me."

Deke wanted to ask more, but Gene was tugging his sleeve to hush him, for at that moment, a tall, young figure stepped onto the platform edge. Rodge Schneider held a striking resemblance to his father but held no resemblance to his siblings. His eyes were crystal blue, so blue that they could see it from on the ground. His dark, almost black, hair was cut moderately, not nearly as long as Whip's, and curled in several places but had a maturity to it. His face was strikingly handsome with darker tones to his skin than the paleness of his siblings. His lips weren't full like Whip's but had expression, maturity, and great talent about them.

His eyes penetrated everyone who looked directly at him, and he held a very striking figure in the dim light of the town square. He was rather tall, almost taller than most of the boys in the crowd, and he was slender in build like a well-trained dancer.

"Um ..." Gene started, leaning over Deke to whisper to Whip, despite the fact that he had just told Deke to be quiet, "how old is Rodge?"

"Almost seventeen," Whip replied. "We actually had a sister between him and Seraphina, but she died several years back from cancer."

129

Deke quickly pushed Gene off of him, for at that moment, Rodge had taken his place on the far-left edge of the platform and was taking deep breaths, preparing to sing the anthem. The silence was beginning to ring in Gene's ears, and then suddenly it happened: a voice full of energy and feeling rose up out of the silence ... an almost-rocky voice that sounded both enticing and dangerous at the same time, not too deep, nor too high, but just the right tone that haunted everyone's ears as he sang:

"The flower of Gerhenia doth wave in the breeze. It shakes those who go against it and scream in it's wake. Faulty blows and torrents do fight to withhold but none can bend the strength of the tall tree told. Stay on dear flower, stay on free. That on the day when hearts do melt, you will stand thus free. Do no let those oppress you or haunt your very soul for yours is that of purity and of Gerhenia's blythe."

When he finished, there was a momentary silence. The song had been so soft ... so heartfelt, that everyone was taking that moment afterwards to feel and think of what that song stands for. At that moment, Gene looked up at Emma, who was standing next to him, and realized that the tall girl was crying. She wasn't sobbing, but tears were streaming down her face and she was biting her bottom lip.

"What is it?" he whispered, standing on tippy toe in the attempt to make his whisper heard.

Emma surprisingly heard him from his short stature compared to her giant size. Smiling at him through her tears, she rubbed her sleeve across her cheeks, reddening her face more. "Whenever Rodge sings, it makes me cry . . ."

Emma's choked reply had been loud enough for Deke to hear, and the two brothers looked at each other in puzzlement. Rodge's voice was stunning, and they couldn't see any reason for Emma to cry over it.

The questions building up in their minds were left unanswered when Seraphina reached across Whip and took Deke by the hand. "Let's get out of the crowd . . . then I'll explain," she whispered, wiping away her own tears.

The two boys at once began to follow Seraphina and Whip through the tunnel of tall people who were beginning to move again. Roy, Reed, Oliver, and Denise were close behind, with Emma bringing up the rear. Deke and Gene were beginning to feel like hamsters in a tunnel when Seraphina finally brought them out into the open near the alleyway that led back toward Mr. Wetherby's house.

"So?" Deke inquired. "Why is everyone so emotional about the song? I mean, in case you hadn't noticed: you guys are the only ones who were crying."

"Maybe we should wait for Neil," Roy suggested. "We won't want to repeat it a million times. By the way . . . where is Neil?"

"He's over with all the older kids by the stage. I think he is talking with them . . . from what I could see," Whip replied, "if talking is on his agenda. You know, he didn't even say hello when I ran into him earlier."

Denise rolled her eyes and tossed her red curls, almost flapping the twins in the face. "Could you stick to the subject, Whip?"

All eyes slowly turned toward Seraphina, who had been hugging her arms around herself, trying to almost keep herself as far from everyone else as possible. Then her face went a deep red and Deke realized why she had been dubbed "the shy one." Brushing a handful of long hair behind her ear, Seraphina rubbed her arms with her hands as if to warm them.

"That box that Silver gave you, Gene . . ." she started in a low voice, constantly glancing about her, "there's more to it than meets the eye. The box belonged to my grandfather, as you well know . . . but there is a reason why he wrapped up his journal in a box and left it in Uncle Nielson's care."

"So, it was a journal," Gene whispered to himself, not realizing that he had spoken aloud. "What was so special about the journal?"

"It contained answers," Emma replied, having just joined them. "Answers to Res Schneider's painful story . . . and why he only had one child that was his own."

Deke was about to look over at Gene, but his eyes fell upon Oliver, who was leaning silently against the wall near them. He was watching them quietly . . . and something about his eyes seemed to know everything that wasn't being said.

"Maybe it would be betht if we let Mr. Thchneider tell them himthelf," Reed suggested.

Seraphina smiled a relieved smile at Reed, and something in her eyes told Gene that she wanted to avoid being the one to explain as much as possible.

Also, just at that moment, Neil hurried through the crowd and without even acknowledging the people around him, said, "Gene, Deke, we've got to go. Mr. Wetherby wants us home by nine and it's almost that."

Deke, being the nearest to Neil, was already being pulled back through the busy crowd by his older brother. Gene, seeing that he didn't have much time, quickly gave Emma, Seraphina, and Whip a quick hug and waved a farewell to the others.

Just as Gene was about to follow his now disappearing brothers, Oliver caught hold of his hand. Turning toward him, Gene couldn't see the boy's eyes in the darkening light, but he felt Oliver place something in his hand before letting him go. The object in his hand felt rough like paper but surprisingly thick. Stuffing the paper into his pocket, Gene gave everyone a final farewell before hurrying off, yet his mind was racing at what Oliver had given him.

The boys reached the house about fifteen minutes later and quietly treaded down the hallway toward the stairs. Neil and Deke were already upstairs. Gene was now left alone in the hallway, slowly making his way down.

He didn't know why, but when he passed Mr. Wetherby's office, something told him to hesitate. Maybe it was his curiosity as to why the light in the office was still on or maybe he needed to stop walking so his mind could concentrate on whatever it was thinking of.

He felt his hand go instinctively to his pocket, where he still kept Oliver's piece of paper. Just as his fingers brushed the paper, Mr. Wetherby's office

133

door slowly opened and light illuminated the section of the hallway that Gene occupied.

Mr. Wetherby smiled down at the young boy as he glanced down the hallway. "Where are Neil and Deke?"

"They are already upstairs," Gene replied.

Nodding, Mr. Wetherby considered the passive look on Gene's face. There was no expression on the boy's face, and that was enough to worry Mr. Wetherby. If the boy had an expression, he would have been able to figure out what was on the boy's mind, but since there were no signs or clues, it troubled the old man.

"Did you have a good time at the party?" he inquired, trying to find the root of Gene's absentmindedness.

Gene's head suddenly shook as if he had been in another world and was just waking out of it. "Oh . . . yes it was great! We saw the Schneiders and the Fischers . . ."

Mr. Wetherby continued to look straight into Gene's eyes and that was when he realized what was going on. Gene's mind was preoccupied with a confusion . . . a question that Gene couldn't quite place. He had seen it before.

"Why don't you come in, Gene?" he inquired softly. "I think there is something you should know."

Chapter 19

Gene was on pins and needles. The look that continued to pass between Mr. Wetherby and himself kept telling him that all of his questions were about to be answered. When Mr. Wetherby nodded toward the other chair, Gene gingerly sat down as if ready to escape.

"You cannot seem to piece everything together . . . is that it?" Mr. Wetherby inquired, fingering his beard.

Gene started but instead of leaping out of his chair, he leaped further into it. Whatever Mr. Wetherby had to say, he wasn't going to miss any of it. "That's exactly it! There . . . there seems to be so much connected to this place and the people here . . . but there is always something missing . . . something that isn't being answered."

Nodding slowly, Mr. Wetherby reached across his chair to the desk and picked up a small notebook. Opening it on his lap, he fingered through a handful of papers that were stuck on the inside cover. Finally, his fingers fell on one piece of paper that was thicker than the rest. Pulling it out of the stack, he held it toward Gene, who slowly took it.

The piece of paper was a drawing or what looked like a blueprint of something. The first thing that Gene realized was a large blue bird-like shape that took up most of the paper. The head of the bird was pointed, and each wing had six "feathers." The tail was normally shaped but with two halfmoon shapes attached to the end that curved inwards toward each other, making a circle separating them. In the center of the bright blue bird drawing was a white square about twenty times smaller than the bird.

All around that square were twelve other squares, all different shapes and sizes, but all smaller than the first square. Each was labeled with a different number. Attached to the front of the number 1 square were two halfmoon shapes, just like on the end of the bird tail but these were three times smaller. Between the two halfmoons was the number 4. Next to the drawing was a list of names, each numbered just like the squares; obviously the list was what each square was.

Gene slowly looked up to realize that Mr. Wetherby was no longer sitting in his chair but had risen to his feet and was walking back and forth, his hand tapping his desk.

"There is only one thing you need to know so that you may understand . . . everything here," Mr. Wetherby said at last, stopping long enough to meet Gene's gaze. "The Society of Hichester Enterprise."

The boy looked back down at the sheet of paper in his hand, then back at Mr. Wetherby. "SOHE . . . that is what everyone has been talking about. Is . . . this . . ." he started, nodding toward the paper in his hand.

Mr. Wetherby crossed the room and placed a hand on Gene's shoulder, his other arm resting on the back of the sofa. "That is where the Society has lived, worked, begun . . . and grown for decades. The building is Hichester Headquarters, but the members rebelled several years ago because HHQ is difficult to pronounce, so everyone calls it SOHE. In truth, Gene, the Society is the main reason why people live here in Hichester District."

"Woah," Gene remarked, waving his hands. "Pull it back a few years. Can we start at the beginning?"

Mr. Wetherby rubbed his beard, considering the question. "There really isn't a beginning to the Society . . . where would you like me to start?"

Gene turned around in his seat so that he was sitting cross-legged, facing the arm of the chair. "Maybe start with why SOHE was started and what it does now."

Mr. Wetherby glanced up at the ceiling as if searching his mind for files that might have flown away. "SOHE is a society that was started by the members of HUDGE. After . . . after they lost two of their members and many of their friends, they decided to create the Society of Hichester Enterprise to help people who were just like them: different.

"SOHE is basically a camp, in a way, that runs through the school season where kids of all ages— from babes to eighteen year olds—can feel secure and . . . wanted. I won't go into the details on what SOHE teaches, but in a way, it is a safe haven for children and teenagers who are treated differently in the real world," Mr. Wetherby continued. "I think that is the best I can describe it, Gene, without placing you in the society."

As soon as those words escaped the man, Gene's head snapped up. "What do you have to do to enter SOHE?"

Mr. Wetherby smiled kindly. "I doubt that is something you three brothers need to worry about. Even if you chose to not enter for another five years, you would still be admitted without any ado."

"How come?" Gene inquired, brushing his hair to the side. "Isn't there anything that we have to do? Something we need to bring or do before we can enter?"

"It isn't what you do, Gene . . . it's who you are."

Gene turned his head to the side, trying to show that he was getting lost in all this. Mr. Wetherby pretended to not notice and held out his hand for the paper. Gene returned it, and Mr. Wetherby began to place the paper back into the stack where it had been before.

"Have you ever wondered, Gene, why it's so painful for you to grow?" he inquired.

Watching Mr. Wetherby's calm face, Gene realized that he was waiting for him to reply. However, he didn't even need to reply, for the look on Mr. Wetherby's face told him that the man already knew. As if just mentioning it brought back the pinching in his back, Gene reached to his back as far as he could and rubbed between the back of his shoulders, where the pain was always worst.

"How did you know?"

Mr. Wetherby slowly raised his eyes to meet Gene's with a calm, satisfied but serious look. "*You cannot see the stars if they are hidden behind a cloud.* That was something that Mrs. Schneider once told a friend long ago. At the time she meant it when she was referring to goodness hidden inside of people, but it can mean many things . . . even physical things."

If Deke had been the one listening, he would have stood there considering the reply and trying to figure out the magical truth that Mr. Wetherby had just pronounced. However, the first thing that the

139

man had said was enough to tell Gene what he was talking about.

Bending his arm and reaching to touch his back, he ran his hand under his shirt and felt his back. It was true that he had never thought about it, but part of his back felt different than the rest of his skin.

"But . . ." Gene started, "Deke and Neil are the same . . . Doesn't everyone . . ."

He stopped, for the sad look that appeared in Mr. Wetherby's eyes told him that what he was thinking had all been a lie. " . . . Doesn't everyone have leather stitched to their backs? Was that what you were going to say?"

Gene didn't need to nod; Mr. Wetherby already knew. The boy had been raised, just like his brothers, to believe that the large piece of thin leather stitched to his back was really part of his own hide. Shaking his head sadly, Mr. Wetherby wondered why people would keep the truth from such young souls.

Slowly walking over, Mr. Wetherby knelt down in front of Gene and put a hand on his shoulder. "There is nothing we can do about it just yet, Gene. We don't have the necessities to remove it, especially since your body has been growing around the leather for almost six years. All I can tell you is that Father Fischer knew about it, and that was why he decided to bring you boys here and why I agreed to have you live here."

Gene swallowed the saliva that had been building up in his throat. It was like there was a wall between his mouth and throat so that nothing could come out and nothing could get in. Mr. Wetherby smiled as he felt the tremor in the boy's young body.

140

"It's late. You should go upstairs and get some sleep. We'll talk more about it on the morrow. Besides, it is only two more days until your first day of school, so you should be ready for a busy weekend."

Chapter 20

The pillow was too fluffy, the blanket too hot . . . the room too bright. Everything seemed terribly off for Gene. He glanced over at the clock on his nightstand: 3:20 a.m. He still hadn't gotten any sleep. It was as if someone had injected him with pure caffeine! Rolling onto his side, he tried a different position. It was as if that leather that usually didn't aggravate him too much was itching a hole down his spine. He couldn't get it off his mind.

Kicking the blankets off, Gene lay flat on his back, looking up at the ceiling. He turned his head to look at the door across the room. There was no light under the door . . . everyone was fast asleep by now, even Deke and Neil. There was nothing for it; he needed to do something to get an answer!

Climbing out of the bed silently, Gene slipped on his blue bunny slippers and slowly slipped toward the door. Opening it, he saw that there was not a soul in the hallway and just the single night light that Phillipa kept on at the end of the hallway, so the boys could find their way to the bathroom if need be. Closing the door behind him, Gene slowly headed down the padded hallway to the bathroom.

Once he was inside, he switched on a light, locked the door, and began to search the cabinets for something that he could use. The first thing he grabbed was a washcloth, just in case things got messy. He then began to search the first aid kit until he found a pair of clean tweezers and a safety pin. He also grabbed the bottle of cleaning alcohol and poured some of the liquid into a cup. He dropped

142

the tweezers and safety pin into the alcohol to disinfect them.

He waited about fifteen minutes before he poured the liquid out and removed the two objects, rinsing them in water and drying them off. He then kicked off his slippers and climbed onto the sink counter so that he was sitting next to the sink. He turned so that his back was to the mirror but turned just slightly so he could see most of his back.

He quickly removed his nightshirt and stared dejectedly at the large piece of leather that took up most of his back. Running his hand down the edge, he felt the place where the leather was stitched to his skin. He had to try with three different fingers before he could feel the stitches that held the leather in place. Grabbing the tweezers and a small pair of first aid scissors, he grabbed the first stitch that he could find and pinched them with the tweezers. It took him several tries before he could catch hold of the small stitch, but he finally managed it and pulled on it. He felt a searing pain run down his back, but he bit it back. Grabbing the scissors, he wedged them between the loosened stitch and the leather and snipped it.

He was there for a good half hour snipping at stitches. After about five stitches, his arms were getting sore, so he stopped. Setting down his instruments, he reached back with his fingers and grasped the corner of the leather. He couldn't really find a good grip, so he pinched the corner of the leather. He began to pull at it and that was when he let out a sharp gasp and released it. The pain was too great, and the leather was not giving way! It was as if the leather was now a part of his skin!

143

He rested his forehead in his hands and let out a deep sigh. "I cannot do this by myself."

He allowed himself to catch his breath and waited for the pain to stop before he hopped off the sink. Switching off the light but leaving his mess, he slipped out of the bathroom and down the hallway to Deke's room.

"Deke," he whispered as he gently knocked on the door. "Deke, open up!"

He was considering opening the door and physically shaking the boy awake but Deke was a soft sleeper and after a moment the door handle began to move. When Deke opened the door, it was obvious that he hadn't really been sleeping. His hair wasn't mussed, and his eyes didn't show tiredness.

"You're awake too?" he whispered. "Let me guess, you forgot to eat at the party?"

Gene shook his head. "We never had a chance to eat anything before Neil brought us home. I need your help with something, Deke."

* * * * * * * * * * *

"I don't know about this, Gene," Deke whispered. "If it hurt you the first time, it will hurt just as much the second time."

Gene turned around to give his older brother a stern look. "Just do it, Deke. I cannot wait for Mr. Wetherby to find someone to do it! I need to know now!"

Deke considered his brother, sitting there on the toilet seat with his back facing him and his hands gripping the towel rack. He looked down at the scissors and tweezers that Gene had placed in his hands. He felt like a doctor in an operating room and to a nine year old, that was a frightening thought.

"I'm sure there is a better way to do this though than to just yank it off," Deke whispered. "Believe me, after what you told me, I want to know just as much, but I don't want to hurt you."

Gene grinned at him over his shoulder. "I'll take full responsibility if you kill me."

That was all that was needed to get Deke riled up. Lowering his eyebrows, he decided to take his little brother up on the dare. Bracing himself, he grasped his weapons as he knelt behind his brother. "Let me know if the pain gets too much."

Taking Gene's silence as a good enough answer, Deke began to snip away at the stitches. They were surprisingly large as if someone had used sewing thread instead of the right material. He removed about eight more stitches before he grasped the corner of the leather.

"Okay hold on there, brother," he whispered.

Gene quickly stuffed the edge of his sock into his mouth and bit down on it hard and closed his eyes, grasping the towel rack. Deke took a few breaths and then began to pull. He opened his eyes once as he pulled to see that Gene's back was tense, his shoulders and back muscles bristling in the attempt to fight against Deke's pull. Sweat was pouring down the boy's neck and shoulders, and his head was leaning on the towel rack.

Deke continued to pull, biting his lower lip when suddenly he felt something give way. He opened his eyes to see that a corner of the leather had come free . . . but Gene's back was bleeding . . . bad! Letting go of the loose corner, Deke leapt up and grabbed a towel. He quickly drenched it in water and placed it on Gene's back, pressing down with as much pressure as he could while his mind began to whirl at the sight of the blood seeping through the towel.

"Did that hurt, Gene?" he whispered, trying to not let Gene see the blood. "Gene?"

There was no reply . . . the boy was just sitting there, his forehead on the rack and his body sweating and bleeding. Deke realized that he was trying to ignore the pain, so he set to work cleaning up the blood. Holding the towel in place with one hand, he fumbled with the first aid kit and found a large bandage and bandage tape. He removed the towel but wiped at the remaining blood, so he could see the wound.

For a split second there was no bleeding, then it began to flow afresh right where the leather had become wedged underneath the skin over the years. It was right next to the wing bone. Quickly placing the thick gauze over the bleeding wound, Deke taped it down. He had to add another layer before the blood stopped seeping through the layers. He took a washcloth and wiped away the rest of the blood that had gotten all over the leather and Gene's back.

"Okay, we're good." Deke sighed, sitting back on his heels. "Maybe we should stop for right now, Gene, that was a lot of blood . . . Gene?"

Deke jostled his brother's shoulder . . . but no reply, not even a reaction! Deke slowly rounded the toilet and grabbed Gene by the shoulders, lifting his head off the rack. Gene's eyes were closed, his face a deathly pale, and the sweat was pouring down his face.

As Deke lifted his shoulders up, Gene's head slumped against his shoulder . . . he had passed out! Deke wasn't as level-headed as Gene when it came to emergencies, but since he was the only one present and it was his brother who was in trouble, he was able to keep his cool. Gently pulling his brother off the toilet seat, he propped him against the cabinet.

Deke quickly washed the tools off and put them back, cleaning up the mess and stuffing the bloody bandages and washcloth into the bottom of the trash can where no one would see them. He then grabbed the towel and stuck it in the sink. He then began to rinse the blood out as best he could. The sink turned red, but he was able to wash that out. Finally towel just looked a peculiar pinkish, gray color and the sink was clean.

He tossed the wet towel into the laundry basket and then picked up Gene's slippers and shirt. Deke was surprised at the sudden strength he had as he grasped Gene under the arms and began to carefully drag/pull him down the hallway to his room. Once the two were inside Gene's room, Deke closed the door and locked it from the inside.

He dragged his brother to his bed and, with difficulty, threw him onto the bed on his stomach. Deke decided to not try to put Gene's shirt back on, for he didn't want to worsen the pain or loosen the bandages that were holding on pretty well. He began to cover his brother with the blanket when he noticed something. The tiny corner that had come loose was lying limp by the bandage.

Deke was no longer exhausted after that horrifying encounter and his curiosity was electrified so he carefully curled the corner over and started . . .

what he could see under the tiny corner wasn't skin . . . it was smooth . . . rough . . . and not leather.

He covered his brother with the blanket and situated himself on the sofa. He didn't want anyone to know what had happened, so he would stay watch over Gene until the boy woke up. Before he realized it, he was fast asleep on the arm of the chair. And two hours later, someone was dragging him back to his room and launching him onto his own bed without rousing him.

Chapter 21

Deke's eyes slowly cracked open. At first, he didn't realize where he was, then it became clear that he wasn't where he had been several hours ago. He was lying on his bed, perpendicular over it with his head and feet dangling over the sides. He jolted up, almost hitting his head on the end bedpost, and quickly brushed his hair out of his eyes.

His room was dark, but light was beginning to stream in protest at his window. Crawling across his bed, Deke turned the clock to look at the time and realized that it was almost lunch! Leaping out of his bed, he quickly changed into a green-and-red plaid shirt, pants, and socks. He didn't bother brushing his hair nor putting his shoes on but grabbed his shoes and bolted out of his room.

The first thing he did was stop at Gene's door. He knocked several times, making sure that Gene could possibly hear him. He was just about to rap a third time when he heard a voice mutter his name behind him. Spinning around, he saw Gene standing behind him, wearing a dark blue long-sleeve shirt and pants. Considering the fact that he had socks and shoes on and his face was slightly red, Deke realized that Gene had already been outside.

"You were tired," Gene remarked calmly. "No one wanted to wake you for breakfast, so we decided to try later. I was just coming to get you for lunch."

Deke stared at his brother as the boy reached into his shirt and fished out the key. He inserted it into the lock and pushed his door open. "Come on in," he remarked calmly. "I would rather not let Neil hear us talking."

Gene had just closed the door behind him and switched on the light when Deke spun around to confront him. "How did I end up in my room? I fell asleep on your couch."

Gene twirled the key on his finger before dropping it down his shirt, where it hung around his neck. "I woke up at about six and found you there. You looked pretty uncomfortable, so I dragged you back to your room. I went back to sleep for another hour, but my back was starting to feel sore, so I spent until breakfast reading."

Deke slowly sank onto the bed, fully relieved that it wasn't Neil or someone else who had found him. If they had, he would have had to explain what had happened that night. "Sorry about last night, Gene. I didn't realize it hurt you so bad! You didn't even cry out."

Gene nodded slowly. "I don't remember much. I just remember it starting to hurt really bad, so I bit on my sock harder . . . then everything went black. I suppose the pain overcame my voice before I could warn you . . . By the way, why did you stop?"

Deke had been fingering the blanket on Gene's bed but now he snapped his head around to give his brother a firm look. "Gene, I may not be the most level-headed when it comes to wounds and emergencies, but I know enough to tell you that you shouldn't even think about doing that again! You blacked out, Gene! The leather has become part of your back, just as much as it has for me. There is no way we can remove that leather without Novocain. Well, we probably could, but if you blacked out from the small bit that we did last night, you would die of pain or bleed to death if we removed it. We

151

need to let someone more skilled handle this, Gene."

Without replying, Gene grasped his desk chair, turned it around, and sat backwards on it, resting his chin on the back of the chair. "I suppose . . . I just wish we didn't have to wait so long! I suppose my curiosity overcame my good judgment. Maybe it's because I am desperate to know if whatever the leather is hiding is what I need to become part of SOHE . . ."

Deke slowly cocked his head the side. "Why all the interest in it all of a sudden?"

Gene ran his finger over the paint on the chair. "I suppose it's because almost everything in Hichester revolves around SOHE . . . I mean, if we are able to get into it without any difficulty, I'll definitely do it! Anyway, we should go down to lunch. Though I should warn you to not bring up the subject of SOHE in front of Neil."

"How come?"

"The last time I brought up the subject to Phillipa at breakfast, Neil almost had a rage fit . . . I don't know what's up with him."

* * * * * * * * * *

"Now, don't get out of this bed," Deke whispered to Gene.

His younger brother considered Deke for a moment. Gene was sitting on his bed cross-legged while Deke stood in the open doorway like a sentinel. A smile creased his face and he nodded. "All right, Deke. Just don't fall asleep on a couch this time."

Rolling his eyes, Deke closed the door and headed across the hallway to his own room. He had just entered his darkened room and was about to lock it when something struck his mind. He remembered several years ago when Neil's toenail had become infected because the nail had dug into his skin. The nurse who lived across the street from the Church had come over to look at it. Much to Neil's horror, she had removed the nail so that the skin could heal without the nail causing more damage.

However, Deke remembered that before she removed it, the nurse had soaked Neil's foot in warm water and salt. Slowly he sat down against his closed door and fingered the key in his hand. He racked his brains, trying to remember why the nurse had done that . . . it was something that had greatly intrigued the three boys, but he couldn't remember it.

Then suddenly, it came to him. The nurse had soaked Neil's foot to loosen and relax the skin. After soaking it in salt and warm water, Neil's skin had become soft and relaxed so the procedure of removing the nail hadn't been so painful and much easier.

Reaching up with one hand, he turned the doorknob and pushed the door open just a crack. Peeking out, he saw that no one was about, and the others had just finished using the bathroom. Now was his chance!

Chapter 22

Deke carefully pushed the door of the kitchen open and peered inside. It was pitch black, completely deserted. Everything was as clean and tidy as a pin with all the dishes clean and put away and the counters and table scrubbed clean. Soft blue light from the moon outside shone through the window above the sink, giving the room a bluish, gray look.

Deke pushed the door open just enough for him to squeeze through, scraping his chest against the edge of the door. He decided to leave the door open just in case he needed to leave quickly. As he stood in the doorway, his eyes scanned the kitchen, searching for the right place.

His eyes fell on the large pot that lay on the kitchen stove, ready for the next day. Quietly busying himself, he located the jar of salt and emptied it into the pot. He then filled the pot with water and set it on the stove to warm. In order to not draw anyone's attention, he kept it on as low as he could and didn't use the gas burner. He stirred the salt occasionally and didn't remove the pot from the heat until it had all dissolved. He then poured the salt water into a large dish, which he then placed on the floor.

Not sure how else he could do it, Deke lifted his nightshirt and carefully laid his back into the shallow dish. He at once felt his back sting from the heat of the water, but he fought the pain by biting his lip. He looked around as best as he could (he soon discovered that lying on his back on the floor wasn't the easiest and most comfortable thing to do) and located the clock on the wall: 12:13. He would give it fifteen minutes, maybe another extra five just to be safe.

He felt his hands suddenly begin to cramp after a few moments. His legs became sore, and his back was cold. He could barely feel the warmth of the water now, for his skin was so numb from the warmth and possible cold of the now cooling water.

"Eight more minutes to go," he whispered to himself, trying to keep his mind off the cold.

However, at ten minutes and fifty-three seconds, Deke's attention completely flew from the cramps in his legs to the sound of footsteps outside the door! Someone was coming. Not knowing what else to do, Deke leapt from the floor and threw his shirt back on. He didn't have time to move the bowl, so he slid it under the table in the hopes no one would notice it.

As Macaroon entered the darkened kitchen, the first thing he thought was why he had left his bed to come to the dark and cold kitchen for a glass of water. Slowly making his way sleepily toward the sink, he didn't see the small figure who was hiding behind the door. If he had turned around just then, he would have seen Deke slip out of the door and up the stairs.

Deke didn't stop running until he was in his room with the door soundly locked from the inside. He pressed his back against the door, trying to catch his breath. When his heart stopped beating so fast, he let out a deep breath. Then, he thought of his experiment. Quickly reaching under his shirt he felt the skin around the edge of the leather . . . it was slightly wet but now damp and tense again. The run from the kitchen to his room had hardened his skin again!

"My experiment failed ... everything failed! I never got around to talking with Gene about the whole thing because he went to bed early last night and then he passed out and that was on my mind all today and then I was preoccupied thinking about trying the experiment myself ... Oh, what am I going to do?"

Deke sighed. "Maybe Gene was wrong ... maybe we should all work together. After all, all three of us have the same problem ... and maybe with three pairs of hands we can figure it out."

Sighing, Deke flopped back onto the covers and looked up at the dark ceiling. His eyes felt extremely exhausted and heavy, but he could barely think of sleep with these thoughts going through his mind. "I can't try to continue tonight. Mr. Wetherby is leaving for three days and we're to spend the rest of the weekend preparing for school ..."

Before Deke realized it, he was out, lying perpendicular over his bed yet again.

* * * * * * * * * *

Deke was woken out of his sleep by a pounding on his door. He felt as if he had just fallen asleep, which was pretty much true, for it was barely seven in the morning. Light was just beginning to appear through the window.

"Deke?" a voice called through the door. "Deke, if you're awake, Whip and Seraphina Schneider came by a while ago. They wanted to know if we would like to go with them to the river for a fishing

156

morning. They said that they'll be back in an hour to pick us up to give you time to wake up. Neil isn't really interested so he is going to stay here, but I want to go. Macaroon won't let me go unless you do too."

"I'll be right there, Gene," Deke replied sleepily. "I'll be down for breakfast."

About forty-five minutes later, the two boys were sitting side by side on the front step watching for Whip and Seraphina. They wore matching brown pants, sneakers, and long-sleeve dark blue shirts. Gene had a leather jacket tied around his waist in case it got cold, while Deke's was in his knapsack, which was swung over his shoulder.

Deke glanced over at Gene, who was watching the front gate contently, the wind blowing softly at his blond hair. Gene was uncommonly calm that morning. This was strange for Gene because he was very social.

Gene turned to return Deke's gaze, which caused Deke to quickly look away just in case Gene could see answers in his eyes. However, Gene didn't need to look Deke straight in the eyes to know what was going on. Smiling to himself, he looked back at the gate. "How did your experiment go last night?"

Deke snapped his head around and stared at his brother. "Wha . . . What in the world? How did you know?"

Gene smiled, turning to look at his brother. The look in his blue eyes showed mischief. "I was on my way to the bathroom when you came running back to your room. I suspected you were up to something, so I went downstairs. I found Macaroon in the kitchen and figured that he had scared you off. I saw the dish of saltwater under the table and put two and two together."

"Did ... did you tell Macaroon?" Deke inquired, rubbing the back of his neck nervously.

"Not at all," Gene replied, patting his brother on the shoulder. "I managed to send Macaroon back to his room and dealt with the salt water. There is no evidence left . . . except our memories."

Deke reached down and picked up a small handful of pebbles from the drive. "It didn't work. By the time I got to my room, my back was no longer soft. It was all a waste of time."

Gene grinned. "It wasn't a waste of time! We now know something we didn't know when I tried it. If we could get Neil to help us, we might be able to accomplish something, but we need to work together!"

"Hey, Mecarnin!" a voice called from the street.

The two boys leapt to their feet at the sound of Whip's bright voice. Closing the front door behind them, they hurried down the gravel drive to where the two Schneider kids were waiting for them. As they slipped through the side gate, Seraphina looked over their heads at the door.

"Where is Neil?" she inquired in her soft voice.

"He . . . he isn't coming. I don't think he's really that interested," Deke replied in a soft voice. "I think he is kinda in a rough mood."

Gene and Whip exchanged knowing looks but quickly erased the looks when two familiar figures hurried over to them. "Howdy, guyth! Whip thaid you might join uth."

"Hello, Reed . . . You too, Roy," Gene greeted with a smile. "I didn't know you guys were coming along."

A smile lit up Seraphina's face which startled the two brothers because she always had a shy and faraway look in her eyes. "The whole gang always comes when we go to the river to fish!"

"No kidding!" Roy remarked, rolling his eyes to heaven. "They are regular ducks out of water . . . wait . . . that was the wrong word!"

Whip cleared his throat loudly, causing the conversation to quickly stop. "So who else do we have to pick up?"

"Oliver and possibly Emma," Seraphina replied.

"What about your brother Rodge?" Gene inquired.

Deke, who was walking ahead with the twins, looked back at his brother in confusion. It seemed that almost everything Gene had spoken of that day had been mainly associated with Rodge Schneider.

Seraphina smiled at the young boy. "Rodge only comes for short visits. He lives with my mother's cousin . . . he lives in the northmost part of Gerhenian. Rodge has been living there with him since Rodge was about ten . . . for various reasons."

"Which are . . ." Gene inquired, showing that he was curious.

"Gene," Deke called back, "maybe it's none of our business."

Seraphina smiled and shook her head. "Oh no, it's fine. One of the reasons was because Rodge was never able to enter SOHE because he didn't have the necessities. He also felt kind of out of place here. Besides, there's a great school where second cousin

Cameron lives that teaches things like art, dancing, fencing, and those kinds of things. Rodge is really into those things, so Mom and Dad thought it best that Rodge go where he felt best. He comes down often for weekend visits."

After the gang had picked up Oliver and Emma, they headed toward the river. It was a good fifteen-minute walk, so the gang split up into groups of two and walked a few feet in front of each other, so they could carry on multiple conversations. Deke managed to pair up with Emma. He felt that if anyone was acting strange within the group, Emma was the one who would know why.

"Gene is acting kinda strange," he whispered, glancing behind him at Gene who was walking with Whip. "He isn't as chatty as he usually is, and all he really wants to talk about . . ."

". . . Is Rodge Schneider," Emma finished.

Deke looked up at her in surprise that she had read his mind. The tall girl grinned cheekily and began to button up her coat as it was getting colder. "You're not just imagining it, Deke, but there is nothing strange about it, either. Gene is most certainly not the first person who has a strange curiosity associated with Rodge."

Deke ran his hand through his hair, brushing it out of his eyes. "There are others?"

Emma nodded. "Mostly it's the people who are most observant who take an interest in Rodge. Oliver, Silver, your brother, some other kids from school . . . even adults! However, it's mostly kids who show complete curiosity with Rodge. It's not their fault, and it has nothing to do with them . . . it's

160

just that those who are more observant discover the special thing about Rodge."

Deke glanced over his shoulder to see that Whip and Gene were out of whisper earshot. "What do you mean?"

"Rodge has a gift, Deke," Emma whispered, obviously noticing that Deke didn't want to bring anyone else into the conversation. "People are fascinated with him . . . interested in him, and in awe of him . . . I can't explain it correctly because I don't fully understand it myself."

Sighing, Emma folded her arms as they continued to walk down the road. "Rodge has a way of causing people to feel drawn to him, not by his own efforts but completely by accident. Rodge doesn't even know about this! It's just the way he is . . . he is smart, talented, kind . . . but different. There is something different about him that no one can seem to place. That is why Gene is so curious about Rodge just like everyone else . . . it's because there is something about Rodge that no one can figure out . . . not even Rodge!"

"Hey, Seraphina!" Whip called ahead, breaking the conversation. "If you would keep up, we're almost there!"

Chapter 23

"He hasn't come out yet," Deke whispered. "He didn't even say hello!"

The three boys were hiding behind the door of the hall closet that was across the hallway from the library. The boys had snuck downstairs before eight after Cook had finished in the kitchen. However, on their way there, Phillipa and Cook had come flying down the hallway toward the library. They barely even noticed the three boys, who were dressed in pajamas and barefoot.

Curious, they had followed the two toward the library, but Phillipa had refused to let them enter. They had been able to catch a glimpse of Mr. Wetherby (who had returned from his business trip fifteen minutes before) but nothing else.

Neil crossed his arms and leaned against the wall of the closet. "If we're going to do the experiment, we need to get it over soon. I don't want to be cooped up in here all night!"

His two brothers barely heard him, for they were listening intently for the sound of voices from the library. "They can't stay in there forever," Deke whispered. "Phillipa should return from the kitchen soon . . . Maybe we should go ask her about it."

Neil rolled his eyes and let out a disgusted groan. Right away he had his brothers' full attention. "Do what you like. I think all of this is just a lot of nonsense."

With that, he pushed past Gene and headed down the hallway toward the front door. Gene and Deke crowded their faces to the door, watching him go. When they heard the slam of the front door, they looked at each other in the dark closet and sighed.

There was a strong breeze outside as Neil stepped onto the front cobblestones. His bare feet felt a stab of cold run up his legs as they touched the stones, but he ignored it. He leapt off the front stoop onto the stretch of grass on the left side of the drive. The grass was damp and cool but soft to his feet.

"They won't let anything go!" he groaned to himself, kicking grass with his feet. "They have to investigate everything that doesn't make even the slightest bit of sense!"

He kicked a long clump of grass and at once felt his large toe cry out in pain as it struck a small rock. The stone appeared from the grass and went flying across the drive into the shadows near the brick wall. Neil bent down to clutch his screaming foot.

Letting out a disgusted grunt, he angrily walked back up the steps and into the house.

The lights were on in the kitchen, but there was no sign of Phillipa, Cook, or even Macaroon. Neil knew that Deke and Gene were probably still in the closet looking for any clues, so he slipped into the kitchen unnoticed. He located a plate of cookies on the counter and dove into them.

As he rammed two large gingersnap cookies into his cheek, Neil sat down at the stool by the table. He rested his head on the edge of the table, so he was looking at the floor. He felt his eyes slowly flicker shut. Before he knew it, he had dozed off sitting at the table.

A vision flashed before his eyes. Beautiful green grass, fresh water, and trees lining the river. He recognized it as the river that flowed near the old

Church where he and his classmates would go swim in their free time during the summer.

Neil was about to look around to see if he recognized anyone when he felt a surge of sudden horror . . . he was struggling . . . in the water! Immediately Neil recognized the scene from two years back when he had almost drowned in the river. If Neil had been awake, he would have furrowed his brow in concentration . . . Almost . . . He had almost drowned. That meant that he didn't . . . how did he not drown? It was so long ago, Neil racked the back of his brain files . . . Why hadn't he drowned?

He was so busy trying to remember that he forgot that he was drowning. He thrashed about madly and cried out, but his voice didn't make a noise. His body barely moved either, and then he remembered that he was dreaming. He let out a pitiful squeak and wanted to dearly smack himself for not trying harder.

The small noise that had left his throat was answered by a strong voice that echoed around him like a comforting bird that continued to chirp the reply.

"I'm coming!" the voice called again.

Neil turned his head, finding that it was almost impossible to open his eyes. However, he barely needed his eyes to recognize the pile of bright blond hair, the bright blue eyes, and the small figure that came darting down the grassy hill toward him.

Gene leapt into the water with one swift movement and disappeared under the blue water. Neil continued to struggle but made no progress in not drowning. Then, feeling like a rush of warmth had entered him, Neil realized that someone had *grabbed him by the chest and was dragging him toward shore.*

Neil sat straight up . . . he had been dreaming. He was still in the kitchen and half the cookies were gone. He slapped his face twice to make sure he was fully awake. He knew that scene . . . it had been a memory! That had been the day before summer break ended two years ago. He had completely forgotten about it.

The day had been kinda rusty. Deke had gotten his head stuck between the railing outside the Church again. The bullies had begun to pick on him and Gene had come out to help his brother. Neil remembered he had been sitting on the Church step, reading and merely watching the scene blankly. He had seen Gene wedge his brother's head out of the railing and then deal with the beating from the bullies.

Neil felt a twinge of regret . . . of pain at himself. He had let his two brothers face taunts and strikes . . . and yet, when he had nearly drowned later Gene had come and saved him. Gene had barely been four then . . . and he had saved him! Was it just him, or did that sound an awful lot like what had been happening the past few days?

He was just summing up the similarities when the door of the kitchen flew open to reveal Deke and Gene standing in the doorway. Neil stopped, his hands poised over the cookie plate, and the side of his face creased from resting on his sleeve.

"Where have you been?" Deke demanded. "We were looking all over for you!"

Neil glanced at the plate of cookies then back at his brothers. "I was outside . . ."

165

Deke nodded, obviously satisfied with that answer, but Gene was more interested in his face. "Did you fall asleep . . . if you don't mind my asking?"

"Well . . ." Neil started to reply but then stopped. The last thing Gene had said suddenly caused him a great deal of anxiety. Maybe he had been too harsh and unkind to his brothers lately, so much that Gene was afraid to anger him with a question.

Instead of answering, Neil pushed the plate across the table toward them and smiled, indicating that he was offering the cookies. Deke stared in perplexity while Gene rushed over to grab a few before Deke ate the rest.

"We didn't mean to annoy you earlier," Gene remarked quietly, "but while Deke was squashing me, I found your favorite pair of socks that we lost last wash day."

"Thanks, Gene," Neil remarked. "I'm sorry if I was unkind to you guys recently . . . I know that you cannot help being curious about this place."

Gene grinned up at his brother. "That's all right."

Deke was preparing to agree when the kitchen door opened again, and Cook entered. She took one look at the scene before her and at once began to busy around like a mother hen. "Out of here, you shenanigans! Back up to your rooms!"

She fairly pushed the boys out of the kitchen and closed the door behind them. With nothing else to do, the boys started down the hallway toward the stairs, intending on finding a game to play before bed. They were stopped halfway there when Mr.

Wetherby came out of the library and almost ran into them.

"Mr. Wetherby!" Deke squeaked. "Sorry! We didn't mean to run into you!"

The old man looked down at the boy a moment, seemingly considering the situation. All three boys were worried that he had guessed they were spying. However, his face at once turned sullen and he placed a firm hand on Deke and Gene's shoulders. "There is something I need to show you boys."

Chapter 24

Mr. Wetherby's large figure blocked the boys' view of most of the interior of the library. All the lights were on, giving a warm and bright feeling to the large-sized room, reflecting a sort of orange glow to the walls and a deeper crimson to the red carpet. The papers on the walls looked even more mucky and dusty than usual but the boys weren't paying attention to that.

"Thank you, Phillipa," Mr. Wetherby was saying. "You may go."

The girl came into view and squeezed past Mr. Wetherby. The boys watched her go, and once she turned around to give them a cheeky grin which erased some of their worries. Mr. Wetherby then pushed the door all the way open and gave the three a nudge into the library.

Neil had been the first one to enter the room, and since Deke and Gene couldn't see over his shoulder, they peered around their tall brother and their eyes widened immediately. Sitting on a straight-backed armchair near the reading table in the center of the room sat a young girl. She was about Neil's age, but the way she looked, she might have been older. Her knees were drawn to her chin, and she was clutching them to her. Her shoulders were shaking, and the boys could barely see her face and the soft whimpering sounds she was making made her seem even younger than she really was.

A long mane of jet-black hair was shielding most of her face from view and hung in tangled, soiled layers about her shoulders. Her full, round lips were blue and vibrating as she rocked back and forth on the chair. She was incredibly skinny and rather tall, probably just a few inches shorter than Neil.

As they entered, she slowly turned her head to look at them, giving the boys a quick look at her small oval, dark blue eyes. Her eyes were almost like the rest of her face, completely shielded by long black lashes that seemed to want to hide everything.

"Boys," Mr. Wetherby said in a soft voice as he entered the library, "I would like you to meet Eileen Gerasimov."

The girl stared at the newcomers without moving or making a sound. Her dark blue eyes seemed to penetrate their souls, making the three feel suddenly fidgety. Deke was the first to step closer, but when he reached out his hand for her to shake, the girl shrunk back from it and clutched her knees closer to her chest.

"What happened to you?" he asked in a soft voice.

When the girl didn't reply, Deke looked over his shoulder at Mr. Wetherby. The old man nodded. "We haven't gotten a word out of her in over twenty-four hours. You see, on my business trip, I was scheduled to meet five other colleagues, one of them being Eileen's father . . . however, no one was there, and I found Eileen like this near my car when I came out."

"What is that pouch she's holding?" Neil inquired.

Everyone turned to see that Eileen was indeed holding a decent-sized pouch against her chest. It was about the size of an average human's head and just as soiled as Eileen. Deke, the one standing closest to her, reached out to touch the pouch when the girl let out a shriek and backed up farther.

"Maybe she hit her head," Neil suggested, "and lost all her common sense. It's like she doesn't want to talk or anyone to touch her! For crying out loud, who says we're going to hurt her?"

"Who says we're not?" Gene inquired with a firm tone in his voice, at once getting the attention of everyone in the room. "She doesn't know if we'll hurt her. Besides, she isn't holding that pouch like she is jealous over it; she wants to protect it. I think the reason she doesn't speak and why she is so jumpy is probably because she is still recovering from a shock or scare."

Deke grasped a wooden chair from the other side of the table and drew it up near Eileen. Sitting on it backwards he considered the girl. "I think you're right, Gene. Whatever happened to her obviously left her in a state of shock. I think it will just take a lot of trust to get her out of it."

Nodding, Gene pulled himself onto the table next to Eileen and sat cross-legged on the edge. He slowly reached out his hand—not too quickly. He saw Eileen's eyes follow his hand until it was just about a foot from her face.

"I'm Gene," he said in a soft voice.

The girl looked up at him, then back down at his hand, then back at his face. Gene smiled brightly and nodded gently to show that he wasn't going to hurt her. Eileen looked back down at his hand and slowly removed her right hand from where it was wrapped possessively around the pouch. She was just reaching up to shake Gene's hand when she suddenly drew it back fast and cowered against the chair.

170

Gene looked around, trying to find out what spooked her. He saw that Neil had taken several steps closer but had stopped as soon as Eileen began to whimper again. Gene looked back down at Eileen to see that her eyes were fixed on Neil and were wide with fright.

"Hey, Neil . . . I think she's afraid of you," Gene whispered.

Neil raised an eyebrow at his brother. "What makes you think that?"

Deke had been watching the whole thing and at once his eyes widened. "He's right, Neil! Eileen shows no fear of Gene, though it's evident that she shows a little fear of me. You and Mr. Wetherby are older than her, so she is completely afraid of you two. I think it's because she believes that if someone is older or about as big as her, they can cause more damage to her than Gene and I can."

Neil was about to object when Mr. Wetherby placed a hand on his shoulder. "I think the boys are right, Neil. That would explain why Gene has been able to get a reaction out of her better than the rest of us. I think we should leave the two boys alone with Eileen for a while."

Neil rolled his eyes and spun on his heels, trying to show his aggravation. "Fine! Just make sure to tell me everything that happens."

Deke and Gene grinned as Mr. Wetherby and Neil left the room. As soon as the door closed, the whole atmosphere changed. Eileen sat up straight and pushed a strand of hair out of her eyes so that her face was slightly more visible. She had high cheekbones, an upturned chin, and her jet-black, long lashes turned slightly upwards at the corners giving her a sort of exotic look.

She looked from Gene to Deke, and then she opened her mouth to speak . . . but no words came. Instead she began to make a strange noise that neither of the boys had heard before. It sounded like she was calling for a bird, but she wasn't whistling, just making a chirping sound in the back of her throat.

"What in the world?" Deke whispered. "That is the strangest thing that I have ever heard!"

He looked up at Gene to see if his brother was also confused, but Gene was no longer on the table. The boy had leapt off the table and was standing in front of Eileen, looking slightly up at her in amazement. His turquoise eyes were wide open, and he was mouthing something as if reading in his mind.

"I can understand her!" he remarked in a hoarse voice.

Deke looked at Eileen to see that she was looking directly at Gene, still chirping but with a more confident look on her pale face. He looked down at Gene, who was still staring at Eileen in wonder.

"Now that is *definitely* the strangest thing I've heard," Deke remarked. "May I ask what language she is speaking, professor?"

Gene held up a finger to show that he needed Deke to remain silent. After about another second, Eileen stopped her chirping, and Gene turned to look at Deke. "It's the most amazing thing! It isn't a language that any human knows . . . it's like a whole other language . . . but I understood it! I don't know

172

how . . . that is the first time I have ever heard it, but I understood every word!"

"What did she say, then?" Deke inquired, not quite sure if his brother was pulling his leg.

Gene looked back at the girl. "She asked who we were and if she could trust us."

Deke's eyes widened. He knew his brother was not the lying type, but if he could understand that much out of that blabbering sound Eileen had been making, then obviously something was going on.

Gene slowly pointed toward himself and Deke. "I'm Gene and this is Deke. We're brothers. You don't have to be afraid. We're here to help you," he whispered in a soft voice.

Eileen glanced over at Deke who returned her surprised look. Then she looked down at Gene and a small smile appeared on her face. "Thank you."

Gene and Deke started. Those were the first words they had heard her say. She spoke in a very soft voice and it had a slight high pitch to it like that of a baby girl.

"I haven't been able to find someone to trust ever since my father died."

Chapter 25

"So, she's an orphan?" Neil inquired, running the comb through his long black hair one more time. "How did you get that much out of her?"

Deke grinned, knowing that Neil could see him in the reflection of the mirror. "We got a lot more out of her, too. Apparently, her father was killed about two weeks ago and her mother died giving birth to her."

Neil stopped, mid stroke and stared at his brother in the mirror. "She said all that?"

Gene nodded as he lifted his face from the sink, dripping with soap and water. "Yeah. And she said that her father wanted her to protect the pouch with her life. Someone obviously wants that pouch because when she went to tell Mr. Wetherby at the meeting, she saw someone beating up those other people Mr. Wetherby was going to meet. She was seen, and they beat her up so that she wouldn't tell but they didn't know that she had the pouch."

Neil tossed a towel to Gene to dry off his face. "That sounds ridiculous!"

Deke nodded as he took the comb from Neil. "That's what Mr. Wetherby thought when we told him. He thinks that maybe her father just died, but she got hurt or hit her head and maybe her mind has been messed up to think that all those things happened."

"Personally, I agree with him," Gene remarked. "It makes the most sense."

Neil rolled his eyes as the three brothers left the bathroom, all groomed and ready for the first day of school. They each wore clean, ironed, long-sleeve, stiff collar shirts that Cook and Phillipa had pressed the night before. Neil's was burgundy, Deke's was navy blue, and Gene's was dark green. They also wore clean black dress pants, clean sneakers, and leather jackets.

"Do you know if she'll be coming to school today?" Neil inquired. "I mean, is Mr. Wetherby going to let her stay here?"

Gene and Deke both shrugged. "Mr. Wetherby said that if she feels up to it, she can come along. I don't know if she has any other family . . . I'm not sure if she will stay here, either. Besides, she told me that she's in third grade like me, so she won't feel too out of place," Deke replied.

Suddenly, the sound of Phillipa's voice erupted from the bottom of the stairs: "Boys! You had better hurry up! Eileen is waiting on you!"

When the boys came sliding down the railing, they found Phillipa and Eileen waiting. Eileen looked much more refreshed than she had the night before, though she still looked hidden behind her hair. Her long black hair was brushed, clean, and shining. Her face was clean, and she wore the outfit she had been wearing the night before, though it had been scrubbed clean. It was a white blouse underneath a burgundy sweater that matched the knee-length burgundy calico skirt. She also wore white stockings and her black shoes were scrubbed.

"Morning, Eileen," Deke and Gene remarked in unison.

Eileen smiled, though barely looked from behind her curtain of hair. "Good morning . . ."

Deke smiled as he pulled on his coat. "Did you sleep better last night?"

Eileen nodded but didn't reply in words. The boys decided to not push it too much further and instead buttoned up their jackets and tied their sneakers.

Phillipa quickly returned from the closet, carrying the caps that the boys had obtained from Break Neck Creek. They were clean as well and didn't carry the mothball smell from before. "You had better hurry. You don't want to be late for school! Mr. Wetherby is awful busy this morning, so he apologizes for not being able to walk you to the schoolhouse," she remarked.

The boys took their hats and clamped them on. "It's all right, Phillipa," Gene remarked. "We can find our way. Whip showed us where it is when we went fishing."

Before long, the four were heading at a brisk pace down the road toward the schoolhouse. It wasn't until they reached the curb at the end of their street that they realized how many kids actually lived in Hichester. Kids of all ages, from four to sixteen year olds, were running down their lanes and joining groups of other kids that were all heading the same direction.

"I wonder what the hurry is," Neil remarked. "Maybe we should ask someone."

Almost by magic, Roy and Reed appeared out of the crowd of kids and ran back toward the four. "There you are!" Reed panted. "We were wondering what had happened to you! We're going to be late!"

"But doesn't school start at seven? I mean . . . that's how it was at our last school," Deke pointed out.

Roy and Reed's eyes grew, and both shook their heads. "Sorry, bro," Roy remarked, "but in Hichester, school starts at six-thirty! It gives us an extra half hour to finish our homework."

"Does that mean we finish school earlier?" Eileen inquired, just as puzzled as the brothers.

The twins had barely noticed Eileen and now that she spoke, they stared slightly up at her in surprise. "Oh," Gene remarked, "Roy and Reed, this is Eileen Gerasimov. She's staying with us a while."

The twins grinned brightly and spoke in unison, "Nice to meet you, but we still have to hurry!"

Roy grabbed Gene and Neil by the hand while Reed took Eileen and Deke and the twins bolted off toward the schoolhouse. "We'll explain on the way."

"Hichester is the complete opposite of every other place in the world, even when it comes to school," Roy panted. "School starts at six-thirty and ends at two, sometimes one if it isn't a busy day. Bentley School teaches its students as if they were homeschooled. They teach the lesson, then give us thirty minutes or so to do the lesson for that day before we go to our next class."

"That way we don't have homework when we get home and then we have plenty of time to go to thothiety," Reed added. "By the way . . . are you three going to join thothiety?"

The brothers weren't able to look at each other since the twins were dragging them at such a pace. Instead, Deke answered straight out, "We're not sure. Mr. Wetherby hasn't mentioned it."

The twins nodded together as they dragged the four up the brick stairs into the schoolhouse. "You

177

had better find out soon," Roy remarked. "Society starts tomorrow."

The schoolhouse was not very large, though it suited the small size of Hichester District. It was only two stories high and each grade was separated into different rooms, with each having about eight to ten students at the most. The kindergarten classroom was the largest, with eleven students, while the smallest was the fifth graders who only had seven.

The left-hand wall of both floors was lined with wooden lockers that looked like they had been hand carved! The lockers, though, looked slightly new or at least recently sanded. On the top of each locker was a number or letter that designated the grade of the student who owned the locker. Since all four of the kids, including the twins, were on the first floor, most of the kids in the hallway on the first floor were their age or younger or only slightly older.

Roy and Reed released their prisoners as soon as they were halfway down the hallway where it wasn't as crazy. That was when Gene was almost knocked over by Whip, who appeared out of nowhere. He wore a bright red shirt, dress pants, and his knapsack flung over his shoulders.

"I'm glad the twins got you here early! Come on, there are quite a few lockers still empty. Before the rush arrives, choose one that is close to mine!" the boy cried.

Gene could barely catch his feet as Whip dragged him slightly down the hallway to the first graders' lockers. The locks were unlike anything Gene had ever seen. Attached to the narrow door was an iron ring about the diameter of the average man's thumb. A similar ring was attached to the edge of the locker so when the door was closed, the two rings were aligned, one on top of the other.

"You'll have to go to the principal's office for your lock. The rule of the school is you have to let at least one person know your combination, preferably the principal just in case something happens to you or something," Whip explained.

Gene opened his locker and peered inside. It wasn't really tall, especially since they were two-tier lockers and the top lockers were barely two feet taller than Gene.

"What schoolbooks will we need for our first class?" Deke inquired.

A small voice replied, "Your math books."

Everyone turned to see that more of the gang had appeared, and Seraphina had been the one to reply. Emma was nowhere to be seen, but Oliver and Denise were there. Denise and Seraphina wore similar clothes to Eileen, but Denise wore dark green and Seraphina wore purple. Oliver had a light blue shirt that looked slightly wrinkled, and his glasses were slightly crooked. From the look of things, someone had probably dragged him to school.

"Deke, you, Oliver, and Denise are going to be in the same room," Whip explained. "Gene and I are together. Neil . . . I don't know who's in your room, but I think the twins are in the room across from you."

Neil nodded. "I'll make do," he remarked with sarcasm evident in his smile.

Seeing that there were no more questions, Whip grabbed Gene's hand and sprinted down the hallway with the rest of the gang following (everyone dragging someone else). The group pulled to a harsh stop outside the principal's office which was the first door on the right by the front entrance.

"Morning, Whip," the voice inside remarked.

Whip dragged Gene though the door into the small office. The office reminded Gene of Mr. Wetherby's office: full of papers and books but extremely neat. At the desk sat a tall man. His hair was a sort of gray/brown color which was a type of hair color the boys had never seen before. His eyes were small and black but full of humor. His nose reminded Gene of a rabbit, for it twitched and turned with curiosity.

"I'm Bill Wadsworth. I'm your principal this year . . . and any future years unless I'm fired," the man remarked kindly in a sarcastic Falfinian accent.

As soon as Gene heard the familiar accent, he perked up. "Thank you, Mr. Wadsworth . . . I'm Gene Mecarnin."

Mr. Wadsworth grinned. "Don't worry, Gene, Mr. Wetherby was by the other day and told me that you boys would be coming. There are locks in that box over there."

The kids at once crowded around a large cardboard box on the end of the desk. It was piled to the brim with locks, each a different color. They all grabbed the one that was their favorite color and returned to Mr. Wadsworth. One by one they handed him their chosen lock. He read the number on the bottom, looked through a log book and gave them a slip of paper that had their combination on it.

"Memorize your combination or write it somewhere where no one will find it," Mr. Wadsworth instructed, "then rip the paper up and burn it, throw it away, or eat it with your lunch."

Deke was just taking his lock and paper from Mr. Wadsworth and when he heard that, his eyes widened. The principal seemed pleased that Deke had actually believed him and let out a snort of laughter. "Just kidding, Deke."

Chapter 26

"Okay . . . it's fat," Roy remarked, staring down at the card that he held inches from his face.

He glanced over the top of the card to see that everyone else at the lunch table was staring at him blankly and with no amusement. The twins, Oliver, and Emma (being the oldest members of the gang and preferably the founders) had created a game that they would play during lunch which had no specific name.

They normally called it the "Guessing Game" where someone would draw a card from a rather thick deck of old mix-matched board game cards that had numerous words (mostly nouns) on them. The person would then have to give clues as to what the object or word was, and the other people would have to guess it. Sometimes it got so competitive that the gang would bet chips or pickles on whoever got the word right first.

Neil, Deke, and Gene had been rather intrigued by the game but after the first few tries, they realized that Roy was the last person anyone wanted to be "it."

"It looks like Reed," Roy whispered under his breath. However, this remark didn't go unnoticed, and his brother socked him in the arm.

"Okay, okay; it's not red . . . Unlike Denise," he continued, though the next boxing he got was much worse than his brother's.

Roy looked back at the others to see that they were completely lost. He then looked back down at the card, then back at them. "Should I just give it away?" he whimpered.

Neil glanced up from his turkey sandwich to see that Whip was making hand motions at him. The boy was pointing at Roy, then the card and other signs that eventually made sense to Neil. "Uh . . . Try something else," he suggested, suddenly pretending that he was choking on his food.

This was the distraction Whip needed, for Neil's hysterical coughing caused everyone at the table to either try to rap him on the back or ask him if he was all right. Neil thought that he was carrying on too far when he saw Whip give him a thumb's-up.

As everyone sat back down, Whip got the attention of everyone on the other side of the table though making sure to not let Roy see him. He then mouthed the answer to them while he pretended to have trouble opening his milk bottle.

The others nodded, but Deke was the one who accidently spoke his mind, "OH!"

"Yeah . . ." Roy started, though he realized that he hadn't given another hint. "Wait . . . do you know?"

Everyone shook their heads and took on innocent grins. Roy looked down at the card, then back at them several times before pouting. "I didn't even say it was a donkey yet . . ."

At the same moment that he clapped a hand over his mouth, Reed let out a rather loud snort which sent everyone else laughing. Whip's laugh of course was considerably louder and when Roy realized that the boy was sitting at just the right angle to see the card, he leapt up from his seat and charged after Whip, who made a quick excuse to use the bathroom.

Once they were gone and their shrieks of horror and laughter were barely audible, the laughing at the table quieted down. "Are schooldays here always this . . . eventful?" Gene inquired.

Emma smiled. "It depends. However, every day at Society is always an adventure. You guys should seriously consider joining. I mean, there is no fee and it's just down the road . . . The building, I mean."

"It sounds really intriguing," Deke confessed, fingering his lettuce in the sandwich. "Do you think we'd like it?"

He at once had everyone's attention; even the kids at the table near them turned around to look at Deke as if he had just named a new law. The boy quickly retracted and felt his neck getting hot.

However, Emma grinned brightly. "You would definitely have fun, Deke! That is something you don't have to worry about. Almost every single kid in Hichester District goes to Society . . . though there are a few who don't. Silver and Destiny don't go but they don't really mind. They prefer to go down to the barges and spend the day with the bargemen. They're pretty handy on those barges."

"That's another thing," Neil remarked, placing his elbows on the table. "How come those guys stay on the barges? I mean, don't some of them protest about not having better lives?"

Seraphina immediately dropped her shy act and perked up. "Actually, Neil, they have really amazing lives. They live here, safe from the outside world and the persecution that they had once faced. They live in a little village down the river near the waterfall . . . it's actually pretty neat. They build thatch houses on

184

the river and they can row their barges right underneath their own houses!"

"We go down there sometimes on the weekends when we don't have anything else to do," Denise added. "I've never heard a complaint from any of them, and many of them have begun to raise families . . . though the strange thing is . . . their children are just like them."

Gene glanced at Denise, then at Emma for an explanation. "It's true," Emma remarked, seemingly puzzled. "You know how the member of HUDGE saved the bargemen by healing them with water prosthetics? Well, no one ever thought that would affect their families . . . but the bargeman who brought you: Lyle? Well he has three kids . . . and they all are like him . . . I mean, they have water limbs and parts of their faces that are water . . . It's almost like the water has become a part of them!"

"Almost like they're their own . . . race?" Deke gasped. "But that's impossible!"

Emma and Denise glanced at each other and smiled. "Nothing is impossible with God!" they called in unison. "Isn't that right everyone?"

Before the boys knew it, every kid outside at the lunch tables were crying agreement. When the noise died down and everyone returned to their lunches, Emma looked back at the brothers. "You see guys, the HUDGE members; they had special gifts that were bestowed on them by God. That is why people hold the memory of them in such respect because they know that everything that they did, they did in God's service."

185

Neil ran his hand through his unruly spiky black hair and rested his chin in his palm. "By the way . . . which HUDGE member cured the bargemen?"

Denise tossed her mop of curls from her eyes and held her head up, "My grandfather. My dad's father was one of the HUDGE members: Timber Nielson."

As soon as that name was out of her mouth, the large iron bell began to ring, and everyone leapt up from their seats. Whip and Roy appeared from the bathroom, steering clear of each other but not trying to kill each other.

Whip caught hold of Gene's arm and grabbed his own trash. "Come on! We have just two more classes before school's out! Then we've got a surprise for you!"

* * * * * * * * * * *

When the bell rang to let school out, there were hollers of cheers from every room and every door opened at the same exact second. Kids poured out of the rooms and swarmed down from the upstairs classrooms, filling the first floors. Gene felt himself getting trampled, but Whip found him before peoples' feet did.

The boy pulled Whip over toward their lockers and opened his own, tossing his books into his bag and locking the door. "Word of warning, there is only one day out of the year that this happens."

Gene glanced at him in confusion. "What happens?"

"This chaos!" Whip hollered over the roar of other people talking. "Every other day each

186

classroom files out two by two in order of youngest kids to oldest. Since we're in the lower grades, we'll get out of the building sooner than the older kids. However, there is no holding everyone on this day of the year!"

"But why the first day?" Gene demanded. "I would think that everyone would go ballistic on the last day of school!"

Before Whip could reply, the twins appeared from the crowd with Oliver close behind. "Welcome to Hichester District Gene," Roy hollered. "Everyone here mourns the last day of school and celebrates the first day!"

Deke, Denise, Eileen, and the rest of the gang appeared and pressed themselves against Whip and Gene's locker so that they didn't get run over by kids trying to get to their own lockers. "Why is that?" Deke hollered. "What is it about this place that makes everything go upside down?"

Seraphina's face lit up and she reached into her locker, producing a handful of paintbrushes, all different sizes. The largest was about the size of her hand and the smallest was barely bigger than a needle. "On the first day of school every year, when we choose our new lockers, we get to paint them! No matter what design or color, just as long as they aren't flammable paints, and no rude comments. Knock-knock jokes are all right, just as long as they're innocent. Oh! And the president doesn't want any neon colors."

"Is this a new thing?" Neil inquired, not as loud since the noise was dying down in the hallway. "All the lockers are paint free . . . did they just decide to do it this year?"

Seraphina suddenly drooped her shoulders and took on a mournful look. "That's why we mourn on the last day of school, because all the men in Hichester come in with sanding tools and remove all the paint! This is how the lockers look all summer until we get back here in the fall and spice them all up again!"

Deke, Gene, and Neil's eyes expanded in amazement. "Seriously?"

Whip grinned and grabbed Gene's hand. "You better believe it! Everyone is on their way to Widow Ethel's. She makes homemade paints that aren't flammable and don't soak the wood! They are always on sale the first day of school, that's why there's a rush because you cannot beat the price of five cents per bottle! The brushes are usually a dollar each, that's why Seraphina keeps her collection all clean."

Chapter 27

When the three boys, Whip, and the twins pushed their way back into the hallway, there was barely a whisper in the whole building. Old canvases covered the floors and from the look of them, they had been used for years because there was every color of paint on them from previous years of locker painting. There was a kid by every locker with a plate full of different paints and a paintbrush in hand.

The six boys found their people halfway down the hallway where the girls and Oliver were standing over Seraphina, who was seated cross-legged on the floor with a chest in her lap. The chest was about the size of her head, plus Oliver and Neil's and it was overflowing with paintbrushes! They were all perfectly clean as if they were just bought and of all sizes.

"Where did you get those?" Deke asked in amazement, setting his bottles of paint in front of his locker. "The kids at Widow Ethel's were buying one or two but all of those must be worth a hundred dollars!"

"Actually, two hundred, twenty-five dollars, and eighty-five cents worth," Oliver corrected.

"You counted them?" Denise asked, raising her eyebrow in disbelief but showing sarcasm in her eyes.

Oliver nodded and that was a good enough answer for everyone. They all knelt down and selected the paintbrushes they would need, then returned to their lockers. There was not a noise in the hallway for over an hour. Principal Wadsworth stopped to watch the painting on his way out the door.

It was almost four when Deke spoke up, "What are you painting, Gene?"

Gene was wiping off his hands on the canvas and stepped back to reveal his locker. It was completely painted a soft sky blue with clouds along the sides. The front though was definitely stunning. The view was of the underside of a tree canopy as if the viewer was looking up at the tops of the trees. Then, smack dab near the top of the locker door was a huge bird shape.

Deke furrowed his brow at the bird shape. It was obvious it was a bird because there were the wings, the tail, and the beak, though the tail looked peculiar and it was just the outline of the bird, as if Gene had painted the shadow but had made it golden colored.

"What about you, Whip?" Gene inquired, bending down to pick up his supplies.

Whip stepped back to admire his work. "I do the same exact thing every year! I think the cleaning lady has begun to realize that the same exact locker is here every year, just in a different place. I think she believes that my locker has feet."

His locker looked like a very elaborate Scardihn Caan soldier outfit. It was covered in brown, dark green, and dark gray blotches, giving a camouflage impression, though there seemed to be some definition in the center of the door. Gene leaned over and squinted at it. "What is that hiding on your locker?"

Whip grinned, pleased that it was hard to see. "It's a whip-poor-will bird! Have you ever wondered where I got my name?"

Gene glanced back at the locker, then at Whip. "Seriously?"

"No," Whip replied, pretending to be disappointed. "It's just kinda coincidence . . . Hey! How did you know that symbol?"

Every one of the gang looked up from their painting to see Whip hurry over to Gene's locker. He reached out and touched the dry golden bird shape in the center of the locker. "How did you know it?" he asked again.

Gene looked at the shape, then at his brothers timidly. How was he expected to tell them that he knew something they didn't? "Mr. Wetherby showed me the blueprints of the society . . . building. That's where I got it. Also, Oliver gave me a copy of the shape at the Welcoming party . . . so I didn't have to memorize it."

Whip whistled. "That's probably one of the coolest lockers I've ever seen! I wonder if Roy and Reed are doing cotton candy and candy corn again this year. They vowed to do that every other year and all other years they would do rainbow and zigzags."

As Whip and Gene turned around, everyone else stepped back to reveal their lockers. True enough, Roy's was cotton candy while Reed's was candy corn (the top white, middle yellow, and bottom orange). Oliver's was quite peculiar, looking like a bookcase. He had painted what looked like shelves on his locker exterior and filled the painted shelves with books and even labeled the binds. Most were Shakespeare, Plutarch and all those books that Gene and Neil steered clear of and left them to Deke.

Denise had made a vast view with the viewer on a grassy hill near a waterfall, overlooking autumn-colored trees and a huge blue moon rising in the distance. Deke had painted an ocean scene with dolphins, sharks, schools of fish, and the shadow of a boat up near the top of the locker and seagrass at the bottom. Eileen's was rather striking: a winter scene in a forest of silver birch trees with the snow falling.

Neil's was a mountain scene beside a small trickling river. There was no living creature or being in sight except for the odd squirrel or snake and a view of blue mountains far off behind the trees. Seraphina's, of course, was the one that made everyone think theirs was terrible. She had taken a collection of soft colors: light green, light pink, soft blue, light purple, gray, white, silver, and even light yellow and had made a huge swirl of these colors in the center of her locker door, then had expanded it until it covered every inch of her locker!

"Where have you been my whole life?" Neil demanded.

Seraphina's face at once turned a bright pink and she partially hid her smile behind her long blonde hair, that is, until she heard the rest of Neil's remark: "I wish you had been there two years ago when we had to paint the fenceposts outside the Church."

No one noticed (that is, everyone but Gene and Oliver) that Seraphina's pleased look at once looked disappointed and almost rejected. Gene was puzzled by this look and wondered what Neil had said to hurt her feelings. Unless she took his first question the wrong way.

Emma looked down at her wristwatch and let out a holler. "Oliver, we've got to get home! It's almost dinner time and Mom will have a fit!"

At that announcement, everyone grabbed their paintbrushes and handed them to Seraphina, who stuffed them in her chest which she left in her locker. No one knew what to do with their paints except Oliver and Emma, who gave them to Seraphina. Soon Seraphina had everyone's extra paints lined up on the shelves in her locker.

Once everyone had closed their lockers, left their books in the lockers, and grabbed their knapsacks, they all charged out of the schoolhouse and headed toward their houses. At the four-way fork that turned left toward Mr. Wetherby's, everyone stopped to say goodbye because that was where most of them parted.

"See you tomorrow, Gene," Whip called. "Remember to come earlier than yesterday so you don't get stuck with the twins bringing you!"

Gene nodded and waved as Whip and Seraphina disappeared down the left-hand fork. Oliver and Emma waved just as Destiny and Silver caught up to them and the four headed home. Denise waited until Seraphina had left before she turned back around and hurried back the way they had come, for she had passed her street earlier, but she wanted to say goodbye to Seraphina.

The three boys, Eileen, and the twins waved goodbye to everyone before they started down their own street toward home. The twins waved goodbye at their gate but kept calling reminders and farewells until the boys and Eileen were inside their own gate. Then the two boys had the nerve to stand on each other's shoulders, so they could see over the brick wall and continued to call to the four until Neil closed the door behind them.

"If they follow us upstairs," Neil remarked, "I'm going to lose it!"

Deke grinned. "If your window is open, they'll definitely try to carry on a conversation."

Gene was about to agree, when Eileen let out a short gasp and galloped up the stairs without a word of explanation. When the boys caught up to her, they found her in the bedroom across from Neil's that Phillipa had prepared for her. The girl was bending over her bed, where the large pouch was nestled snugly in a pile of her pillows.

"What is going on?" Neil demanded. "Why on earth would your father ask you to guard that pouch with your life? What is so special about it?"

Eileen slowly turned around to give Neil a hurt look. To show that she didn't appreciate the question, she replied to Neil's question but while looking at Deke instead of Neil, "My mother had found it when I was a baby. I always wondered the same thing, but my dad told me that the reason why he was killed and why his friends were hurt was because the time was close . . ."

Deke shivered as Eileen slowly lowered her voice but Gene, intrigued, stepped over to Eileen and sat down on her bed. "What do you mean?"

Eileen glanced uncertainly at the door and Deke, seeing the look, closed the door behind him as he and Neil came to sit on the other side of the bed. Eileen pulled herself onto the bed next to Gene and hugged the pouch to her.

"He said that the time would come again when evil would take on a new face and begin to take over the world . . . but as evil will begin to rise, the light will rise to challenge it," Eileen whispered. "Did you ever find it strange that whenever something terribly evil like a war happened, the good always won out in the end?"

The three boys slowly nodded. It had intrigued them especially when it had to do with politics. Eileen hugged the pouch closer. "That is because it was the work of God. My father said that God always made sure that there would be someone to oppose the evil every time that it returned. The war may be over, but there is still work of evil at play. They may not seem so evident, but the evil is coming . . . and at the same time, God is preparing an army to oppose it."

Neil scratched his black hair, ruffling it slightly. "That doesn't answer the first question."

Eileen glanced over her shoulder at the door before leaning toward the boys. Automatically the boys leaned forward too until their heads were all touching. "Daddy told me that there was a legend about the HUDGE members. The legend states that there were eight characters known as the 'second-hands' who worked alongside the HUDGE members. It was rumored that the 'second-hands' were mythical creatures."

All three boys reacted differently. A smile appeared on Gene's face, but he remained still. Deke's eyes grew in amazement and supposed horror while Neil prepared to laugh out loud, but Deke and Gene both clamped a hand over his mouth.

"What kinds?" Gene inquired in a low voice.

A smile appeared on Eileen's face and she began to explain in whispers but excitement evident in her voice, "No one really knows because whenever someone asked the HUDGE members or their children, they would reply with the same answer: "Only God knows." Some people think that they say that because they don't want to lie and say "no," but they don't want everyone to know. However, some of the rumors are that most of the 'second-hands' were regular animals like wolves or something, but unusually large! Other rumors say that there were some flying animals like giant birds, flying beasts, and even dragons!"

Eileen looked down at the pouch that was nestled between her crossed legs. Opening the flap, she slipped both hands in and drew out a small object that was barely bigger than her palm. It had been surrounded by scarves and rags, making the pouch seem larger than the contents. The object was a rather large egg, filling Eileen's hand, but this wasn't your normal egg. It was a bright violet and had a glassy look to it as if there was a layer of glass around the shell. There were soft white speckles near the top and bottom and the pale light in the room reflected off of the shiny object.

"My dad is quite sure that this is no ordinary birds' egg," Eileen whispered. "He thinks it may belong to one of the 'second-hands'!"

Gene slowly held out his hands and Eileen gently placed the egg in his palm. He turned the egg over, then rapped it softly with his finger. "It sounds and feels like an egg . . . did he try candling it?"

Eileen nodded. "He did but the shell was so thick it wasn't as clear as normal eggs . . . but there was definitely something inside! It was hard to see because the shell was so thick but there was something moving inside."

Gene handed the egg back to Eileen, who slipped it back into the pouch. "But if your mom found it when you were a baby . . . how come it still hasn't hatched?"

Eileen shrugged. "My dad thought that maybe if it is a mythical creature, they incubate much longer. But you see, my dad isn't the only one who thinks that this egg is genuine."

The three boys slowly nodded and all four of them shivered at the thought. "Okay . . . now that my comfort zone has been shot," Neil remarked, rubbing his arms as if cold. "Could we concentrate on the issue of SOHE? If we're going to act, we need to do it tonight!"

* * * * * * * * * *

Gene glanced across the bench at his brothers. Neil was looking from Gene to Deke, exasperated. Deke was twirling his fingers nervously while Mr. Wetherby looked at them expectantly where he sat at his desk.

The boys had prepared a "speech" where they would hint at joining SOHE and they had assigned parts for each of them. Deke was supposed to do the first part, but the boy was all tense and had sudden stage fright. Gene had the inkling to pinch him to get him going but that would only make Deke more nervous.

Mr. Wetherby was beginning to look rather impatient, so Gene began to consider starting the conversation with his own part. What Gene didn't know was that Deke was just overcoming his stage fright. As soon as Gene began to speak, Deke regained his courage.

"We were wondering . . ."

"What would . . ."

Neil slapped his forehead into his hands in exasperation while Mr. Wetherby smiled at the boys while stifling a laugh. "Maybe one at a time?"

Gene looked over at Deke who took that as a hint that he had waited long enough. "Uh . . . we were wondering how long society lasts . . . throughout the year?"

While Mr. Wetherby was considering the question, Gene and Neil were giving Deke confused looks since that was a shorter version of the part they had assigned him. Usually Deke was a boy of many words but obviously not at that particular moment.

"Well, it starts tomorrow as you probably know. I'm not sure about fall, winter, and spring breaks but I know it ends three days after school ends in the spring," Mr. Wetherby replied. "Why, are you thinking about doing it?"

None of the boys were looking directly at Mr. Wetherby when he asked, so they didn't see the excited look on his face. Gene rustled his hair as he spoke, trying to not sound too hopeful. "Well . . . we were . . . but we weren't sure what you thought about it and if Eileen could do it."

Gene was almost jolted out of his seat when Mr. Wetherby erupted with a loud shout that sounded more like a hoot than a shout, "Gene Mecamin, of course everyone would love to have you join! That is what Hichester District is all about! Eileen could certainly do it . . . if she is interested."

Neil rolled his eyes to heaven. "That's the only problem. She was enthusiastic about it until she realized that her visit here might only be temporary. Then she said that she doesn't want to get too connected to Hichester."

"Well you can march right back upstairs, young man," Mr. Wetherby remarked, sitting down in his chair, "and tell her that her father was one of my closest friends and until the day that Eileen tells me that she wants to leave Hichester, this will be her home if she wishes it so."

The old man was prepared to go on, but for just a split second he looked away and when he turned back around, the three boys were gone, and the door of his office was slowly closing itself. Smiling to himself, he listened to the sound of the excited feet that sprinted upstairs to bring the good news.

Chapter 28

"Honestly, Phillipa," Neil remarked, "I can button my own jacket . . . I am ten, you know."

Phillipa nodded. "I know that, youngster, but I also know you. I can tell you this: you'll be thanking me later when you come out of Society tonight when it's almost dark and it's blistering cold. You'll be thankful that I gave you your scarf this morning!"

"And I also know that school doesn't wait for its students," Deke remarked from down the hallway. "If we want to beat the school rush, we need to leave now!"

"Don't forget your meal bag," Phillipa called to them, hurrying into the kitchen.

Gene patted his backpack carefully. "We already have them, Phillipa."

The girl whisked out of the kitchen, carrying three brown paper bags in her long slender hands. "That is your lunch laddy. These are your dinners. In case you hadn't noticed, society doesn't end until five and that is a full hour past supper. Cook made sure that the soup and potatoes won't spill, but you'll have to use the SOHE oven to heat it up just like all the other kids. I would suggest you have one of the girls help you, not the boys."

"How come?" all three boys inquired at the same time.

Phillipa hurried from boy to boy, slipping their dinner bags into their knapsacks. "You weren't here last year so you didn't hear about the time that Roy and Reed Fischer almost blew up the kitchen. You can ask them about it later."

The boys exchanged knowing looks. That sounded about right when it came to Roy and Reed, though they wouldn't have been surprised if it had been Whip either. If anything, they would ask Oliver to help them out.

Phillipa disappeared into the kitchen again and returned with a fourth paper bag. "Here is Eileen's," she remarked, handing it to Deke. "She's waiting outside for you. I think she didn't want to have a huge ceremony over school this morning since it would also involve talking about society. I think she is still unsure about it."

* * * * * * * * * * *

School was barely out when the whole school was empty other than the teachers and principal. Almost every kid in the school had left in a rush. There was very little separation and instead of the kids splitting into dozens of groups to head to their own streets, they separated into two completely uneven groups. The smaller group which consisted of about five kids (Silver and Destiny among them) headed toward the river while the rest of the kids from Hichester which numbered to about thirty, hurried in the opposite direction toward the furthest part of town.

As they walked, the three boys began to realize that the once huge group was now separating out into smaller groups. Before they knew it, they were walking with the kids from their own classrooms from school. Gene, thankful that he had Whip to talk to during the fifteen-minute walk, squeezed past the other kids his age 'til he was walking beside the boy.

"So, what usually happens on the first day of society?" he inquired.

Whip grinned mischievously. "Well, the first day is always kinda slow and easy, especially if there are new students. I think this year we have eight new students, which is pretty good. You three boys and Eileen are the only new people to Hichester. The other four new students didn't enter SOHE until this year because they weren't quite old enough. I mean, you only have to make sure that you're not in diapers and you can tie your own shoelaces! Anyway, the first day is usually when the new students are sent to the apothecary for analyzation."

Gene slowly glanced at his friend to realize that Whip was grinning at him. "I know what you're thinking," Whip remarked. "It's not going to be like it was at Break Neck. You see, most every kid here in Hichester is what we might call: free. That is why when we first joined, we only had to go to the apothecary to make sure we were sturdy and able to handle the days in society. For you guys . . . it might be different."

"Different in what way?"

Whip slowly reached behind Gene and tapped his back, right in the center of his back. Gene cringed, for his back was still sore from the expedition he had with Deke a few nights before. Whip didn't see the cringe, but he didn't tap too hard. "That thing on your back."

All at once, Gene felt his blood racing and his mind was beginning to fill up with questions that had been waiting patiently for so long. "It's going to get removed? Do you know why I have it on? Why is it that you don't have it? Where do we . . ."

Whip clapped a hand over Gene's mouth because the motions he was making with his hands weren't enough to tell Gene to stop. "Easy, pal. I'll explain everything that I can, but some things I cannot answer . . . they're things that cannot be said."

Whip removed his hand slowly just to make sure Gene wouldn't erupt again. When the boy didn't speak but merely nodded, Whip relaxed. Shifting his knapsack on his back, Whip sighed and began to answer the long list of questions that had been thrown at him. "First off, yes, it is going to be removed. You cannot be part of SOHE if it isn't. That is what will happen at the apothecary. It's pretty much what you'll be going through today. The reason I never had that, nor anyone else in the gang and most of the kids here in Hichester is because . . . my parents weren't afraid. You see, either your parents or some adult who was in charge of you when you were a child decided to hide something from you by covering it up with that leather. That's as much as I can say on that matter, buddy."

Gene had been looking at Whip with earnestness and complete concentration, though he hadn't been watching where he was going. He did, however, come out of his state of concentration when he almost collided with the kid in front of him and he felt his arms almost get ripped out of socket by his two brothers.

"Gene . . ." Deke cried, but then in a whisper he added, "I've seen this place before."

Gene's vision was completely barred by the kid in front of him. He took Deke by the hand and squeezed through the crowd 'til he was on the front of the group of kids. Neil and Whip followed closely. When they came out into open air, the three boys stared at the scene before them in stunned bewilderment.

A vast lake lay before them, but the strange thing was: it was crystal clear. There had been a lake down the road from the Church where the boys would go swim on the hot days, but it was always mucky and soiled. This lake was so clear, they could see almost perfect reflections of themselves in the water. They could see the other side of the lake, for it wasn't as large as some, but it wasn't shaped like most lakes and ponds: it was the shape of a bird!

The diagram that Mr. Wetherby had shown Gene had been the diagram of SOHE; however, Gene hadn't realized that the bird shape had actually been water! As soon as this raced through his mind, Gene looked across the lake and, to his surprise, there in the center of the lake was a cluster of buildings.

From the distance they were at, the sharp details of the buildings were hard to see, but from the shore, it was evident that these buildings were carefully built and had an almost regal design to them. The rooftops were pointy cone shaped and covered in dark red shingles. All of the buildings were made of dark brown stone and each building a different size. The largest building was the one in the center and on its roof rose two tall towers that were the tallest of them all. That building definitely had a castle look to it.

"Where in the world did you see this, Deke?" Gene demanded, not taking his eyes off of the scene.

Deke didn't reply right away, which caused Gene to look at him. Deke slowly glanced at him and there was evident concern in his eyes. "In ... in that dream I had in Break Neck, Gene ... you know when ... I thought I saw things from the past ... and the future? Well ... I saw this too ... at the very start."

Gene stared at his brother for a long time. There was a sort of strange realization and truth in Deke's eyes. If he had seen the society in his dream and it had actually come true, would the other things in his dream come to reality one day? They didn't have time to think on this further, for the rest of the gang appeared from the crowd and grabbed their hands.

"Come on, slowpokes," Denise called. "We don't want to miss the boats."

The gang pulled the three bewildered brothers and Eileen farther down the shore, where several of the other kids were heading. Gene was trying to picture the diagram in his mind, figuring out where exactly they were, when he saw that they were approaching narrow sections of the lake that were like the platforms on the barge river. There were several long narrow slits in the lake that Gene realized were the "feathers" of the bird. They were a good twenty feet from each other and about ten feet wide and thirty feet long. There were two boats in each "feather" or dock that were tied by ropes to iron posts on the shore.

The boats were simple outrigger canoes with the balancing pole attached to the side, making them much wider than usual canoes. Kids were piling into the canoes, eight each since they were considerably long. The gang hurried to the furthest dock, since no one had arrived there yet, and leapt into the boats as if it was as easy as climbing stairs. Neil and Eileen slowly inched into the same canoe, going on their hands and knees, but ended in hitting their chins on the side. Gene didn't go on his knees but sat on the edge of the shore and put his feet in before throwing all of his body into the bottom of the canoe.

Deke hesitated on the shore, watching as the twins, Whip, Oliver, and the girls leapt onto the balancing pole and into the canoes. He didn't want to look cowardly or weird, especially if he fell into the water. He decided to try the way the rest of the gang had done. He knew that going too slow would result in his falling, so he leapt off the shore and landed on the balancing pole. His first reaction was horror and fear as the pole slightly dipped into the water under his weight; however, the others in the canoe caused it to stay relatively steady.

Seeing this, he leapt the rest of the way and collided square on with Denise. The girl pushed him off of her with a huff and tossed her curls out of her eyes. Deke tried to get to the back of the canoe, but the others in his boat (Roy, Reed, Gene, and Emma) were trying desperately to congratulate him on almost getting the landing perfect on the first try. Deke glanced at Denise, who was sitting in the front, but the girl rolled her eyes and grabbed a paddle.

There were four paddles per canoe, so with four people paddling strongly out of the docks, they were moving at an incredible speed. Deke found that he wasn't rowing, which made him feel weird since everyone in his boat was rowing except for Reed. However, he didn't exactly feel guilty, especially when he saw all the other canoes, twenty-four to be exact, come soaring smoothly out of the branches and into the open water of the lake. It looked like an armada of small vessels heading to meet the enemy.

Before he knew it, Deke's admiration at the spectacle grew when the canoes lined up, two by two, and slowed their pace. That was when Deke looked ahead for the first time and realized that they had just arrived at the buildings. They were much larger up close than they had been on shore. They seemed to rise up out of the water like stone glaciers. He also saw that they were approaching the dock that was attached to the front of the largest building.

The dock was shaped just like the end of the "tail" of the lake, but it was stone. It rose out of the water almost four feet, just like all the other buildings, so when the canoes pulled up alongside the inside of the crescent dock, the dock was much higher than their heads. Deke's boat was the second to pull up (Neil and Eileen's was the first). Denise, being the person in the front of Gene and Deke's boat, stood up and grasped the edge of the dock with her hands, pulling the canoe close to the side.

Roy, Emma, and Gene then set down their paddles and slowly rose to their feet, using the stone dock to balance themselves. Emma led all of the passengers in their boat, except Denise, almost to the front of the boat. That was when the boys realized that there were chiseled steps in the side of the dock that were large enough for one's feet. The twins were the first to leap forward and climb up the steps to the top of the dock. Gene and Deke were next, with Emma close behind.

Deke was about to ask Denise if she was coming when he saw that one person in each canoe remained to row it out of the dock and tie it to pegs on the outside so that the other canoes could row in. Emma led the four to join the rest of the gang, who then hurried around to the other side of the dock where Denise and Oliver were climbing out of their canoes and tying them to small posts that were drilled into the stone dock.

Oliver was just helping Denise out of her canoe when Whip caught up to Gene and the others. Then, with a dramatic wave of his hand he motioned toward the huge double oak doors that stood before them. "Welcome to the Society of Hichester Enterprise."

Chapter 29

Everyone was on pins and needles, waiting for all the kids to file out of their canoes and tie them to the anchor pegs. Deke had moved his knapsack from one shoulder to the other at least three times before Denise impatiently told him to stop the fidgeting.

It seemed ages before all the canoes were tied down and the kids were all crowded on the dock (which was too small for almost thirty kids) waiting for something to happen. Sudden, the huge doors began to echo a creaking noise across the lake and one of the two doors slowly creaked open just slightly.

A man in his late thirties, early forties, slipped out of the door and closed it behind him. He wasn't a very tall man; in fact, he was barely taller than the ninth-grade boys. His skin was a dark, rich tone of brown, and his hazel, cat-like eyes scanned the crowd of kids. He was slightly on the round side, and his legs seemed too short and slender for his decently rounded figure. His arms were also small and slender, reminding Neil of a character from comic strips in the newspaper.

His hair was the same goldish/sandy color as his eyes and stuck out from his head in a large mop of straight hair. There were several locks of hair that fell over his forehead, covering his eyes partially, but he never strived to move them aside. He wore light brown pants that came to his ankles and were tucked snuggly into small boots that came just above his ankles. The boots were slightly curved upward at the toe and the same color as his hair. He wore a relaxed, white starch, long-sleeve shirt with no collar (if he had one it would be smothering his round face), and over that he wore a wrap like the simple ones from Break Neck Creek, but instead of rough brown material, it was a silky, light tan fabric.

"Welcome, everyone," he remarked in a soft voice that was barely audible. Since it was so hard to hear, the ones who did hear it passed it on to people behind them.

The first time that the little man had spoken, the three boys and Eileen had started; for someone of his peculiar stature, his voice was extremely soft but also high-pitched and slow.

"Is everyone here who should be?" the man inquired.

He was obviously waiting for a particular answer because no one spoke; however, several kids began to step aside to let a tall boy through: Oliver.

"Yes, sir," Oliver replied in a soft voice that was almost as quiet as the man's. "Everyone is here."

The little man nodded, and Oliver stepped back to stand out of view behind a bunch of kids. The little man turned around and put both of his small pudgy hands on the huge double doors. "Welcome back, then, to the Society of Hichester District."

With that, he pushed inward at the doors and they slid open, away from the kids, with such ease, it was amazing that the weight of the doors didn't cause problems in opening them. The little man strode in with fast, short steps, and the kids followed him inside.

Eileen had been holding onto Gene's hand, while Gene had been holding Deke's, but now they dropped each other's hands in amazement as they stepped into a huge open room. The floors were just

213

recently polished, for they reflected everyone's shoes. Beneath the thick polish was a dark rustic brown/golden color. Huge marble pillars, that had the diameter of eight feet, emerged from the floors at every corner of the room. The ceiling was so high up that the kids felt even smaller than they already were. The hall that they found themselves in opened up into an even larger part of the building that had a huge open space in the center and a huge wooden chandelier in the center of the ceiling. Two flights of spiral stairs stood on either side of the huge circle opening in the room. They both met at the second floor that was practically an indoor balcony overlooking the hall.

Neil slowly leaned over and whispered in Roy's ear, "What is this place?"

Roy grinned. "It's the Hall of Organization. This is where the headmasters and senate of SOHE work and meet. If you need anything that the headmasters or instructors cannot help with, you can find help here. We don't come here that often during regular days unless we have strange questions or we're in trouble."

"I didn't know there was a senate for SOHE," Deke pointed out. "What do they do?"

Seraphina had heard the conversation and now squeezed over to explain before the twins confused them, "The senate of SOHE is half made up of members of Hichester government and half of past members of SOHE. They are in charge of everything here in society. They make the changes, make the rules, discipline the kids who are misbehaving, decide for or against new developments. The headmasters and instructors are the same thing, but there aren't as many headmasters as there are instructors. Besides, the headmasters are more like 'elite' instructors if you get my drift."

The boys were about to comment on her "drift" when a strong voice broke their concentration. Everyone looked up to see that about ten to fifteen grownups had appeared on the balcony and were looking down at them. Right away they recognized one of them to be Principal Wadsworth. The one who had spoken was a tall, slender man who looked pretty ancient; even older than Mr. Wetherby. His hair was gray, and his beard came almost down to his waist. He reminded Deke of Abraham Lincoln because his legs and arms were long, and his face looked weatherbeaten but kind. He wore long black pants and a long black robe with thick, wide sleeves that were almost too long. The robe came almost to the floor and pretty much consumed the tall gentleman.

"Welcome back, everyone, and welcome to those who are new here," the man continued. His voice was strong and carried a long way, but there was a crack of age in it. "I see you have all met William Shakespeare Grant."

Neil quickly covered his mouth to hide a snicker. His brothers glared at him, so he leant over to explain in their ears, "I just didn't expect someone so small to have such a strong name."

Of course, Seraphina heard, and she got in an explanation before anyone else spoke, "That might be his full name, but it is rarely used. Everyone calls him Willie. He's a retired scientist. A regular genius. Kinda explains why he and Oliver get along so well."

"First I will begin by acquainting the new members with the instructors and professors," Mr. Walker called loudly. "I am Mr. Walker and I am your headmaster. I attend to any of the needs associated with the society so if you have any questions, please let me know. Mr. Grant is my secretary and the vice-president. If I am not on hand, you can ask him whatever you need."

The man then turned to a woman who stood beside him and rested a hand on her shoulder. "Mrs. Schneider is the regular Aerial Development teacher and works mainly on Aerial techniques and growth." Then, turning to another woman next to him, he continued. "Mrs. Keith is your Individual Derivation teacher and her job is to teach you your ancestry and the history of the society."

He then turned around to the three people who stood on his other side and waved a hand toward a young man. "Bill Wadsworth, who you know as your principal from school, is the Substantial Education and Progression professor. In better words, he is your PE teacher."

There was a slight groan from the kids in the crowd, but it died down when the man turned to a younger man. "Quintin Quaker is your Suppression of Physicality professor on concealing things that should be concealed."

Mr. Walker then turned to the last two people, who looked almost older than him. "Mrs. Fischer is your Terrestrial Consideration teacher on land techniques and will assist the Wer division. Mr. Nielson teaches Nautical Expansion and works with the Mer division."

Deke gently nudged Seraphina and the girl nodded. "Haraus Fischer is Roy and Reed's grandmother on their father's side. Mr. Timber Nielson is Hummer Nielson's father and Denise's grandfather."

The old gentlemen continued speaking but Deke wasn't really paying attention. He was busy trying to squint at the other adults. He quickly leaned over, meaning to ask Seraphina something but almost knocked heads with Denise. "Who is that?"

"The one standing next to Mr. Walker, on his left; that's Mrs. Schneider. She always asks that we call her by her first name only: Elys."

Deke studied the woman who was at least in her fifties. Her strawberry blonde hair was beginning to gray and though it was braided, it came well past her knees. Her deep brown eyes seemed to hold millions of answers and stories . . . mysteries. She wore a dark blue dress that wasn't from this time period. Obviously, it was the style that women wore during her childhood. He could see a striking resemblance between Elys Schneider and her son: Colton Schneider. He couldn't see if she had resemblance to Seraphina or Whip because of the difference of age.

Standing beside her was a man, Mr. Nielson. The man was about the same age as Elys Schneider with graying red wild hair that was brushed up out of his face. His eyes were a bright blue and seemed to have a great deal of energy. He was extremely tall, compared to the petite Elys Schneider. He wore an outfit that looked slightly old fashioned: relaxed white shirt, brown pants tucked into knee-high

217

leather boots, and a leather jacket, that wasn't buttoned up, over the white shirt.

Deke wished that he had more time to figure out who the other grownups were, but at that moment, Mr. Walker finished speaking and there was a roar of applause from the kids. Deke hadn't heard what the man had just said, but Gene grabbed his hand and pulled him toward the front of the group of kids. On the way, Neil caught hold of Eileen and pulled her forward until the four of them were standing in the very front with four other kids who were about five years old.

"Mrs. Schneider will show you where the apothecary is," Mr. Walker remarked.

Deke felt a surge of excitement. They were going to officially meet one of the eight HUDGE members! But then his heart sank when he realized that by going to the apothecary . . . their leather would be removed. He suddenly remembered the issues he and Gene had encountered, and he shivered at the thought.

Gene felt the shiver run through Deke's hand and he smiled at his brother. "It'll be all right, Deke," he whispered. "These people know what they're doing . . . unlike us."

Chapter 30

Neil could tell that Gene and Deke both were trying to walk as close with Mrs. Schneider as they could. He didn't want to say anything to embarrass them, but it was kind of irritating at how Eileen had to keep rushing over to catch Gene and Deke from falling into the lake because they weren't watching where they were going.

Mrs. Schneider led the four children out of the Hall of Organization and took them directly to the left. At the end of the platform that connected the front of the hall, there was a plank that was barely three feet wide. Leaning slightly to the side, Neil could see that the plank was supported by wooden pillars that disappeared into the water.

Mrs. Schneider, Gene and Deke right away began to cross the plank with Eileen and Neil following uncertainly. The other four little kids were walking ahead, racing before the others but then stopping and waiting for them to catch up. As he stepped across, Neil glanced to his left to realize that the platform that surrounded the Hall of Organization went all the way around, even to the back and there were several planks leading from the platform, to other platforms that surrounded the other buildings.

To his left, about thirty feet away, was another plank that went directly over the water and connected to a long rectangular building. There was a wooden sign hanging above the door of the building that said: Steeple Hall. There were two more planks that were connected to the other side of the Steeple Hall platform that connected to two different buildings: Benvor Hall and the Aquarium.

Neil had hoped to see what the other buildings were and how he reached them, but they had just arrived at the other end of the plank and were standing on the platform surrounding the Apothecary. The building had a more relaxed and welcoming look to it, different than the vigor and almost castle-like design of most of the buildings. There were several windows that were wide open, flowers of all colors growing in the window sills, and vines literally had overtaken the whole outside of the building.

Mrs. Schneider pushed the door open and strode inside without a word. The kids followed her, one by one and soon stepped into an open, dim lit room. The only light in the room was the light that came from the open windows. The floors were wooden but not polished like they were in the Hall of Organization. The interior (just like the exterior) of the place was rustic and old fashioned. There was a handmade wooden table on either side of the door with rocking chairs, stools and benches surrounding it with several books and papers to read, obviously while one was waiting to be seen.

Opposite the door was a flight of stairs that looked narrow and the type that creaked excessively. Beside the stairs and almost underneath them was a desk which was the only place not organized. Sheets of paper, folders and books were piled in clusters over the desk. A vase of flowers stood to the side, apart from the mess but they looked two days old.

"Livonia?" Mrs. Schneider called in a soft voice.

A head popped up from behind the desk and then the person stood up to reveal a rather tall woman who looked young enough to be Mrs. Schneider's daughter, but not young enough to be her niece. Compared to petite Mrs. Schneider, this woman: Livonia, was a giant. Her skin was a dark rich brown and her eyes, though almost black were full of feeling and kindness. Her medium length black hair was pulled out of her face into a ponytail that flipped about her face when she turned her head.

"Oh, it's you, Elys," the woman remarked in soft voice that seemed to come from a far-away place. "From what Willie told me, it sounded like Viggo was going to send Bill to bring the kids."

Mrs. Schneider smiled but the smile seemed half-hearted, as if there was something else on Elys's mind. "I have to return to Mt. Kyvers. I still have to clarify the members on the new developments as far as rules."

Livonia nodded and waved her hand. "Don't worry about us, Elys. I'll see that they're taken care of."

As Mrs. Schneider began to head out the door, she paused with her hand on the doorframe and glanced back at Livonia. None of the kids noticed this except Gene, who saw Mrs. Schneider point toward Neil, Deke, and Gene before making a movement with her mouth that he wasn't fast enough to read. Gene quickly turned around to see Livonia nod her head in understanding before Mrs. Schneider left the apothecary.

"All right, everyone," Livonia remarked in a bright tone as soon as the door was closed. "I am

Livonia Spring, first off, and I am your apothecary here at society. If you have any issues: sprained ankles, colds, splinters ... anything, you just let me know. While most of the other buildings are locked and closed after society hours, I am usually here several hours after closing, so if you forget anything here you can ask me, and I'll help you."

The kids nodded to show that they understood. Livonia then walked from behind the desk and grabbed a clipboard and pen as she did so. Her outfit was one that reminded Gene of a swan. She wore a lovely white silk blouse with sleeves that came to her elbows, but then lacy tails that hung from the hems. She wore a long dark brown skirt which came from high on her waist, down to the floor and slightly flowed on the floor behind her. Her feet were invisible beneath the long skirt but from the sound of it, she wasn't wearing heels.

"All right," she remarked, opening her pen. "Let's start with the four youngest."

She led the four other children over to the table and had them take a seat. "My friend, Marianna will be down in a moment to see to your needs," she explained.

Turning to the others, her eyes fell on Eileen, who was trying her hardest to not be seen. "Eileen," she said in a soft voice, "you can stay here with the young ones. Marianna will help you."

Eileen nodded and gladly took a rocking chair in the corner of the room. The boys barely had a moment to take this all in, for Livonia quickly ushered them up the stairs and true enough, they creaked loudly. At the top, she led them down the hallway and into the last room on the left. Once inside, she switched on a light, which lit up the small room.

It was virtually empty except for three beds that lined the walls. The beds were identical to the ones in the health check cabin at Break Neck Creek. The walls were lined with pictures and the room looked very welcoming for some reason.

"Each of you choose a bed," Livonia instructed. "Let's see what you have here."

Neil was the one who hesitated because he hadn't really heard much about the whole deal with the leather. Gene and Deke of course fairly flew toward the beds and leapt onto one each. As Neil was slowly, cautiously making his way to the empty bed, Livonia stepped over to Gene and sat down next to him.

"Mr. Wetherby spoke to you about this, I suppose?" she inquired in a soft voice.

Gene slowly nodded, looking directly into the woman's eyes. Livonia smiled kindly at him, surprised at his calm but inquisitive look. "This is a painful and difficult procedure. That is why we have to do it while you're asleep. That way you don't feel the pain and it doesn't affect your nerves. Don't worry because we've done this before. There have been several members in SOHE who also had leather stitched into their skin."

Gene shivered at the thought. "Are you going to remove it?"

Livonia smiled at him. "Of course . . . but there is something you need . . . all of you need to know. You might be sore for a few days and seeing how long you've had the leather on . . . it might take a lot to keep up with the exercises in society."

The three boys nodded in understanding, which caused Livonia to take on a serious mode. She patted Gene on the shoulder and stood up. As she began to rummage in the cupboard on the wall, Gene slowly lay back on the bed and looked up at the ceiling. Was this the right thing to do? What did all of this mean? Obviously, nothing that had happened the past week wasn't anything "normal."

"Here you go," Livonia remarked in a soft tone. "This will make you sleep, and it will numb your body, so you don't feel the pain."

She held out a small cup that held barely a teaspoon of a clear liquid. The boys each took a cup and slowly sipped it. There was no taste and it was cold. When they had finished, Livonia took the cups from them and placed them in a small bucket that sat near the door.

She then continued to rummage in the cupboard and began to draw out small objects that she placed on a tray. From where they lay on the beds, the boys couldn't see what the objects were, but they guessed they were surgical tools. Livonia then began to wash her hands vigorously as if her life depended on clean hands.

At that moment, the door opened, and two women stepped inside. They both were half Livonia's age, barely nineteen, and reminded the boys of Livonia. They looked almost just like her, at least in height and dress. Their hair was also dark, but their skin was fairly lighter.

"This is Robin and Cary," Livonia explained, introducing the two women. "They'll be helping me today, so we can get you all finished at the same time."

225

Gene had been watching Livonia steadily, but once Robin and Cary had entered, things had begun to change. His vision became blurry and his eyes felt heavy. He felt woozy and suddenly exhausted and his mouth was dry. As Cary and Robin stepped into the room, closing the door behind them, the room began to swim and waver around as if Gene was falling off the bed . . . Then everything went black.

* * * * * * * * * *

The first thing that ran through Gene's mind was: they were swimming. The room seemed to swim back into vision, twisting and turning like a spiral. It reminded him of the design Seraphina had painted on her locker. Slowly the room began to come into focus and stop wavering. It was just like he had remembered: but he couldn't see Livonia, Cary, or Robin. The room was a different brightness: slightly dimmer than it had been when he fell asleep.

Gene slowly turned his head, thinking that maybe Livonia was sitting in the corner. There was someone in the corner, but it wasn't Livonia; it was Whip. Roy, Reed, and Oliver were also sitting in the corner, but on the floor since Whip had claimed the chair.

Gene made a move to sit up, but his back cried out in protest. He felt like he had been vomiting for a week, and his ribcage and back were exhausted and sore. Something felt strangely different, despite the sore and tired feeling . . . it was like something was missing. Then it came to him: he had been asleep because the leather was being removed from his back.

226

"What happened?" he asked in a dry voice.

At the very sound of his voice, Oliver leapt to his feet and fumbled for a cup of water. He helped Gene take a drink without choking and then sat down in the chair since Whip had gone to sit on the end of the bed.

"You've been out for at least two hours," Whip remarked. "Everyone else has gone home. The girls are waiting downstairs, but we're the only ones here besides Livonia. You've had quite an interesting first day of society, Mecarnin."

Gene slowly reached up with one hand to rub his eyes and he felt his shoulders cry. "I didn't even get to see the whole place."

Roy leapt up from his seat. "Oh, we can show you around. I'm sure Livonia wouldn't mind us lingering around for another few moments, after you guys have found your feet."

Gene glanced around and saw that Deke and Neil weren't where they had been before. "Where are the others?"

"They had to be moved," Reed replied. "It wath kinda crowded in here, and Deke was bleeding like crathy! Neil wath even worthe!"

Considering that, Gene quickly looked down at the sheets around him, expecting to see blood. Whip leaned over and patted his knee. "Don't worry, you barely bled. From what Livonia told us, since Deke and Neil are older, their bodies have begun to grow over the leather more than you. It will take them longer to recover than you."

Gene slowly reached for the wall with his hand and slowly sat up. His back cried out, but he pushed it out of his mind. He was about to reach behind him to feel his back, then stopped. He looked at Whip, then at the others. Oliver was the only one who understood his hesitation.

"Livonia cleaned out your wounds. You won't bleed anymore unless you overdo it."

Nodding, Gene reached behind him to feel his back. His fingers touched the collar of his shirt and began to travel down his back when he stopped . . . this wasn't the shirt he had been wearing when he came in. He felt further and realized there was a huge slit in the back of the shirt from the collar, almost down the bottom.

Gene swung his legs off the bed and slowly pulled himself to a standing position. For a split second the world swam as he had risen too fast, but he bit his teeth hard together and it stopped. When he felt that he wasn't going to topple over from exhaustion or nausea, he looked over his shoulders.

He couldn't see anything since he wasn't an owl and couldn't turn his head all the way around. He was about to reach back again when Whip spoke up. "Hey, buddy . . . could you do something for me?"

Gene slowly nodded, deciding that they knew what was going on better than he. Whip got off the bed and walked over to him. He grasped Gene by the shoulders and looked directly into the boy's eyes. Then gently he dug his fingers into Gene's shoulders and moved his hands so that he caused Gene's shoulders to turn back just slightly. Gene cringed, for it caused a shoot of pain to run down his spine . . . but then another strange feeling . . . a feeling of being able to move. He wondered why but it felt like he had been immobilized in some way until then and now he could move . . . but why?

Slowly he looked behind him and just stared. Now he knew why . . . now he knew why the leather had been there . . . now he knew why he suddenly felt powerful: protruding from his back, just between his wing bones, were two objects. They weren't huge but seemed just the right size for him. They were almost velvet and the part closest to his back was fluffy and gray while the ends were black with marks of white and gray.

He slowly moved his shoulders inwards and they folded up, and when he moved his shoulders back again, they rose into view . . . true enough: he had wings! Then, right there and at that moment . . . he fainted.

Chapter 31

"Gene!" a voice called from somewhere far off. "Gene Mecarnin, open up!"

Gene's eyes slowly fluttered open. He couldn't recognize where he was . . . it wasn't where he had last been. Shaking his head, trying to stop the room from swimming before him, he sat up. Right away he realized that it was a mistake for his back seemed to refuse to work with him. It no longer hurt unbearably but was uncommonly sore. It reminded him of the time when he had gone to play baseball with Neil's schoolmates years ago and the next morning his shoulders and forearms were sore.

Looking about him, he realized that he was in his own bedroom, the windows and shutters closed. He saw a clean outfit already on his desk chair with his school knapsack packed and ready to go.

"Gene," the voice called again, followed by sound knocking on the door. "Are you awake yet?"

Gene forced himself out of bed and strode slowly to the door. He had barely opened it when he was welcomed by the brightly lit hallway and his brother Deke's face. Deke flew into the bedroom and began rushing around. He grabbed Gene's clean clothes on the chair and tossed them into Gene's face.

"Hurry and get changed," he cried. "We barely have ten minutes before we have to go."

Gene didn't bother to remove the light nightshirt that he wore but pulled his clothes on over it. It would give him a good reason to not have to use his jacket all day. As he was pulling his shirt on, he realized there was something different. Turning it over, he saw that there was a row of buttons down the back that wasn't there before. Looking up, he realized that Deke's shirt had the same thing.

"Hey, Deke," he remarked as he pulled it on. "What's the deal with the buttons on our shirts?"

Deke grabbed Gene by the shoulders and stared him directly in the eyes. "Gene, you know how terrible my sight is. Now, I'm not sure if this is an illusion of my imagination or my eyes playing tricks on me, but . . . Is there really a fin on my back?"

Before Gene had time to take this in, Deke had turned around and unbuttoned the buttons on the back of his shirt. When he unbuttoned the last one, a long, slender object broke free from underneath his shirt. It was long, coming almost to Deke's waist and stood out a good two feet from Deke's back. It was slender and almost webbed like a duck's feet. The ribs between the leathery parts were a slightly lighter blue color than the rest of the dark, navy-blue fin. Gene didn't have to be a genius to know that Deke did in fact have a sailfish's dorsal fin.

Gene reached over and touched the tip of the fin. It was rough and almost sharp in a way. "Yeah, Deke . . . I'm pretty sure that it's not an illusion of your imagination."

Deke let out a deep breath that he obviously had been holding since he had entered the room. Reaching back carefully he pushed the fin underneath his shirt and buttoned it back up. If Gene didn't know that it was there underneath his shirt, he wouldn't have guessed that the boy had a dorsal fin attached to his back. However, a sudden thought struck his mind.

"What . . . What about Neil?"

Deke was just picking up Gene's knapsack when he turned to give Gene a distressed look. "He's determined to attend, Gene. When Eileen pointed out that he might not be able to participate the way he is, he fairly flew at her in a rage. Mr. Wetherby said that there is nothing wrong with him trying, but he warned Neil that it will be difficult."

Deke headed toward the door and was opening it when Gene put a firm hand on his shoulder. "What do you mean, Deke? Why would society be hard for him?"

"Because ..." Deke started, taking his time clearing his throat. "Neil never returned from the apothecary. Livonia had to keep him there because ... he has only one wing ... and it's ... it's as if the thing is disfigured."

* * * * * * * * * * *

"Are you sure about this, Neil?" Livonia inquired. "The salve has worked to relax your back and shoulders, but it hasn't fixed the bone."

Neil nodded. "I'm sure. I asked Mr. Walker and he said that it is fine if I attend, just as long as I get your 'okay' to leave the apothecary."

The door of the apothecary flew open and the gang burst in, led by Gene and Deke. The twins almost knocked over the table that stood between Livonia and Neil, but Deke was able to hurry over to stop it in time.

"Guess what, Neil," Roy remarked. "Today we get to learn about the differences of categories."

"We have only a few minuteth before thociety thwarts," Reed added.

232

Emma and Seraphina were calmer in their approach, so they got Livonia's attention first. "Would it be all right if Neil joined society today? Our instructor doesn't want us to miss too many of the first days."

"Who is your instructor?" Livonia inquired, rising from her chair.

"Mr. Wadsworth," Whip replied. "Though he is really adamant about us calling him just Bill. It's weird."

Livonia smiled. "He is a strange one. And if I know Bill, he is going to throw a fit if I keep Neil here any longer. Tell him that Neil is free from hospital quarantine, but he needs to take it easy until his wing builds up strength."

The kids nodded and once they got the slip of approval from Livonia, they left the apothecary with all haste. They waited until they were crossing the plank to the Hall of Organization until they started chattering.

"How are you feeling, pal?" Deke inquired, patting his brother on the back kindly.

Neil shrugged but put on a defiant look. "It wasn't fun ... And it's kinda strange feeling like a disfigured being, but I'm going to get through this."

Deke slowly leaned over to give Gene a confused look. Gene merely shrugged, just as surprised at their brother's determination as Deke. This was obviously a new high for Neil.

Whip, seeing that the conversation had died down, began to pick up his pace. "Well, I'll see you guys at Mt. Kyvers!"

The boy started off at a sprint and disappeared around the building. The twins were close behind him, and Emma would have joined them if Deke hadn't stopped her by grabbing her arm.

The girl turned to see a look of slight confusion and sudden realization in the boy's eyes. "This . . . this is the answer isn't it? The reason why . . . everything here is different? Why Hichester is so protected, why there are so few inhabitants . . . Everything?"

A smile lit up Emma's face and her deep dark eyes smiled at him. "That's right, Deke . . . the whole of Hichester District revolves around the rareness of its inhabitants. Hichester District is known by most . . . at least those who know about it . . . to be the home of changelings."

Gene hurried over from where he had been listening at a distance. "What are changelings?"

"You are changelings . . . all three of you. Even Eileen is a changeling. Everyone here in the society are changelings and many of the adults in Hichester are changelings. The thing that makes us different from humans are not only the physical differences like wings, fins, or other things . . . but also our hearts. The greatest trait of changelings that makes us so special . . . is a gift that was given to us by God when we were born, and that is love. Changelings are their own race. They aren't considered humans, but they are mortal just like humans. They have the human form . . . and also partial forms of changelings, but the thing that really distinguishes us is our natural instinct to do good. It is very rare that a changeling will do something terribly wrong or use their unique differences to do evil. We all have our bad hair days just like any mortal. We're all sinners just like humans, but just like birds have very strong instincts to care for their children, changelings have very strong instincts to do the right thing rather than the wrong."

Gene, Deke, and Neil looked at each other in puzzlement and strange understanding. Everything was starting to make sense now. The pieces were beginning to blend together.

"Is there anything else we need to know?" Neil inquired, giving Emma a sarcastic grin.

Emma pretended to think about it, rubbing her chin thoughtfully. "You'll need to understand the differences of Aerobeasts, werebeasts, and merbeasts, but that will be explained in depth later today. Oh, you'll also have to learn about the founding of Hichester District."

* * * * * * * * * * *

"All right, listen up," the man called out loudly. "Today we're going to be concentrating on understanding the differences between the different beasts."

There were about ten kids in the classroom, all sitting in a circle on the floor of the spacious room. Mt. Kyvers Hall had turned out to be a building full of classrooms that were all dedicated to a different "lesson." The kids then had been separated into three different groups, each a different size, and led off to different buildings. Gene, Whip, Neil and Seraphina had been led with the largest group to Steeple Hall on the other side of the lake. Denise, Oliver, and Reed had gone with the smallest group to Benvor Hall while Deke, Eileen, Emma, and Roy were sitting in the medium-sized classroom with their "instructor": Robert North.

Robert North was a tall young man in his mid-twenties. He was of slender build with straight brown hair that fell over one side of his forehead, and he was constantly brushing it back. His eyes were a striking blue and his handsome face was full of mischief that reminded Deke of Whip.

Robert turned around to face the blackboard that hung on one side of the wall and took up the entire wall, reaching from the floor almost to the ceiling. He began to scribble down some words near the top (as far as he could reach), which gave Deke time to look around the room.

There were small desks and chairs piled up on the left side of the room, out of the way. They were there for "classes," but today Robert had explained that they would only be there for a short time and needed space. The other side of the room was lined with books and bookcases, while the back of the wall had all different kinds of scales and measuring equipment attached to the wall.

Robert stepped back to reveal what he had written on the board: **Aero Mer Wer.**

For a second, Deke believed that they were learning Latin. Robert stepped to the side so all the kids could see the words, twirling the chalk in his hand. "Now, who would like to demonstrate what signifies Aero from the other two categories?"

A young boy near the front lifted his hand uncertainly and at once Robert nodded toward him. "Come on up, Charles, and write down the traits."

The boy, Charles, rose to his feet and took the piece of chalk from Robert. He was probably Neil's age with slick red hair that made a slight almost crest on his head. His eyes were dark brown, almost black, and his face was a rosy color. He quickly scribbled a list of words below the word **Aero:**

Flight
Wings
Keen Sight
Smell

Nodding his approval, Robert took the chalk from Charles who quickly returned to his spot on the floor. Robert circled the first word: Flight.

"That is an important trait for Aerobeasts. It is the most common category of changelings and there are always twice as many Aerobeasts as werebeasts. All Aerobeasts are able to fly. The ones that cannot are sometimes a mixture of Aerobeasts and the other two categories. An example would be Danny York. He has the wings of a penguin but as you all know, penguins do not fly. In that case he usually works with the Aerobeasts most of the time but spends some of his time with us."

He then circled the next few words. "It is true that all aerobeasts have wings and that is the most distinctive difference. Their sight is twice as good as most of us, though the sight of merbeasts can sometimes challenge them especially when the merbeasts are under water. Aerobeast sense of smell is also extreme."

Robert then skipped: **Mer** and went on to: **Wer**. He called up a young girl of about twelve to write down the traits of werebeasts:

Keen hearing
Ability to walk on all fours
Mostly land mammals

237

The girl didn't wait for Robert to take the chalk from her but left it on the table and sat back down. Robert didn't push the subject but began circling each part and explained each as he did so: "Werebeasts are distinctly separated from Aero and Merbeasts because of their ability to walk on all fours. It is true that the majority of werebeasts are land mammals, but there are also some land reptiles as well. Certain ones have keen hearing, but each of their specific traits varies."

Emma was then called up to write a list for **Mer** and when she sat back down, Robert had to check the board twice to make sure he wasn't seeing things:

Ability to swim
Able to breathe underwater
Great speed underwater
High sense of hearing
High sense of smell
High sense of sight
Some have echolocation
Electroreception

As Emma sat down, many of the kids grinned at the girl, but Deke was the only one who brought to light what everyone was thinking. "I don't think Robert was expecting that long of a list."

Robert cleared his throat, getting everyone's attention. "Well . . . as Emma was so kind as to show us: Merbeasts do have a long list of gifts. They are able to breathe underwater and they have extreme sense, including the sixth sense known as electroreception, which is basically detection of certain movement in the water. However, we won't go into great details since you will have plenty of time

238

to experience that later today in the Aquarium. For the time being, class is dismissed."

Chapter 32

The next three weeks were ones that the boys wouldn't easily forget. They were sent into a series of exercises and drills by their instructors that helped them get the basics of their different categories. Deke, who had always been slightly afraid of the water, had now overcome his fear ... though through some tough days. The first day he nearly drowned, mostly because he thought that he couldn't breathe, and Emma had to retrieve him. He almost had a heart attack the next week when Roy and three other kids came swimming from underneath him and, having slight trouble seeing in the water, he thought they were real sharks.

Gene's time was not much better. The first three days he had several cases of falling into the lake on takeoff and a few times he tripped and ran into someone else. He got stuck in a tree and Whip had to retrieve him since Gene's shoe was stuck between two branches. Gene then collided head-long with twelve-year-old Vicky who made it plain that he had better work on his flight.

When Neil discovered it was virtually impossible to fly with one wing, he began to just watch the other fliers and took notes. Before long all the other Aerobeasts caught on to the fact that he had all the information that was said and was learned, so they asked him for help on their flight techniques. Soon Neil was busier than anyone in the whole society and having a much more productive few weeks than his brothers.

On the third Friday, the kids were let out an hour early so all of them went home for dinner before heading over to SOHE. Gene had finished his dinner sooner than Deke and Neil and decided to go ahead and walk to society alone since they took forever to finish their turnips that Gertrude had made.

As he approached the lake, he saw Whip waving his arms impatiently as he came into view. Smiling, he pulled his knapsack further onto his back and hurried over to the boy. "Hey, Whip. How long have you been waiting?"

Whip shrugged. "Probably about ten minutes. Seraphina headed over to the Wagner's to wait for Emma and Oliver. Personally, I think she was trying to avoid Vicky."

Gene grinned. "I don't blame her. You barely have to come within five feet of Vicky to get on her bad side. What did Seraphina do?"

"Oh, I don't know if Seraphina is in trouble with Vicky," Whip replied. "Personally, Vicky is only really nice to girls and she seems okay toward Seraphina. I think Vicky has gotten on Seraphina's bad side . . . though I don't know how."

"But I saw Vicky and Seraphina talking just before society ended yesterday," Gene pointed out. "Is it a recent thing?"

Whip shook his head. "I doubt it. It seems to change each day. Yesterday she wasn't on good terms with Vicky all morning, then during lunch they were okay . . . until you and Neil came over, then Seraphina was put out with Vicky for the rest of the day until right before we left."

Gene removed his knapsack and set it on the ground, propped against his feet. "Maybe it's not Vicky . . . maybe Seraphina is just having a rough time and it seems that she is on bad terms with Vicky."

Shrugging, Whip set his own knapsack down and began to remove his jacket. "Come on, Gene; we have a few minutes before everyone else gets here. Let's work on that roll turn."

"Oh, come on," Gene groaned. "That is the one that is causing me the most trouble."

"Which is why you should concentrate on it most," Whip pointed out as he began to unbutton the buttons on the back of his shirt.

After a moment of having trouble with the buttons, his wings slipped out and he fanned them open several times to warm them up. "Besides, as a very impressive waxwing aerobeast changeling, you need to be able to fly without any trouble. You know you are the first waxwing AC in about fifty years?"

Gene removed his jacket and tied it around his waist. "I might also point out, Whip Schneider, that as a whip-poor-will AC, you can be rather chatty and obnoxious, especially in early morning and late afternoon."

Whip grinned, running his hand through his wild hair. "I aim to please! Now remember, relax."

Without another word the boy braced his legs and then leapt into the air from a standstill and rose up, aiming for the clouds. He was almost out of sight, just a dot in the sky, when he stopped and leveled out to wait for Gene.

"Try the roll turn on your way up," Whip called. "There isn't much wind, so it shouldn't be too hard for you!"

Rolling his eyes to the sky, Gene took several steps back before taking a running leap toward the pond. His feet were millimeters from the water as he took off. He began to build his altitude by turning his face heavenward and building with steady, slow but strong flaps. When he was about thirty feet above the lake, Whip began to call down to him.

"Now try the roll turn and don't tense up this time!" he called down. "Relax and make sure you don't come out upside down again! If you do, turn back around."

Gene glanced back at his wings and considered the command. To do the roll turn, he had to tuck one of his wings close to his body while turning his other wing back just slightly. This made him go streamline but with the unbalance, it would cause him to roll over. However, the issue with Gene every time was that he spun out of control and when he finally got out of it, most of the time he was upside down. This was all right . . . just as long as he could get right-side up which was something that proved impossible for Gene.

Looking back up toward Whip, Gene curled his left wing in close and turned his right wing back. At once he began to roll, at first nice and slow . . . then all of a sudden it sped up within a split second and there wasn't even a gust of wind! He began to spin out of control until he forced his wings open and he stopped . . . upside down!

Groaning in defeat, Gene kept his wings wide open for a moment, allowing the world around him to stop rocking back and forth. "That worked," he remarked to himself.

Whip flew down to about ten feet away from Gene. "Maybe you moved your wings a certain way. I honestly cannot tell because each aerobeast is different. Something I might do to make mine roll correctly might make yours go ballistic . . . everyone's flying depends on their own methods. Maybe it's . . ."

Suddenly a voice interrupted the conversation. "Hey, you two!"

Whip turned his head to look down at the shore where the voice had called from. Gene was about to do so but realized he was upside down. He then instinctively tried to sit up as if he had been lying on a bed . . . but that let his guard down and he began to plummet. The wind whistled in his ears and for all the strength in his body, he couldn't level out! It was as if his wings wouldn't respond!

He could see the lake water nearing and that was the last place he wanted to end up in on that particularly cold day. Finally, he reached back to his wings and grabbing them with both hands and fanned them out. It felt like someone had just socked him in the stomach when his wings stopped his fall just inches from the water.

He was perfectly exhausted and didn't have the energy to fly to the shore, so Whip descended and taking hold of his shirt, he dragged Gene through the air to the shore. When he set him down, Gene looked at the person who had caused him to let down his guard and realized it was Deke. The boy's hair was windblown, his eyes were wide, and there was a strange look on his face.

"What's up with you, Deke?" Gene inquired. "You look like you did last week when the twins invited you to test a blood sample in their dad's lab to see if it had signs of blood poisoning."

"The only reason he was freaked out was because, it turned out, they wanted to use *his* blood," Whip pointed out. "But Gene's right, Deke . . . what's wrong?"

Deke clasped the sides of his head and shook it sadly as if trying to empty his mind. "We're in trouble, guys."

Whip rolled his eyes. "Aren't we always?"

"But this is different," Deke pointed out. "You know how Eileen has been acting really uptight and icy the past few days? Well according to Denise and the other girls, it's because Vicky has been picking on her."

"That figures," Gene remarked. "I would react uptight and icy if Vicky was picking on me. Luckily I haven't gotten into that much of trouble."

Deke grabbed Gene by the shoulders as if to stop Gene from changing the subject. "But that's the problem! Do you know why Neil has been so adamant about being a part of society even though he is kinda an outcast with his single wing? It's not the attention he's getting like we thought! It's because he has a crush on Vicky!"

Gene and Whip were lucky that it was autumn, or they would have caught flies when their mouths dropped open. Whip had been picking up his backpack but on hearing that, he dropped it with a loud thump.

"Vicky . . . the same Vicky I know?" Whip inquired. "Okay . . . that is really weird and all . . . but what does it have to do with Eileen?"

"Eileen was fed up that Neil kept bringing up Vicky and finally she told Neil about Vicky's bully traits," Deke pointed out.

Whip and Gene exchanged concerned looks. "What did Neil say?"

"He said that Eileen is just a 'child' and knows nothing of life! Eileen has locked herself in her room and has refused to let anything or anyone in or out. But that's not the worst of it," Deke remarked in a rushed voice. "When Neil insulted her, Eileen socked him in the shoulder . . . and the reaction he gave wasn't your usual groan."

"Translation?" both boys inquired together.

Deke glanced over his shoulder as if he didn't want anyone to hear. "Macaroon and I finally managed to get a good look at Neil's wing . . . Gene, it's not good . . . I'm afraid that it's infected."

Whip shivered at the very word. Gene bit his lower lip, but then a thought struck his mind. "What makes you think so?"

"You know when Neil's toenail was infected, and the nurse had to remove his nail?" Deke whispered. "Well, the nurse had told him that if the infection got too bad, it would spread to his bloodstream and there would be red streaks on his foot . . . then it would get really dangerous and difficult . . ."

The two boys didn't even need to hear the rest to know what Deke was going to say, but he said it anyway: "I have pretty poor sight, but if I was able to see bright red streaks all over my brother's back, then it's obviously bad."

"What are we going to do?" Whip whispered in almost a whimper. He was clutching his arms around his chest as if trying to keep this horrible truth away from him.

Deke looked directly at Gene. It was obvious that Deke didn't know what else he could do. Gene

247

looked over at Whip, shivering at the thought and then back at Deke, who was waiting patiently for a suggestion. Sighing, Gene shook his blond head. "Whip, go tell Livonia that we need her at our house pronto . . . Deke, we're going to have the hardest job of keeping Neil at the house 'til Livonia arrives."

Chapter 33

Deke had never bitten his nails his whole life. He was the only one of the three brothers who didn't have any nervous habits like that. Gene was the one who bit his nails 'til they bled, and Neil was the one who would pace. However, standing in the library with everyone else sitting silently in chairs, Deke was pacing back and forth, gnawing at his fingers.

Phillipa and Macaroon had decided to go to the kitchen to help Cook with clean up, rather than watching the peculiar scene in the library. Roy and Reed were watching Deke walk back and forth in front of the door. The strange thing about that was that Roy was moving his head with Deke, while Reed was moving his head in the wrong directions so every other rotation of their heads, they would collide their skulls but then keep going as if they would never learn.

Denise was attempting to untangle a lock of curls but in the process, she had made more of a tangle. Finally, Emma had to help her out but discovered that red curly hair was much different than wavy brown hair. Oliver was knee deep in books piled around him and his head was half concealed behind a full edition of Charles Dickens. Seraphina, finding that she couldn't paint the books, was making movements in the air with her hand as if she was painting imaginary paintings in the air.

Gene was sitting on the floor between Oliver and Denise, looking from one to the other. He would watch Denise in misery with Emma untangling her hair, then he would look over at Oliver completely content in his books.

"I have a question," Whip remarked out of the blue.

No one else had noticed Whip sitting, bored, in a chair across the room from the others. Everyone looked up from what they were doing, except Deke who continued to pace.

"If someone is really getting on my nerves, should I kick him in the shins?"

Gene, Emma, and Denise raised their eyebrows in confusion, while Oliver returned to his books. Obviously, it was a conversation he wasn't interested in.

"I don't think kicking said person would be necessary," Gene remarked.

Whip shrugged and slouched back in the chair. The room was silent for a few seconds before he sat up straight again and spoke up, "Here's another question . . . what if I already did?"

At once he had everyone's attention, but that attention was short lived, for the library door opened slowly and Livonia stepped in, closing the door behind her. Everyone dropped what they were doing (except Oliver who kept the book tucked under his arm) and hurried over to the woman, making a perfect half circle in front of her.

If she had been Gene, Whip, or one of the other gang members they would have bombarded him or her with questions. However, Livonia was the kind of person that they didn't want to rush or annoy. In that case, they waited silently.

Livonia didn't make any eye contact with the children when she first entered. She walked clear across the room and sat down in the same chair that Whip had just left. She leaned back against the cushions and looked up at the ceiling. Taking in several deep breaths, she turned her head to look at the children who were standing in front of her. The boys were leaning on the backs of the chairs while the girls were sitting on the floor in front of her.

"There is something I need to tell you . . . and it will be really hard to hear," she remarked in a low voice that seemed to crack with worry. "Neil won't like it . . . but he needs to know the truth. That is why I need you, Gene, to tell him. I think he'll take it better coming from you."

Gene slowly swallowed. "What am I going to tell him?"

Livonia looked around at all the faces watching her. She wished that she didn't have to tell them, but it was the only thing she could do. These children before her were the ones closest to Neil. If anyone needed to know, it would be them.

"Neil's wing . . . would never be able to work even if he had two," she started, trying to find the right way to get it out. "I don't know how, but . . . Neil's wing has been broken and seriously infected ever since the leather was stitched onto his back. Now, the broken bones have continued to grow, but they were never reset so the wing has grown crooked. I could rebreak the bones and reset them . . . but the infection is what I cannot cure."

Deke slowly removed his fingers from his mouth where he had been gnawing on them. "How bad is it?"

Livonia looked across the room at him and the look of deep distress in her eyes caused Deke to shiver. "The infection was never treated . . . over time it spread throughout the wing. The whole wing is infected . . . there is nothing we can do to stop it."

"Well that's not so bad," Whip remarked. "He just won't be able to fly."

"He won't be able to attend society," Livonia interrupted, at once getting everyone's attention. "The infection in the wing is now spreading into his bloodstream and the only way we can stop it from taking over his body and causing some serious health problems . . . is to remove the wing."

The silence that followed was so painful that Livonia couldn't look at the kids. The girls had gone pale while each of the boys either dropped their jaws or just stared.

"You're right," Roy remarked. "Neil isn't going to like it."

* * * * * * * * * * *

"If you're going to tell me something, you might as well do it," Neil remarked.

Gene quickly took on an innocent look, trying not to reveal why he was in his brother's room. "Who said I had something to tell you?"

Neil glanced up from where he had been studying his fingernails. "When you're the only one who comes, usually it's because you have to tell me something I won't like."

"Well . . ." Gene started, " . . . you see . . . Livonia said . . . I mean we . . . you . . . ."

Neil slowly raised one eyebrow at his brother. Gene was the most level-headed of the three of them, but now he was stammering, which was something he never did. "Get it out, Gene!"

Gene stopped his stammering at the sound of his brother's voice and merely stared at Neil. Slowly he lowered his head 'til it was resting on the back of the chair (he was sitting on the chair backwards). "Livonia says your wing has to be removed before it causes physical and health problems."

The next things that happened were so fast and vague that Gene barely remembered them. The first moment Neil was sitting across from Gene on his bed and the next moment, Gene was on the ground and half of the room was overturned.

"So, you are expecting me to be glad about that? You're right, I don't like it! No wonder they sent you in here by yourself or Livonia would have a houseful of broken arms to take care of!" Neil hollered at the top of his voice.

His face was a red that made his hair look blacker than it was. His hair was already a mess from his tossing his head from Gene, then back to whatever he was throwing about. Gene slowly tried to get to his feet, but the look on his brother's face and in his eyes scared him. It wasn't just fury that was in Neil's eyes . . . it was also complete horror.

Gene was slowly making his way to the door when Neil stopped throwing his books across the room and turned to face him. Neil strode across the room faster than Gene could blink. He grabbed a hold of Gene's shirt and lifted him completely off his feet. By the time Gene realized what was going on, his face was level with Neil's and his back was pressed against the door, Neil holding him almost a foot off the ground.

The next thing he realized was that Neil was holding him up with one hand and preparing to draw his other hand back. Gene looked directly into Neil's eyes and stared a hole clear through them. He made no expression on his face, but merely looked at Neil as if he was a wall of white paint.

Neil at once felt something that felt like lightning strike his body. He couldn't move . . . it was as if he was frozen to the spot with his right hand drawn back, prepared to strike his brother. Those light blue eyes were looking directly up at him . . . with no fury . . . dejection, or even fear. There was only one look that stabbed a dagger through Neil's heart: pain. The pain-filled look in Gene's eyes told everything . . . answered all the questions. For two years since Gene was old enough to attend the school across the road from the Church with Neil, he had been pushed around and bullied because he took everything that came his way with silence. For two years Neil had stood and watched as his little brother had been picked on and pushed around . . . then he wouldn't even say anything to him as he brought Gene back to the Church bruised and sometimes with a bloody nose.

That silence . . . the horrible silence that now filled Neil's ears brought back too many memories. Whenever Neil had seen the other boys holding Gene against the brick wall of the public school, Neil hadn't heard any of the taunts that the boys threw Gene's way. All he heard was the silence . . . the steady breathing . . . the muteness that would come from Gene . . . the silence that was louder than any taunts.

He couldn't understand. He couldn't see why or how his brother would bear a childhood of being bullied with perfect silence. A quick memory flashed before Neil's eyes of the day before Father Fischer came for them. Gene had been sitting alone at an empty lunch table when Neil's buddy Jeff had stridden across the yard and grabbed Gene by the collar. Gene hadn't even moved, flinched or even changed his calm and almost bored disposition as Jeff dragged Gene to the brick wall and pressed the boy against it.

The brick wall and the door of the bedroom . . . Jeff and Neil . . . it was the same exact thing . . . same exact story . . . Neil suddenly realized that he was just one of many, one of the group. The memory of Jeff beating up Gene slowly began to change: the brick wall and Jeff disappeared to reveal the bedroom door and Neil.

Neil's hand that held Gene's collar seemed to go numb and he let go of his brother. Gene tumbled to the floor but didn't even flinch as his feet struck the floor. Neil stepped back several steps as if Gene had just bitten him. His eyes were wide now . . . not with fury but of horror. Something had happened to him . . . he had almost struck his brother . . . what was happening to him?

Gene watched his brother as Neil slowly backed away from him. Neil's horrified expression didn't change . . . until he was barely an arm's length from the window . . . then he just froze. Slowly Neil's eyes rolled into the back of his head and he flopped forward. Gene stared at him in sudden confusion, his expression changing for the first time.

Then, as Neil flopped onto the floor, Gene saw a shape squatting on the windowsill. The sun was shining brightly through the window, so Gene could only make out the rough outline of someone squatting with a long tail curled around his legs and two small ears emerging from a headful of wild hair.

"Thanks, Oliver," Gene remarked, letting out a deep gasp of air. "That was probably the most frightening thing I have ever seen."

Oliver smiled as he slowly climbed through the window into the room. "I don't think Neil saw the fear in your eyes. He only saw that you were willing to take his fury."

Gene slowly shook his head as he knelt down beside his unconscious brother. "I don't want to accept the fact that my brother is furious, but if showing no dejection toward him helps erase the fury . . . I'll do it."

Chapter 34

They were sitting against the wall of the hallway, across the door of Neil's room. There was occasionally the sound of Livonia speaking to Macaroon or Phillipa, but it was always muffled.

Roy finished tying two locks of Denise's hair in a knot without her knowing and turned to find something else to do. He looked from face to face and seeing that no one knew what to do, he tried to strike up a conversation.

"Hey, Reed, have you ever tried to sneeze and yawn at the same time?"

Reed raised an eyebrow. "No . . ."

"Try it," Whip and Roy remarked together.

Reed slowly swallowed and smoothed his wild hair back, revealing the brown scaly spikes hidden beneath his hair. "Uh . . . okay."

The noise that he made was partially covered up, luckily for him because the door of Neil's room opened, and the three adults emerged. Everyone in the hallway leapt to their feet and waited for some news.

Phillipa was carrying a basket of linens which she kept above the kids' view. She and Macaroon quickly disappeared down the hallway before any questions were asked. Everyone then turned to Livonia who gradually walked over to Gene and Deke.

Slowly she placed a hand on each of their shoulders and crouched down so that she was level with their faces. "He'll be sore for several days . . . the infection should go away. I've instructed Macaroon and Phillipa on how to clean the wounds. I'm afraid Neil will be in a state of depression . . ."

"For how long?" Seraphina inquired in a soft, concerned voice.

Livonia smiled sadly and shook her head. "I honestly don't know. If he is able to move on with his life with the loss . . . it shouldn't be too long. Just try to be encouraging. I've put a salve on his wounds to help draw out the bacteria. I've also given him pain reliever, but it will keep him asleep for several hours. Just keep an eye on him for the next twenty-four hours."

The kids slowly nodded. Livonia smiled and, rising to her full height, she slowly headed down the hallway. When she was out of sight, Whip put an arm around Gene's shoulders. "We'll help you, pal. We can take shifts in watching Neil. My parents aren't strict about curfew. I'm sure they'll be all right with it."

Seraphina and the twins nodded in agreement. Emma and Denise, however, shook their heads. "I'm afraid I cannot help, Gene," Emma apologized. "Oliver can, but I am going with my mom to visit my cousins in Gerh. Denise is going with us too . . ."

Deke smiled kindly. "Don't worry about it, Emma. With the boys and Seraphina helping, it'll be fine. We'll make a sleepover out of it since Mr. Wetherby is gone for the weekend."

"Hey, Gene," Whip remarked, cocking his head to the side. "Did you want to say something? You've been standing there with a strange look on your face."

Everyone turned to see that Gene did in fact have a peculiar look on his face. It was as if something had just dawned on him but was puzzling him. It took him a moment to answer and almost seemed to have not heard. "Sorry, guys . . . that sounds great. Why don't you guys think of a shift schedule . . . I'll be right back."

* * * * * * * * * *

"You'll do fine, Deke," Whip encouraged. "It's not the end of the world if you have trouble on the test today."

"Easy for you to say," Deke remarked, shrugging his shoulders in defeat. "You don't have trouble transforming your feet into a fin!"

Emma looked over Whip's head (which wasn't difficult for her) and glanced at Deke. "Is that what you're having trouble with? I thought we mastered it last week."

"That was the breathing," Deke corrected. "I still cannot see underwater and my feet won't transform, no matter how hard I try!"

"And I still have to do running take-offs. Whenever I try stand-still takeoffs I make a new enemy in the poor soul that I collide with. Also, I cannot turn and roll for the life of me!" Gene remarked. "I think I've fallen in the lake more times than the merbeasts!"

Denise snapped her fingers. "That's what I've been meaning to tell you. I thought you aerobeasts can stop your falls."

"We can," Whip, Seraphina, and Gene chorused.

"But for some reason I cannot get my wings to fan out when I'm falling," Gene pointed out.

Seraphina quickly hurried over to put an arm around Gene's shoulders. "Don't worry about it.

259

Your wings are probably still trying to get used to being . . . wings. It will take time to strengthen them."

"Hey, guys," Roy hissed. "I think we have stumbled onto something."

Everyone looked up to see a small handful of kids that were standing around an even smaller group of kids who were obviously going head to head (with words).

"It ith Vicky," Reed whispered in Gene's ear, "and her couthin Walt . . . and Barret!"

"Let's see what they're doing," Denise encouraged, hurrying ahead.

The twins and Whip didn't hesitate in following her to the ring of kids. The others followed at a calmer, more leisurely pace. It took a moment to squeeze under and around the taller kids but finally the gang made it further into the ring to where they could see Vicky and Walt Langley and Barret Stevens.

There was another kid in the ring who they were obviously teasing. The girl was probably about Gene's age and was probably smaller. Her shoulder-length auburn hair hung in flowing waves from a ponytail that rested comfortably on the back of her head. Her small, rather pretty oval face showed a great deal of defiance. Her chin was pointed and slightly upturned. Her nose was small, and round and her slender eyebrows showed expression and concentration. Her mouth was perfectly shaped but turned down in fury. She was a slender, rather petite girl but the most striking thing about her was the energy and fire in her bright blue eyes.

"You choose the wrong group to annoy Salerno," Barret was saying. "You do realize that I could have easily clobbered you earlier without any difficulty."

The girl raised her eyebrow in defiance and placed her hands on her hips. "That is your opinion, *Stevens*. But I will say this: Mentor Haraus wouldn't . . ."

Right then, Walt let out a rather rude snort through his nose. "Mentor Haraus is a cry-baby, Zara. Besides, she's not here to get us into trouble this time, even if we beat you up. Besides, I don't think we'd get into much trouble with a big-headed lunatic."

That seemed to snap all the tense cords. The fire that was building up in the girl's eyes suddenly flared and she flew across the small space that separated them and doubled into Walt. The boy hadn't expected this assault and was knocked completely off his feet. Zara pinned his arms down on either side of his face, but the strength of the boy was twice her own and before she knew it, he had knocked her off of him and Barret had grabbed her by the shoulders.

Walt rose to his feet and approached Zara who was wiggling under Barret's grip behind her. He drew back his right arm, but by leaning back it made the job all the easier for Zara. She used Barret as a bar and struck Walt square in the chest with her feet, knocking him back again. This extra weight and movement knocked Barret out of balance and he and Zara both tumbled to the ground.

Vicky, seeing that her partners were having trouble, leapt forward and grabbed Zara by the hair. The girl let out a loud howl as Vicky dragged Zara to her feet, allowing Walt and Barret to do the same.

261

Walt tossed his mop of brown hair and lowered his eyebrows at Zara.

"I think you've just about wasted my patience, shorty!"

Whip had been watching the scene from between the legs of a taller boy. He had given up trying to jump to see over the boy's shoulder, so he was half lying, half sitting on the ground, watching the scene from a lower perspective. However, when he saw what else was coming into the scene, he almost wanted to screech.

"Gene, what are you . . ."

Sure enough, Gene had broken from the crowd and was now approaching the scene from the side, keeping his eyes completely on Walt. It was evident that if Gene did anything foolish, he would have a boy twice his size to deal with.

"Hey, guys, what's going on?" Gene inquired in a calm, almost friendly tone.

Barret's eyes grew wide and then narrowed. "You!"

Walt and Zara looked at Barret in confusion. "Who?"

"Mecarnin," Vicky concluded, answering their questions. "What are you doing on our territory?"

Gene glanced down at the wooden platform below his feet and gave Vicky an innocent look. "I thought the society belongs to the whole of Hichester."

"Well you're not one of us, so this isn't your territory," Walt pointed out. "Now scram, shorty."

"I will," Gene replied coolly, "as soon as you let your guest go and, Vicky, would you be so kind as to release her hair?"

When Vicky let Zara go and the little girl tumbled to the platform, the onlookers thought that the three older kids would actually obey Gene. However, what very few people noticed was that Barret had circled around 'til he was almost behind Gene. That way, the boy couldn't see all three of his opponents.

What Gene did see was Walt's fist come around and head toward his face. Gene leaned back, rather than ducking, but this was a mistake. Barret had bent down just behind his legs, so Gene went flying head over heels toward the edge of the platform. His heels weren't even over his head yet when he struck the platform and skidded toward the side. For a moment, everyone thought that he would stop but the skid was a little too smooth and Gene toppled over the side of the platform and disappeared from sight.

Walt brushed his hands off as if satisfied in beating up a boy half his size and half his age. As he turned back around to continue his bullying of Zara, he felt a horrible feeling run through the side of his head. At once his left ear began to throb and he felt his knees buckling underneath him. He glanced up to realize that a figure was standing over him, and after recognizing the person, he felt all of his confidence go out the window.

"I hope that will teach you to pick on someone your own size," Elys Schneider remarked in a firm and obviously furious voice.

Walt slowly nodded but his head hurt too much to talk. As Mrs. Schneider stepped back away from him, Barret and Vicky quickly grabbed Walt by the arms and dragged him off before they suffered the same punishment.

At once, the crowd of kids who had been watching dispersed within seconds. Soon there was only the gang and Mrs. Schneider in front of Benvor Hall.

All the kids had their mouths hanging open, but Whip's eyes were probably wider than his mouth. He had barely seen his grandfather's sister-in-law appear, and she had given Walt a boxing on the ears so fast that all Whip could remember was the ending part.

Mrs. Schneider didn't make eye contact with any of the kids but strode toward the edge of the platform. Kneeling down, she reached over the side and began to pull someone up. As she drew Gene back over the side of the platform, it was evident that he had hit the water. His hair was flat against his face, wet and dripping. He was shivering slightly from the cold water and it looked like he had tried to unzip his coat because one of his wings was sticking out while the other was still safe under his jacket.

"Are you all right?" all the kids asked together.

Gene slowly shrugged and began to wring out his shirt. "I guess . . . but I can say one thing: this is the start of a week that will probably be the worst in history."

Mrs. Schneider stepped over and helped young Zara to her feet. The girl brushed her hair out of her eyes and squared her shoulders. "Thanks for stepping in . . . I don't believe I know you."

Gene smiled and held out his hand toward the girl. "I'm Gene Mecarnin. It's a pleasure to meet you, Zara."

Deke glanced from Zara to Gene. They were both grinning at each other, but the grin on Gene's face wasn't one that Deke recognized. Deke didn't know Zara well enough to know if the girl smiled that brightly at everyone, but the smile on Gene's face was so bright that Deke didn't think he had ever seen that kind of smile on his brother's face before. Especially not recently.

Chapter 35

"Neil, we're back," Deke called as they climbed the stairs.

There was no response. On any other day, Deke would repeat the announcement but from what he had seen that morning: Neil wasn't in the mood to reply.

In fact, he hadn't been in the mood to reply to almost any remark or question for the past two weeks. He would stare at the teacher all day in school and without any farewell, he would walk home while everyone else went to society.

The three passed Neil's room on their way to their own rooms and saw that the door was open. Peering in with curiosity, they found Neil leaning against his pillow on his bed, reading a book.

"How was your day?" he inquired.

It was the same question every day, the start of the same conversation that occurred whenever the three returned from society. It was almost as if Neil had a list of things that he would say and those were the only things you would ever hear out of him.

Usually, Eileen and the boys would quickly tell about the things they learnt in society. Then Neil would inquire about the rest of the gang and the three would update him on that. However, after Neil asked the question, neither Gene nor Deke replied.

It was almost a full five minutes before Neil realized that they hadn't answered him. Glancing up just slightly, he gave them a look that held no interest . . . not even feeling. "Well? How was it?"

Eileen looked down at the two boys beside her just in time to see the two of them exchange hurt looks.

"It could have been better," Deke replied.

Neil had returned to his book but now he looked up to give Deke an agitated, almost confused look. All other days, Deke was full of chatter. Even if Neil had already heard about their day, Deke would carry on for hours. Deke didn't meet Neil's gaze for long but slowly turned from the door and headed down the hall to his own.

Shrugging helplessly, Neil looked back down at his book. "How is everyone?"

Deke was always the one to answer that question first and since he had left, Eileen was about to reply. However, a volcano erupted beside her and something happened that she had never seen before.

Gene's face went a bright crimson; a color that he never turned. His eyes flashed with fury and his small hands clenched into fists until his knuckles turned white.

"Why don't you ask them yourself?" he hissed in a tone that none of them had ever heard. It was like a deep, guttural growl with a tint of a cat-like hiss.

Neil's head snapped up and it was apparent in his face that he was shocked and confused. "Well I didn't . . ."

"No, I know you didn't mean to carry on the exact same conversation every day for the past few weeks," Gene snapped. "And I suppose you didn't mean to leave your whole life in a box and live a half-life and neglect those who care about you the most!"

Neil's mouth flopped open like a box of marbles. Eileen was about to do the same but instead, she bit her lip hard because she knew the exact reason why Gene's cool had just erupted. The boy spun on his heel and bolted down the hallway, rushing into his room. A second later the sound of his door slamming could be heard, and it caused Neil and Eileen to shiver.

"What was that all about?" Neil inquired, looking Eileen directly in the eyes.

Eileen shook her head gently, biting her lower lip. "They have had a really rough time at society. Gene is having trouble flying and Deke cannot transform his feet . . . I'm afraid they're giving up."

Neil shrugged and glanced back down at his book. "Are they expecting me to fix everything for them? It's not like I'm their babysitter."

As he glanced back down at his book, he was expecting Eileen to either leave or reply . . . but she didn't. Stepping into the room, she pulled the door shut behind her with ferocity, causing Neil to look up at her.

The girl who was always shy and barely spoke, hiding her face behind her mane of straight hair, now stood looking directly at him with a look of complete determination. Tossing her long locks of hair behind her shoulders, the girl placed her hands firmly on her hips and pursed her lips together tight.

"No, Neil. They're expecting you to be the brother that you are supposed to be to them! If you're wondering why Deke isn't talking and why Gene lost his patience, I can tell you! It's because you are letting weakness overcome you! This is a time when your brothers need you to be strong, not just for them but for yourself. They are concerned about you and your mental health. The other day,

Deke was just saying how he's afraid your state of depression will lead you to do something foolish or rash. You have been a strong brother their whole lives and that is how they have been able to survive. Even though you pushed them around, ignored them, and bickered with them, they were able to go off of your strength and stubbornness."

Neil looked up at Eileen, puzzled. It had never dawned on him that his brothers even looked up to him, especially with how he sometimes neglected them. Eileen seemed to read his mind and answered the question.

"Gene has stood up to every bully, including yourself, with passiveness because you were never strong for him. You were strong for yourself, but never for him so he had to make his own strength. Just like Deke never got any wisdom that you kept for yourself but had to make his own. Those two boys have been prepared to look up at you for years. Every day they hope that tomorrow will be the day that you start acting more as a role model and example rather than just another person in their life. They don't think of you that way, Neil, but by allowing yourself to be swallowed into depression, it is becoming obvious to them that you really don't care! You don't care if you live in depression your whole life, and you don't care if it affects your brothers because you don't think it will! You have dug so deep into yourself that you don't even realize that whatever you do and however you act affects someone, especially your brothers!"

Neil quickly looked away from Eileen because the fire in her eyes was scaring him. "What are you trying to say, Eileen?"

The girl relaxed her gaze, deciding that she had lectured him enough. "Your brothers need you to be strong, Neil. That is all I can tell you. I most certainly can't tell you how to treat people and how to interact with your brothers, but I will say this: if your brothers' dejection toward you made you feel any remorse, then I advise you think of why it hit you so hard."

Eileen stepped away from the bed and opened the door, stepping halfway out. Just as she was about to leave, she turned to look over her shoulder. "By the way, even though tomorrow is Friday, the boys don't want to come back for dinner. They want to head over to the lake early so they can practice their flying and swimming. The rest of the gang agreed to come along as support. Just to let you know, if you want to join, there is a slot open."

Neil nodded slowly, the look on his face showing almost pain like a dog who had been disciplined for chewing a blanket. "I'll think about it."

* * * * * * * * * *

"Have you heard?" Denise inquired of Gene.

The boy glanced away from the water just long enough to acknowledge the girl. "Heard what? Hey, Deke, try it with your feet in the water."

"The news," Denise pointed out impatiently. "Everyone at school was talking about it."

"Oh, you mean Ivan Olsen? I don't know him, but I've heard he's pretty nice," Gene replied, shielding his eyes against the sun to watch Eileen, Emma and Deke in the water.

Roy nodded from where he, Reed, Oliver, and Whip were sitting on the side of the platform. "Yeah, I heard that he disappeared. It's not the first time though."

Whip raised his eyebrow quizzically. "I never heard about Ivan disappearing before. I thought this was the first time."

"It is," Denise replied. "It's not the first time, though, that someone in Hichester has disappeared. This is actually the third time."

Everyone on the platform, except Gene, nodded, remembering hearing the news. "If I remember correctly," Reed remarked, "they were Cathy Martin, Luke, and Ithabella Walker. I don't think they found them."

Gene cocked his head to the side, sitting down between Roy and Oliver. "They didn't? Does anyone know where they went?"

All heads shook negative. "The funny thing is," Seraphina remarked, "all three of them were members of society . . . for a long time. Cathy should be thirteen in a few weeks . . . Luke turned twelve shortly before he disappeared, and Isabella was ten. The amazing thing about them was that they had been members of society most of their lives and they were exceedingly talented. They were also really good people . . . with really strong characters and full of energy. It doesn't make sense that they would run away."

"Well, we know that Ivan didn't run away," Oliver pointed out. "Nothing was missing except him . . . and the clothes he was wearing."

Presently, the sound of heavy breathing could be heard as the three swimmers approached, wiping water from their faces. Eileen and Emma pulled themselves out of the water and onto the platform beside the others. Deke remained in the water but put his chin and arms on the side of the platform.

"How did that go?" everyone asked together.

Deke shook his head. "I don't get it . . . I mean, swimming is a lot easier now that I can breathe underwater and all, but my sight is still poor and without a fin, I'm not as far as I could be."

Emma shrugged. "I think it's because you have gone so long without thinking you can do it, that you've convinced yourself you can't."

"But how would that affect his transformation?" Whip inquired, leaning over to see past the others.

"By convincing himself he can't do it, he is unable to convince himself and his body that he can. The transformation doesn't happen because we want it to or because we make our bodies change through our minds . . . it works through our souls and our hearts. If Deke has convinced his mind that he can't do it, he'll start to feel the same way in his heart and soul and then he'll never get there."

Whip was leaning so far over that he began to fall into the water. However, Deke reached up with one hand and pressed his two middle fingers against Whip's forehead, stopping his fall. Whip clumsily grabbed the side of the platform and pulled himself back to a sitting position.

Gene considered Emma's wisdom thoughtfully. "Do you think it could be the same case with me?"

At once, Whip and Seraphina smiled. "No, Gene," Seraphina assured him. "Your difficulty is the fact that you still haven't found your balance point. Each aerobeast is different because we are all different in body and in wing. We are also different in how we learn things and how we see things. The advice we are giving you is probably not helpful because our way of flying could be the complete opposite of yours. You just have to find the correct way to look at flight and then you'll get the hang of everything."

"Well I hope you have the correct way at looking at bullies," Roy remarked. "Because it looks like Vicky is coming this way."

All heads turned to look at the far side of the platform. Sure enough, Vicky was trotting toward them.

"Hello there," she remarked, the kindness in her voice tinted with a bit of iciness. "Still having trouble swimming, Deke?"

"Well, I . . ." Deke stammered, not sure what he was to say to that remark. He didn't want to say something that would cause an argument or possibly make him look like a fool.

"I'm having trouble, too," Gene remarked, trying to get the tension off of his brother. "I still cannot turn right or take off from a stand-still."

Vicky raised an eyebrow in amusement, obviously interested that Gene would admit to having problems as well. "Good luck trying to find a balance point."

Seraphina had been glowering at Vicky since she walked up, but now she rose to her feet and glared up at the girl. "I don't think it will help the situation by teasing him, Vicky."

For a moment, Vicky met Seraphina's infuriated glare but then rolled her eyes dramatically. "It's the truth. His balance point is probably dead. It probably died when his brother almost boxed the life out of him."

Seraphina would have gone for Vicky's hair if Oliver and Emma hadn't caught hold of each of her hands and held her back gently. However, Gene had been listening to Vicky's every word with a look of passiveness on his face. Suddenly, his expression changed to that of surprise and sudden realization.

"You know what ... You're right!" he cried, leaping to his feet. "I know what I need to do!"

Chapter 36

The knocking at the front door continued. "Roy, could you get that?" Mrs. Fischer called from the kitchen. "My fingers are covered in flour!"

"Sure, Mom," the boy called, rushing down the stairs from his room.

As he approached the door, Reed poked his head out from the living room. "Who ith it?" he inquired.

Roy rolled his eyes. "Maybe if you had offered to see who it is, I wouldn't have to tell you."

Reed smiled innocently. "Thorry, bro, you got the job."

Grumbling to himself, Roy opened the front door and stepped out just slightly to see who was knocking. He had to step back because Gene was standing almost inches away from the door. The boy grinned at Roy, a look of complete excitement on his face. Over one shoulder he was carrying his knapsack that seemed to be bulging and under his other arm was a parcel wrapped in brown paper.

"Hey, Roy, I hope I didn't catch you at a bad time," Gene apologized.

Roy quickly drew his head back into the house and glanced at the clock on the wall. "It's eight in the morning on Saturday. Unless you're referring to my mom's crazy cooking antics on Saturday, then you're fine. Come on in."

Gene stepped in and Roy closed the door behind him. Reed poked his head out of the living room again and raised his eyebrows in surprise. "Hey, neighbor! What are you doing here tho early?"

Gene gave the boy a lopsided grin and nodded toward the parcel under his arm. "I was wondering if you could do something for me."

"Like what?" both boys asked at the same time.

Gene glanced over his shoulder uncertainly and right away the twins realized what he was worried about. Both grabbed hold of one of his hands and hurriedly pulled him off away from the kitchen door. After about five minutes Gene found himself standing inside the twins' room. He thought Neil's room was untidy. This was beyond untidy.

Cloths were piled in ugly bundles all over the room in the strangest places: on top of their dresser, under the bed, in front of the door, the window sill and so on. Their knapsacks were thrown over their desk chairs and their beds were unmade. From the look of the quilts, it seemed that they had burrowed caves into their beds and then emerged, deciding to use their past cave for the next night.

"So, what did you need from us?" Roy inquired, jumping onto his bed, causing the springs to scream in annoyance.

Pushing the thought of the untidy room out of his mind, Gene reached down to the bundle he carried. Walking slowly over, he made a space between two piles of clothes on the floor and lay the bundle down. Reed knelt down on the other side of the parcel while Roy leaned over the end of his bed to watch.

Gene untied the string around the parcel and began to unfold the brown paper. As he drew the last flap back, the twins leapt back in surprise and shock.

"Where on thith good earth did you get that?" Reed demanded.

Not sure what to make of the long, black wing that lay in the brown paper before them, the two boys kept their distance and merely stared at it in confusion and shock.

"Macaroon was going to toss it," Gene explained. "Then naturally he forgot to close the lid of the can, so a bunch of racoons got into it. They dragged it to the backyard. I thought it best to not bring back up Neil's . . . dilemma."

"What are you going to do with it?" Roy demanded, rather perturbed by the presence of the broken, destroyed wing.

Gene looked up at the two from underneath his eyebrows and the smile on his face faded slightly. "I need you guys to keep it hidden here. I don't want Neil to find it or Phillipa and Cook to find it when they clean the rooms."

"But why?" Reed inquired, raising his voice and then receiving stern glares from the two boys, he lowered his voice. "Why do you want to keep it? Why don't you throw it away?"

Gene looked down at the wing once, then began to wrap it back up in the brown paper. "Because . . . I need answers. There is something about this wing that doesn't add up. Why are the three of us changelings? Why did Neil seemingly fall short? But most importantly, why was his wing broken?"

"Those are all good questions . . ." Roy remarked, pressing his chin into his hands, " . . . what are the answers?"

Gene lowered his eyebrows in impatience but kept the glare in his eyes from spreading to the rest of his face. "I have a feeling that they might be connected to this wing. I need you to keep it until I

278

can find out the answers to my questions. I don't want to destroy the evidence."

Roy and Reed slowly looked at each other, then back at Gene. Reed slowly cleared his throat, causing Gene to arc an eyebrow. "Tho . . . do you want uth to keep thith quiet?"

Gene nodded vigorously. "Most certainly!"

* * * * * * * * * *

Gene was resting his chin on the side of the boat, watching the water slowly ripple past below him. It was late in the afternoon on Tuesday and the whole gang was watching the merbeasts practice swimming. Gene was sitting with Reed, Whip, and Oliver in one of the canoes while Denise, Seraphina and a few other kids sat in another, a good ways across the lake. There were about eight other canoes out with the rest of the aerobeast members and some werebeasts which were scattered about the lake.

The exercise that day was the art of awareness and stealth. The merbeasts had to practice stealth while the aerobeasts and werebeasts worked on awareness. Gene was determined to not let Roy sneak up on him, especially after what had happened the day before. The three boys were almost late for school since they had worked through the night in the Fischer garage on cleaning Neil's wing. To get back at Gene for causing them to miss beating the rest of the gang to school, Roy had almost caused Gene his first heart attack when Gene fell into the water.

Gene's flying was still up in the air, or in better words: in the water. Flying straight was no problem, nor was landing but take-offs and turns were his downfall. Like Emma and Seraphina had explained before, there wasn't much other people could do. Only Gene knew how to control his flying . . . but so far, it seemed that not even Gene knew.

The boy was pulled from his daydreaming by a face that was slowly coming into view below the water surface. Gene quickly leaned over, trying to see who was creeping up on him.

"Hey, Reed," Gene whispered, "I think someone is over here."

Reed, being the one of the two twins who reacted a little hastily, leapt across the canoe to the side where Gene was sitting. Gene was already leaning rather far over the side and with the sudden unbalance and extra weight on Gene's side, the canoe rocked strongly. With a sharp cry of surprise, Gene went tumbling into the water head first and Reed was knocked off of his feet by the movement in the canoe.

All eyes on the lake turned to the canoe that was one person short. Everyone had heard Gene's cry, and some had seen the splash . . . but now the whole lake was enveloped in silence. The water on the lake was like glass . . . not moving or even rippling in the light breeze.

Reed felt the back of his neck burn in embarrassment, for he knew that the headmasters and instructors were on the dock, watching the whole exercise. Suddenly, he felt a handful of water strike his face and he turned to see a figure emerge from the water, dripping and panting.

"I got him!" Gene panted, holding up what looked like a fin.

Gene turned slightly to see if Reed saw, but the horrified looks on his friends caused him to look back at what he had just caught. Glaring at him from beneath a pile of seaweed were two piercing eyes. Gene might be the calmest person toward bullies, but he was no fool in realizing that if he didn't get away from Walt, he was going to have issues.

Letting go of the boy's fin, Gene quickly paddled over to the canoe and began to pull himself over the side. Reed reached down and helped pull the boy in, dripping and shivering. No aerobeast was used to swimming in ice-cold water.

"We need to dry you off," Whip speculated, "before you catch your death. Come on, I'll help you to the apothecary."

Gene raised a wet eyebrow in amusement. "I'm not dying yet, Whip."

The boy tossed his brown hair and grinned at his friend. "After a few seconds of being in that water, your lips are already blue. I'm not going to give you a diagnosis, Gene, but we need to get those wet clothes off of you."

As if in agreement with Whip's point, a shrill whistle blew, indicating the end of the exercise. All the canoes began to turn around and head back to the dock. As Whip and Reed set to the oars, Gene sat at the other end of the canoe, seething in annoyance.

Whip quickly grabbed the edge of the dock and held it still so the others could climb out. Reed was the first out with Gene following closely. Gene was halfway onto the dock when he glanced across the dock where another canoe had pulled up. Without a single word, he leapt onto the dock and hurried off into the crowd.

Whip and Reed exchanged confused looks. Whip shrugged. "Just get him to the apothecary," he remarked. "I'm going to kill him if the fever doesn't already!"

Deke was pulling himself out of the water a little ways down the platform when he saw his brother run around to the other side of the dock. Pausing, half on the dock and half in the water, Deke saw Gene approach one of the canoes and reach a hand down to help someone.

After a second, he saw his brother pull Zara Salerno onto the dock. Deke scratched his wet hair in puzzlement. There was something strange going on. Shaking his head like a damp dog, Deke grasped the side of the platform and pulled most of his upper body over the side. A hand appeared out of nowhere and grasped his wrist.

Deke wasn't able to look up at the person before he was pulled all the way onto the platform. As he brushed his wet bangs out of his eyes, Deke looked up into the face of his older brother.

"Neil . . ." Deke started, not sure whether to smile or just stare, so he did both, "what are you doing here?"

Neil shrugged, thrusting his hands into his coat pockets. "I thought I might come down . . . see how everything was going. Eileen told me that you guys are having some trouble . . . adapting, that is."

Deke nodded, suddenly feeling at ease with his brother. "Yeah . . . I think it's taking a harder toll on Gene. I mean, I'm still able to swim without my tail fin, but I think Gene is starting to give up . . .

especially since he is such good friends with Whip . . . who is much better than he is."

Neil glanced across the dock at where the other society members were beginning to separate into their separate groups and disperse to their different buildings. "What are you guys doing the rest of the day?"

Deke shrugged. "We merbeast members are pretty much done for the day. The werebeasts usually have longer days than the rest of us . . . We were planning on watching the aerobeast members. They have to drag the canoes by ropes to gain strength in their wings. You're more than welcome to join us."

A small smile appeared on Neil's face and the almost distant look in his eyes told Deke that he appreciated the thought.

"Hey, Neil!" a loud voice erupted from across the platform.

The two brothers turned to see Whip and the rest of the gang hurrying toward them. Emma and Whip were the first to reach them, both giving Neil a hard clap on the back.

"How are you doing, man?" Whip inquired. "Good to see you again."

Neil smiled. "You too. Where is Gene?"

Whip tossed his head, nodding behind him. "He's talking with Zara."

Neil leaned over, looking around Whip at where his little brother was chatting with the small girl near the canoes. Smiling to himself, Neil straightened himself out. "I have to say, that interesting stunt in the water was pretty humorous to watch."

All eyes turned to Reed, who quickly cowered behind his twin. "Don't look at me!"

The gang at once broke into series of laughter. Deke looked at Neil, unsure whether his brother would join in but was relieved when he saw a bright grin appear on Neil's face.

The laughter was suddenly interrupted by the sound of loud footsteps and a bright, loud voice: "What do we have here?"

Neil, Deke, and Eileen turned around hastily, not sure who had just approached, but the rest of the gang knew that voice and quietly groaned to themselves. They didn't even have to turn around to know that Vicky was standing there, arms crossed over her chest and an evil look twisted into her eyes and mouth.

Neil felt his face get increasingly warm and his throat dry out. Deke saw this and impulsively stepped closer to his brother, hoping to make his brother feel less out of place. He knew that Neil had a strong liking to Vicky and he also knew that Vicky had a strong liking to bullying which wasn't a good combination.

"How are you, Vicky?" Seraphina inquired in a soft voice.

Neil and Deke glanced back at her for a moment, surprised at the softness in her voice. Vicky raised an eyebrow and rolled her eyes. "I didn't come over here for pleasantries, Schneider. I have an issue to settle with Shorty."

"You mean Gene?" Deke inquired, taking a step closer. "I'm afraid he's busy."

Neil, Whip, and Emma alike were prepared to grab Deke and pull him back, but his sudden stern voice and impulsiveness surprised them. Vicky was equally interested, but then her swarthy flounce quickly returned.

"Sorry pip-squeak but 'busy' isn't in my vocabulary and I will talk with Shorty, now, or I'll have to deal it out with you," she remarked, lowering her eyebrows angrily at Deke and taking a step closer to the boy.

The gang was watching the tall girl and the small boy in frozen worry, but this was doubled when Eileen stepped out of the group and placed herself beside Deke. Placing a hand on Deke's shoulder, she gently pushed him back toward the gang.

"Absolutely, Vicky. I'm sure Gene would love to have a pleasant conversation with you," Eileen remarked, brushing her dark hair out of her face (something she never did).

Vicky sized Eileen up and down. Tall and slender, the girls were not much different except Vicky was slightly taller and probably stronger than the delicate, almost fragile Eileen.

"I will not waste my time being delayed by a pip-squeak and a lily-livered orphan," Vicky snapped. "Now scram, or I'll . . ."

"Or what Vicky?" a strong voice snapped.

Everyone turned to look at the strong voice that had erupted to see Gene standing probably an arms-length from Whip who was trying desperately to get his friend's attention.

A smug look appeared on Vicky's face, obviously pleased that she finally had her adversary before her. This look didn't last long because Gene slammed his knapsack on the ground and began to approach the girl, an almost dangerous look on his face.

None of the kids had ever seen a furious look on Gene's face like that before and it scared them. His eyebrows were down almost in a "V," his blue eyes glittered with fury, and his mouth was twisted into a disgusted scowl.

"This is a new low, Vicky," Gene remarked. "Even for you."

Eileen felt a strange impulse to step out of the way, making room for Gene to stand in front of Vicky. It was a strange scene, watching such a tall girl look down in confusion at a boy half her size and half her age.

"So instead of beating up girls," Gene continued. "You've now resorted to criticizing people your size and belittling boys who deserve better."

"You have nothing over me," Vicky retorted, unsure of how she was to stand her ground. "I am a very nice person, so there is nothing wrong with my teaching some people a few lessons."

Gene allowed a smile to appear on his face as he ran his hand through his wet, blond hair. "Impressive . . . But I fail to see the truth in any of that."

Deke reached over and took Neil's hand with worry. Neil looked over at Deke, confusion and fear evident in his own eyes. They never ever heard Gene debate with someone, let alone a girl who could easily beat him up.

Vicky seemed also equally surprised but tried to hide her confusion. "Prove it."

Gene glanced over at the gang for a moment, considering what to say. Turning back around, he looked Vicky directly in the eye which caused the girl to feel fidgety.

"If you had the job of deciding the fate of someone who had just committed a murder, what would you do?" he inquired.

This was the last thing Vicky expected but decided that waiting too long to answer would make things worse. "I would choose a just punishment. If the murderer killed the other person while defending himself, I wouldn't make the sentence as harsh but if he murdered the person for the wrong reasons, I would sentence him to a series of years in prison . . ."

Gene nodded, a soft smile appearing on his face. That was exactly what he wanted to hear. He was glad that Vicky had good in her. If she didn't, he would worry that she was following a path that she could never escape from. However, this glimpse of justice in her was a relief.

"Now I have another question. Say this person murdered the victim for the wrong reasons, but during trial he said that he should be pardoned since he is a doctor, he volunteers, and helps the poor. What would you do?"

Vicky looked over Gene's head at the rest of the gang. They were watching her expectantly, but she didn't know what to say. Shrugging, she shook her head. "That doesn't sound just . . . even if he did volunteer and help the poor . . . that has nothing to do with the bad things he did."

Before the words were barely out of her mouth, Gene slapped his hands together hard, causing the girl to jump. "Exactly! Now if I remember correctly, not two minutes ago you said . . . and I quote: 'I am a very nice person, so there is nothing wrong with my teaching some people a few lessons,'" Gene explained. "You just proved yourself wrong. The good things we do in our lives don't excuse the bad things we do. We cannot excuse evil because evil might have some goodness to it. The only way we can convince ourselves that we are being just and fair is simply knowing that it was wrong."

Vicky stared down at the boy, too speechless to say anything. She didn't even dare to look at the gang but slowly stepped away and left the quickest way she could. When she was gone, Deke raced over to his brother and grabbed him by the shoulders.

"How did you do that?" he demanded.

Gene shook his head. "Do what?"

"You just showed Vicky the thing that everyone has been trying to show her for three years!" Whip replied, hurrying over to join the two boys.

Gene shrugged innocently. "It's not impossible. Everyone has goodness in them and because we are changelings, we are supposed to have an even stronger understanding of goodness. I knew that if I could tap into Vicky's goodness, I could show where she had tripped. There is always a light, even in the darkest place."

Chapter 37

The next two weeks were truly miraculous, or so it seemed to the headmasters. For three full days, the whole gang showed Neil around and introduced him to everyone they knew. Then during lunch while everyone was eating, Neil would go around and make friends with all the other kids. Sometimes he wasn't welcome at some tables but there were quite a few kids who welcomed Neil at their table and soon everyone caught on to how well Neil could carry on a conversation and before they knew it, there was more talking in the refectory than before.

Neil was present during every exercise, especially the ones concerning the merbeast and aerobeast members. He would watch the students constantly in dead silence and take notes on everything that happened. During break hours and even after everyone left the society for the evening, Neil would stay with Deke and help his brother on his transformation.

Deke was beginning to lose hope, but Neil soon discovered the issue. Due to the fact that Deke was a sailfish, his tailfin would thus beat horizontally rather than vertically like a dolphin's. Because of this, Deke's feet needed to be on top of each other rather than side by side.

Even after figuring this out, Deke couldn't quite get his feet to transform so Neil spent a good hour each day convincing Deke that he was capable of doing it. Just like Emma and Seraphina had supposed, Deke had almost convinced himself that he couldn't do it, so Neil had a tough time teaching him otherwise.

Once Deke mastered his transformation, his progress in the society sped up but there was a considerably noticeable tension with Gene. It was obvious that he was getting disheartened with his failure.

Neil was the first to notice this, so he decided it was about time to act. He chose the perfect moment while he and Gene were having a leisurely morning in the library. Deke had left as soon as the twins brought the newspaper (Ivan was the usual paper boy but now that he was indisposed, Roy and Reed had the job).

"Gene," Neil remarked. "Could I ask you something?"

Gene glanced up from the book he was reading. "Sure Neil . . . what's on your mind?"

Neil leaned forward. "Why have you never fought back . . . I mean when you're being bullied and stuff . . . why have you just let them beat you up and never fought back?"

Gene furrowed his brow but tried to concentrate on his book. "Mostly because I think I get hurt less that way . . . but also because I don't know how to fight back."

Gene had hoped that would answer Neil's question but the silence that followed his reply was only minor for Neil lifted him to his feet and planted him squarely in front of him. "Then I'll teach you."

"But . . ." Gene started. "Do you think this is a good idea?"

"Why wouldn't it be?" Neil inquired. "You'll be able to defend yourself if anyone was to bully you again."

"I could always use Deke as a shield," Gene retorted.

Neil gave his brother an amused look and grinned. "That is an option . . . by the way, where is Deke?"

"He said he had to talk to Oliver about something."

The kids had been let out earlier the day before due to fall break beginning. They had a full week off from school which was a blessing in disguise, but society would also be closed for a few days starting the next day.

"Funny," Neil remarked. "I wonder what it was about. Now let's concentrate. The most important trait when fighting is to be aware and to try and avoid as many hits as possible. That way you last longer."

Gene lowered his eyebrows, trying to look unamused. "It doesn't look like I'm going to last long anyway."

"Come on bro, you've got this," Neil retorted, grasping the top of Gene's head by the hair and shaking his head as if trying to knock the negativity out of his brother. "Now concentrate. If you cannot get out of being punched, you lift your arm to block the strike."

He reached over and grabbing his brother's wrist, he lifted his arm up to demonstrate. "Now you have to be careful because they might come around for a side swipe, so you have to be quick and give them a good hit in the stomach."

Gene looked up at his brother, then down at where Neil was guiding his hand to demonstrate. "Is fighting always this complicated?"

Neil shrugged. "Sometimes . . . why?"

"Now I know why I never learned how to fight before now."

*　*　*　*　*　*　*　*　*　*　*

"Now don't lose your nerve today," Neil whispered. "This is the last day before society is closed and we won't be able to practice out here."

"Well if I happen to get wet today, you had better have a good excuse," Gene remarked.

Neil smiled mischievously. "I don't, which is why you had better not get wet."

Gene rolled his eyes and removed his jacket. "This had better be worth coming out here an hour before society starts. The twins aren't even here!"

Neil climbed into one of the canoes and began to push off. "Don't be such a baby. You'll do fine."

Gene watched as Neil pushed off of the shore with one of the oars and paddled into the center of the lake. 'Be calm and relax' Neil had told him at least three times that morning. Taking in several deep breaths, Gene began to warm up his wings.

"Okay, Gene," Neil called from the canoe, "let's start with the takeoff. Take three more steps away from the water."

Gene glanced over his shoulder as he stepped back. When he was almost five yards from the edge, he stopped and looked back at Neil.

"Now try doing a stand-still takeoff there," Neil hollered.

Gene braced his legs, lifted his wings so they were slightly above his head then leapt into the air. He began to flap his wings frantically in an attempt to build altitude, but it was as if he didn't have wings

293

and he struck the ground, three feet closer to the water.

"Okay," Neil called. "Try this: when you are about to take off, relax your whole body as if you're about to just fall off a cliff. Crouch close to the ground so that your hand can touch the ground. Then, lift your wings as high as they can go."

With nothing else to do but obey, Gene crouched low to the ground, reaching down to make sure he could touch the ground with his hand. Taking in a deep breath, he relaxed his body and lifted his wings so that they were almost perfectly vertical.

"Now, when you take off, use just one strong powerful flap and then keep your wings close to your body so that you're streamlined. Don't do more flaps than that. Also, when you jump, try to use your legs more," Neil called, cupping his hands around his mouth so Gene would hear him.

Gene looked down at his feet, shifting them slightly so that they were further apart. He was just doing that when Neil called again, "No, keep your legs close together. The closer they are together, the more they'll work like a spring. If they're too far apart they won't give you enough leverage."

Shrugging, Gene moved his feet closer together and closed his eyes. He checked his feet, his hand and his wings before letting out all of his air. Saying a quick prayer in his mind, he leapt into the air. His wings flapped down with a strong powerful stroke that made Gene feel like something had erupted. He curled his wings close around his body and kept his feet close together.

When he had entered the air, he had closed his eyes, afraid that he would strike the ground or water. However, that never happened. He felt himself suddenly begin to plummet and naturally, he opened his wings to stop his fall. His fall stopped, and he began to hover. This was strange because all the other times he had tried, he had been too low for his wings to hover.

Opening his eyes, he glanced down and almost cried out. The water was far below him and Neil was barely visible. He could almost not see Neil's eyes. Neil was grinning up at him, waving wildly.

"You did it!" he hollered. "You did it, Gene!"

Gene smiled and waved back. "I guess I did."

Neil sat back down so as to not rock the canoe. "Now let's work on that roll turn. I think you're curling your wing in too close. This time do not move your wings! Move your feet! Try raising your right foot and lowering your left."

Cocking his head to the side, Gene glanced back at his feet. Slowly he lifted his right foot and lowered his left. All at once, he spun around to the left. He would have been turning left for ever if he hadn't leveled out his feet and he stopped turning.

Glancing down at Neil in the water, Gene smiled. "My feet! How did you figure out that it wasn't my wings?"

Neil shrugged but it was barely visible to Gene. "I was reading about birds when I was . . . you know, depressed. Well, apparently, their wings only change their altitude, not their steering. Their tails do that."

These words were barely out before a voice called from the platform in front of the hall of organization. "Neil! Gene!"

The two boys turned to see Deke, Oliver, Whip, Seraphina and Eileen standing there. The looks on their faces spoke volumes of worry.

"What happened?" Neil called.

"Ivan has returned home," Whip called. "So have Cathy, Luke, and Isabella . . ."

"That is great!" Gene hollered.

When Gene's enthusiasm was met with looks of worry, the smile faded from Neil and Gene's faces.

"They've returned," Whip continued, "half dead."

Chapter 38

"Half dead?" Denise demanded. "Did they say where they had been?"

"You don't seem to understand," Eileen retorted. "They were found on the doorsteps of their houses ... seemingly drained of all life. They weren't starved or dehydrated ... but ... depleted."

"That doesn't seem right," Gene remarked. "Were they able to talk when they were found?"

Everyone shook their heads. "Livonia says that there is a pretty poor chance that they'll survive."

"How sad," Seraphina remarked in a low voice. "I wish we could find out what happened to them."

Neil looked around the group of friends as they sat on the edge of the platform. He thought he saw Deke and Oliver exchange knowing looks and at once he brought it to attention.

"Is there something you two want to tell us?"

Deke shifted nervously on the edge of the platform. "Actually ... we do know something about what happened to them."

Immediately Deke had everyone's attention. "Oliver and I noticed a strange article in the newspaper last week that really caught our attention. It was a report about how some mad-man had escaped from jail and was on the loose in Gerhenia. Now that isn't what caught our attention. Halfway through the article it said how the man had been arrested due to being part of a ring of men who are trying to create a war-weapon. The authorities have been trying to capture the ring for a long time but every time they do, the guys escape."

"Tho, what?" Reed insisted. "That hath nothing to do with Ivan and the otherth."

"Actually, it does," Oliver interrupted. "Deke noticed the next day that there was another article on the subject on how the man had been questioned about the machine and that he had revealed when they had finished the machine."

The gang felt that whatever they were going to hear was something possibly frightening so they braced themselves as Deke spoke. "May third this year."

Whip furrowed his brow in confusion. "What might be special about that date?"

"It was the day before Luke and Isabella were kidnapped. Two months before Cathy was kidnapped," Deke replied. "Don't you see a kind of rhythm here?"

Everyone slowly shook their heads, so Deke continued. "Don't you think it's strange that every two months, someone here in Hichester has disappeared . . . on the same day of the month? Luke and Isabella were kidnapped May fourth, Cathy was taken July fourth and now Ivan disappeared October fourth!"

"Deke," Gene began. "Are you going to say what I think you are?"

Deke shrugged. "That depends on what you're thinking."

"I think I'm thinking what you're thinking because I know I'm thinking what you're thinking about," Gene replied, not waiting for anyone to think on that. "You're saying that Luke, Ivan, Cathy, and Isabella were kidnapped . . . because of the weapon?"

"But they aren't responsible," Seraphina objected. "None of us even knew about it!"

Oliver shook his head. "They weren't taken *because* of the weapon . . . but *for* the weapon."

Deke nodded in agreement. "For the past week, Oliver and I have been keeping close attention to the newspaper and in yesterday's paper, there was an article about how the man that escaped was interrogated. According to the paper, he mentioned that the weapon was only missing it's 'batteries' and when he was asked how many . . . he said five."

"Five batteries?" Roy demanded. "That isn't even enough to charge a car, let alone a war machine."

"That's what we thought," Deke replied. "But then we also noticed that the man had said that the weapon would be functional December fourth."

Whip's eyes grew wide. "Okay that is a little weird . . ."

Denise leaned forward, furrowing her eyebrows in concentration. "But wait . . . December fourth would be exactly two months after Ivan's disappearance . . . and December fourth is in two weeks!"

Deke and Oliver nodded together, long and slow. "And if there is something strange about that . . . someone might disappear December fourth and that would be the fifth person to disappear from Hichester District."

Everyone waited for a moment, trying to think of what Deke and Oliver were trying to say. Gene was the first to realize and almost knocked the twins into the water. "The fifth person . . . The fifth battery . . .

they aren't using batteries to charge the machine . . . they're using people!"

"Changelings none-the-less," Roy remarked. "But that means . . ."

"That meanth any one of uth ith the next victim!" Reed hollered.

Whip and Gene both clapped a hand over his mouth so that no one would hear him. People were beginning to arrive at the society for the last evening of society before break and they didn't want everyone to know.

"What are we going to do?" Seraphina whispered.

"There is nothing we can do," Deke replied. "I heard from Livonia that the police are going to investigate the grounds for clues that the four might have left before they disappeared."

Whip shivered. "And it's perfect that this all has to happen tonight while my parents are gone to visit Rodge!"

"Well you can spend the night with us," Neil quickly offered before his brothers could do the same. "The twins and Oliver were already coming over."

The boy and Seraphina smiled happily. "Thank you for inviting us . . . that sounds great!"

"Why don't you all come over?" Eileen inquired, speaking up for the first time. "Denise, you too! We can even get Emma over."

"I don't know about Emma," Oliver replied. "She is a little behind in her schoolwork, so she might have to skip this time."

* * * * * * * * * * *

301

Considering what the kids had been talking about the whole day, you would have thought that they would be busy chatting quietly when they arrived at the Wetherby house . . . they weren't. Mr. Wetherby was sitting in his office, the door open when he heard the front door of the house open . . . followed closely by a torrent of loud chattering and calling.

For a moment, he thought that the whole of Hichester was in his front hallway. However, when he poked his head out of the door, he could see that it was just the boys and the rest of the gang, trying to carry their school knapsacks and duffle bags down the hallway. Naturally, the kids tried to carry on a conversation with each other as they headed down the hallway and up the stairs . . . but even after ten minutes of getting seriously stuck, they didn't realize that the hallway wasn't built to fit a handful of kids with duffle bags trying to squeeze close together.

"Neil," Deke hollered. "You guys are blocking the way!"

Neil glared at his brother over his shoulder. "In case you hadn't noticed professor . . . we're kinda stuck!"

True enough, Neil, Whip and Seraphina were stuck tight at the bottom of the stairs. The strap of Whip's duffle bag was caught on Neil's jacket buttons and while trying to get it untangled, Whip had dropped his knapsack without realizing that the button on his bag had gotten tangled with his sister's hair.

Gene was standing in the back with Oliver and Eileen, watching his eldest brother and best friend trying to get untangled. Deke, Denise and the twins were not much better for when Neil and Whip got tangled up, all four moved to help but their shoulders wouldn't allow four people to move at once.

Dropping his knapsack on the floor, Gene got down on his hands and knees, crawling between Roy's legs to the other side of the first jam. Realizing that he was the only thing between the front tangle and the back tangle, Gene had a moment of regret and doubt. However, Seraphina was now hollering because Whip was trying to pull the knapsack button out of her hair.

Hurrying over, Gene began to help the three out while trying to talk some sense into the others. "Deke! You and Denise step back and let the twins out first!"

The four began to follow this suggestion but Reed let out a girl-like squeal. "We're thtuck! My bag ith tangled up with Roy'th!"

"And Deke got his hand tangled in my hair," Denise screamed. "Gene, we need you back here!"

Gene glanced over his shoulder and sighed. "Oh, come on! Try to figure it out! I have to help Seraphina before she kills her brother!"

"But I'm not the one in her hair," Whip complained.

"I know that, Whip," Gene pointed out. "The button is in her hair, and Oliver is in the hallway . . . ah, can you wait a minute? Oliver! Can you get the twins untangled?"

Oliver had just stepped over when a familiar sound erupted from down the hallway. Everyone froze at the sound and listened to the steady ring of the doorbell.

Naturally, Gene, Deke, and Neil fought over who got to the door first but this time it only caused more mayhem. When Neil tried to hurry back down the hallway to get the door, he stumbled over Gene and pulled Whip and Seraphina down with him. Roy and Reed had just broken free of their tangle but were right in the way of Whip's fall. The three boys went down like a trail of dominoes and struck Denise and Deke who were trying to get to the doorbell as well.

Oliver stood there, watching this whole eruption with a calm, sincere look on his freckled face. Using one finger he brushed his spectacles further back onto his nose and considered the mess. "I'll get the door."

The pile of kids watched as the tall boy walked to the front door and opened it. At first, he opened it just a crack so that he could see out; then seeing who it was, he opened it wider. There stood Destiny and Silver.

"Hi, girls," Oliver remarked.

Destiny quickly returned the welcome and poked her head inside. "Have any of you seen Emma?"

Several heads popped up to look at the visitors. "No, Destiny . . . didn't she go home after Society?" Deke inquired. "We saw her head home . . ."

Destiny shook her head with determination. "She never came home. I went back to society to ask Livonia, but she said that no one was there. I called at all the houses who know Emma . . . she isn't around."

"But it's not even December fourth," Whip began to mutter to himself.

He wasn't able to speak this louder for Gene quickly pushed down on his friend's head, muffling his words. "We'll help you find her, Destiny."

With Silver and Destiny's help, they were able to untangle everyone and leave the knapsacks and duffle bags piled neatly at the end of the stairs. Once outside, the kids suddenly realized how cold it was and pulled on their jackets.

"Now," Destiny started, "I think we need to split up into groups of two and ask at every house . . . every building."

Everyone nodded in agreement. That sounded like a reasonable idea since it was getting dark and no one wanted to be by themselves out in the dark.

Soon, Neil and Roy were paired up, going west. Gene and Seraphina were heading east, Reed and Oliver were going north, and Destiny and Denise were bearing south. Whip and Deke decided to take the river while Eileen and Silver took the society.

It was getting dark by the time that they were thirty minutes into their search. Gene and Seraphina were beginning to jump at the movement of the shadows. Whenever they saw the lights of a house, they made a beeline for it and tried to take their time leaving the safety of the lit porches.

On one such occasion, they had just left one house with no luck and the sun was now completely gone. They had their arms looped together so as to not lose each other in the dark but this only showed each other that they were both shivering, not from the cold but from fear.

"How many more houses do we have?" Gene whispered.

"One more," Seraphina replied. "If we cannot find Emma there, we'll have to hurry back to your house. Hopefully the others had better luck than we have."

A pale light began to appear and at once the two began to relax, though their pace didn't relax but quickened. They were barely a throw's distance from the front porch of the house when a large figure leapt out of the darkness and touched Seraphina's shoulder.

The girl let out a sharp scream and jumped clear out of her skin. Gene thought that his heart would stop beating but luckily, he was able to make out the person's features in the pale light.

"Golly, Eileen . . . you scared us!" he panted. "Silver, why didn't you stop Eileen from scaring us?"

Silver shrugged and shook her head. "Don't look at me. If Eileen has her mind set on something, there is no way I can stop her."

"Did you have any luck at the society?" Gene inquired while trying to calm Seraphina down.

The two girls shook their heads. "It was like a tomb! Unless Emma has a key to any of the locked buildings, she's not there. How about you?"

"We just have to check this house before we meet back with the others," Gene replied.

"We were going to before you scared us out of a week's sleep," Seraphina replied in a harsh voice. "Honestly."

Silver didn't reply to this but turned her head slightly as if listening. She ran her foot back and forth on the brick road, then glanced back up at the others. "You do realize that we're standing outside your house Seraphina?"

Seraphina's face at once showed surprise, but of course Silver couldn't see that, so she quickly composed herself. "Of course I did. I'm not as bad as the twins! They couldn't recognize their house in daylight!"

"Then how do they make it home?" Gene and Eileen asked in unison.

Seraphina looked at the two in distress, obviously trying to get out of where she found herself. "Let's just go check. Emma might have dropped by to see my mom."

"I thought you said they were away visiting Rodge," Gene pointed out.

"Well . . ." Seraphina started. "They must have not left yet . . . or the light wouldn't be on . . . right?"

The other three shrugged, deciding that obviously someone must be home. Heading up the porch steps, Seraphina rang the bell briskly.

There was a long wait while the four waited with stomping feet on the front porch. Presently, the porch lights were flicked on and the door opened wide. The kids had to look far up at the tall figure that stood in the doorway, taking up most of the doorway itself.

"Rodge!?" Seraphina cried. "What are you doing here?"

Her brother gave her a sidelong grin, rustling his dark brown almost black hair. "I was about to ask the same of you Seraphina. Mom said that you and Whip were over at Mr. Wetherby's for a sleepover."

Seraphina nodded. "That's right . . . but you still haven't answered my first question."

"Oh," Rodge remarked. "Well I decided to surprise Mom and Dad by meeting them in Break

307

Neck instead of having them come all the way up to Gerh. I'll be here for about five days . . . but what are you guys doing out so late?"

"We're looking for Emma," Silver explained. "We cannot find her anywhere and she never returned home from society."

Rodge raised one of his dark bushy eyebrows in perplexity. "But Emma never goes somewhere without telling someone . . . are you sure she didn't leave a note or something?"

The four shook their heads. "We have been high and low on this road," Gene replied. "We're hoping that the rest of the gang found some clue . . . we were wondering if she dropped by here?"

Rodge shook his head. "Sorry, little man . . . I haven't seen Emma, and no one has been here . . . other than you guys."

Seraphina pursed her lips in thought. "This doesn't look too good . . ."

The other three nodded in agreement. "Maybe she returned home while we were gone," Eileen suggested. "We should check on our way back."

Presently, Rodge reached back into the house and flicked a switch, causing more porch lights to turn on. Stepping out of the house and closing the door behind him, he peered at the four kids.

"I don't believe I've met you two," he remarked, looking from Gene to Eileen.

"Oh, these are our new friends," Seraphina explained. "This is Gene Mecarnin . . . he and his brothers just recently moved in with Mr. Wetherby. This is Eileen Gerasimov, a friend of ours who is also new to Hichester."

Rodge reached down and shook Gene's hand heartily. Gene grinned up at the tall man in admiration. Rodge then turned to Eileen and held out his hand in greeting. Eileen shyly reached out and shook it. Instead of pumping her hand like he had for Gene, Rodge shook her hand gently and smiled down at her.

Eileen looked up from behind her mane and smiled back. Seraphina was busy racking her brain for ideas of where to look for Emma, so she didn't see the exchange between Eileen and Rodge. Gene did though, and he believed that Silver did too . . . or she at least heard or felt the change of attitude in the atmosphere.

As soon as Eileen smiled up at Rodge, the young man's face completely changed. He stared down at the girl, not wide-eyed but almost surprised. Eileen was looking up at the older boy with equal amazement and curiosity. Gene had no idea what the two were thinking but obviously they were thinking the same thing.

"Hey, Tchaikovsky," Seraphina remarked out of the blue, breaking the silent exchange. "Keep an eye out for Emma, would you? We have to head back."

Rodge nodded, grinning at his sister. "Will do. And stay out of trouble."

"That would better serve directed toward Whip," Gene pointed out.

The older boy grinned at that observation and nodded in agreement. "Probably. Be sure to carry it on."

309

Chapter 39

Neil was leaning against the brick wall, watching for the others to return. Destiny and Denise had returned with absolutely no luck just shortly after Neil and Roy had returned. Not long afterwards, Reed and Oliver had returned with nothing that had any form of a lead. They were now waiting for Gene, Seraphina, Whip, Deke, Silver and Eileen to return.

The dark-haired boy had grown tired of watching Roy testing to make sure he was just a smidge taller than his twin while Oliver just watched the two silently. If Oliver wasn't so quiet, Neil guessed he would have commented on the fact that it didn't matter if Roy was taller than Reed because Oliver definitely towered over both without effort.

Neil reached to his belt and pulled out the torch that he had obtained from Macaroon. He shined it down the left-hand street, and seeing nothing, he shined it down the opposite side of the street. At once he was greeted by protests from several voices.

"Turn that spotlight off," Whip called. "Are you trying to land a plane or something?"

Neil quickly turned the torch off and stuck it in his pocket. "Sorry . . . I was just checking who it was."

"Well it was us," Deke objected. "Any luck?"

Neil shook his head. "We were waiting for you guys . . ."

The group shook their heads. "Not a thing."

Silver quickly appeared from the back of the group. "We even checked back home on our way back . . . she's not anywhere!"

Gene saw Whip take in a breath to comment on Silver's form of grammar but after Gene gave Whip a meaningful sock in the stomach, Whip stopped.

"What does Oliver think?" Seraphina inquired.

Neil arced an eyebrow in confusion. "Oliver . . ."

"We all agreed on our way back," Reed explained. "We are pretty thure that Emma wath taken . . . but Oliver hath to give the final thay."

"Why Oliver?" Neil inquired.

"Because he is the oldest . . . By three months," Gene pointed out, choosing his last words carefully."

Neil rolled his eyes to heaven and stepped back. "Oh fine! Let's ask Oliver."

* * * * * * * * * * *

Phillipa found the kids in the library, all spread out at different parts of the room. None of them were talking . . . they were all staring off into space with depressed and worried looks on their faces.

The girl quietly slipped into the room and set a tray of cookies down on the center table, hoping that it would cheer the kids up some. When she saw none of the kids move, she sighed deeply and thought of something to say.

"Maybe she went to Break Neck Creek," she suggested.

Seraphina shook her head. "Emma would never go that far without asking first."

Phillipa nodded and glanced around at the other kids. "Where are Silver and Destiny?"

"They had to go home," Whip replied. "They needed to let their parents know that Emma wasn't found."

The tall girl decided that she had stayed long enough and began to turn toward the door. She paused with her hand on the doorknob. A sudden thought came to her mind, so she turned to look at the kids.

"Mr. Wetherby says that the police are going to search the society tomorrow for clues," she remarked.

Neil scoffed, barely lifting his eyes. "Good luck with that!"

"They won't even be able to check the girls' bathroom," Denise pointed out. "And since none of them are aerobeasts or merbeasts, they won't be able to check the aquarium and flight exits."

Gene lifted his head quickly and looked across the room at the girl. "Flight exits?"

Denise nodded. "Once you reach your third semester in society, you are allowed to use special exits high on the roofs of the buildings. However, only aerobeasts can reach those exits."

"It's a pity the society will be closed for five days," Roy groaned. "Or we could go and investigate."

At that suggestion, Neil, Deke and Gene looked up at each other and realized that they had all thought the same thing. However, there was the issue that Mr. Wetherby wouldn't allow it.

"Oliver," Deke remarked, getting everyone's attention. "How good are you at chess?"

Oliver looked up from the book he had been reading with no change in his expression. "Okay . . . Why?"

A smile appeared on all three boys but the only one who understood the smile was Denise. "Now wait a minute," she remarked sharply, standing up. "If you three are cooking up some sort of mischief, I am not going to have anything to do with it!"

"Oh, come on Denise," Neil remarked. "It's not that bad! Oliver can distract Mr. Wetherby long enough for us to sneak out without him hearing us."

"And what exactly are we going to do when we 'sneak out'?" Whip demanded.

For the next five minutes, the three boys explained their 'bullet-proof' plan (Which was what Neil called it, though if he had let Denise speak, she would have called it 'life-proof'). When they finished, half of the group nodded in agreement while the other half shook their heads in uncertainty.

"What do you think Phillipa?" Gene inquired. "You've been watching us quietly . . . do you think it will work?"

The tall girl slowly stepped over and sat down on the couch next to Seraphina. "Honestly . . . It sounds fine except for the part about breaking into the society. What if you're caught? You will all get expelled for breaking the most important rule."

There was a momentary silence while the group considered this observation.

"Well how about this?" Eileen suggested. "We get as many of the society members as we can and have them help. If we explain everything to them, they will probably agree. If we get a majority of the members to help us, then if we're caught, we won't get expelled."

"There is nothing stopping the council and headmasters expelling all of us," Deke pointed out.

Eileen shook her head, indicating that she hadn't finished. "They won't expel the majority of the society members! That would cause a great deal of issues. If anything, they will suspend us or something, but they won't expel 99% of the school, especially if they know the reason why we broke in."

"How are we going to sneak out the front door without Mr. Wetherby seeing us through the window in his office?" Roy inquired. "You do realize that it faces the front gate."

Gene reached over and stuffed a cookie far back into his mouth, so his next words sounded muffled. "Who said anything about going out the front door?"

Huge grins quickly spread over Whip and the twins' faces. Denise leapt up from her seat and shook her head vigorously, tossing curls everywhere. "That does it! There is no way you are going to convince me to do this!"

If Denise knew what the three boys decided to have her do, she would have stayed silent. After about five minutes of fool-proofing the plan, the kids hurried up to Neil's room while Oliver went to engage Mr. Wetherby in a chess game. They decided to leave by Neil's room because it was the only one that descended down into the back yard. They would then climb over the brick wall into the small stretch of trees that separated the wall from the houses on the next street.

Denise peeked over the side of the sill at the ground. It seemed so far away. "I don't know about this, guys."

Deke gave a large thumbs up to her from inside the room. "You'll do fine! If Seraphina and Whip can't get you down, Gene will be below to catch you."

"That makes me feel much better," Denise mused aloud.

"Just get going," Roy hissed. "We need to get down before Oliver finishes the first game and loses Mr. Wetherby's attention."

Sighing deeply, Denise slipped her feet out of the window and sat on the sill. Grasping the frame of the window, she began to slowly lower herself out of the window. Seraphina and Whip, who had been flying nearby, flew over and held out their hands for support.

Denise reached over with both hands, allowing the two to grasp underneath her armpits. Slipping completely off the sill, she felt a surge of fear as her body hung with her arms being the only thing holding her to the two fliers.

Seraphina and Whip made a quick but smooth decent to the ground and let Denise go. Once on the ground, Denise felt much more relaxed and assured while watching the two carry down Eileen and Neil.

The twins were slightly rustier, and Gene had to help by flying directly underneath the two boys just in case. Finally, everyone was down, and Gene locked the window from the outside before joining his buddies on the ground.

The world around them was dark and unwelcoming. The eerie silence was unnerving, and the kids jumped at every unusual sound.

Making their way quietly across the yard to the back of the brick wall, the kids began to assess where they would split up. They decided that it would be best if they used the pairings they had used earlier when looking for Emma and they would search the same streets. However, this time they would only knock at the houses where members of the society lived, pretending to be still looking for Emma as a way to keep suspicion down.

When they approached the wall, they realized it would be some job getting everyone onto the other side. The gate was surrounded by flower beds but fearing that they would leave prints or trample some of Cook's flowerbeds, they chose the part of the wall that was lined with bushes.

Neil carefully found a space that was large enough where he could stand and bend over slightly. Eileen, being the tallest of the group (besides Emma and Oliver) climbed onto his back and grasped the top of the wall. Neil stood up slowly, giving Eileen extra leverage to climb onto the top of the wall.

"All right send up the first one," Eileen whispered. "But make it quick and quiet ... the moon is just about to come out from behind that cloud and we'll be flooded in light."

Deke quickly climbed onto his brother's back and Eileen grasped his elbow, pulling him up. When he reached the top, Deke slowly turned around, so his lower body was dangling over the other side. Taking a quick look at the other side of the wall, he let go.

When he struck the ground, it wasn't as bad as he thought. The wall was only about ten feet tall at the most and by holding onto the top of the wall with his hands before dropping, it wasn't more than a five-foot drop. However, Deke felt much more pain when Roy landed on top of him, having not looked before he leaped.

Eileen constantly checked the sky, watching the moon as it slowly began to appear from behind the cloud. The only one who knew they were leaving was Phillipa so if Macaroon or Cook saw them, they would report it to Mr. Wetherby.

"Hurry, Neil," Eileen whispered. "The moon is almost out."

Meanwhile inside, Oliver and Mr. Wetherby were concentrating on a serious game of chess. Oliver kept his ears sharply tuned for the possible sounds of the others leaving, hoping that he would have time to distract Mr. Wetherby.

"Oh man," Mr. Wetherby remarked, causing Oliver to jump. "I spilt milk on my shirt. I should go wash it off."

Oliver felt his face go suddenly cold. To get to the kitchen, Mr. Wetherby would pass by the hallway window that looked out at the back yard!

"Oh, I can go get a washcloth sir," Oliver quickly remarked. "I'll be right back."

"Oh, don't worry about it," Mr. Wetherby remarked. "I'll go with you."

Oliver wanted to say more but he knew that Mr. Wetherby wouldn't miss a beat if he seemed too suspicious. Without anything to do but hope, Oliver followed the huge man out the room and down the hallway.

As they passed the window, Oliver glanced out, hoping to not see the others. Biting his lip in worry, he could plainly see Eileen struggling to pull Neil over the wall! The moonlight was flooding around them, making it quite easy to see them.

"What are you looking at, Oliver?" Mr. Wetherby inquired, causing Oliver to shiver.

"Oh, nothing, sir," Oliver replied but he was too late.

Mr. Wetherby stepped over and peered out the window. Oliver closed his eyes, waiting for Mr. Wetherby to ask why Eileen and Neil were climbing on the wall. However, the next thing he said caused Oliver to let go of the air he was holding in. "I cannot see clearly without my glasses. That looks like a huge bird!"

Mr. Wetherby fumbled with his glasses, Oliver watching him with bated breath. He ran a short prayer through his mind, hoping that the two would disappear. Mr. Wetherby pulled on the glasses and peered out the window again. "Huh . . . I wonder where it went."

Oliver snapped his head up and looked out the window . . . the wall was flooded with light but there was not a soul there! He felt his heart suddenly relax and the sweaty feeling on his forehead disappeared.

Nevertheless, outside Neil and Eileen were feeling the exact same thing. They were both hanging onto the edge of the opposite side of the wall, having just managed to hide before Mr. Wetherby looked back out the window.

"That was a close one," Neil whispered.

Eileen nodded. "Too close."

Glancing below her, Eileen waited 'til the others were out of the way before she dropped. She quickly backed up, so Neil could drop. Quickly counting heads, they hurried down the strip of trees to the road.

"All right listen up," Neil whispered. "Stay off the roads. You'll be more obvious there. Walk next to the road but among the bushes and trees. Stay in the shadows. Go to all the houses on your assigned streets that have society members. Act like you're still looking for Emma but secretly tell the members about the plan. Don't tell them where we're meeting until they agree to help us."

Everyone nodded silently, peering about them in frozen anxiety. Neil nodded in return, feeling there was nothing else he could say. "We'll meet up at the town square as soon as we're done. Good luck."

Repeating the farewell, the kids quickly split up into their groups of two and disappeared into the darkness.

Chapter 40

Eileen and Denise pressed their backs against a couple of trees, worrying that the street lights ahead would reveal their position. "This is our first stop," Eileen whispered.

Denise nodded. "This looks like the Salerno's."

"Well hopefully we can get Zara to help at least. Maybe even her sister," Eileen whispered back, quickly slipping out of the shadows and hurrying across the street.

As she dove into the nearest clump of shadows, Denise joined her nearby. "Remember," Eileen hissed. "Don't mention our meeting place until after they agree."

"My mouth is sealed," Denise whispered back. "I'm great at keeping secrets."

Eileen slowly raised her eyebrow in amusement. "Sure, like the time you told Neil I had put fresh pickles in his lunch? You didn't keep quiet then."

"I was younger then and had less self-control," Denise objected.

"It was last week, Denise," Eileen pointed out. "Now let's go."

The two broke from the darkness and hurried onto the porch silently. While Denise peered through the side window, Eileen tried to look through the small stain glass window on the door. "I see Zara in the hallway," she whispered. "I'll try knocking."

She knocked gently on the door and watched as Zara approached the door. The girl opened it partially, then seeing who it was, she opened it wider.

"Hello, Eileen," she greeted kindly. "What are you doing out so late?"

"Are your parents around?" Eileen inquired in a low voice.

Zara looked over her shoulder. "They're upstairs . . . do you want me to get them?"

Eileen shook her head. "I need to know if you can help us . . . you know how Emma disappeared?"

Zara nodded. "Well, we think we know who took her, but we need some more information. We're planning on sneaking into the society to find clues."

Zara's eyes grew wide, but she quickly composed herself and stepped onto the porch, closing the door behind her. "Sneaking in? That's against the rules! You could get expelled!"

"I know," Eileen whispered. "But we figured out that if we could get the majority of the members to come with us, the council won't try to expel most of the members."

Zara nodded, considering the reason in the plan. "I don't know if I can get Vivian to go, but I'll try . . . where do you want us to meet you?"

"If you could meet us in the next five minutes by that tree in your front yard, that would be swell," Eileen whispered.

Zara glanced down at her wrist watch, then at Eileen. "I'll be there."

* * * * * * * * * *

"It's been almost half an hour," Deke whispered to Neil. "We should give Gene another five minutes before we send a search party."

The whole gang, minus Gene and Seraphina, were waiting in the shadows of the town square. Almost every shadow was occupied by one or two kids. There had been only two instances where the members declined but they had sent encouragement and support in words to the group. They had almost all of the members and when Gene arrived, they would be able to see who was missing.

Neil turned to see Zara Salerno heading his way with her sister Vivian behind her. Neil smiled at the small girl whom he recognized as one of Gene's friends but stared in surprise at Vivian. The girl was obviously about two years older than Zara and had nothing in common with Zara except the dark blue eyes. Vivian's naturally black hair was dyed a medium gray, almost silver color with tints of darker gray throughout her hair. She was surprisingly pretty, and she wore a dark red slouch hat that was similar to Emma's style.

"Hey, Neil," Zara whispered. "I'm Zara ... Gene told me about you."

Neil smiled at the girl and nodded. "He has told me about you too."

"This is my sister Vivian," Zara continued. "We were wondering if Gene was with you."

Neil nodded. "He should be back soon."

Almost as soon as he said this, the sound of Whip's voice came across the silent square. "He's back."

Everyone turned to see a handful of kids hurrying into the square and diving into shadows. Neil could see Gene's light hair as the boy crept over to him.

"You took your time," Neil whispered. "What happened?"

"Seraphina didn't think we should ask Vicky so there was a moment of uncertainty," Gene replied.

Neil felt his face going red. "Did you?"

Gene nodded. "I felt that I might give her the benefit of the doubt. She's here with us. She's on the other side with Deke."

Gene saw Neil glance once across the square but then quickly shrug off the thought. The little boy knew that Neil's perspective of Vicky had drastically changed but there was still that feeling.

"Are you ready to go?" Gene inquired. "We had better hurry before anyone is missed."

Neil looked back at his brother, having barely heard the question. He had been too busy chastising himself in his mind for being fooled by someone like Vicky. "Sorry . . . I wasn't paying attention."

Over Gene's shoulder he saw Zara pull her hair out of her face and tie it in a quick ponytail on the back of her head. Zara reminded him of a little lick of fire, full of energy and determination. "She wouldn't have trouble taking care of herself," Neil thought to himself. Beside Zara, Neil saw Vivian smile at him sweetly through the darkness and he felt his confidence return. "Come on."

If anyone on the road to the lake had looked out their window that night at midnight, they would have possibly seen a few obscured figures hurrying along in the shadows, trying to hide the outrageous amount of space that many kids took up.

They were like a herd of racoons sneaking through town. Once they reached the shore of the lake, their self confidence in the dark had returned and they felt more at ease especially since there weren't as many lights out by the lake.

"Now what?" someone whispered out of the darkness.

"We cannot use the boats," Deke whispered. "If someone was to follow us, they would know we came here especially if the boats were gone. We'll have to go across a different way."

"What, swim?" Denise demanded. "Do you realize how cold that water is?"

Deke was preparing to answer her, but Eileen stepped up out of the darkness, resting a soft hand on the boy's shoulder. "Not to us merbeasts."

"But we're not all merbeasts," a young boy of about ten pointed out. "What about the werebeasts?"

"I think we could easily give the werebeasts a ride," a young voice remarked.

The group turned to see Zara standing there, hands on hips and her face turned in a side smile. "Come on, guys. If we were able to fly with canoes tied to our waists, then we can do this!"

None of the kids needed further encouragement. As if by magic, all of the aerobeasts lined up on the shore of the water while the werebeasts lined up behind them. Seeing that the majority of the werebeasts were teenagers, half of the aerobeast members paired up into groups of two so that carrying one teenager per pair wouldn't be as painful as doing it alone.

Eileen hurried over to Neil and touched his arm. "See you on the other side," she whispered.

Neil nodded in agreement, giving her a smile of encouragement. Eileen stayed long enough to return it before heading after to the rest of the merbeasts who were making their way to the water's edge.

"Come on, Neil," Gene whispered out of the darkness.

Neil turned to see that all the aerobeasts and werebeasts were sorted out and slowly beginning to take off, one at a time. Neil caught sight of Denise, Reed and Seraphina leaving. He knew that Deke and Roy would be with Eileen, so he didn't bother looking for them. He turned back to acknowledge Gene who was standing on the edge of the water.

"I'll give you a ride," Gene offered. "Just as long as you don't fidget."

Neil slowly approached his brother, unsure how to explain the situation to the boy. "But I'm too heavy."

"Oh, tosh," Gene remarked, waving his hand to emphasize his remark. "I'm not that much younger than you."

The older boy was preparing to object again when the last aerobeast took off, carrying a werebeast by the shoulders. Gene arced an eyebrow and gave his brother a mischievous grin. "There's no way out of it now, bro."

Neil turned to Gene, fully defeated but still with a spark of defiance. He wasn't going to let Gene get away with this. Gene ignored his brother's threatening glare and walked around Neil so that he was standing behind him.

With Gene standing behind him, Neil felt strangely concerned and was about to turn around when he felt strong hands wrap underneath his armpits and lift him off the ground. He let out a startled cry as the ground slowly disappeared into the darkness and the glare of moonlight on the water became the only thing beneath him.

"Gene, what are you ..." Neil started but he stopped himself. He knew that Gene would come back with a simple reply. Neil decided against asking and instead looked over his shoulder at his young brother.

"You're really unbalanced," he whispered. "If you carry me any longer like this, you're going to nose dive."

Gene didn't move his head but looked down at his brother with his bright blue eyes. "If you would keep your feet still, I might be able to even you out!"

Not sure what that meant but realizing that he was fidgeting, Neil stopped moving his feet. He felt the speed at which Gene was going slowly decrease 'til they were hovering. Neil wasn't sure what was going on until he felt like he was falling. He was about to cry out when he felt his ankles grabbed by something and lifted so that his stomach was facing downward.

He realized that Gene hadn't let go of his arms and looking behind, he could see that Gene had wrapped his own feet around Neil's ankles, holding him completely parallel to himself.

The landing was the thing that Neil really worried about. He wasn't sure how Gene would land with his feet preoccupied. However, Gene had the whole flight over the lake to think of a plan so when they neared the dock, he released Neil's feet and used the extra weight of Neil's body to lower themselves onto the dock with some force but not more than a bruised knee and sore hands.

"That was good," Neil remarked, not meaning it in a bad way but rather that he was glad they hadn't died.

"Neil!" a voice called from nearby.

The two boys turned to see the rest of the kids rushing over to them like a swarm of bees. Half of them were drenched in water while the other half were windblown. It wasn't a pretty sight.

Whip broke free of the crowd and rushed at the two. "We have a problem," he whispered.

"What, the police are here?" Gene inquired, feeling the blood drain from his face.

Whip shook his head. "Someone blew their cover?" Neil added, trying to aide his brother in guessing.

Whip shook his head again, so Gene began to think that he was pulling their legs. "You need to use the lavatory?"

The brown-haired boy lowered his eyes at his friend but quickly shook his head, allowing the fear in his eyes to overcome his annoyance. "We forgot that every building is locked . . . we cannot get in!"

Chapter 41

The door rattled again as Denise shook the door handle violently. She pressed her shoulder against the door to push as if it would add to the effect.

"It's no use, Denise," Roy groaned. "We've been here for ten whole minutes."

Denise slammed the toe of her shoe onto the door in disgust and slumped down on the platform next to Seraphina. "After all this work and it's all for nothing."

The blonde shook her head, causing a rustle of long hair as she did so. "We made it across the lake. I think that is a pretty good accomplishment."

"Thanks, a heap," Denise groaned. "Where did Gene and Zara go?"

"They went to check the other exits," Roy replied. "Here they come now."

Gene and Zara appeared around the corner of the building with several other kids with them. The long gloomy looks on their faces already answered the question everyone was thinking.

"Maybe we should call it a night?" Reed suggested.

"No," Neil snapped. "We can figure this out."

The gang looked over at Neil, sitting on one of the anchoring posts, his hand rubbing his jaw thoughtfully. "There is always a way in."

As soon as he said this, several voices murmured back a well-known saying. "Whenever a door closes a window opens."

"Window!" Deke cried, leaping to his feet. "We could get in through the windows!"

"But the windows are never open, Deke," Zara pointed out. "If we wanted to get in through the windows, we would have to break either the locks or the glass and that would leave suspicion and marks."

Nodding slowly, Deke realized that there was no sense behind the suggestion. "Still ... things can sometimes be confused or misinterpreted because of a different point of view."

Neil let out a loud, distressed groan. "Gene, why don't you guys just check the windows in case one happens to be open. Don't pry anything open though."

Gene smiled, glad to have something to do. "Ten four."

"No, it's twelve-fifteen," Roy objected, glancing at his wrist watch.

There were several kids who snickered at the joke, but this only caused Neil to groan further. "Just check the windows!"

Gene quickly saluted and started off around the corner of the building with a handful of kids following. Their footsteps had just died down when the sound of rapid footsteps sounded, and Gene returned at a brisk pace. "Wait ... you said windows, right?"

Neil snapped his head up, glowering at his brother. "What am I talking? Egyptian? Windows, Gene. The things that you can open and close and get through if need be?"

Gene nodded. "I know what you're talking about ... but I just remembered what Deke said about things being seen from different points of view."

"I was referring to when someone deliberates I am aphorism approximately otherwise and I exceedingly intended something different," Deke objected.

Neil slowly raised his head to give Deke a confused glare while Gene merely stared at Deke as if the boy had just recited the laws of life.

"Anyway ..." Gene continued unsurely. "I meant about how we were going to check the windows ... well, doors and windows aren't the only ways into buildings."

"The society doesn't have chimneys if that was what you were going to say," Denise pointed out glumly.

Gene shook his head and raised one hand before someone could interrupt again. "I was talking about another form of exit that we're sitting on."

Roy and Reed quickly looked beneath them while Neil rolled his eyes. "Translation Gene?"

"The flight exit?" Gene inquired, trying to emphasize what he was trying to get at.

"The flight exit!" Denise and Whip cried in unison.

"Forget it," Seraphina pointed out. "The flight exits have scanners that pick up anything that passes through the exits that have extra bones. That is how none of us can leave without permission because it keeps track of what and when something left through that exit."

There was a brief silence while everyone groaned inwardly. Neil was about to yell at Gene to go back and check the windows when he became aware that a pair of eyes was staring down at him.

Neil quickly peered through the darkness and saw that the pair of eyes belonged to Seraphina.

Neil felt himself begin to get fidgety under the girl's gaze when finally, she spoke. "Neil . . . you're not a changeling . . . you don't have extra bones like the rest of the changelings. The scanner wouldn't pick up you are passing through!"

* * * * * * * * * *

"Next time I want to be on the top," Roy hollered from the bottom of the pile. "The human stack up was my idea!"

Neil slowly glanced down from where he was slowly scaling the human tower. Roy and Reed were the two on the bottom with Oliver on top of them, then went Seraphina, two older kids, Whip and finally Neil.

"Stop wiggling!" Neil hissed. "It feels like I'm on a sapling in a gale!"

Pressing his hand onto the top of Whip's head, the boy pushed himself further onto his shoulders and grasped the edge of the flight exit. Pretty much it was like a huge circle window in the very top left tower of the Hall of Organization. The average-sized human could stand up inside without scraping his head on the roof of the exit.

Neil peered over the edge and reached down with one hand to unclip his torch. Switching it on he scanned the interior of the exit. He could see plainly that there were small radio like objects on the top, bottom and on both sides. It would be difficult to go through without setting one off, but he had to try.

Setting his torch on the inside of the exit, he grasped the edges of the ledge. Glancing down at the others below him, he pulled himself onto the edge and pulled his left knee over the side. That secured the fact that he wouldn't slip. Pulling his other knee over, he dragged himself in and grabbed his torch. Placing one hand on the left-hand wall, he flashed the light about to see where the scanners were.

Seraphina and the other aerobeasts had told him that the scanners are set off when they see a large object, within three feet, move through the exit at least five miles per hour. In that case, he would have to move slowly and out of range of the scanners. The exit wasn't small at all and was as wide as it was high. In that case, to not set of the scanners, he would have to choose one side and walk as close to the wall as possible.

Stuffing his torch into his pocket, Neil pressed his back against the right-hand wall. Keeping a close eye on his feet and the scanners, he began to walk sideways, keeping his back against the wall. For one horrid moment his foot slipped, and he was afraid that the movement would set the scanners off. However, nothing happened but the rest of the time Neil was on edge.

When he reached the other end of the exit, there was a door. He was relieved to find out that the door opened up onto the balcony overlooking the grand hall where the headmasters had stood when the kids first arrived. The drop was only about five feet. In that case he lay down in the exit on his stomach and lowered himself down. When he was sure his feet were on firm ground, he closed the door over the exit and pulled out his torch.

The light immediately fell on the stairs that led down to the first floor and he quickly hurried down. He hurried straight to the front door but then realized that he still didn't have keys. He tried to rack his brain about where he had seen keys . . . then it came to him. They were in a small cupboard underneath the stairs that he had just run down.

Hurrying back, he found the cupboard and opened it. Shining the light on the row of keys, the light reflected back into his eyes slightly. He read the labels that were tied by string to each key. Some of them opened up private storage rooms and feeling that those weren't important, he grabbed the keys that opened the classrooms and main buildings.

Choosing the key to the front door of the hall, he inserted it and quickly unlocked the door. As he slowly swung the door open, he was met by a tall dark figure that was silhouetted by the moonlight. Neil almost had the urge to jump but the figure at once became visible as he stepped inside.

"You took your time," Roy whispered. "Where are the rest of the keys?"

Glancing over Roy's shoulder, Neil could see the rest of the kids all crowding on the platform outside the building. He stuffed his hand into his coat pocket and drew out a handful of keys.

He handed one to Roy. "This opens Benvor Hall. Go there with five other people and search thoroughly."

As Roy nodded and hurried off, Neil stepped out of the building and began to hand keys to each of the gang members. He sent Whip and six other kids to Steeple Hall, Seraphina and three other kids to the apothecary, and Reed and four others to the refectory.

The light in Neil's torch suddenly gave out and he had to wait for Deke to fish his own out of his coat. Once Neil had steady light on the handful of keys, he continued handing them out. Soon Denise and her group were heading to the PE building, Gene and four kids to the library, Zara took three to the viaduct, Vivian and five kids to the storage building, Deke and the last six kids to Mt. Kyvers hall, leaving only Neil left.

Neil glanced down at the two keys in his hand. One was to the aquarium and the other was to the aerial observatory. He decided to start with the observatory first.

Chapter 42

Neil considered the observatory a moment. It was the only circle building on the lake and was the one furthest away from where the boats were held in the docks along the shore. It faced the pointed part of the lake which was the 'head' of the bird. The walls were windows rather than walls. There was only a small fraction of wall space in the building which was about three feet's height nearest to the floor.

The boy always felt unsure about the building especially since the floor was also glass, looking down at the water below. For the longest time Neil wondered how the building was held up above the water. Then Deke revealed to him that the perimeter of the base of the building was held up by stone while the center wasn't. Due to the fact that the floor was glass and people usually didn't walk on it, the building didn't need as much support.

Neil smiled to himself, imagining Whip, Gene and Seraphina flying about in the observatory. Whip and Seraphina had before but Gene hadn't since his first encounter flying inside had ended in a sprained ankle his first week. After that Gene was banned from flying indoors until he could learn how to turn. Now that Gene had mastered that, Neil felt suddenly proud of the fact that Gene would be able to fly in there.

Even though the observatory was the smallest building at least in diameter, it was a great privilege to fly in there just like it was a privilege to be a merbeast working in the aquarium. Having to work outside and in the lake was okay, but after a while the kids began to long for the obstacle courses that would be set up in those two buildings.

Neil slowly stepped back off the glass. There was no way anything could have happened in there without someone seeing or obvious marks left on the glass floor and walls. Neil sat down in the doorway and began to pull his shoes back on. Hoping to not leave marks, he had removed his shoes and had walked across the floor in his socks.

He was just pulling his last shoe on when he felt a hand touch his shoulder. He turned around hastily, staring into the dim light to see the face of Deke slightly above his own.

"Any luck?" Neil inquired.

Deke shook his head. "Not a thing. We didn't turn the main lights on, but we were able to check everything with our flashlights . . . there was nothing."

Neil began to nod in understanding when he saw another face behind Deke's that was vaguely familiar but covered in a look of full concern. "Denise . . . what's wrong?"

Deke spun around in surprise, having not heard Denise enter and finding that she was standing beside him caused him to shiver. "You guys need to hurry! We found something . . ."

"Something good?" Deke asked hopefully. He wasn't sure how many more heart attacks he could bear in one night.

"Something bad," Denise corrected, not changing the tone in her voice.

Deke grimaced in defeat. "How did I know you were going to say that?"

By the time the three arrived at the PE building, all the other kids had arrived as well. The PE building was one that everyone loathed. It was a huge open gym separated into different stations. On the far-left corner there was a huge pile of haybales, covered in targets. The targets either had footprints or handprints on them where mostly the aerobeasts had to practice striking the targets in flight to help their steering.

In the opposite corner there were different sized harnesses that the kids would wear during exercises. Each was weighted with sand and each a different weight depending on the person's size and age. There were also punching bags, lifting weights and pads on the ground where they could do stretches and calisthenics.

Neil and Deke had barely entered the building when they saw where the commotion was. Everyone was crowding about to see whatever everyone was looking at, opposite the door. Neil knew right away that opposite the door on the other side of the building were the bathrooms.

Pushing their way through the crowd, ducking under some arms and legs, the two finally made it to the center of the group to find that there was much more room to breathe. In the dim light Neil could make out the faces of all the gang members and some other familiar faces.

"What's up?" he inquired.

Whip flashed his light around, striking Deke in the eyes with the light before he finally found what he wanted Neil to see. Leaning forward, Neil squinted in the torch light to see that on the frame of the door of the girls' bathroom were three long scratches. Whatever it was had torn a good-sized piece of wood off the frame as if trying to open the door.

Neil right away turned around and his eyes fell on Seraphina. "Did anyone check inside?"

The girl nodded, a serious look on her face. "The doorknob on the inside was almost wrenched off the door. It looked like someone had been pulling really hard on it. Everyone here though promises that they haven't done it, nor noticed it 'til now."

"What do you think it is Neil?" a small voice inquired.

Neil turned around to see who had spoken and found himself face to face with one of the first-year students who was barely eight years old. The girl's jet-black hair was pulled back in a thick black braid that fell over her left shoulder and a handful of side bangs flopped across the side of her cheek. Her eyes were a deep blue and seemed to hold a great deal of worry in them.

"What is your name?" Neil inquired, smiling at the girl kindly.

"Maeve," the girl replied, brushing her bangs behind her ear as she replied.

Neil sighed. He didn't want to break the truth, but he had to. "It seems that someone was trying to get into the bathroom and my first guess is, Emma sensed trouble and hid in the bathroom. When the person tried to open the door, she pulled the doorknob almost out while trying to hold the door shut."

"But who left the scratches?" Denise demanded, finally getting through the tight crowd. "Those aren't any knife marks."

"They almost look like claw marks," Roy mused aloud.

"Or teeth marks," Whip remarked.

Neil had been listening intently to the suggestions everyone was giving out when he heard a sharp gasp go off behind him. Looking over his shoulder he saw that all eyes, except those of Deke and Gene, were staring at Whip in aggravated disbelief. Neil had no clue what all those looks directed at Whip meant, but he knew one thing: neither he nor his brothers knew why Whip suddenly turned pale and lowered his head in shame.

Gene as well was puzzled, but his reaction was quicker than his brothers. He began to scan the crowd for some sign of someone who wasn't as infuriated but had some sort of understanding about the situation. His eyes fell on the tall, delicate girl who stood with her face shrouded in black locks of hair.

"Eileen," he said in a soft voice.

All eyes turned to Gene, then to the tall girl who was meeting Gene's gaze tranquilly. Reaching up with one hand, Eileen brushed a handful of hair behind her ear and out of her eyes.

"I was hoping that we didn't have to break it to you guys like this," she replied in a soft, almost shaky voice. "We were hoping that you three would be satisfied in simply knowing that you guys are changelings ... I suppose it was a mistake we all made in assuming that you wouldn't one day figure that there was something missing."

"What was missing?" Gene inquired, his voice firm and almost dominant, trying to get higher ground in this peculiar conversation. "Eileen ... if

340

there was something you refrained from telling us, I think now is the time for you to do so."

Eileen glanced around the crowd of kids. Some of them had their heads down, wishing to not be a part of this decisive moment while others were fearfully nodding their heads, not sure whether this was a good idea or not.

"You went looking for answers, Gene," Eileen began. "You left Neil's wing in the twins' hands because you hoped that it held answers . . . it did."

She stopped to let those words sink in. She knew right away that Neil's eyes would widen and turn to his little brother in puzzlement. She allowed Gene to burn under Neil's quizzical stare before she continued. "Neil's wing wasn't broken by accident. He fell . . . Far. Before you were born, Gene . . . Neil took a terrible turn and fell from a cliff . . . when he fell, he was frozen in sleep for three months, and during that time, he lost three years of age. Neil is really thirteen . . . But because of the fall, his mind, body . . . his whole life retracted three years."

Deke's mouth fell open and hung there for a long time. Beside him, Neil was staring Eileen full in the face with a look of shock as if a horse had just struck his chest. Gene, however, had no expression. His eyes were watching Eileen's patiently as the girl slowly explained.

"The fall wasn't an accident . . . there was a kid stuck on the side of the cliff . . . Neil tried to save the kid and did . . . but the consequence was that he fell and couldn't save himself. That cliff would never have crumbled under the weight of that small child

341

. . . but the BP's made sure that the cliff was unstable when Neil helped."

At once, Deke's mouth clamped shut and both he and Neil took on peculiar faces with eyebrows furrowed down and their mouths twisted in bewilderment. "BP's?"

Eileen turned her head slightly to lock eyes with Oliver. Oliver had managed to sneak out of the house and join the others at the society. The boy met her gaze steadily and nodded. Eileen reverted her eyes back to the three brothers and bit her lip as she spoke. "The Birds of Prey . . . are known as the BP's. They are the reason we are here . . . in Hichester. They are the reason why the society was made, why there is so much security . . . and why Emma has disappeared."

Deke opened his mouth, prepared to ask for an explanation, but Whip was losing his patience. He had been listening to Eileen slowly explain the situation to the boys but now his patience was running on reserves. "As you know, changelings have a natural instinct to do the right thing and to recognize good and evil more clearly than humans . . . the trouble is . . . there have been times when changelings have chosen evil over good and turned to the seductive evil of darkness. When a changeling begins to turn evil, the first thing you notice is that his or her behavior changes; he becomes aggressive, uncaring, and soon he begins to show violence to those closest to him. The second symptom is the eyes . . . you might not know this, but changelings have a special gift where their eyes have an unusual sparkle to them. It's hard to notice when you're not looking for it . . . but when a changeling begins to

342

turn evil, their eyes turn a horrid gold . . . and gold that seems to glare . . ."

Whip had to stop to swallow the saliva that was building up in his mouth. The pause he took was just long enough for Eileen to jump back into the conversation. "Finally, the changeling will take on the form of a Bird of Prey . . . these are nothing like changelings. They have a craving for evil . . . to do evil . . . and they take on the vilest shapes," she paused to let the boys consider this before she continued. "Vultures . . . hyenas, bats, buzzards . . . and many more. They are the minions of darkness. They work under the iron fist of their master: Nohte Respure, the sorcerer."

Now it was Neil's turn to drop his jaw. "Nohte Respure? But . . . I thought he was a legend! Wait . . . If there is actually such a person . . . how did he survive for the past sixty years!? If the legends are true, he fought in the war of the Black Years . . . But that happened at least fifty years ago!"

Roy nodded. "Nohte Respure is a sorcerer, like I said . . . he has his ways. He also has his ways of stating revenge and remembering that vow of revenge even sixty years later."

"Woah, pull everyone back onto the field," Deke remarked, holding his arms up. "Revenge? Why would Nohte want revenge against Emma and the others?"

Denise blinked once, then shook her head. "He doesn't want revenge against Emma and the others . . . he wants revenge against someone who has haunted him for years."

"Let me guess ... that's ..." Deke started, holding a finger up. " ... okay I give up ... who can defeat a sorcerer?"

Seraphina lowered her eyebrows, giving Deke a firm glare. Once she was sure Deke was over with joking, she turned back to the other two boys, trying not to encourage further interruption with Deke. "You all know the legend I assume ... the legend of Hichester?"

The three boys nodded while all the other kids did as well, even if it wasn't necessary. "That's true," Neil replied. "Though when we were growing up it was called the Legend of the Black Age."

Whip nodded. "That tends to be a popular name. Anyway, because Bentley Hichester felt that he had power to control things, he was punished ... punished with a curse and a revenge wound. Nohte would haunt his children and the world the rest of eternity because he dealt in dark magic and did the evil thing rather than the good. Bentley's descendants would be cursed with the inability to age. Some people thought that wouldn't be so bad ... but once you've watched your great-grandchildren die ... you find no pleasure in life."

"So ... All of Bentley's descendants are still alive? That is kinda creepy," Deke remarked, quickly regretting those words.

"No, Deke, eventually they died from sickness or other causes. The fact was, unless they died from sickness or other causes, besides old age, they would live on until the end of time. Bentley didn't think much of this curse ... until he realized that the revenge was just as serious. The legend stops short when it comes to the outcome of the war of the

Black Years. No one knows the truth to what happened . . . Except a few."

"And you might be one of them?" Gene inquired, his calm expression still not changing.

Eileen nodded. "Myself and all the changelings. The truth of the legend was handed down to us from our parents . . ."

Neil quickly held up a hand and shook his head. "Wait a minute . . . I feel like this has gotten off topic. Okay it's great to know that we have a guy somewhere who is determined to finish his revenge vow on the poor descendant of Bentley and that he has a lapful of evil changelings . . . but what does this have to do with the marks on the door and Emma's disappearance?"

"I was getting to that," Eileen remarked, breathing deeply so that she kept her patience. "When . . . when I arrived at your house several months ago . . . it wasn't by accident."

Finally, Gene's expression changed as his eyebrows went down. "Hold on . . . I thought Mr. Wetherby found you at his meeting place and brought you home."

"That's what we wanted you to think," the girl explained. "I actually arrived at the house at the same time Mr. Wetherby returned home . . . I came here because . . . because there was something that I knew that everyone thought had been forgotten . . . the revenge vow."

Oliver slowly walked over and put a hand on Eileen's shoulder as she slowly shivered. "Eileen had been running for her life . . . her father was a secret agent for Hichester District and he kept tabs on the suspicious things going on outside of Hichester. He was preparing to warn Mr. Wetherby of the suspicious disappearances and the connection to this 'war machine' . . . but the Birds of Prey found him first. Eileen had to deliver the message . . ."

All three boys opened their mouths to ask the same question, but Eileen's firm look into their eyes already said what she was going to confirm. "I have been trained . . . Been trained since childhood to be a secret agent, guys . . . You wonder why I always seem to have a secret. The fact is . . . I came to warn Mr. Wetherby because I knew he had decided to foster you three for a while before possibly adopting you . . ."

The last part didn't get straight to Deke and Gene, but it did for Neil. "Wait . . . why would you have to warn Mr. Wetherby about us?"

Oliver shook his head. "Not about you . . . *For* you . . . It was by sheer luck that Nohte's minions didn't choose one of you three boys as the last victim."

"Why may that be?" Deke croaked, barely a whisper. His heart was in his throat and he believed his lungs had changed places with his feet. He couldn't feel half of his body and his mouth was horridly dry.

"Because . . ." Eileen started then had to stop and swallow before breaking the news. " . . . because the revenge vow Nohte made wasn't a vow to destroy Bentley or his descendants . . . It was a vow to destroy the changeling, Gianna's, male heirs. Guys . . . your mother was Gianna's only living descendent . . . Nohte is looking for you three."

Chapter 43

Whip continued to slap Deke's face. He thought it was pretty absurd that the boy was lying there, eyes closed and his body limp. Finally, Neil put a hand on the boy's shoulder. "That's enough Whip. If Deke set his mind on fainted five minutes ago, there is no way we can wake him up 'til he's good and ready."

"I'll get a bucket of water," Seraphina offered, hurrying off with the twins following.

Neil turned around to see Gene sitting some ways off in the hallway, his back pressed against the wall. Slowly walking over, Neil squatted down in front of Gene and placed a hand on the boy's knee. "Hey . . . Are you all right?"

Gene slowly nodded but didn't look up. Neil decided that he needed to get Gene talking. "It makes sense though . . . I mean . . . the fact that mom was an aerobeast. It makes sense why we would be changelings too even if dad wasn't a changeling . . . that probably also explains why I fell short."

Gene still didn't speak but kept his head bowed, his straight blond hair shielding his eyes from Neil's gaze. Neil was beginning to give up. He began to rise when Gene slowly spoke. "All the signs . . . they were all there Neil."

Neil turned around to look back at his brother. "What do you mean?"

Gene looked up and his young eyes showed agony. His bottom lip was trembling, and tears were welling up in his eyes. "Why? Why did all these things have to happen? We have lost five of the best people in the world to Nohte . . . we lost mom and dad because the BP's were really after us and killed mom and dad instead . . . Eileen lost all her family and almost lost her own life . . . and now . . ."

Seraphina had returned with a bucket of water and had seen the two boys in the hallway. As soon as Gene's voice broke into sobs, she hurried over and put an arm around the young boy's shoulders. She began to gently stroke his arm and hair like a mother crooning over a frightened baby.

After a moment of trying to calm him down, Seraphina caught hold of Gene's hands and forced his head to look up at her. "Hey . . . hey, Gene. None of this is your fault. Even if some of these things have happened because you three are wanted by Nohte, they aren't your fault. You didn't choose your ancestors. But I will tell you this, you might not be able to change your past, but you can do something about your future."

Gene ran his sleeve across his face, sniffling back the tears. "How can I do that?"

A mischievous smile appeared on Seraphina's face . . . something he had never seen. "Eileen wasn't trained to be a secret agent for nothing. She didn't tell you everything that her father knew . . . he knew the location of the Birds of Prey secret base here in Gerhenia. It is known as the Smothering Marshcs."

The boy looked over the girl's shoulder at his brother who was smiling down at him, waiting to see what he would decide. Gene looked back into Seraphina's kind brown eyes. "How soon can we get there? It'll be dawn soon."

The smile on Neil and Seraphina's faces increased but a voice rang out from the other end of the hallway. "I was wondering when someone would say that!" Whip hollered.

* * * * * * * * * *

"You weren't kidding when you said that bog boots would have been a good idea," Deke hissed through the reeds.

Denise rolled her eyes, giving Deke a teasing grin. "If I was kidding, I would have been smiling when I told you."

Deke considered the statement a moment before nodding. "That suits you."

"Would you two lovebirds be quiet?" Whip hissed from ahead. "Unless you want to explain to Nohte when his men bring us before him how we happened to be spotted trying to infiltrate his secret base."

The two quickly decided to not argue with Whip just yet but began to build up shocking remarks to shoot back at him when they got the chance. The three were in shoulder high reeds. The water that the reeds grew in was ankle deep, but it had already soaked their shoes and socks, leaving them shivering as the water ran shivers of cold up their bodies.

"Can you see anything?" Denise whispered. "Neil said he would give us five minutes before the rest of them would join us. We don't want them to join us just five meters from the front gate!"

Whip glared at the girl over his shoulder and parted the reeds in front of him. "There is no one in whispering earshot. I can't see any guards . . . I hope Seraphina gets that covered." The boy glanced up into the sky, thinking he might just see his sister

350

flying high above, scanning the countryside from an aerial point of view. Of course, he didn't so he continued his quiet investigation. "The portcullis is down the river . . . It is half submerged in the river . . . I don't know if it goes all the way to the riverbed."

"So, it would be perfectly fine if we joined you?" a voice whispered right behind Whip.

The boy released the reeds and spun around to see Neil grinning down at him. "Ugh! Don't do that again Neil! You gave me a heart attack!"

"Well that is payment for causing Deke to have another heart attack after you dumped water down his shirt earlier," Neil whispered back. "Draw back a little so they don't see us. We need to assess the plan."

Whip nodded and silently followed the tall boy further back into the tall reeds. After a moment they came upon a relatively open space in the rushes where all the kids were huddled together, trying to stay quiet.

"All right listen up," Neil whispered. "Seraphina and Zara will be back any minute from scouting out the place. In the meantime, I need to give you merbeasts the head."

Deke and Eileen, huddling together to keep each other warm, nodded. "Okay . . . so . . . it seems that the drawbridge goes partially underwater. We don't know if it goes all the way down. We've sent Roy ahead to see if it touches bottom. If it doesn't, that will make our life easier. If it does however, we're going to have to be prepared to wait in the shallows of the river while Gene and his posse raise the portcullis enough to let us through."

"But how will we do that without anyone noticing?" one of the older kids inquired.

The reply he got was a small pebble hitting his head and he quickly brought up a hand to touch the slightly stinging part. He turned to see who had thrown it and saw Whip grinning at him. "Nothing a little distraction cannot fix."

Several people rolled their eyes to heaven. Most of them knew how mischievous Whip was and his experience in the arts of pranks. That was a job well shaped for him.

Suddenly reeds nearby began to move, and everyone held their breath, hoping that it wasn't an underbeast. However, as the reeds parted, they saw Seraphina, Zara and Roy quietly hurrying toward them. Everyone wanted to ask questions as the three approached, but they kept their excitement down long enough for Neil to ask the first question.

"Well?"

Seraphina and Zara nodded together. "The base is mostly just walls, no roofs ... But that is the problem. Since there were no roofs we could see inside and there is no sign of Emma. There is however one place that is entirely enclosed."

"Where?" several voices whispered.

"In the very back of the base, near the edge of the forest," Zara replied. "It's the biggest part of the base ... and the hardest to get into. There is only one door and that is on the inside of the base."

Everyone was silent for a moment, considering this observation. "What about the river?" Deke inquired. "Does it run into the building?"

The two girls nodded. "It does . . . but through a pipe," Seraphina replied. "It's barely bigger than my arm."

Gene quickly raised his hand to get everyone's attention so that he had time to ask his question. "What is the landscape right behind the back of the building?"

Seraphina didn't know this answer for she had been concentrating on the interior of the base, rather than the walls. However, Zara's face split into a grin. "It's dirt . . . but really mucky. I think the water drains out there but afraid to put a drain there, they just let the water seep under the walls naturally."

"Excellent," Gene and Neil remarked at the same time.

"Listen up," Neil whispered, leaning forward. "We're going to split up into three groups, aero, mer and wer. The werebeasts are going to wait in the back of the base. When Whip has the guards distracted, they are going to dig into the muck and under the wall. If I'm guessing right, then there will be no floor inside the building just water, so it won't be hard to dig our way in. The aerobeasts are going to slip in through the door the best way they can and get Emma out of there and the merbeasts . . ."

Roy quickly interrupted with a loud clearing of his throat. "Actually . . . I meant to tell you Neil. There is no way they can get in under the portcullis . . . it goes all the way to the bottom of the river bed."

Gene quickly waved his hand. "No problem. Zara and I can tackle that. Whip are you all right with distracting the front guards as well as the back guards?"

Whip raised a hand in mock salute and grinned. "Armed and ready captain."

Everyone nodded, realizing that there was no point that hadn't been answered . . . yet. Neil quietly clapped his hands, getting everyone's attention. "All right, off you go . . . and Godspeed."

Chapter 44

The guard's patrol was routine. Walk the length of the wall, occasionally scanning the countryside to his left which was the rushes. There was no need to scan his right because that was where the wall was. When he reached the end of the wall, he checked to make sure the guard on the other wall was all right before scanning the front once, then going back to walk the length of the wall.

If the guard had any unique intelligence, he would possibly check upwards occasionally. However, having not been told to check up, he didn't find any reason to and didn't even think of doing so. If he had looked up, he might have just seen the two shadows that passed over the moon a few moments earlier as silently as owls. He might have also seen the shadow that sat crouched on the top of the wall, watching his every move.

Whip was savoring this moment, seeing the guard just walk back and forth, unaware that his eyes were burning a hole in his head. The boy occasionally glanced over his shoulder to see if Gene and Zara reached the portcullis controls. There were underbeasts all over the place inside, sleeping, talking and sitting around fires. None of them even looked up to see Gene and Zara walking along the walls silently toward the portcullis wheel. Nor did they see the shape that almost looked like a poised gargoyle on the base wall.

Whip reached down into his knapsack. He had supplied himself with all sized rocks. His fingers brushed against the largest stone he had put in there. He would save that one for a special finale. Finally, he chose a relatively large stone and tested its weight. It wasn't that hard but considering the size, it would make enough noise. He looked back over his shoulder just as he saw Gene and Zara's shadows slip through the unguarded control door. 'Time to get to work' he thought.

The guard was halfway down the length of the wall. He stopped, scanned the countryside and began to walk again. His foot stopped in midair when a rather loud rustle in the reeds was followed by a loud thud and splash. His head snapped around and he peered into the darkness.

In the glare of the torch he carried he couldn't see into the darkness like that. The bat underbeast might have had the strong enough hearing to hear that noise, but he didn't have the sight to see through the darkness.

Grasping his torch with his left hand, he reached down to his belt where a savage looking black blade was stuck into the leather of his belt. Whip smiled to himself as he saw the guard begin to walk carefully into the marshes, careful as to not strike the reeds with his torch.

Whip grabbed his knapsack and began to hurry to the other wall. He needed to get that guard distracted as well. Whip reached into his bag and pulled out a smaller rock, barely bigger than his hand. He lifted it onto his shoulder and prepared to launch . . . then he stopped. He looked back over his shoulder to where the other guard was journeying further into the marshes. He looked down into the inside of the base . . . no one was in earshot.

He felt the weight of the stone and ran his finger over it. It wasn't too heavy, nor was it sharp but it was hard. He moved the rock off his shoulder and held it out over the side of the wall. If Gene had been looking, he would have thought Whip was dropping a twig into a river, however the rock hitting helmet made a different noise.

Whip lifted his wings as far as he could as a signal and waited long enough to see Zara acknowledge that the coast was clear.

* * * * * * * * * *

Deke was feeling increasingly nervous. The cold water soothingly flowing past his body did nothing to calm his worry. He peered through the dark water to see who was beside him. It only took a moment to see the blurry figure of Roy swimming beside him. Roy had always scared Deke, at least when he was in the water. The huge shark fin, the tall waving tail made Deke's skin crawl.

Deke slowly swam ahead to check the portcullis again. It hadn't moved. He felt the wet, semi squishy wood that was covered in algae. He ran his fingers down to the bottom where they struck the riverbed and the end of the portcullis. Deke had tried earlier to squeeze through the squares, but they wouldn't allow his shoulders through.

He had wanted to go up to see what was going on, but Eileen refused to let anyone emerge until the portcullis lifted. That would give the signal that the guards were distracted. The only ones who were even allowed to float near the surface were the mammal merbeasts who couldn't breathe underwater. They were waiting in the shadows of the river where no one would see them rise occasionally to breathe.

Deke slammed his forehead on the drawbridge. There was no noise that followed but his head hurt. His stomach was churning with anxiety and he wanted to just get it over before he erupted. Suddenly, he felt his head being lifted and he realized that the drawbridge was lifting! The other merbeasts waited impatiently until the drawbridge was barely two feet from the riverbed before slipping underneath. It was a tight squeeze but by going between the pikes, they could fit through. Deke held back and slowly rose to the surface.

He poked his eyes out and rotated, looking all around him. The place was dark and unwelcoming. The grass was dead and trampled underfoot and the outside walls were lined with torches. There was no hiding in the shadows on the ground outside the walls!

Deke turned around once more and felt his heart stop for a split second as he found himself staring up into the dark eyes of the underbeast guard! The boy retracted right away but his murmur of horror was cut off by a light chuckle that was coming from the underbeast!

"Oh, Deke, you are so easy to scare," the underbeast remarked.

Deke lowered his eyebrows in concentration and considered the underbeast. He was dressed in the black clothing that looked like he had gone through a shredder then was dipped in tar. The huge helmet that the hyena underbeast had worn was there . . . but there was something different about this underbeast . . . the voice was too . . .

"Don't you know me, Deke?" the underbeast asked. "It's me, Whip!"

The underbeast reached up and lifted the helmet enough to let Deke see the mocking brown eyes and mop of mad brown hair. He felt a rush of relief run over him and he wanted to spit out a furious insult at the boy, but Whip nodded toward the portcullis. "Don't you think you should catch up?" ·

Deke glowered at the boy. "We're not done with this conversation!"

Meanwhile, inside the base, pressed against the wall in the shadows was Denise. She was on sentry duty. It had surprised her how easily Oliver had dealt with the two sentry underbeasts standing outside the door. They were bound and gagged, locked in a crate in the far corner where Denise could keep an eye on them. Oliver and Reed had stripped them of their armor, not their clothing, and given them to Denise.

The helmet she wore was rather cumbersome and built for a hyena underbeast. There was a special design for the attire of each different underbeast since there weren't as many different species as there were for the changelings.

The hyenas were almost considered the fast running infantry. They wore light armor over black outfits that hung about their body like small shreds, giving them the impression of fur. Their helmets covered their chin, nose, forehead and the back of their head where two metal ears poked out. The nose of the helmets was much larger than any normal human nose and the part of the helmet where the cheeks would be concealed was replaced by black leather that smelt to high heaven.

Denise looked to her left where the crate was situated in the shadows. She then looked to her right where the river veered off its straight path to a sharp left and disappeared down a drain pipe that was (true to Seraphina's word) no bigger than her arm. It made a soft gurgling sound as it rushed down steadily into the drain and probably inside the building.

The girl felt strangely uncomfortable being the only werebeast (other than Oliver and Reed) inside the walls while all her other wer mates were outside the walls, digging in knee deep muck and mire. Unlike the other girls of the gang, Denise would have easily found digging in mud much more interesting than standing guard.

She didn't even know what was going on inside the building. The only glimpse she got of the interior was when Oliver wrenched the door open and hurried all the aerobeasts inside. It was a long black hallway, lit up by torches on the wall. That was pretty much all. Denise felt strangely disappointed that the underbeasts' form of decoration didn't meet Denise's standpoint.

Denise was suddenly caught off her guard by a soft whisper behind her. Turning around, Denise saw a face peeking out from behind the door. The girl squinted in the darkness but in being a fox werebeast, Denise was able to see that it was none other than Vicky poking her head out the door.

"What do you want?" Denise asked, trying to calm her voice from the snappish before Vicky got angry.

Vicky however didn't seem to notice Denise's angry tone and her eyes darted back and forth in a frenzy that at first looked like fear, but then Denise had to remember this was Vicky she was thinking about.

"You need to get Gene and Neil in here quick," she whispered in a hoarse, rushed voice.

Gene and Neil, feeling that they would only get in the way inside, agreed to act as lookouts in the tower above the portcullis once Whip got rid of the guards. Denise wondered strangely why Vicky would want the two in the building.

"Why?" she demanded, keeping her voice low.

"I don't know why," Vicky replied. "But I have a feeling something bad is going to happen."

Denise raised one eyebrow, lowering her other one. "Sorry, Vicky, but I'm not endangering Gene and Neil without proof that they are needed."

Vicky turned her wavering eyes to Denise and gave her a firm look. "Okay, listen, Denise, I know you have no reason to trust me, but you have to understand . . . something is going to happen . . . I can feel it! This expedition has gone too perfectly . . . it doesn't feel right."

Denise turned her back on the girl and crossed her arms sourly. "If you want to convince me of that, send someone I trust."

Vicky let her shoulders shrug, but the shrug never reached her eyes. They were full of fear . . . and strange determination. "I don't want to do this Denise, but you leave me no choice."

Denise spun around to see what Vicky was talking about, but a hard object struck the back of her neck and the world went black. Vicky watched as Denise crumpled to the ground. She felt a tinge of regret. She didn't want to have to knock the girl out, but she had no choice. She had to signal Gene and

Neil. She knew that lifting her wings would be suspicious since Gene and Neil would wonder what happened to Denise. In that case, she grabbed the helmet and armor Denise was wearing and pulled it on.

Gene and Neil were sitting calmly in the tower, both facing different directions. Neil was watching the guard off in the marshes with contentment. The man had discovered that obviously he needed to return to his post but had a hard time returning without burning down the rushes. When he did return to his post, Whip took on a deep voice and pretended to scold the underbeast for leaving his post.

"Hey, Neil," Gene whispered. "Do you by any chance remember that signal?"

Neil turned around and looked at what Gene was pointing at. There was Denise, waving at them with both hands, then motioning for them to hurry over. Neil and Gene had worked out a series of signals with Denise earlier about how to talk to them, but that was nowhere in their list.

"She must be in a hurry," Neil whispered. "I'll go see what she needs. You stay here."

Gene nodded as Neil quickly slipped through the window that led down to the wall. He could see Neil's dark shape hurry along the wall until he reached the stairs, then he slowly descended into the depths of the base.

"What is it Denise?" Neil demanded.

Denise clapped a hand to her head and pointed to the door. "There's something wrong. Seraphina doesn't know what it is, but she can sense something is wrong."

363

Neil didn't need further encouragement, so he hurried through the door into the torchlit hallway. On his way down, he wondered why Denise had sounded kind of funny.

Outside, Vicky lifted the helmet off her head and let it drop to the ground. She walked over to the shadows in the corner opposite the crate and considered the wiggling shape there in the shadows. "Hey, at least I didn't send Gene in there too," she remarked to Denise, who glared at her from behind the gag.

Chapter 45

"Hey, Seraphina," Neil whispered as he approached the group.

All the aerobeasts, Oliver, and Reed were crowded around the door at the end of the hallway, peering through all the cracks they could find. All eyes turned to Neil in surprise, but Seraphina pushed through the crowd to the boy.

"Neil ... what are you doing here?" she inquired.

"I was told you needed help ... something wrong?" he inquired, worrying that Denise may have heard wrong or was playing a prank on him.

Seraphina nodded angrily. "Everything is wrong! There is no way the merbeasts can get in without being seen ... and there is no way we can free Emma without getting caught."

Neil shouldered his way through the crowd until he reached the door. Oliver was standing near the slightly ajar door. He moved aside so Neil could peer through. What Neil saw stayed with him always. The room was huge, and circle shaped. There was a balcony that ran along the whole interior. That was where the door opened up to. About twenty feet below the balcony was the water which took up all corners of the room. He could see vulture underbeasts lining the balcony, crossbows on their backs and worst of all, pistols on their belts.

After the war, Neil was hoping he would see less guns, but he felt that maybe there was no telling. The vultures made him twist his face in disgust. They wore helmets like the hyenas, but they were solid metal with only room for the eyes to peer out and the front of the helmets were shaped like a huge vulture. They wore a red hood that was kept snug to their head and tied under the helmet. Their outfits were black cotton shirts, pants and leather boots with long cloaks that concealed their weapons and were covered from top to bottom in ugly black feathers.

"I'm afraid there is nothing you aerobeasts can do in here," he whispered after closing the door.

Everyone's eyes grew wide with worry and sudden fear that they had failed. However, a smile appeared on Neil's face. "Though, I think there is something else you guys can do."

* * * * * * * * * *

"I doubt this is going to work, guys," Roy whispered.

Deke looked over his shoulder long enough to give Roy an annoyed glare. "Do you have a better idea?"

Roy shook his head. "But I doubt pulling on that drain pipe will work either."

True enough, Deke, Eileen, and two other teenage merbeasts were pulling vigorously at the drainpipe from underwater. Seraphina and Zara were stationed nearby as sentries, hoping to catch any suspicious movement in the other sections of the base.

Deke quickly began to separate his feet, so they reverted back to his feet rather than his fin. Placing one of his feet on the side of the drainpipe, he began to put his leg strength behind it. Eileen followed suit, with the other two pulling them.

367

Suddenly, they felt it give slightly. Deke squinted in the dark water to see that the pipe was almost out of the wall. Water was making a spiral as it tried to slip into the crack between the pipe and the wall. "Almost there," he whispered.

The other merbeasts quickly drew back as the four tumbled backward as the pipe came loose. Roy pushed forward, hoping to catch any mistake that they might have made. The water was pouring through the hole and the rocks surrounding the hole seemed to be shaking at the strength of the water.

Eileen quickly pulled Roy out of the way as Deke and the two teenage boys began to work at the stones. One by one the rocks began to come out and they would toss them out of the way onto the riverbed. Deke seemed to be having trouble with one particular rock, so the two boys gave him a hand. Eileen was watching from about two feet behind when she suddenly felt herself being pulled out of control.

Everything was a blur from then on. The merbeasts felt themselves being tossed and turned, spun around upside down. They struck things with all parts of their bodies, especially their arms and legs. They felt like they were being swallowed down a tube when suddenly . . . it stopped.

Deke slowly cracked one eye open to see that Eileen was swimming beside him, looking up at the surface of the water. Deke looked around, but the water was too dark to see through. All he could see was a reddish light above the water.

Carefully he swam toward the surface, only allowing his eyes to emerge. He found himself inside the building! They were inside! He turned his head, hoping to see Neil and sure enough he saw his brother peering out of the crack in the door, smiling at him. Deke continued to scan the room, hoping to see some sign of Emma.

Presently, Eileen touched his arm and pointed quietly. Deke leaned over to see around Roy's head and sure enough, Emma was bound hand and foot to the wall opposite the door where Neil was hiding behind. She looked exhausted, expired but relatively okay.

Meanwhile, in the hallway Seraphina was whispering to Neil. "What do we do about the underbeasts? They cannot save Emma with those guys there."

Neil nodded. "That's where you guys will come in handy."

Seraphina lowered her eyebrows at the boy, not sure if that was a compliment or an insult. Deciding to trust that it wasn't the latter, she followed Neil and the other aerobeasts back outside. When they reached the door which led outside the building, Neil stopped them.

"We need to get as many of those guys out of there. I'm going to cause a commotion, so they think something is happening. I want you guys to get out of range of those crossbows and bullets, but continue to make noise," Neil remarked, then seeing that Reed was about to ask a question, he interrupted. "Whatever noise they choose Reed. If you could make sounds like an air raid, I think that would work best. You can throw rocks or whatever, just stay out of range. You are just the distraction, not the target."

All heads nodded, definitely agreeing with the last part. Neil nodded as well, feeling inclined to show he was glad they agreed. Stepping out of the way, Neil let them out and turned to Oliver and Reed.

"Now, let's try to practice our best underbeast voices," he teased.

Up in the tower above the portcullis, Gene was sitting in his chair, his leg over the arm. Neil had been gone too long. He couldn't see Denise at the door like she was supposed to be and now the whole base was alerted to something or other. He had seen the aerobeasts sneak out and then take to the skies, but he didn't know why they were making such horrid noises. It was obnoxious. He recognized several voices that were trying to take on different pitches and sounds.

"Psst, Gene," Whip called from down below.

Gene hurried to the window and looked down at Whip. "I don't know what they're doing, Whip," he whispered, guessing Whip's reason for calling him. "I'll let you know when I find out myself."

Whip nodded and saluted, deciding that carrying on a conversation might not be wise, considering who Whip was impersonating.

Chapter 46

Neil smiled to himself. The plan was working perfectly. He and the two boys had hidden in a side corner until after the underbeasts had left the building. They were now crouching in the shadows on the balcony, watching the merbeasts cautiously make their way across the huge 'pond' to Emma. They weren't sure if anyone would return at any given time, so they were being slow and careful.

Reed leaned over and mouthed something to Neil. The boy couldn't quite read it since Reed did it so fast and he had a lisp, but he seemed to be saying: "Book the vanity." Neil wondered if Reed was trying to send him a coded message or something. However, Neil didn't even know what "vanity" meant.

Furrowing his brow, he shook his head at Reed, indicating that he didn't understand. Reed's eyes opened wide now, showing horrible worry and shock and was pointing with his hand to the other side of the room.

Neil turned and thought he saw a brief movement on the other side of the balcony. Leaning over, careful as to not leave the shadows, he peered at the dark lit room. Suddenly, he realized that there were two vulture archers still in the room! They were hidden behind a corner that was obscured from view from the doorway! Their backs were turned to the room since they were obviously talking quietly and looking at something. They were about a stone's throw away from Emma!

However, Neil wondered what Reed had meant to say, "Book the Vanity." That most certainly doesn't look or sound like "watch out for the vultures" or something like that. Then, spying the other shape that was moving rapidly toward the archers, reality dawned on him: "Look at Vicky"!

Sure enough, Vicky was hurrying along the balcony . . . Straight toward the archers! Neil's mind raced. He had to stop her before she alerted the guards to their presence! If the archers saw Vicky, they would soon notice Neil, Oliver, Reed, and the merbeasts! All would be lost!

Neil grabbed Oliver's wrist and quickly signaled instructions for him to get the merbeasts' attention. Oliver nodded and hurried through the shadows. Neil went the opposite direction, knowing he had to hurry if he wanted to stop Vicky.

Down in the water, meanwhile, Deke and Eileen were bringing up the rear as the group of merbeasts carefully made sure to not disturb the water as they made their way closer to Emma. They made sure to stay in the shadows, just in case someone returned.

Roy was constantly looking back at the two, waiting for them to give him the okay to hurry up and rescue Emma but they wanted to make sure everyone was well hidden, and they were close enough. Eileen looked over at Deke and waited until she got his attention. She nodded her head toward Roy, showing a question in her eyes.

Deke lifted one hand from the water, preparing to give her a thumbs up . . . but something else caught his eye: the two shapes that were about ten meters apart that were running through the shadows on the balcony above them. Then he spied the two archers! Looking back at the shapes, he recognized them as Vicky and Neil. Neil was obviously pursuing

Vicky and Vicky was either running from him or running to the archers.

Eileen was waiting impatiently for Deke to approve the rescue but instead of giving her a thumbs up, Deke pointed, eyes wide. Eileen carefully turned around and looked up. Taking in the scene, Eileen managed to keep her cool by submerging her head once before whispering to Deke.

"Keep going . . . slowly. I'll go help Neil," she whispered.

Deke nodded and began to continue on, urging Roy to keep going slowly. Eileen dove down into the water and began to hurry back toward the wall. She had seen earlier that there was a ladder that led up to the balcony. Not sure what it was used for, she decided it served her purpose.

She had barely made it up five rungs when she heard a slight scuffle above her. She poked her head over the side of the balcony just in time to see Neil grab Vicky by the shoulder with one hand and clap the other hand over her mouth. Vicky began to squirm like an eel, twisting one way then the other in the attempt to break free.

"Stop that," Neil whispered. "You'll give away our position."

Eileen lifted one leg onto the balcony and grasped the rail, preparing to pull her other leg over when Vicky broke free of Neil's gag and whispered in a loud, hoarse whisper. "There is a whirlpool sensor around Emma! As soon as they get within ten feet of her it will go off!"

Neil and Eileen may have had some deep contempt against Vicky but at this moment, there was no time to question her, nor time to consider the horrified look in her eyes. She was telling the truth.

Forgetting all concepts of secrecy, Neil rushed to the rail and prepared to call over the side. He was preparing a loud call for Deke to watch out . . . but that never came. He heard a deep gurgling sound that he thought might have come from his throat . . . but it had come from under the water. A loud click sounded . . . then something like an air raid followed. Neil knew he was too late so the cry that came out was just a croak: "Deke . . ."

Deke didn't hear that croak, but he did hear the gurgle and the horrible sound that began to fill his ears. Yet, both those sounds were soon drowned out when he heard startled cries in front of him. Turning, he realized that the water surrounding him and the other merbeasts was beginning to churn. It was no longer calm and still . . . it was whirling around . . . they were in the center of a growing whirlpool!

Eileen leapt from the balcony, straight into the water. She knew that getting herself stuck in the whirlpool would do nothing to help her comrades, but she knew that she could possibly help them get out. Keeping one hand always on some grip hold, whether it was knitch in the wall or the rung of the ladder, she tried her hardest to reach out to her struggling friends.

Deke was doing the same, though his efforts were working better than Eileen's since he could reach his pals and give them hard pushes out of the whirlpool. That was the best he could do, then they would have to swim with all their strength to get out of the rotter wash.

375

He grabbed a hold of Roy and gave him a hard push back out of the whirlpool. He watched to see if Roy would break free of the current. The boy caught hold of a part of the wall and held on. Deke felt a part of the burden lift off his shoulders. He had to get his troops out before they drowned. He knew that most of the merbeasts couldn't hold their breath for eternity. As he saw Roy crawl his way along the wall, his eyes fell on something above the balcony, close to where the two archers were . . . A switch!

Deke considered where he was, looked around for some escape. Deke turned, treading water as he went, rotating around and taking in his surroundings. As he turned more to the left, facing the door, his left eye was blinded by a sudden light that was blaring in his eye. Covering his eye with his hand, he opened his right and peered up at the light.

It was a small twinkling light coming from a crack in the roof. Light was pouring in . . . though he didn't know where it was coming from. Suddenly, Gene's words ran back through his mind: *There is always a light, even in the darkest place.* Deke quickly swam to one side, trying to see where the light was pointing at.

There, glittering under the light was a long object protruding from the water. It hadn't been visible before because the calm water had covered it. Now that the water was moving, it was just visible. Deke grabbed a kid nearby and dragged him through the water. When Deke's fingers closed over the object, the flicker of light disappeared, and he felt a strange sensation of peace run over him.

The object was strong, not swayed by the strong current. Deke pulled the boy closer to the pole so that the boy could hold on.

"Hold onto that," Deke whispered. "Don't let go. Try to get the others to join you but don't get the archers attention. You'll be dead meat."

The boy nodded solemnly, making Deke smile. The boy was probably three years younger than him, about Gene's age. Patting the boy's arm, Deke pressed his foot against the pole and pushed off away from the hard current.

On any other occasion, Deke would have passed out from exhaustion and allowed himself to fall asleep. However, this time it was different. Forcing himself to not relax, Deke raced to the nearest ladder. Scaling it, he caught sight of Vicky and Neil rushing through the shadows toward the door. Probably in search of some switch. However, from their viewpoint the switch wasn't visible.

Deke pulled himself over the side of the balcony and rolled further on, hoping that he wouldn't fall in. When he was sure that he was safe, he climbed to his feet, wet and dripping. Taking in his new view, his eyes fell on the switch. It would be faster to go to the left rather than the right which would take him all the way around the circle.

Keeping an eye on the archers and staying in the shadows, Deke hurried toward the switch. He had wished that Emma would be close enough to get to but, to get to Emma he would have to go into view, down several steps where the girl was closer to the water than Deke was.

Deke's eyes locked on the switch, which was less blurry than it had been before. He reached out one hand, prepared to grab it as soon as he was in reach and pull it down. His fingers brushed the red painted wooden switch when suddenly, all the soft noises in the room were overridden by a loud, wicked laugh.

Deke had the urge to faint or scream, but he forced himself to slowly turn around and face the tall figure that stood behind him. Deke was working a picture in his mind of what Nohte might look like . . . but what he saw was the complete opposite. A tall woman stood before him, dressed in a long black gown that flowed behind her. The dress looked dreadfully heavy and thick with a long silver stripe down the front and the back. Her black curly hair looked like it was daily dipped in oil, then run through a blender. It fell past her shoulders slightly, but she kept it pushed out of her face.

Her skin was deathly pale though she didn't look ill, other than the fact that her dress and hair looked sick. Her cheekbones were uncomfortably high and though she didn't look unhealthy, her facial features stood out a little too rigidly. Her black eyebrows were twice the length they were supposed to be and her eyes . . . were golden. Her nose was slightly long and crooked and her mouth, a bright red, was twisted into an evil smirk.

"So, you're behind all this are you?" she inquired, lifting one hand as if holding a platter. "Not what I expected."

Deke's mouth opened and closed, not sure what to say. "Are you . . . Nohte?"

The woman's eyebrow shot up and her mouth twisted even further. "Of course not, *child.* Nohte wouldn't spend his days in a place like this. I'm his colleague and accomplice: Dorsa."

"Two of you?" Deke inquired, feeling that things couldn't get worse. "Just great."

Deke didn't know what happened, but he felt someone suddenly push him over and striking the railing of the balcony, Deke went tumbling over the side. As he went, his foot struck the large lever and pushed it up.

Dorsa had seen the boy suddenly go catapulting into the air and she heard the click as the switch turned off. Fully infuriated, Dorsa turned to see who had interfered to find herself confronted by a boy barely taller than Deke but holding a large stick in his hands.

"No one gets to pick on my brother," the boy growled. "Oh and by the way . . . my name is Neil."

Chapter 47

Deke had barely struck the water and regained his composure before Reed and Eileen had dragged him to the surface. Deke shook his head, trying to shake off the shock of striking the water upside down. He looked around and felt strangely dazed.

"What is going on?" he asked, his head wobbling back and forth.

Eileen and Reed exchanged concerned looks. Eileen handed Deke over to Roy, who grasped the boy beneath the arms. "You get him through the tunnel, quick. I'll get Emma."

Roy nodded, taking a breath and diving under. Eileen paddled through the slightly upturned water toward the stairs that led up to Emma. The girl was tied by ropes which were strung through rings in the stone wall. Eileen reached Emma out of breath, dripping wet and her hair a mess. Emma's eyes were closed but Eileen didn't want that to cause her to make a wrong decision.

Grabbing a hold of the knots, she saw that the knot was simple, but impossible to untie when you were the one tied. She quickly released Emma's left hand, then realizing that the girl was limp, she untied her feet first. Then she removed the bonds that held her right hand, allowing Emma to fall against Eileen limply.

The girl looked over her shoulder down at the water. Roy hadn't returned yet from getting Deke out, so she called to one of the older boys. As he looked up at her, she released Emma and the unconscious girl went tumbled down into the water.

Eileen catapulted herself into the water and landed near the boy. Nodding, she took Emma from him and dove under the water. The werebeasts had completed their tunnel, digging all the way under the wall and into the bottom of the pond which wasn't as deep as the kids thought. The oldest werebeast: Fred, had brought a torch and was shining it through the water so they could see the tunnel.

Eileen knew that Emma was a mammal merbeast and needed oxygen, so she kicked as fast as possible down into the tunnel. She felt like the dark tunnel never ended and her greatest fears was that it would collapse. Then, she struck air and pulled Emma free of the water.

Looking up, her eyes were met by several smiling werebeasts all with flashlights at the entrance to the tunnel, knee deep in mud. Eileen had to admit, even though they were covered in mud, she had never seen happier faces.

Meanwhile Neil's hands were spread out away from his body, feeling the wall to his right and the balcony rail to his left. He was slowly taking steps, one at a time backwards as Dorsa continued to approach him. "Keep her distracted 'til everyone is out, then you can dive in," he kept repeating in his mind.

Then his left hand struck something hard behind him . . . Dorsa had backed him into a corner! The only corner in the room! Before he had time to assess this, the two archers whom Neil had seen earlier had become aware of the situation and were standing, one on either side of Dorsa.

"You walked nicely into my trap Neil," Dorsa mused. "Do you think I was dumb enough to have two guards stand watch over that runt without having radios? Oh yes, they might have been tied up hidden away in a crate, but they were still able to communicate."

Neil was screaming in his head, chastising himself for not thinking of that. As Dorsa continued to taunt him, he became increasingly aware of a dark object behind Dorsa. Then he realized that it wasn't an object but a space ... there was an open doorway behind Dorsa! He hadn't seen it before because the two archers had been standing there not long ago!

If only he could get Dorsa in there, he could lock her up and possibly deal with the archers. He was considering how far he would have to push her when he felt a striking pain in his left shoulder as Dorsa pressed a hard object against his shoulder. He realized that she was now holding the staff he had just recently dropped and was pinning him to the wall with one end of it. There went his plan of pushing her into the room.

"You may have walked into my trap kid, but you aren't going to be walking out of it," Dorsa was saying but the last part never came.

A loud thud sounded from somewhere far off and was followed by a crashing noise. It wasn't until after the crash that everyone saw the door on the other side of the room go flying off the hinges. Standing in the now open doorway, arms braced, legs spread apart and eyes taking in the whole scene, was none other than Gene.

* * * * * * * * * * *

Neil's mind was screaming praise and joy in his head while in his heart he was crying in agony: "No, leave, you fool, before you're caught too." Gene of course couldn't hear Neil's mind or heart, so he didn't take any of those in. His blue eyes scanned the room once and he had his plan already assessed. Denise had been right; most of the archers were out. Now there were only two to deal with besides Dorsa. He had found Denise bound and gagged outside the door and after releasing her, learnt everything from the first three words she said (she said much more than three, but Gene didn't wait to hear them). Feeling that Denise needed a break, he told her to get out and join the other werebeasts in the back. She had readily agreed to this.

Gene rushed to the edge of the rail but didn't stop as everyone thought he would. He didn't even grab the rail but leapt up, striking the rail with the bottom of his heel and lifted off into the air. Naturally as the young boy lifted into perfect flight, the two vulture underbeasts reached to their belts for their weapons. Neil prayed hard that they wouldn't choose the pistols . . . but they did. Both fired at the same time but purposely missed the boy as a warning. Gene discarded the warning without even reacting to the shots.

This seemed to infuriate the two underbeasts to the point where they began to fire more shots, directly at Gene. Neil watched, his teeth boring holes into his bottom lip. Gene's face was calm with a slight smile on his lips. His eyes were focused, watching the underbeasts' guns and anticipating where they were firing. He swiveled here and there, ducking up and down constantly avoiding the shots, then ducking when more shots were aimed further up.

Neil feared that all this avoiding with such ease would infuriate the vultures more ... which it did but when they both prepared for another round of shots ... they realized that they were out of bullets. Throwing their pistols down, much to Neil's relief, they grabbed their crossbows. The weapons never left their belts for Gene arrived at the other side of the building and sticking both feet out, he allowed them to strike hard into the chest of the first underbeast.

The man catapulted onto his back, but Gene quickly jumped off, knowing that the man would try to trip him. Instead of jumping back as both men thought, he jumped forward and leaned back on his dominant, left foot. The second, standing vulture saw this as a good chance to knock the boy down. As the man made a strong strike at the boy's head, Gene lifted up his right arm to deflect the strike and drilled his left hand into the man's stomach. This movement caused Neil to grin, remembering when he taught his brother that move.

The underbeast stepped back, coughing and gagging in shock and pain. Gene pivoted on his heel, having heard the other man rising but instead of moving both feet, Gene spun on one foot and lifted his other as he spun so that it struck the man's legs causing them to buckle. The man now on his knees, Gene pivoted back around so that the second vulture was in sight but drew his left elbow back hard, striking the first vulture hard in the nose.

The strike was just as painful to Gene as it was to the underbeast, but it was stronger than both

384

thought. It sent the man staggering back over onto his hands and knees. Gene caught a quick glimpse of the man turning to glare at him, then spinning around to see the second vulture coming toward him. The boy had a moment of déjà vu when Barret and Walt had tripped him from behind at the society.

Gene's eyes scanned everything that was within five feet of him. He spied the lever nearby and the door next to it. Considering the tools that he had: the crossbows on the vultures' belts, a line of rope over the shoulders of the second one and the staff Dorsa held.

If Neil had gotten a glimpse inside Gene's mind, it would have been racing faster than Neil could keep up. All he saw was the final decision as Gene took a step backwards. The boy didn't have to turn around to know that the first underbeast was on his hands and knees, preparing to trip him. Gene's eyes were glued on the underbeast coming toward him, eyes lowered in fury and hand drawn back.

Gene's mind raced back to the day when Neil first taught Gene how to fight. One of the first things his brother had said was: 'don't try to block a straight punch with your arm or hand because the power of it will drive you back over your head'. A small smile flickered across Gene's face as he braced his feet.

The fist flashed forward, a pinpoint heading straight at his eyes. The underbeast had no idea where the hand appeared from, but Gene's hand shot up and blocked the strike just before it came within arm's length of the boy's face. The impact of fist on palm sent a stinging feeling through Gene's wrist and a huge jolt shook his body, throwing him over his head.

He felt his back touch the other underbeast as he rolled over the man's back. Gene remembered how when Barret and Walt had tripped him, he hadn't been able to stop himself because of the force of the strike. As he went spinning over his head, he knew that with partially wet shoes and nothing to grip on the floor, he wouldn't be able to stop in time this time.

His feet struck the floor and he went sliding back, a good five feet away from the two vultures. Reaching down with one hand, he realized there was no grip there so instead he opened his wings with one strong stroke. He stopped on a dime, his head swimming from the jolts he had endured in the past two minutes.

He crouched there on the balcony, one hand on the ground and his wings partially open. Both underbeasts were on their feet now, coming straight at him. The boy lifted his wings as far as he could and braced his feet, preparing to leap.

The underbeasts saw this movement and both prepared for the boy to take to the skies. Naturally they reached to their belts for the crossbows. However, Gene knew they would make that move and the moment their eyes left him to look at their weapons, he sprung. He brought his wings down close to his body with a powerful stroke, throwing himself into the air. As his feet left the ground, he pushed forward with his toes so instead of going up, he went forward straight at the underbeasts.

The first underbeast who was closest to Gene looked up just as the boy did a summersault in the air. The last thing he remembered was a pair of feet crashing into his chest and stumbling back, his head struck the railing, and everything went black. The second underbeast had seen the whole thing happening so he was prepared if the boy tried something similar.

Standing about five feet in front of the huge creature, Gene wasn't planning on doing another summersault. Instead he took a leap forward, reducing the distance between them. As he landed, he didn't plant both feet but allowed his right foot to strike the ground but in a single movement he sent his body pivoting on the foot.

The underbeast had his eyes on the boy's left foot, knowing he was going to trip him with that one. As Gene's foot neared the man's legs, the underbeast leapt up into the air, directly into the path of Gene's extended wings.

Neither Neil nor the underbeast realized how hard a wing could strike someone but when the shoulder of Gene's wing struck the back of the underbeast's head there was a sound thud and the man went stumbling into the wall and crumpled to the ground.

Neil felt a smile spread across his face. He had never deemed that Gene had that kind of fire in him. However, the smile lasted for about a second before it turned to a frown of fear. Neil opened his mouth to cry out, but it was too late. Gene lifted his eyes and found a dark object flashing toward him. He felt his feet go flying over his head, his shoulder striking the railing as he tumbled over the side.

Neil's heart caught in his throat as Gene steadied himself a good ten meters from the railing and began to hover. Dorsa reached down to the unconscious underbeast behind her and drew out the crossbow. She had a bolt ready and aimed at Gene within a second. Gene's wings were spread apart and not that far away, he was a perfect target. The blood in Neil's face drained when he realized that there was no way Gene could avoid the crossbow. Dorsa was no fool. If Gene tried to avoid it, she would aim for his escape.

Gene knew this as much as Neil did. If anything, he knew it better than Neil did. He looked up, he couldn't escape there because Dorsa would guess that as one of his escapes. If he flew to the left, he would strike the wall and the left was another escape Dorsa probably had under control.

Neil saw Gene's blue eyes scan the whole place, then lock with his own. He saw Gene smile at him . . . a sad smile. Gene knew there was no way out and Neil knew that he knew it. Neil had the urge to cry out, but he heard the click of the crossbow and saw the bolt sail through the air, directly at Gene.

Gene took one last look at Neil and a grin replaced the sad smile. With one swift movement he dodged the bolt and missed, but the course he took was a mistake. His left wing wrapped around his body while the other turned back slightly and he plummeted out of sight.

The boy turned his fearful and now infuriated eyes on the tall woman to see she was staring back at him with a smile of contentment on her eyes. "Poor kid," she mused aloud. "There isn't enough distance between here and the water for him to compose himself. And wet wings are almost impossible to fly in."

Chapter 48

Neil felt the blood boiling in his brain. He knew that what Dorsa said was all too true. Gene still hadn't gotten the hang on stalling his fall, and considering the seemingly tiny twenty feet between the balcony and the water, there was no way the boy could make it.

Neil turned his eyes back on Dorsa and lowered his dark eyebrows. "There is no way you are going to get away with this!"

Dorsa tossed her head, sending her hair sailing over her shoulder. "In case I calculated wrong, I've already gotten away with it."

The boy couldn't think of another striking reply to that observation. He was desperately trying to get the pain out of his mind, having realized that Gene was possibly in trouble . . . or worse: dead. Neil's eyes wavered away from Dorsa's and he thought he saw another pair of eyes looking back at him from the shadows behind Dorsa.

He didn't squint for he knew Dorsa would see that and turn around. Instead he looked back at Dorsa for a moment, then looked back at the shadows. They were eyes! Someone was in the shadows looking back at him.

Whoever it was, the person was trying to help him. He had to keep Dorsa's attention on him. Neil quickly looked around, pretending to look for a way out.

"I wouldn't say that just yet," Neil remarked, forcing his voice to take on a vibrating tone. "You may have gotten rid of Gene, but you haven't gotten away with me."

Dorsa raised her eyebrows but the amusement in her features didn't reach her eyes. They were stone hard and as cold as ice. "'You haven't gotten away with me'," she repeated. "I'm afraid your self-confidence has marred you good judgement. Do you think we would bother to kidnap a handful of kids just for you to come and 'rescue' them? Emma has an important job to do before our weapon is completed."

"What weapon?" Neil asked, the blood draining from his face.

"Oh, did I say weapon?" Dorsa inquired, running her fingers through her hair. "I meant to say monster. You see, Nohte has created a fabulous machine that enables him to create underbeasts from scratch. However, to do that, he needs life energy of living, breathing humans. He saw it fit to use strong willed changelings since their natural durability was stronger than most. He hasn't accomplished this yet, but with Emma's help, we'll finish charging the first man-made giant human machine that we can bend to our will."

Immediately, Neil's face turned an uncomfortable purple since it couldn't go any paler than it already was.

Dorsa smiled to herself, glad that her words had worked the reaction she wanted. However, Neil glanced around her just vaguely to see the same pair of eyes looking back at him. He saw a hand extend from the shadows, holding what looked like a lasso. He couldn't see what the person did with it for Dorsa's tall figure blocked his view, but he was quite sure the person had placed the lasso on the floor just behind Dorsa's feet.

A foot slipped out of the shadows . . . but it didn't look familiar. Then a leg . . . then another foot . . . an arm . . . and Vicky stepped out of the darkness of the shadows, holding the end of the rope. The lasso still lay on the ground behind Dorsa's feet on the ground. Neil felt his mind suddenly scream, not at Vicky but at himself for thinking that this was a rescue. However, Vicky's actions were strangely peculiar.

Taking the end of the rope, she wrapped it around the whirlpool lever and carefully slipped it over the side of the balcony.

"What are you looking at?" Dorsa inquired, turning slightly to the side.

Neil's mouth clapped shut but it was too late. Dorsa turned fully around and stared down into the eyes of the tall teenage girl. Vicky cocked her head to the side, looking directly into the woman's eyes without flinching and a smile creased her face. Lifting her left hand up so that it was level with her eyes, she stuck her thumb up as if giving Neil encouragement. What no one knew was that the movement was actually a signal.

Dorsa took an aggressive step forward and as her shoe clicked on the hard wood of the floor, Vicky leapt backward about two steps and cried out. "Now Deke!"

Neil's eyes shot down to the lasso on the ground. It was now wrapped around Dorsa's ankles and was pulling tight with incredible speed. The rope became tight, dragging Dorsa off her feet. As the rope was still being pulled by the end, Dorsa was unexpectantly dragged toward the latch.

Vicky leapt out of the way and as Dorsa slipped toward her, she grabbed the section of the rope that was wrapped around the lever. She pushed it down and the grinding noise of the whirlpool could be heard below. However, having pushed it down, the direction that the rope was pulling Dorsa changed and the woman rolled completely through the doorway.

Neil's mouth was hanging open but as a small body bumped against his arm, it fell open even further which he thought was completely impossible. Gene appeared out of nowhere and ran over to where Vicky was trying to close the door behind Dorsa.

"Hurry," the girl panted. "She's going to get untied soon. We have to get this closed!"

Gene slammed his shoulder against the door and with Vicky's help, the door clicked shut. Gene fumbled with the lock beneath the doorknob, but the blood began to drain from his face. "It's stuck! I can't get it locked!"

The boy left the lock alone as soon as Dorsa slammed her weight against the door from the other side. Vicky wedged her foot underneath the door, trying to wedge it closed. "I'll hold it . . . Get Neil out of here," she yelled through gritted teeth.

Gene's blue eyes flew wide open and shook his head madly. "No, Vicky! I'm not going to leave you here! You won't be able to hold Dorsa long enough!"

The door vibrated as Dorsa slammed into it again. Vicky cringed as the door wedged hard against her foot. "Just go . . . I'll hold her long enough for you guys to get away. You have to trust me, Gene! Do it!"

Gene bit his lower lip, drawing blood. Reaching over, he touched Vicky's shoulder and looked up into her eyes that were half closed from the pain that was running from her foot through her body. Vicky smiled down at the boy and gave him a quick wink.

The boy pivoted on his foot and raced toward his brother. Neil felt his brother grab him beneath the arms and heave him into the air. The two boys seemingly bounced up and down as Gene's wings began to lift them into the air. Gene dragged Neil over the railing and paused, just as they were about to leave Vicky's sight.

Vicky flashed them a smile and with one hand, waggled her fingers at them in farewell. The door at the other side of the building flew open and the vultures returned. Neil felt most of his air leave his body as Gene's arms tightened around his chest.

Gene spun a full 180 degrees and dove head down toward the water. Neil caught a fleeting glimpse of Deke and Eileen dangling at the end of the rope that was still tightly looped around the latch above. The whirlpool howled in his ears and Gene flew directly into the center of it. He felt several hands grab his ankles as they disappeared into the wet and dark abyss.

When Neil managed to wipe the water out of his eyes and focus in the dim light of a torch, he saw dozens of eyes looking at him in surprise. He was drenched head to toe, cold and weak. Gene's arms were still wrapped under his arms and around his chest. The boy was dragging his brother out of the muddy tunnel.

Eileen and Deke released Neil's ankles and climbed out of the mud, grabbing one of Neil's arms and helping Gene pull Neil out. Neil's head was swimming and he couldn't feel his legs. They were completely numb and the only thing he felt was Gene's arms squeezing his chest so hard that it stung.

Through his still wet eyes he could see blurs of lights flashing about and people moving around. He felt himself being laid down on something soft and somewhat hard. Then he felt the object move and he realized he was on someone's back.

Turning his head slightly he caught sight of a mop of orange hair and the glasses resting on Oliver's nose reflected the glare of the flashlights. Neil instinctively wrapped his arms around the boy's neck as the muscles in Oliver's back tensed before taking off.

Meanwhile, at the front of the base, Whip was still walking back and forth, keeping his eyes open for the others. He had noticed that Seraphina and the aerobeasts were no longer circling up ahead and wasn't surprised when he saw them all fly off toward the marshes, heading home.

Whip tore off the heavy armor except the helmet and released his jacket so that his narrow wings could open up. The guard on the other wall had just approached the drawbridge when he saw this. "Hey, dude, what do you think you're doing?"

Whip didn't reply but tearing off the helmet, he leaped into the air. The underbeast only caught a glimpse as the boy disappeared from sight, the dark, starless sky shrouding him from prying eyes.

The door of the back building flew open and Dorsa stormed out, her hair amess with three vulture underbeasts behind her. Her face was twisted into complete rage. "They'll pay for that!"

The next thing that happened was never clear in the woman's mind. She heard a decisive thud that sounded right behind her. As she turned, she saw that one of her underbeast vultures was bending over, clutching at a huge stone that was lying on his foot. If Dorsa had looked up, she would have seen the   white

teeth grinning down from the sky as Whip swung his knapsack back onto his back and flew off to join the others.

Chapter 49

Needless to say, when the kids woke up the next morning in their beds, they discovered that each and every one of them had slept in well past lunch. Lucky for them, it was a Saturday. The police investigation on Emma's disappearance was called off when Mrs. Wagner found the girl sound asleep on the living room couch. They did, however, send Emma and the other four kids to a more advanced hospital in Gerh.

When society continued the next week, the outcome was not what any of the members wanted but they had seen it coming. That week, instead of having the usually fun exercises, they had to clean every building so that it was all spick and span before Thanksgiving.

Emma, Ivan, Luke, Isabella, and Cathy recovered nicely and were soon able to return to Hichester and society. Ivan never got his paper route job back especially since everyone agreed that it kept the twins out of mischief in their free time. Whip was never content with the fact that nothing happened the rest of that year that could even compare slightly to what they had encountered at the underbeast base in the smothering marshes.

The police were sent to investigate the marshes but found the base empty, deserted, and pretty much in ruins. That came as no surprise to anyone. However, it was disappointing especially to the gang and even the other society members who were hoping that they might be able to capture the 'machine human' and destroy it. However, they realized that with Emma back, the weapon would never be able to function.

The gang members were suspended from leaving their houses without permission for three weeks. However, this gave them a good excuse to avoid the council members who were still mad at them for breaking into the society at night, illegally.

Life continued on for the next three years, peacefully and without any outrageous adventures. Things in Hichester did change quite a bit once the mayor decided that the high protection and safety criteria were not as necessary as they thought. More people began to hear about the peaceful town and more people moved into Hichester, causing the once small town to expand even slightly into a more moderate sized town though it still remained a country-side haven.

The information concerning the changeling inhabitants of Hichester were kept very confidential, though many people began to notice that more people were talking once more about the supposedly mythical beings.

Destiny and Silver never forgave the gang for leaving them out of the rescue plan. They even forbade to teach the others how to use the barges. However, they couldn't remain angry with them for long.

The girls began to hang out more together and almost separated from the rest of the gang, making their own tight-knit group which consisted of Silver, Destiny, Zara, Seraphina, Denise and Eileen. Zara was a natural surprise to the group, especially since she seemed to fit in with the boys better than with the girls, but no one complained when she spent equal time with the gang members.

Deke soon discovered a cure for his poor eyesight. Creating a pair of work goggles, he filled them with water. The almost therapeutic alteration that the water did for his eyes aided Deke in almost virtually healing himself of his poor eyesight. However, it was necessary for him to use them when swimming or reading.

Gene gained a reputation amongst the bullies of Hichester as 'the kid you shouldn't cross'. Gene even went on to being better at fighting than Neil which impressed everyone, except Neil who said that he always knew that Gene had it in him. Gene tried constantly to thank Seraphina for teaching him a valuable lesson and talking him into rescuing Emma. However, the girl refused to be thanked and the two kept up a strong brother/sister relationship.

Neil changed dramatically and, in a way, grew out of his old skin. People wondered if he would even stay with the gang since he was kind of a 'fish out of the water'. However, Neil stayed on and spent most of his time at Hichester. He became known as a rebellious, yet freedom-loving type. He never had trouble keeping up with the rest of the gang and began to find interest in sports such as football.

Eileen was adopted by Mr. Wetherby three months after the escapade to the smothering marshes. Even though the two consistently pleaded with the three boys, Neil, Deke and Gene decided that they preferred keeping their true last name but agreed to live in the Wetherby home.

The life in Hichester went on with it's ups and downs, but never with the paths that would curve slightly to the side and lead anyone on a strange adventure. The kids finally grasped that, but it was hard for them to accept. There was still that longing of mad adventure with no limits, a life full of risks. Perhaps the parents cherished the three years of limits and no risks, but when the summer of 1948 rolled by, the kids would get their wish . . . but not in the way they expected.

Chapter 50

The doorbell rang again, more shrilly and with vigor this time. "I'll get it!" Gene called from the library.

He dropped the erector set he had been messing with and hurried from the room. The jacket he wore over his shirt got tangled around his arm as he went. As he opened the door, he began to unwind it. At first, he was expecting one of the gang members to be standing there. However, the late autumn sunshine lit up the tall person who stood there on the front stoop.

"Can I help you?" Gene inquired, quickly unwinding his shirt from his arm.

The man quickly removed his cap to show a large bald spot on the back of his head. He looked to be in his late fifties but the look in his eyes told Gene that the age hadn't reached his heart yet. He smiled down at the boy, who looked no more than nine, though his height suggested that he might be older.

He considered the lad a moment. Obviously, this boy was growing far beyond his young years. His straight blond hair was slightly wet from sweat and waved about his forehead. His bright turquoise blue eyes seemed to hold a mad list of questions that could never be satisfied. He was a strongly built, slender boy whose hands seemed so steady . . . so calm but full of energy.

"I'm Phil Vostro. Is Deke home?"

Gene's eyebrow shot up in surprise. Nodding his head, he turned around and poked his head back into the house. "Deke! Someone to see you!"

Gene brought his head back out and looked back up at the man. "What do you need from Deke?"

The man smiled at the boy, but it was obvious he wasn't interested in revealing all the information to anyone other than Deke. "I'm a lawyer . . . it's a law matter."

The boy's face expanded as his eyes widened in fright. What had Deke done to cause a lawyer to want to see him? As Deke appeared at the door, Gene slipped back inside and headed straight for Mr. Wetherby's office.

Mr. Vostro looked down at the skinny, rather short boy who now stood before him. He knew that Deke was older than the boy who had just left, but he wasn't taller; if anything, he was about an inch shorter. A huge pair of work goggles rested amidst his wild brown hair and looked like they were full of water. A pencil was wedged behind his left ear, and he had a notebook tucked under his arm and what looked like a large piece of metal. The boy wasn't bad looking, but obviously was a late bloomer.

"I hope I'm not interrupting something?" the man inquired, gesturing toward the notebook and metal.

Deke looked down at the objects and grinned. "Oh, no, I was just working on something . . . what can I do for you, Mr. . . . ."

"Vostro," the lawyer explained. "I'm a lawyer and I think there may be something you need to know."

403

Just at that moment, the door opened wider and Mr. Wetherby stepped out with Gene close behind. The lawyer caught sight of a tall girl peering around the huge gentleman and a boy about her size trying to get a good look.

"George!" Mr. Wetherby exclaimed, his eyes widening. "What are you doing here in Hichester of all places? The last time I saw you, you were heading for a position in parliament."

Mr. Vostro nodded. "I'm sorry to barge in at this moment, Wetherby . . . but I came to deliver a message to this young lad," he said, motioning toward Deke.

Mr. Wetherby placed a comforting hand on the boy's shoulder. "What might that be?"

"You are Deke Mecarnin, correct?" the lawyer inquired.

Deke nodded slowly.

Mr. Vostro reached into his coat pocket and drew out a thick envelope . . . that was blue! Deke's eyes widened, and he took half a step back. "Where did you get that?" he demanded in an almost girlish voice.

"You've seen one like this before, have you?" Mr. Vostro inquired, his voice suddenly showing home. "I was hoping as much . . . do you remember the name of the person, lad?"

"A man . . . named Alec . . . I don't know his last name," the boy replied. "Why . . . is he a colleague of yours?"

Mr. Vostro let loose an eruption of laughter which caused Deke to bite his lower lip. He was afraid he had said something wrong. However, as Mr. Vostro wiped his eyes he saw that he hadn't.

"Who's Alec? He is no one's colleague. He is what you might call: 'nobody's friend.' He never got along with anyone except maybe himself. Alec is the brother of a certain Steve Rasmussen. Steve is a well-to-do man who retired from active military some years ago."

"Wait . . ." Deke started, racking his brain for the reason why that name was familiar. "Isn't he that millionaire who lives in Gerh?"

Mr. Vostro's humorous eyebrows slightly lowered. "He's not exactly a millionaire. He might be one of the wealthiest men in Gerh, but he lives a rather quiet life."

"What does that have to do with me?" Deke demanded.

Mr. Vostro peered at the two faces that were craning their necks to see through the door. He was going to ask them to leave but he knew that the kids probably wouldn't agree. It made matters even worse when the older boy stepped out from behind Mr. Wetherby and placed himself directly behind Deke, putting a protective hand on the boy's shoulder.

This boy was obviously a brother. While his eyes were dark, he could see that one eye was a completely different color from the other. His jet-black hair was brushed up and out of his forehead and the arched eyebrows showed great expression but also determination. His lips were slightly open, as if prepared to defend his younger brother but didn't show unkindness. His skin was a shade or two darker than Deke's, obviously showing that this boy spent most of his time outside rather than inside like Deke.

The lawyer had to admit that this was a boy to respect. He might not look like much as a tall, slender boy of thirteen, but his shoulders, hands and arms showed that he was no weenie.

"It has to do with your father Deke," Mr. Vostro finally remarked.

All eyebrows went up at this remark. Everyone knew that Mr. Mecarnin was dead, that was the truth. However, not one of the boys had ever heard the name: Steve Rasmussen, even when their father had spoken of business in the few moments they had with him in their childhood.

"My ... dad ..." Deke started, swallowing at least three times during the sentence. "But he's ... he's dead."

Mr. Vostro cast a quick look at Mr. Wetherby who was trying to not make eye contact. Obviously, the older man didn't want to tell the boy without adult approval, but Mr. Wetherby didn't want to be the one to hold back the fateful truth.

Finally, the lawyer merely held the envelope out to Deke, inches from the boy's face. Deke slowly took it and looked at the front. Through the stinging sweat that was pouring into his eyes, he could barely make out the words on the front: Deke Mecarnin.

Deke felt Neil's strong hand grip his shoulder tighter as moral support. Deke felt a sudden relaxation, knowing that whatever that envelope said, he would have his brothers to help him. He slipped his finger under the flap and tore it open. Inside was a single piece of paper that seemed to be of the highest quality.

He unfolded it and quickly wiped the sweat from his eyes with the back of his sleeve. He scanned the first line and began to read it aloud in a low voice. "To Deke Mecarnin. You are being called to the

406

Gerh on a visit of incredible importance on December 20th ... this year of 1948 ... your lawyer and mentor in this case shall be Mr. George Vostro who bears this message ... signed: Steve Rasmussen II."

The boy wiped his eyes again and scanned the letter to make sure he had read it correctly. Looking up, he waved the letter toward the lawyer. "What ... What does this mean?"

The lawyer locked eyes with Mr. Wetherby, then Gene who stood in the doorway. Lastly his eyes fell on the tall teenage boy who kept his hands protectively on his brother's shoulders and was giving the older man suspicious looks.

Finally, the man sighed and ran his hand through the thin hair atop his head. "Deke ... Mr. Rasmussen wishes you to visit him."

"But why?" Deke demanded. "I don't even know him!"

Mr. Vostro took a step forward but the warning look in Neil's eyes told him that too much closer would be seen as hostile. Finally, he crouched so that he was eye level with the young boy. "Deke ... your last name isn't really Mecarnin ... It's Rasmussen."

He paused to let those words sink in but regretted it as the blood drained from Deke's face and the blood rose in Neil's face.

With nothing else to do, the lawyer put a hand on Deke's shoulder and looked him straight in the eyes. "Steve Rasmussen ... is your father."

I never thought a day would come when I would hear someone admit to my brother that his father was not Frank Mecarnin. Deke would go on to tell

407

me that when he heard that, he felt his mind stop and his legs turn to putty. It was lucky that Neil was there, or Deke would have ended with a bad concussion from hitting the drive.

It was true, and Mr. Wetherby confirmed the fact that Deke was in fact, Neil and my half-brother. I couldn't believe this, and I had no clue how it could be possible. Maybe there was some possible evidence that something was different between the two of us and Deke, but I had never noticed it.

I can say this, it wasn't what we expected. Christmas was coming fast, and November was almost over. Deke would be due to visit his blood father in barely a month and wasn't at all happy about it. I could go further into detail, but I think that is a story for another time.

What I will say, though, is that Deke was lucky that he learnt the truth when he did. If he had learnt it any sooner, he wouldn't have had the strength to even live through it. It was that autumn, three years ago, when the three of us made the closest friends ever. While we may have found the greatest gang to hang out with and be a part of, the greatest friends that we could have ever wanted was in each other. That was what helped us through the trials of that fall, and the trials that we would soon face with Christmas just a stone's throw away.

The End.

Acknowledgements

To everyone who made this adventure possible, especially my parents and siblings who always encouraged my writing.

To Khala, Taylor, Sean, Brenna, Emma, Madeleine, John, and James, who in every way inspired the creation of the "gang." Especially to Sean and Brenna who inspired me in the creation of Neil and Deke!

My best friends: Hannah, Jackson, and Sarah and their family who saved me from myself and showed me a friendship that I had never experienced before.

For everyone at Rivershore, especially Jansina Grossman, who never lost her patience when I constantly changed my mind. Thank you so much for your patience!

And for everyone who feels like they don't fit in or should have a crowd of friends: Do not think that you must have a crowd; it is easier to have a few absolutely amazing friends who will do anything for you.

Last but not least, for my greatest childhood friend: Luke, who was Gene in every way. If it hadn't been for you, I may never have reached this point.

Author's Bio

    Sarah Flanagan had always been inspired to read books, especially fantasy and fiction. It wasn't until she was about nine when she took pen in hand and began to write her own stories. The first stories she ever wrote were imaginary sequels to some of her favorite fantasy stories and some short stories of her own. When she turned fifteen, she began her most intense story that would one day take her on a journey of a lifetime. She originally wrote *The Last Victim in Hichester District* as a novel about four friends who entered a boarding school. However, after a week-long personal adventure, she changed the story into what it is now.

    Presently, she is preparing to enter her Senior year of homeschooled high school and has become intrigued with her future in college. She is also looking forward to a second adventure with the Mecarnin brothers. When she isn't writing, she is helping with her little brothers or taking long walks and dreaming up more ideas for writing.

Rivershore Books

www.rivershorebooks.com
info@rivershorebooks.com
www.facebook.com/rivershore.books
www.twitter.com/rivershorebooks
blog.rivershorebooks.com
forum.rivershorebooks.com

www.ingramcontent.com/pod-product-compliance
Lightning Source LLC
Chambersburg PA
CBHW020928020726
47495CB00002B/391